Elizabeth Kelley

Sunday by Sunday
A Spiritual Journal

A Work of Fiction

Grounded in the Revised Common Lectionary, Year C

Cristy Fossum

Create in Me Enterprises

Copyright © 2007 Cristy C. Fossum
Second Printing, 2008

This is a work of fiction. Names, characters, places and incidents
either are the product of the author's imagination or are used fictitiously,
and any resemblance to any actual persons, living or dead, events or locales is entirely coincidental.

The Scripture quotations contained herein are from the New Revised Standard Version Bible,
Copyright © 1989 by the Division of Christian Education of the National Council of the Churches of Christ
in the U.S.A., and are used by permission. All rights reserved.

Hymn text, "O Morning Star, How Fair and Bright!" - Philipp Nicolai.
Text copyright © 1978 LUTHERAN BOOK OF WORSHIP. Used by permission of Augsburg Fortress.

Hymn text, "Thine the Amen, Thine the Praise" - Text - Herbert F. Brokering, Music - Carl Schalk.
Copyright © 1983 Augsburg Publishing House. Used by permission of Augsburg Fortress.

Hymn text, "Awake, Awake, and Greet the New Morn" - Marty Haugen.
Text copyright © 1983. Used by permission of GIA Publications.

Excerpt from the hymn, *Eternal Spirit of the Living Christ,* by Frank von Christerson,
Copyright © 1974 The Hymn Society. Administered by Hope Publishing Company, Carol Stream, Illinois 60188.
All rights reserved. Used by permission.

Published by
Create in Me Enterprises, LLC
1215 Beaufort St.
Columbia, South Carolina 29201-1401

Cover Art by David Hedges

Printed in the United States of America

Library of Congress CIP data applied for.

No parts of this book may be reproduced or transmitted in any form whatsoever without prior written permission
from the publisher, except in the case of brief quotations embodied in critical articles and reviews.

ISBN: 978-0-9820207-0-8 (previously ISBN 978-1-6053072-4-4)

ACKNOWLEDGMENTS

Elizabeth Hunter was my editor at a *Writing for the Church* workshop where Sunday by Sunday was first conceived. Her encouragement and advice, along with the affirmation and input of fellow writers in my small group, have been significant in carrying me through this project. Thanks also to Bob Sitze and Ted Schroeder for leading that workshop along with Liz, out of their passion for writing about faith.

Judy Aebischer, already a friend and church sister, became my editor once the book was well underway. For her perfect understanding of my vision and intent; her fondness for Rose and Rose's people; her deep experience as a reader, writer, and editor; her patience when the going got frustrating; her probing questions and high standards; her excellent ideas and suggestions; and all the laughs, I am profoundly grateful.

Harvey Huntley Jr., my former husband of 36 years, served as a highly valued theological and biblical consultant when the book was in its formative stages. While he was not involved throughout, the work is better because of his early participation, and I thank him.

The ever-changing community of Lutheran Theological Southern Seminary supported me through the kindness and affirmation of its people walking together in faith daily. The interest of those who knew I was writing a book was most gratifying and encouraging. Ginger Barfield wrote, in my opinion, the perfect foreword (with one arm in a cast!). I am deeply indebted to her for the gift of her insights, writing skills, and willing spirit. Dr. Robert Hawkins, Professor of Worship and Music, helped me gather my thoughts together in regard to the cover and David Hedges, Graphics Designer, used his considerable talent to create artwork and a cover design which expressed our ideas. Others helped me with bits of scholarly information. Thanks, everyone!

Charles H. Cook, Esquire, has expedited the publication process in a professional and expert manner. I am very pleased to be setting out on my writing career solidly established for business as well as creative expression, thanks to him. Charles' personal interest in the project along with his kindness and wit and his own churchmanship have made him a true partner as well as a valued attorney.

Judy Jolly—friend, church sister, and enthusiastic reader of rough drafts—joined the team by agreeing to proof the final manuscript. If we have accomplished the hard-to-imagine feat of no errors, Judy is part of that perfection, and I thank her for her time and support.

The several congregations of which I have been a member are very dear to me; the people of those places, many of whom have joined the saints eternal, are a part of me and therefore a part of this book about life in the Church. I am so grateful to them for letting the light of Christ shine through them into my life.

My family and friends have been intrigued and encouraging in regard to the writing of <u>Sunday by Sunday</u>; now, they are as excited by its publication as I am. Many thanks to my mother, daughters, siblings, cousins, aunts and uncles, and dear friends for urging me on. I hope you all like it. Don't forget—any similarities are purely coincidental!

FOREWORD

If you have ever gone to church, ever kept a journal or diary, ever sat on a bench and observed the peculiarities of people, ever thought spiritual questions that maybe you were afraid to speak out loud—you will find something in this book that resonates within you.

Rose Harris, the quintessential church lady of St. Timothy's, invites us into her life, her family, her faith and narrates a wonderful story through the characters in her journal. Somehow we know Rose and her friends from somewhere in our lives. Rose and the characters in her journal reflect the joys and struggles of our own ups and downs with life.

We walk our own long-term grief with Rose as she talks to her husband, Charlie, who has been dead for years. We know what it is to miss someone so much that we can still feel that presence in our lives long after they are dead and buried.

We laugh out loud at the on-going saga of the people populating the membership of St. Timothy's. What is it with their tendency to blame it all on the pastor? What a motley crew they are! And, oh how many of them we have met before—the gossipers, the arrogant pious ones, those who are just there for appearance sake, the ones who swallow all that faith stuff hook-line-sinker, the doubters who will never believe any of it. We know these people—we are these people.

We wrinkle our brows at the dysfunction of Rose's own family. A daughter who never bought into Rose's devout beliefs, a granddaughter whose life reflects Rose's spirit though her lifestyle is so 21st century, and a son who struggles with divorce and alcoholism, but who unfailingly shows up for Rose.

And then there are the vagabond characters who drop in out of nowhere. Garfield and Mindy do not fit within the boundaries that many of us set for people in our lives. Somehow these kinds of folks find their way to us nonetheless, and their presence certainly makes our lives more entertaining.

Perhaps the most unique part of this book is its organization. Rose's journal entries are written every Sunday, Sunday by Sunday, and include her reflections on the lectionary texts and Pastor Sauer's sermon for the day. There is, then, a devotional sense that ties all the stories and people together into God's great story. And, ultimately, that is what binds the disparate lives and actions into one sweeping read. Not just for them, but also for us—their stories, God's story, and our stories. You will find something in this book that resonates within you.

The Reverend Dr. Ginger Barfield
Lutheran Theological Southern Seminary

For my grandmother, Clara Nelson Cristy, and my mother, Bobbie Cristy Fossum, whose lives of faith lived out in the Church nurture and inspire me.

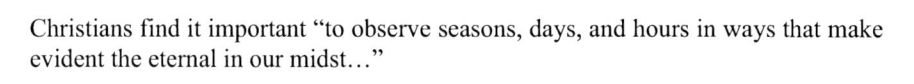

Christians find it important "to observe seasons, days, and hours in ways that make evident the eternal in our midst…"

>From Calendar, Christ's Time for the Church
> By Laurence Hull Stookey

Sunday by Sunday
A Spiritual Journal

First Sunday of Advent

Jeremiah 33:14-16
Psalm 25:1-10, 14
1 Thessalonians 3:9-13
Luke 21:25-36

    I cannot believe I laughed when Florence's wig blew off this afternoon! We went with Pastor Sauer to the Advent Service of Lessons and Carols at the cathedral in the city. On our way back to the car, Pastor was between us, holding our arms to steady us into a wicked northern Indiana wind gusting down Broad Street. Dirt and dust were blowing into our faces, Grapes of Wrath-like. I was already burning with anger and sadness to see my favorite friend and church sister for over 50 years struggling like that, balded and weakened by diabolical cancer. And then, just as we turned a corner, she reached up to adjust her wig and away it went!
    Pastor took off after the wig, of course, chasing it down the street as it continued to elude his desperate grabs. Florence hasn't lost her sense of humor, though, and we held on to each other, laughing until we cried and then crying until we laughed. Finally, Pastor stomped on it and then waved it over his head in triumph. On the drive back to Shippensforge, we took turns recounting the whole fiasco, adding more details each time. After a few quiet seconds of looking out our windows, we would all break up again.
    So why am I sitting here weeping at my kitchen table? I get awfully weary of going up and down, like mercury in a thermometer. *Charlie, when I opened the front door after Pastor dropped me off I could smell the toast I had burned at lunchtime, which primed the pump of my tears. You would eat properly toasted toast if you had to, but you really loved it burned. I've not been very good at widowhood, I'm afraid. I miss you as much right now as I did right after you died, I think, and that's going on five years.*
    I built a fire in the fireplace and lit the first candle in the advent wreath, which helped a little, and settled in the recliner with Cute Baby—nothing like a furry feline to sooth my troubled soul. But then, the lead story in the Sunday paper was about a man ambushing his wife yesterday as she and her children returned from Christmas shopping. He shot her three times in the chest, then put the gun against her head and shot again as she begged for mercy and the children watched. Dear God. Words that we sang in worship this morning no longer seem archaic: "Sin's dreadful doom upon us lies; Grim death looms fierce before our eyes." (Koln)
    Only God in Christ, a mysterious power that defies physical laws and human logic, can save us from such horror—receive that woman, heal those children, save

the lost soul of that despicable murderer. God comes in a baby, loves the universe, suffers and dies for it, and then conquers death. Nothing less will do.

I have tried several times not to believe in Jesus Christ. Faith seemed an embarrassment of emptiness, a relic of childhood. At such times, maybe four or five of them in my 79 years, I have thought, "Okay, God, I've had enough of Jesus. The story is too preposterous and the agonies of the world too much to bear."

The truth of Christ, nonetheless, hit me full force once again this afternoon. As Pastor and Florence and I watched from a balcony, the elaborate gospel procession made its regal way down the center aisle. Hundreds of believers turned to encircle the written Word of God: "In the beginning was the Word, and the Word was with God, and the Word was God." My entire being resonated with the truth that God's power revealed in Jesus Christ is stronger than the sinfulness of this world. I believe in Jesus because nothing less will do. What less can conquer the evil that overtook that murderous husband? What less can overcome the evil that fuels terrorism, killing innocents and toppling skyscrapers, or the evil of economic policies that cause people to suffer and die?

How I wish I could bottle the glory and majesty of worship and drink of it later. It doesn't have to be cathedral level worship. What we do at St. Timothy Sunday in and Sunday out is just as true, if less extravagant and sprinkled with comedy and error. There we sat this morning, the only church in town not decorated for Christmas, I'll bet. The advent wreath and evergreens in the vases on either side of the altar are all we will see until Christmas Eve. Pr. Sauer is unyielding on this. No Christmas carols until Christmas, either. IT'S ADVENT. I was one of several who used to argue strenuously with him.

"Oh, come now, Pastor. What would it hurt? There's so much sadness and hardness in this world, why not use the whole month of December for joy and celebration?"

"Rose," he would reply calmly, "only by facing the darkness can we fully appreciate the brilliant light of hope which God gives us in Jesus the Christ. From the dawning of time, human beings have used the natural cycle with its coldness and darkness to come to terms with in-born fears and anxieties. When the days began to get longer..." Yakkity-yak.

The funny thing is, I agree with him now, after twelve years of experiencing this approach. Many are still complaining, the ones who gripe about everything Pastor Sauer does, but I've come to appreciate the simplicity as a nice contrast to the "Ho! Ho! Ho! Buy! Buy! Buy!" atmosphere out there. The barren nave is in sync with my soul as I read the horror stories in the paper and deal with Florence's cancer and with missing my soul mate and all the rest of it. For the four Sundays of Advent, we gather together and square off against evil, knowing the wonder that is coming, that is here.

I liked (i.e. agreed with) the sermon this morning: God is always present, appearing to break into the world dramatically when especially needed. Pastor reminded us that there hasn't been a time in history when people have not been hurting and longing for an end to suffering and sorrow, and God always comes. To Babylon, to Thessalonica, to the United States, to Iraq. God comes to us here, now, Emmanuel, God with us in Christ. Pastor urged us to be on the alert to recognize divine activity.

The world is on the alert all right. Since September 11, 2001, we live with grief and uncertainty in the United States in a way that we have not known before. Another attack could come anytime. Even WW II didn't hold this kind of imminent, random danger. Since last week's raising of the security level to orange, Stephanie Rose is having a terrible time trying to decide if she will fly to New York for her friend Colleen's wedding—and as a loving grandmother, I certainly share her concern. Steph hates flying anyway, and it didn't help that her friend's cousin was on the plane out of Boston that was brought down on 9/11.

In the midst of our complicated messes, it is definitely reassuring when Jesus asserts: "Heaven and earth will pass away, but my words will not pass away." No evil, no mistake, no mystery or misery can withstand God's gracious love, ultimately. Amen! Come, Lord Jesus. Hurry!

Pr. Sauer surprised me by asking me to visit Mindy Lucas. She joined St. Timothy sometime last summer but hasn't been back. I believe Mindy was in Stephanie's high school graduation class; maybe she'll go with me. I certainly don't know what to say to a young woman who doesn't want to come to church anymore. I wish Pastor hadn't asked me. Eek.

Second Sunday of Advent

Malachi 3:1-4
Luke 1:68-79
Philippians 1:3-11
Luke 3:1-6

"The Church is like an old woman with no teeth, sitting in a corner muttering to herself, and nobody is paying her any attention."

I heard an Anglican bishop make this statement, which rings very true to me, I'm sad to say. And yet, I love that old woman. She keeps me close to God and therein close to myself. I don't care that many of the people I know ignore the Church, consider it—at best—harmless, because each time my soul empties I can go there, and I am filled again with the graciousness and joy that make all of life bearable, if not splendid. Worship this morning was closer to the bearable. God Almighty seemed a bit weary of his people. He sent messengers to help prepare the way—refine, purify, repent, perfect. Sermon title: "Prepare and Repair." Make our worship, and our lives, pleasing to God.

Well, I don't have to look too far to know that we need to sharpen up our reverence around here. Madge Humphrey, for example. Why in heaven's name does she write her offering check right as the sermon begins?! Then she tears it out a millimeter at a time, and it sounds like it's coming over a microphone for about five minutes. Every Sunday she does this!

The Townshend family lit the advent wreath. Poor Claudia. I'm so grateful to know her through Lydia Circle, and be friends with such a smart, strong lady. She's a wonderful mother, too, but her daughters put her on the spot this morning. They had a little tussle over who would read the scripture and who would light the candles. Michael, the dad, stood by while Claudia firmly and quietly told Rebecca to read, which she did, pouting the whole time. When Rachael, the older girl, went to light the candles, Rebecca "helped" her, jiggling the handle of the lighter with a mischievous smile until her dad had to pull her away. I felt for Claudia; her face was beet red as they made their way back to their seats.

And while I'm on my little tirade, I might as well mention that people creeping in after months of absence bother me too. They show up about now so they can get in on all the Christmas festivities. We won't see them again until Easter or maybe a week or two before. Not much of a living faith, in my opinion. Maybe they're just paying homage to the old lady in the corner.

When I quoted the "Church as an old lady" statement to Virginia the other day, she chuckled knowingly, which irritated me, I guess because she's not an "insider."

(So then why did you even mention it to her, Rose?) Virginia's last day to attend worship regularly was the June Sunday when she was honored as a high school graduate. *Remember what she said, Charlie, when you went to wake her the next Sunday? "Dad, I've gone to church enough to last me the rest of my life."* So far, she has been true to that statement.

Virginia harps on the Church as "empty ritual" and "hotbed of hypocrisy," so unlike her brother. Except for his college years, Stephen has rarely missed Sunday worship, even when he had bad hangovers and even when he was traumatized by his and Denise's divorce. At least Virginia is honest. She freely admits that she comes on Christmas and Easter only because of family tradition. I am so grateful that she and Barry allowed us to take Stephanie with us to St. Timothy.

I understand why people stay away. Faith is not so simple, not always satisfying. Besides that, there is too much bickering, too much majoring in minors, as Pastor puts it. Merciful heavens, I have seen arguments in the church over crosses, carpet, signs, steeples, flowers, altars, toilets, and the Holy Eucharist itself. Big, hateful, mean arguments. Poor Jesus must want to spank us and send us to time out. Sometimes I wonder why I stay, but I can do no other. Life apart from this ragtag group of believers is unthinkable for me. I simply cannot live with any measure of true peace without the crazy Church. I'm convinced we never would have recovered from the tragedy of Charlie's accident without it.

So, I understand people being unchurched or dechurched or antichurched or whatever. Nevertheless, God knows how much I pray that Virginia, and many others, will be drawn back. And I wish I could convey to her the deep and abiding joy that goes so far beyond a pleasurable life and even beyond the precious happiness provided by family. She is a caring person; why doesn't she want to join with others against the sadness and horrors of this world? When will she be blessed to know her need of God? Of course, when I feel most sad and even desperate about my own child's absence from the community that gives me life, I hear a divine chuckle with the message, "Relax, Rose. I have this covered."

Mindy Lucas didn't show up this morning, not that I had any reason to expect that she would. Stephanie didn't want to go with me to visit her, so I went alone last Thursday. I was a little nervous as I walked up to her apartment. I took some deep breaths and prayed that the Lord would be with my mouth.

I rang the bell, then knocked, then knocked again, and was halfway back to my car when I heard a high-pitched, "Yoo-hoo. Here I am," and turned around to see a skinny, tallish young woman with thick-lensed glasses and a wild mop of burgundy-colored hair. She was waving frantically and looked like she had been quickly put together in a rumpled sweat suit.

Mindy is not much of a housekeeper. She had to clear away a place for me to sit. When I squeezed between the coffee table and the chair, I upset a half cup of cold coffee.

She exclaimed, "Oh, shit, I'm so sorry! Oh! and for my language too!"

"No, my fault. Oh dear, what a mess I've made," I apologized.

"Well, if the cup hadn't been sitting there, you wouldn't have spilled it," she countered, bringing a sour smelling dishcloth to wipe it up.

That was a great way to start.

She settled on the sofa, and we traded awkward smiles.

"So, you go to St. Timothy?" she asked.

"Yes, I'm a charter member."

"What's that mean?"

"It means I'm an original member; I was there when the church started 53 years ago."

"Wow. I just joined in July. I was in the pits, big time. I had just gotten fired, which was actually a good thing, and I'd broken up with my boyfriend. Come to think of it, that was a good thing too. But none of it seemed good right then, you know? I knew Pastor Sauer—he'd helped me out through some tough times—so I decided to try church. People were real friendly and nice, it was just what I needed. Now, I've got two pretty good jobs, one at a day care and one at the video store, and I've sworn off men. And, best of all, I'm taking classes to be a radiology technician," she said, sitting up straight. "I'm in pretty good shape now, but I'll probably be back at church for Christmas and maybe bring Regina, that's my mother, on Mother's Day. I like St. Tim."

"My St. Lord!" I thought, using one of Stephanie's early attempts at cursing. I wanted to say, "Well, you little snip. You just think you know it all, don't you?! You don't understand the first thing about true faith."

Instead, I said, "We'll be glad to see you anytime," and smiled politely, then engaged in small talk for a few minutes and made my exit.

"Good-bye, Miss Daisy," she called behind me.

I turned and said evenly, "It's Rose. Not Daisy. Rose."

"Oh," she giggled, "I knew you were a flower."

Why in the world did Pastor ever ask me to go see her? Bad idea.

Merciful heavens, I'm negative and glum this afternoon!

Charlie, if you were here, you would listen to all this with that little half-smile, and when I was all ranted out, you would look at me for a minute and say, "Whew, Rosie! It's a good thing you got those sour apples out of your system." I know you would, and then we'd laugh, and it would be over.

I would take myself for a walk if it weren't so chilly and rainy. I've got to do something. Maybe I'll put on some Quincy Jones and dance like Florence and I used to do after card club before the men got home. Or play the piano. Or I could invite some folks to come over. I hate to impose on anyone though. Life is so busy. This may be the first night Virginia and Barry have had to themselves in a long time, and Stephen told me at church this morning that he's heading for Chicago on business. Stephanie, our Associate Professor of Women's Studies as of June, is probably grading essays or exams. Florence oughtn't to get out in this weather.

Let me end this entry on a positive note (pun intended): what a gift are the songs in Luke! When Vivaldi and Handel and Bach, and contemporary composers as well, got hold of them, wow! We sang Zechariah's "Benedictus" as the gospel canticle. The simple melody flowed smoothly with its powerful promises of deliverance, salvation, light, and peace. Those promises are still real for me on this dark and dreary afternoon and still real for a world continually threatened by danger and uncertainty. Still real, even if many in the world ignore the promises— or don't believe them—or have never heard them.

Later
I'm so glad I found the energy to make some phone calls. Florence and Stephanie and Virginia and Barry came over. Popcorn around the fire and catching up with what we've all been doing was just what I needed! Barry, the storyteller, was hilarious telling about getting rear-ended in slow traffic on the interstate the other day by people who didn't speak English. The woman kept saying, "Too sorry! Too sorry!" Of course, Florence and I told about the wig incident, sometimes unable to speak for laughing. Stephanie was still uncertain about whether or not to fly to New York after Christmas.

"Oh, for heaven's sake, Steph! Get on the damn plane," Virginia said. Stephanie decided to go. May she "be saved from our enemies and from the hand of all who hate us."

Virginia will be honored as the top-selling realtor in her district again, must be at least the third or fourth time. *We're not surprised, are we, Charlie? And while we're always proud, we know her elbows have knocked out some teeth along the way to her success. I don't know how, judging by us, but she was born with a strong competitive streak. Remember when she was a little girl on her way to a birthday party or whatever, we'd say "Bye. Have fun!" and then want to call after her, "And remember, Virginia—life is not a contest!" Wherever two or three were gathered, she organized some kind of winner-loser activity.* Anyway, gathering around the fire was a fine way to spend a winter evening.

I've decided I can't give up on Mindy. Pr. Sauer (who knows? maybe even God!) has put us together for a reason. When I told Pastor about the initial contact, he smiled and said, "I'm glad you're a person who doesn't give up easily." He has so much confidence in me! Pastor and I knew upon our first meeting that we were kindred spirits, and our close relationship has developed from there. I am almost embarrassed sometimes by his high regard for me, when he speaks of me in public as "a Shakespeare scholar and gifted lay theologian." That's laying it on a little thick, I'd say.

Anyway, I must find a way of sharing the good news of the gospel with this young woman, Mindy. Maybe I'll bake a loaf of sweet bread for her and stop by this week.

Dear God, grant me wisdom and grant me courage for the living of these days. Amen.

Third Sunday of Advent

Zephaniah 3:14-20
Isaiah 12:2-6
Philippians 4:4-7
Luke 3:7-18

 The "brood of vipers" gospel has never been the same for those of us who remember Pr. Herbert's rendition of it about twenty-five years ago. After we had sung "Glory to you, O Lord" before the reading, he took off his robe. He was dressed in some kind of camel's hair costume, and he let us have it. "Prepare the way of the Lord!" We didn't respond like the crowd in the Bible and ask what we could do, but he told us anyway. "Give money to global ministries instead of getting new carpet! Put on a Christmas dinner for the poor! March in the 'Justice for All' rally!" We were very uncomfortable—except for Louella Rutledge, of course—and considered his behavior highly inappropriate. *We talked for years about how good it would have been if we'd done what he'd suggested though, didn't we, Charlie?*

 And then there was that time he seated himself with his back to the congregation until the sermon, his point being that the congregation was looking backward instead of forward, I think. Poor Pr. Herbert. After just six months at St. Timothy, he went into a psychiatric ward. The last I heard he was selling vacuum cleaners. Merciful heavens, I hope he is not still doing that. Unless he really likes it.

 Today was the day of the pink candle in the Advent wreath, joyjoyjoy. Notwithstanding cousin John's fiery message, joy and hope and the presence of God pervaded the service. Nowhere was the divine presence more evident than in the lighting of the advent candles by Susie and Pete Wakefield and their grandson, Gene's little boy. It hasn't been a year since Gene was crushed to death by a backhoe on a construction site while he was tying his shoe. I know they're still in agony. Joy makes no sense for those parents, yet Susie will be the first one to tell a great joke or laugh heartily at someone else's. She and Pete love to talk about Gene, love to hear others tell stories about him. The apostle Paul certainly had no reason to pray with joy from prison either. *Charlie, the first time you laughed, I mean genuinely laughed, after the accident, I knew you were seeing the light of God's grace again. You hadn't laughed for over a year.* I agree with Fra Giovanni: "Joy is the most infallible sign of the presence of God."

 Now here's something. I sat next to Claudia this morning. During the confession of the creed, it sounded like she was saying some extra words a couple times. When we said the Lord's Prayer, I distinctly heard, "Our Father-Mother" instead of "Our Father." Claudia and I need to talk. I'll have her over for tea.

I'm trying some of Pr. Sauer's far-out ideas. I've been fasting these Sunday mornings in Advent. I felt a little weak and shaky when I stood up to go to communion, but when I knelt, some kind of metaphysics took over. From that little bit of bread, strength flowed through every part of my body. That swallow of wine warmed me with a powerful sensation of well-being. Thank you God, Christ, Holy Spirit.

These are the truths that I so badly want to get across to Mindy, but I sense she would not understand or is not ready. When I dropped by with a loaf of pumpkin bread yesterday, she didn't even invite me in. She was still in her bathrobe at 11 o'clock. Obviously, the child needs help, needs direction, needs to delve into life more deeply. I wish she would let me help. How can I communicate God's love to her?

Later
Florence and I went caroling at Rutledge Home, as always, but I halfway wish I hadn't. First of all, several were grumbling because Pastor didn't make it. Louella came as usual; after all, the place is named after her father who gave the money for it ever so long ago. The youth group was supposed to come, but only Stuart Brown turned up, bless his heart. I was happy to see Eugene and Danny Bennett. Some people seem to feel uncomfortable with Danny's Down's syndrome and the childlike behaviors that go with it, but I find his innocent frankness refreshing. Madge Humphrey was there, of course, acting like she was in charge. Actually, I guess she was, and things were nicely organized. That woman is such a perfectionist! I'll bet she flosses her teeth right before she goes to bed and again as soon as she gets up.

Anyway, I'm afraid the effort was not very uplifting for anyone. We gathered around Kathryn Bjorklund's recliner, and she cried and gave a self-pitying speech about how no one visits her, except at Christmas time. She can't make the connection between her crankiness and people not visiting. Besides, I'm there every month; am I nobody? (whines Rose).

Poor old Bill Jackson is completely bedridden and can hardly hear or see. His bowels moved while we were singing "Angels We Have Heard on High." The smell was almost unbearable and Danny kept saying, "Whew! S-s-tinks!" and waving his hand in front of his face. We moved out quickly singing "Gloria!" As we walked down the hall, I heard Florence telling young Stuart that Bill used to be on the Parish Council, etc.

We couldn't rouse Mrs. Wheaton, and Mary Thurgood didn't even turn around, just kept staring out the window. Sam Benshaw was a bright spot, as usual. He shared his Christmas poem with us. At the age of 97, he's experimenting! This was the first poem he has ever written that doesn't rhyme, a haiku:

God's new baby boy
Sleeping sweetly in cow trough
Loves us like a dog

Now, here come the Sunday night blues again. *Charlie, I miss you! I feel like a widowed goose honking alone in the cold moonlight. And how strange to think that I loved you passionately for 50 years when you irritated me more than any human being I have ever known.*
What irritated me the most? His chiding me about alcoholism every time I indulged in a glass of wine? (Actually, he stopped doing that after Stephen blew up at him once—"You have no idea what alcoholism is Dad, and neither does Mom!" he'd said with fury.) Or Charlie's obsession with roller-skating? Or how he would ask for my opinion when he had already made up his mind? Or 25 other habits? I'd take all 25 at once to have him back. I can't believe I'm saying this, but I even miss his flatulence. In fact, for months after he died I would hear his ghost "let 'er rip" and instantaneously break into a sob.

Florence was my angel, one of several through my first year alone. She knew exactly what was going on, having lost Arnie two years before. She gave sympathy and support for a reasonable length of time; then she tough-loved me out of abject grief. Even though it's been awhile, I remember it like it was yesterday…

"It's time for faith, woman! I've had about enough of your moping, and I expect the good Lord has too. Charlie would be disappointed in you, Rose."

She seemed unaffected as my muffled sniffles increased to hands- over- my- face sobs.

"Tomorrow night you are coming to my house for a turn- the- corner dinner, so you pull yourself together between now and then! I'll see you at six." With that she left, the kitchen door slamming behind her.

I sobbed for another five minutes, then marched to the bathroom, resolutely washed my face, and dialed her phone number. My heart was beating rapidly as I planned my speech.

"Florence Lawrence, I will not be manipulated into your little do- gooder dinner. I am working through my grief in my own way at my own pace. I am deeply hurt that you don't understand, or at least accept that. I sincerely hope that this will not be the end of our long friendship, but I am in too much pain right now to talk with you anymore. I will be back in touch when the time is right."

Then I would hang up on her, fully assured that we would never break up; we could blackmail each other several times over.

Drat. No answer. She hadn't gone straight home. I fueled my anger with tears and self- pity and tried to call three more times. As emotions subsided, I resigned myself to appreciating her intent and indulging her with her little plan but not enjoying the experience. I would be distant and patronizingly patient with my insensitive friend.

So, the next night, assuming a pleasant but cool attitude, I rang her doorbell.

When she swept the door open, I thought for the hundredth time about opposites attracting and how this chic, petite woman with perfectly white wavy hair, who loved to smoke and drive big cars and read romance novels, was best friends with me—a gangly, big-boned English teacher with straight-as-a-stick mousey gray hair who cares nothing for makeup or fashions and gets sick at the mere smell of tobacco. When she hugged me around the waist, her head on my bosom, I surrendered into a long embrace. My charade was over.

"I smell apple pie," I said, composing myself as I took my jacket off. "From the market, I presume."

She shook her head.

"Florence, you hate to make apple pie!"

"It's your favorite," she said simply, leading the way to the kitchen.

Over fine wine, she told of her latest standoff with the neighbor's Chihuahua. Hilarious. At the elegant table adorned with shiny china and silver and freshly cut roses, we savored a choice cut and vegetables flavored to perfection. Classical music played in the background. Conversation ranged from books to church matters to the downtown gazebo controversy to memories of Charlie and Arnie and family times together. Over coffee and pie of flakey crust and spicy, tender fruit, Florence presented me with a handsomely tied packet of forty years worth of snapshots, all of which included Charlie. Small wonder it was nearly midnight when silence came over us, and it was time to part.

On the sidewalk in the light of an almost full moon, I remember whispering thank you. Florence breathed a soft, "You are most welcome, dear friend." The Chihuahua next door yapped, breaking us up.

Ever since then, whenever I smell fresh-baked apple pie I immediately feel precious and hopeful. That aroma is sweeter than the most fragrant incense Pr. Sauer could ever burn. Florence was a "little Christ" to me.

But tonight I just plain feel rotten. A gin and tonic is tempting and might give momentary comfort, but I might have to pay with a headache. I don't have the strength to make a call or dance or even switch on the TV. It's no use tonight. My soul and body ache with futility, even in this season of celebration. Even though I am blessed with the finest of friends and family. Even in spite of my fervent beliefs. When the time comes, I will be so happy to go home to God. This sentiment seems horribly sinful, yet I can't deny a death wish, fleeting though it may be. "Would I were dead! If God's good will were so; For what is in this world but grief and woe?" penned my dear friend, Will Shakespeare, sage of human pathos, and so say I tonight.

Oh, God, maybe you need to give me a good swift kick. In the meantime, thank you for holding me in your forgiving love while I wait for a new day. Amen.

Fourth Sunday of Advent

Micah 5:2-5a
Luke 1:47-55
Hebrews 10:5-10
Luke 1:39-45 (46-55)

Mother Mary, "the Mother of God," as the Orthodox say, was the star in worship today which reminded me of the night the Beatles came to Lydia Circle. Claudia led the Bible study about Mary and used songs to reflect the qualities of Mary we were considering. To show Mary as accepting of God's will, she played "Let It Be," which worked perfectly! Since then, I've prayed with Mary on occasion. Last Sunday night in my hour of darkness I prayed with her while I gazed at a Christmas card of mother and child. Like a truly depressed person, I dragged my lanky self to bed to escape into the relief of sleep. As I was lying there, Mary seemed to come to me, saying, "Rose, you're okay. It's all right to be sad. I've known sadness. God is with you. Let it be." For the first time in a long time, I slept the night through, waking at dawn feeling unreasonably refreshed and lighthearted. This morning when we sang "Awake, Awake, and Greet the New Morn," I thought, "Holy smokes, that's exactly what happened to me last week!— 'In darkest night his coming will be, when all the world is despairing, As morning light so quiet and free, so warm and gentle and caring.'" (Haugen)

At the advent tea a couple weeks ago, everyone brought a nativity figure and a thought or poem to go with it. Pauline came from the group home. We're always glad to see her, though we never know what to expect. When it was her turn, she marched up to the table, plunked down a crudely painted ceramic Mary made for her by a friend, and said, "This is Mary. She has tears runnin' down her cheeks." There was an almost audible gasp of surprise; Pauline firmly responded, "That's right. She's cryin' because she knows her son is gonna' get killed for the forgiveness of our sins." She marched back to her seat, and we sat in thoughtful silence for a moment.

And the poetic, majestic Magnificat! But just a minute—who are the proud, the powerful, the rich, who are going to be sent away empty? Us?! If every middle-class Christian—actually every Jew and every Muslim too, because the thoughts and words of the Magnificat come from the Old Testament—wanted to be part of God's kingdom, wouldn't we make radical changes in lifestyle? For example, wouldn't I sell my house and move into a modest apartment and give all the proceeds to those in need, the wounded, the "anawim" (that Greek word I learned at a seminar once)? Even while cherishing Mary's song, I squirm in the pew when I hear it.

Claudia came for tea last week, after we'd gone to Evelyn Blake's funeral. Evelyn was the oldest member of Lydia Circle—I should think so, at 102! Claudia and I marveled at how Evelyn, with her granddaughter's help, had hosted us at her house just a few months ago. And then, as I lit the candles in the advent wreath and poured the tea, I got right to what was on my mind.

"Tell me about using feminist language in worship, Claudia."

"Well," she paused, gazing out into the backyard, then looking me in the eye. "I either modify the language or leave the church; I am increasingly alienated from an exclusively masculine God.

"Rose," she leaned toward me, "I have no doubt in my mind that the Divine is beyond gender. When we assign gender, it is a sign of our limited understanding. We are making God in our image. So, to balance out paternalistic, militant images of an old, angry white male, I add the feminine—Father-Mother…"Our Father-Mother who art in heaven'…'The Holy Spirit proceeds from the Father-Mother and with the Father-Mother is worshiped and glorified.' That kind of thing."

Zounds! In the twinkling of a second, she wiped out thousands of years of tradition, of carefully thought-out and corporately created creeds and theology. Such radical action took my breath away. What does a creed even mean if we each change whatever we don't like or don't quite exactly believe? Shouldn't we either swallow it whole or spit it out? We don't even understand it all, for heaven's sake. But it's our faith, the faith of our fathers going back for centuries. Mothers, too, certainly. A veritable cloud of witnesses who lived their lives, and in many instances, gave their lives, consumed by their convictions. Their God-given convictions.

Not that I wouldn't have added a sentence to the creed if I'd been in on the final draft. I am perpetually amazed that the word love is not uttered when we confess our faith, the faith in which we baptize. After "conceived by the power of the Holy Spirit and became incarnate from the Virgin Mary," I would add, "He lived a life of love." I suppose we can infer that Jesus was motivated by love when he let himself suffer under Pontius Pilate, die, and be buried, but in this most bold statement of the faith of the whole Church, I don't think inference is adequate. Love should be clearly stated in there somewhere, as far as I'm concerned.

I decided to go the next step with Claudia.

"But isn't "Father-Mother" just as genderized as Father? If God is beyond gender, how does that help?"

She nodded. "Using male and female is a bridge for me," she replied, "a bridge I think I'm almost over. Inclusive language is helping me move from the exclusively masculine God to the great Divine Being beyond our imaginations and our definitions. Really, I don't find Father-Mother that meaningful, but it helps me go with the flow in worship.

"Sometimes I alternate the pronoun—'The Lord is my shepherd, I shall not want. She makes me to lie down in green pastures; he leads me beside still waters; she restores my soul. He leads me in paths of righteousness for her name's sake.' Grammatically absurd but theologically more sensible.

"And dealing with the issue is not even that simple, Rose!" her voice rising. "A gender-inclusive terminology would include Goddess; Lord would also be Lady, except for Lord Jesus, of course, and then there's kingdom," she sighed.

My head began to ache; Lord God is a very meaningful term to me—and yet I see her point. I watched this earnest young sister in the faith as she watched the birds at the feeder.

"You may think this is weird, Rose, but I'm going to tell you anyway. Spirits visit me on occasions, spirits of millions of women, ancient and modern, who have been systematically denied the opportunity to be the people they were created to be—composers, writers, architects, scientists, doctors, actors, who were never allowed to develop, to function, to know the exhilaration of expressing their deepest longings and using their gifts to glorify the Creator who gave them their talents in the first place! We're present throughout history, if only we can find where we've been hidden."

"Yes," I murmured as a memory took shape in my consciousness. "My Aunt Beatrice was in med school when I was about 11 or 12 years old. Aunt Bea didn't make it. On her last day, she stopped at our house, forlorn and agitated. She was wearing a brown suit with a brown hat that had a feather. I remember my mother comforting her. I remember them talking about all women as 'us.' She and Mother were sad and angry, and I wondered how in the world anyone as smart as Aunt Bea could ever flunk out of anything."

Claudia nodded, and in a moment her frustration boiled over again.

"And when we try to make amends for centuries of tragedy by changing language, because the masculine deity is part of that oppressive ball of wax, we're met with derision! Inclusive language is treated as an irritating, petty fad that one must occasionally endure in public but can ridicule in private!"

Deep sigh and shake of head.

"But I must get going. It's my day to be home for the girls." When she took my hands in hers and said, "Thanks for this time, Rose," I felt highly honored.

With a hug at the front door, we agreed to keep talking, and as Claudia, woman of faith, danced gracefully down the walk, arms outstretched to avoid slipping on the patches of ice, I wondered what language would come next to help her stay in the fold.

And then there's Mindy. Mindy, Mindy, Mindy. *God, what would you have me do here?* WWJD, to quote popular bracelets. All I want to do is share the marvelous news of divine love and mercy, but she will not hear. I'm about to shake the dust off my sneakers with this child.

I stopped at her apartment on my way home from working at the food pantry the other night to bring her a little nativity scene with a candle in the middle of it. She thanked me sweetly and set it on top of one of several cups on the dusty coffee table. We chatted for a few minutes over the blaring of the TV. I asked how she would be spending Christmas Day. Merciful heavens, I got a soap opera in reply, complete with salty language describing family feuds, telephones angrily hung up, relatives estranged for years. I felt more blessed by my own family with each of her anecdotes.

As she was talking, something on her cluttered kitchen table caught my eye. Whatever it was looked familiar yet strange. Then, I recognized it; it was the pumpkin bread I had brought her, still wrapped in plastic and greenish-blue with mold. I said a quick good-bye and rushed out into the fresh, cold air. What would Jesus do? Well, I'm not Jesus, that's for sure.

Christmas Eve

Isaiah 9:2-7
Psalm 96
Titus 2:11-14
Luke 2:1-14(15-20)

What a night of contrasts! Dazzling and dingy. In the midst of fancy clothes and family togetherness I met a homeless couple. And while cloth of gold adorned the altar and candles glittered everywhere, along with Chrismons and twinkle lights on two huge trees, Pastor Sauer preached, "The people have walked in darkness, and still are, and when we gather next Christmas Eve, the likelihood is that we will still be walking in darkness…"

He went immediately on to remind us that into this darkness a great light shines. He dubbed Isaiah "God's prophet and preacher" who announced the light and proclaimed the coming of the light to people like us, people painfully puzzled by events in their world. On this cold, dark night we gather together to proclaim and to believe that the light shines on us, that it shines into the hell of Iraq, into the dark and dreamless streets of Darfur, into the horrors of homicide all around us, and into wastelands where villages once stood. "The grace of God has appeared in a manger," he declared and talked of the child who grew to a man, offering us everything God has to give. "And the gift is enough," Pastor said earnestly, claiming that the power of love enfolds the cosmos, and we tremble and bow when we recognize that power.

He gave voice to the thought that maybe we're crazy to believe something so outlandish and mysterious as light shining into so much darkness. "Probably some of you sitting here right now think such talk is insane." I sensed Barry's head nodding as Pastor forged right ahead, saying that "we, the Church, carry on the same mission as Isaiah, to help reveal the ferocious grace of Yahweh, the Almighty One. The words addressed to the church of Titus' time repeat the refrain," he said, "bidding us to live strong lives of purpose and hope that give witness to the light.

"And so, like our fathers and mothers in the faith over the millennia, we will sing our song again and again because the message is new, fresh, vital and amazing once more. We do not have to live in the darkness, alone and afraid."

Leaving no room for discussion, he concluded with a shout, "The zeal of the Lord will do this!" *God of Light, this night I thank you once again for the marvelous gift of having Marcus Sauer as my pastor and spiritual friend!*

Dinner at Virginia and Barry's before we all came to the service dazzled as always. Virginia had decorated with gold, crystal, evergreens and just the right touch of mistletoe with its white berries. Her Honey Glow hairdo, stylish glasses, and green velvet pantsuit complemented the scene.

The children surprised me with gas logs for my fireplace. I know Stephen meant it kindly when he said that flicking a switch to have a fire is age-appropriate for me, but *Charlie, you know how I've always loved everything about a wood fire—cutting and stacking the wood, building the fire, cleaning out the ashes. Now I feel like I'm being dictated to about what I can and can't do. I don't know, Charlie, am I being unreasonable, ungrateful? Gas logs will be a lot easier. Gratitude would be a better response than offense, wouldn't it?*

Stephanie gave me an anthology of feminist theological writings which I will look forward to reading and maybe share with Claudia. Significantly, Stephanie's beau, Ethan, joined us this year. Virginia tells me they're living together. I am truly surprised. I expected better of Stephanie Rose.

Worshiping with my family was the crowning glory of the evening (except for that moment when "Oh Come, Let Us Adore Hi-im, Chri-i-st the Lord!" still hung in the air and I thought my heart would burst with joy and I heard Virginia mutter, "Good God, I'd forgotten how much I detest organ music!").

The best gift of the evening was Mindy, not just that she came to worship, much more than that. She was with a couple I assumed were relatives. I found out differently after the service. She rushed up to me saying, "Miss Rose, Miss Rose, do you all have any food around this place, a food pantry or something?"

She explained that she had met Garfield Temple when she stopped for gas earlier in the evening. She didn't exactly introduce us, just tossed her head towards the thirty-something fellow in a grease-encrusted gas station jacket that said "Stan." He has just worked at the station for a couple days. He and his wife, Marie (another head toss), are staying in the motel next door to the station, the Cloverleaf. They are trying to get from Missouri to upper Michigan and having a hard time of it. Mindy invited them to come to the Christmas Eve service.

My family waited patiently outside the kitchen door while I filled a couple bags with groceries for Mindy's new friends. Mr. Temple asked if we happened to have any dog food. I laughed but didn't ask questions. Normally, I would have thought, "What nerve! People in their situation have no business having a dog." In the merriness of the moment, I just threw in a couple extra cans of corned beef hash. *You always thought it looked and tasted like dog food anyway, Charlie!*

Then came the zinger. Mindy asked me what I was doing tomorrow. When I told her I wasn't sure—that Virginia was going downstate to Barry's family dinner and Stephen was going to his girlfriend's house and Stephanie to her boyfriend's— she invited me to Christmas dinner with Garfield and Marie at her place. I surprised myself by saying yes.

As we were getting in the car Virginia said something about who were these people and what in the world was I thinking?! Stephen added that old, tired, "Mother, how do you get yourself into these fixes?"

I could have played dumb, but they would have thrown all those past situations in my face—Linda, who stayed with us a while, along with her fleas and lice; and Andre, who came for Christmas holidays and left in March, still without a job; and of course, Frank and Jan—and their five kids. Oh my, I've known some people, each one precious! *I should say we, shouldn't I, Charlie? You were in on all those. We had some adventures, didn't we?!*

Stephanie told them to leave me alone, I knew what I was doing. Sitting here at 1 a.m. as tired as can be, I'm not so sure I do. We'll take it all up again in the morning.

Christmas Day

Isaiah 52:7-10
Psalm 98
Hebrews 1:1-4(5-12)
John 1:1-14

Of course I went to Mindy's for Christmas dinner, even though a million reasons not to go danced in my head like sugarplums when I was trying to fall asleep last night:
- I'm too old
- the children wouldn't approve
- I'd rather sit by the fire and cry
- she might serve moldy food
- Mindy and the Temples might be con artists
- some of her angry relatives might stop by

Charlie, you and the Holy Spirit cut through it all, saying, "Don't be a silly old fool. Go to the banquet!" You came to me in a dream:
I was in the kitchen (but it was really your childhood kitchen) fixing myself something to eat. I sat down at the table and closed my eyes to say a blessing. You tapped me on the shoulder. I knew it was you even though you didn't speak. I held my finger up to say just a minute. When I finished my blessing, I looked up and saw you walking into the dining room. There was light coming through the doorway and the sound of people talking and laughing. I heard a bird at the window, swishing its wing against the glass. I knew you wanted me to come into the dining room, but I didn't want to. The bird swished at the window again. That made me mad, and I threw something at the window. I realized I was mad because you were having a great time in the dining room when I wanted you to come and sit with me in the kitchen. The bird kept swishing by. I kept throwing something, maybe a fork, but it wouldn't move through the air, it just kept dropping down on the table right in front of me. The bird kept swishing, and I kept throwing. And then, I realized the bird was the Holy Spirit in cahoots with you, telling me to go in the dining room. I woke up laughing and laughed even harder when I saw that a branch of shrubbery was blowing against my window. So, thanks to you, husband, I got up and went to the banquet.

And a banquet it was, although not in physical food, particularly. Mindy burned everything except the cake, which was gooey in the middle. Burned peas, burned rolls, burned mashed potatoes, even. Dry, leathery turkey loaf. We dubbed her "the

Merry Arsonist" because every time one of us would smell something scorching she would squeal and laugh and say, "Not again!" or "Can you believe this?!"

Naturally, the air began to get a little smoky and, naturally, the smoke alarm went off. The deafening screech was piercing our eardrums, but even I couldn't reach the thing. We opened the doors and windows and were freezing, and still the doggone alarm pierced on. We were all laughing like idiots. Finally, we unset the table and dragged it over, and Marie climbed up and pulled the battery out. A collective sigh into the silence brought forth another wave of laughter.

Tramp, their dog, was a perfect gentleman, content to eat leftovers, of which there were several, and sleep under the table.

"People look down on us for having a dog," Garfield commented. "What the heck, I know it doesn't make good sense. But I feel sorry for anybody who might try and take this pup away from us. We've got as much right as anybody to a little extra friend to love. The minute I saw him wander out of the woods behind the gas station, I knew he was ours."

"He's part of us now," Marie chimed in. "I guess he's the child we've never been able to have."

Marie is quite intriguing. She is a strikingly beautiful woman of dark, silky complexion and shiny dark hair pulled smoothly back into a bun. Her face is full and healthy-looking, which surprises me, given the fact that she is essentially a homeless person. She didn't volunteer too much about herself, and I didn't want to nose around. Well, of course, I did, but I restrained myself. She has a certain air that makes me think she is probably educated and had a good upbringing.

I told my childhood holiday story of Mother molding hamburger into the shape of a turkey because we had our own beef from Grandpa's farm but couldn't afford a turkey. They thought that was pretty fascinating and had all kinds of questions about the Depression years and WW II. I told them about my brother Dewayne and how we all thought the war ruined him. I bet I heard Mother say a hundred times, with that pained expression, "He's not the same boy who left here."

"The Vietnam war killed my dad,"˙ Garfield said. "He's not actually dead, but he might as well be. I remember him waking up screaming with nightmares. He kept getting fired from jobs; no one could get it that he was disabled. The war ruined him. Agent Orange, post traumatic, alcohol, drugs, the whole ten yards. I've got this long, drawn-out case going with the V.A. I've got three of the best lawyers in St. Louie on restrainers with it, and I should have about three-quarters of a million in the next year or so." Hm.

You sure didn't have those kinds of problems with war, Charlie. Of course, it was a very different war from any fought since. You couldn't wait to get over there and fight Hitler for the sake of freedom and justice for all. Like your father before you, you've always been proud of being in the service and ready to die, if necessary. You still had nightmares though. "Hell doesn't even begin to describe how awful war is," I've heard you say. Somehow, the horror and hardship didn't twist your insides and break your spirit. The war devoured Dewayne, but you never looked down on him. You were a fine brother-in-law, and I am forever grateful to you for that. I've always wondered if Dewayne would have had the drinking problem if not for the war. Probably, since Dad was alcoholic. Of course, Dad was a victim of WW I. "O war, thou son of hell."

I told them all about you, the amazing Charlie Harris. You seemed to be sitting there beside me, enjoying it all. As shy as you could be, you always loved a party.

I even told them about the accident, Charlie.

Shaking her head, Marie murmured, "How do people keep going after killing someone in a car accident?"

"Only by the grace of God," I said, your wounds and healing wrapped in those simple words. How sweet it was to share you with others. They all said they wished they'd known you.

Garfield brought his guitar, and we sang Christmas carols after dinner. I think we didn't sound too great. His guitar was missing a few strings, and we were missing a few notes and very sketchy on the words. Garfield also sang a couple original compositions. Not bad. Marie watched him with unmistakable admiration. One of his songs was called "Every Day Again," a ballad about the ups and downs of life and never giving up, obviously a good song for old mercurial me.

As I made motions to leave, Mindy jumped up and said we must do something to mark such a special occasion. She had us put our arms around each other and sway and sing "I'm Dreaming of a White Christmas." Another sweet and bizarre moment. I offered to drop the Temples at the motel on my way home.

"This was a more wonderful Christmas than we could ever have imagined, Rose," Marie said, leaning across the seat to give me another hug. Garfield seconded the motion and smooched my cheek from the back seat. Tramp would have done the same thing, I'm sure, but fortunately Garfield restrained him. I'll take cats, thank you.

Stephen and Virginia each called a little while ago and asked me how my day was. They enjoyed all the details and were glad I was home safe, as though I had been in some kind of danger. More than anything, I told them, it was unique to join in intimate festivity with people I didn't even know 24 hours ago.

Thank you God, for that holy time. Thank you, Christ, for coming to me in these people and showing me that I don't have a monopoly on your love. Thank you, Holy Spirit, for beating your wings against my window. Amen.

First Sunday of Christmas

1 Samuel 2:18-20, 26
Psalm 148
Colossians 3:12-17
Luke 2:41-52

Sea monsters, praise the Lord! Snow, praise the Lord! I love that Psalm 148! What a perfectly marvelous picture of the cosmos knowing its Creator. The choir sang a delightful anthem based on it that actually had us laughing out loud. Us! Laughing out loud! That ancient psalm brings to mind a piece by Christopher Smart that I heard Stephanie's college choir sing. I memorized a line in honor of Cute Baby and other felines: "For I am possessed of a cat, surpassing in beauty, from whom I take occasion to bless Almighty God."

In the Old and New lessons, we heard about two twelve-year-old boys in temples, Samuel and Jesus, and two mothers who gave them up to God's service. Samuel was probably three when he went to live with Eli, Pr. Sauer said. How could Hannah stand it, I wonder. She had waited so long for a child and then, just when she can carry on a conversation with him and he can express his thoughts and looks like a little person instead of a baby, off he goes. She saw him only once a year, to bring him the next size gown to wear. Hannah certainly lived out Kahil Gibran's philosophy that "your children are not your children."

Pastor linked Hannah and Mary's dedication of their children with the vows that we parents make at our children's baptisms. In his sermon, he answered a question I've wanted to ask him for a long time, namely, why do we baptize babies when it's quite evident that their parents have no intention of fulfilling the vows? They come all dressed up with an entourage showing off their baby for the baptism and have a big dinner afterwards, but then they don't come back. What's the point? Doesn't that cheapen baptism?

From the pulpit, Pastor shared the struggle. He plans baptisms with the parents, explaining the vows and the expectations. He prays that the Holy Spirit will work through this event to draw the family back or in to the community of faith. Regardless of the outcome, he went on to explain, it is not our role to judge people's intent but only to administer the holy sacrament when requested. The rest is up to God, and the seed planted on the day of baptism may not bear visible fruit until much later. I'm glad I never put him on the spot by asking him. Heavens, I knew the answer—or at least recognized it when he said it.

When Danny Bennett was baptized, about 23 years ago, somebody (I can't remember who) asked what the point was since Danny wouldn't be able to understand the teachings or worship. My, what foolish thinking! Danny often expresses the faith more simply and purely than the rest of us even can. This morning he came running up to me with his Bible.

"R-r-r-read me a st-st-story, R-r-rose," he asked, thrusting it into my hands, open to Exodus.

I said, "This is about Moses."

"Yeah, that's g-g-good. I love those g-g-guys—Larry, Curly and Moses!" Okay, so he won't be a biblical scholar.

Pastor announced the winter spiritual retreat during announcements this morning. The topic is going to be icons. An Orthodox priest will be the leader. Pr. Sauer is bringing icons into St. Timothy more and more. Florence says Pastor Sauer is just too damn religious for us! I heard even sweet old, dedicated, long-suffering George Hapless say recently that he'd seen enough icons to last him the rest of his life and besides, aren't they idols? I don't think Carolyn Sauer cares for them too much either. "Jesus looks like he ate a bad hot dog," I once heard her comment. Personally, I think they're very weird. Some of the hair-dos are ridiculous. Obviously, Pastor gets a great deal of meaning out of icons and several people in the congregation are very attracted to them. He uses them as sermon illustrations, explaining intricate symbolism, but, frankly, I have trouble listening and understanding because my resistance to them is so strong.

So maybe, I thought, learning about icons is one of those experiences God is sending to stretch me spiritually. Okay, I'll go! Haven't missed the retreat in eight years. Why should I let icons scare me away? I thought it would be great if Florence went too, but I guess I tried a little too hard to encourage her into it.

"I'm just not as holy as you, Rose," she finally said, with a mocking smile. I could have slapped her.

Well, I've had my glass of sweet concord grape wine, a frequent Sunday practice since Charlie's been gone. *(Hush, Charlie. I AM NOT AN ALCOHOLIC.)* Combined with fasting before communion, the sweet drink extends the sweetness of grace afforded at the altar. I consider alcohol sacred and am astounded by the sensations of peace and power and wisdom it gives me, all from God. This is a crazy way for a child of an alcoholic and a parent of an alcoholic to talk, but this simply is how I understand and use alcohol—"wine to gladden the human heart."

Then, I spent an hour at the piano, wrestling with Bach's Fugue 20—I don't know if I will master it this side of heaven! I also went to Rutledge Home this afternoon. Pretty much status quo there—Sam was perky, Kathryn was grumpy, Mary Thurgood seemed to be surrounded, as usual, by her own personal "cloud of unknowing." And then I had the shock of my life: Steve Hagendorf is a new resident there—Alzheimer's! Merciful heavens, he can't be more than 60! He was 44, I think, when he became our hotshot new principal. More shot than hot, I always thought. And there he sat this afternoon, a convalescent, "his brain as barren as banks of Libya." I had heard that he had some health issues, but I didn't know it was early Alzheimer's. When I said, "Hello, Mr. Hagendorf," he just looked at me dumbly. Oh! how the pathway of life can twist and turn!

Speaking of pathways, on my way to the grocery store yesterday I saw Garfield and Marie Temple walking along Washington St. where there are no sidewalks. I drove by them first, but then went around the block and offered them a lift. Even though it was bitterly cold, Marie said she wanted to walk. They argued in strained tones for a minute, Marie turning her back to the car. Garfield came back and said no thanks with a helpless smile. His pockmarked face looked especially tired and scruffy with his straggly mustache and dark bags under his eyes. His only coat was that thin gas station jacket.

Dear, oh dear, I'm afraid those two may not be doing too well. And shall I try to help? What could I do? What do they need? Prayers for them have been flashing through my mind continually. I think if I'm supposed to get more involved with them, God will put them in my path, *won't you, God?* I do know that they're in Room 6 at the Cloverleaf Motel. Is that in my path?!

I was still contemplating the Temples' situation after I got back from the grocery store when cousin Josephine called. We hadn't talked since early last summer. She wants me to come down and visit her. I guess I ought to—merciful heavens, another decision! I've always wondered why Josephine is such an odd duck. I never knew her mother, Aunt Somebody-or-Other. She died when Josephine was born, I think. Uncle Ralph, Dad's brother, stayed in Mississippi after being down there in the service. As I recall, Uncle Ralph was pretty strict.

Josephine asked me how everyone was and how I spent Christmas Day. She was quite intrigued with the cast of characters. She spent the day alone, as usual. Out of the blue, in her breathy, slurred diction—a combination of medication and Southern drawl—she said, "Rose, how ah loved yo' daddy!"

Dad/my father/Clarence Brinkley. The Editor, Dewayne and I called him and we loved hanging out at the newspaper office where he was at his best. A man of contradictions: intellectual yet impractical, wise but weak, kind but undependable, courageous yet self-destructive. Named top editor in the state one year, burned down the newspaper office the next. He was a grand human being! Troubled but grand.

"Do you 'member him payin' us a dollah to take his shoes off that tahm? He was so funny," cousin Josephine giggled.

As soon as she said that, I felt like I was eight years old and it seemed like it could have happened yesterday...

Josephine was visiting and we were going to play in the Studebaker. Walking up to the car, I got a whiff of that strange smell that Dad gave off when he was

sick. When the two of us creaked the door open, it was a big scare to see the bottoms of his shoes. He was lying sideways on the front seat, his knees bent and his hands pillowing his head. My heart stopped and then pounded. He looked dead. I was ready to run screaming to Mother, but Josephine tee- heed in delight because she was crazy about him and didn't know anything about his sick times.

He bent his neck up and looked at us.

"Hi, girls," he said, and his head dropped back down and he said, "Rosie, tag my shoes off, would ya', darlin'?" in that lazy voice I hated.

I didn't much want to touch him because I felt like this wasn't really Dad; maybe it was some hobo who had climbed in our car pretending to be him. Josephine was already untying his shoes.

He said, "Thas a sweet girl, tha feels so good," and reached in his pocket and said, "Here, take this for helping me out, my li'l sweet princesses," and tossed a folded up dollar bill toward us.

She picked up the money and I snatched it out of her hand, giggling like crazy, thinking about running to the store and picking out a hundred pieces of candy. But I also knew something was bad wrong and ran in the house and gave the money to Mother and told her what had happened. She put the dollar in her apron pocket, turning away. I saw the tears in her eyes, though, and heard them in her voice when she said to leave Dad alone, that he was sick and needed to sleep.

Meanwhile, Josephine sat in the grass by the Studebaker. I sat with her for a little while, trying to teach her how to make jewelry out of clover, but it was boring for both of us. I walked back up the hill to the house and curled up in the big chair on the porch and sucked my thumb. She sat happily on the running board waiting for Dad until he kicked the door open, knocking her to the ground. She didn't cry, but he did...

So anyway, I guess I should go see my weird cousin.

Okay, God!!! I'll go to the icon retreat! I'll think about what I might do for Garfield and Marie! I'll visit Josephine sometime! Good grief, how about backing off for awhile?! Amen!

Epiphany

Isaiah 60:1-6
Psalm 72:1-7, 10-14
Ephesians 3:1-12
Matthew 2:1-12

All through the service this morning Garfield and Marie kept popping into my mind. Like the people in Isaiah, they are in darkness. Like the poor and needy in the psalm, they have no helper. Like the wise men, they are far from home. God puts foreigners in our path, the preacher proclaimed—or warned. In the kingdom of God, we open our hearts to them. Hm.
 The preacher was our bishop, and he delivered the gospel lesson from memory. We sat spellbound as he articulated each word with proper emphasis in his rich, strong voice, turning and looking into our faces as if he were the gospel writer himself telling the story for the first time. In his sermon, he contrasted the just, righteous, and merciful king of the psalm with Herod, the lunatic king.
 "In which kingdom do we want to live?" he asked repeatedly. He urged us not to fear the darkness for it is in darkness that we are most likely to see the light and know its true splendor. Excellent sermon. I hope I will recall its truth tonight when the sun goes down.
 Chad Brewster was holding his toddler at the communion rail, and the little cherub stared intently at Pr. Sauer when he put his hand on the baby's head and blessed him and then the child let out a shriek of laughter and practically jumped out of his father's arms. What an appropriate response! Jack and Helen were right beside Chad, and it seems not that long ago that Chad was the babe in arms.
 Back to Garfield. He's lost his job at the gas station. They accused him of stealing money, which he denies with sound and fury. He'd called Mindy the other day about getting more groceries, and she called me. There they were, back in my path, and I agreed to go with Mindy and talk with him. Wanting to give them a fishing pole instead of a fish—and trying to keep my distance, maybe—I suggested that they check in at the shelter in the city. I've heard and read about programs there to help people in marginalized circumstances—short-term financial assistance, job counseling, health care, etc.
 "Yeah, we stayed there a couple nights already. I never even want to be downwind from one of those superiority outfits again," Garfield snorted. "Not an option. The first thing they'd do is send Tramp to his own shelter where he would be put down. No way, no thanks."
 Fighting my beggars-can't-be-choosers mentality, I went to the store and bought them $30 worth of food. After Mindy got home from work, she and I

delivered the groceries to the Cloverleaf. That's when Garfield told us about getting fired. He doesn't know what they'll do. He said Marie was out looking for a job.

When Mindy brought me back home, I invited her in for a cup of tea. She thinks Garfield and Marie are decent people—even though he's a "blow-hard, big mouth"—who have had some bad breaks and made some mistakes and now they're down and can't get back up.

"Rose, you ever play Monopoly?" she asked.

I nodded.

"Gosh, I hate that game! Once I get behind I never can catch up. That's what this country is like. I'm working two jobs and going to school, and I'm going to make it if I die trying. But I get really p.o'd when I think of movie stars and CEOs making their millions. They don't work any harder than I do. Then, when you really get down, like Garfield and Marie, and can't wash your clothes and don't have a telephone or a car and don't know where the next meal is coming from, it's almost impossible. People don't even want to look you straight in the eye. They wish you'd just disappear."

She doesn't even care whether or not Garfield stole the money; even if he did, it's not our problem, it's between him and God is her attitude. And besides, she said, who knows what any of us would do in a battle to survive.

Mindy's a bit radical, I'm thinking. My concerns were honor and integrity and the gas station owner trying to run a business—and Garfield's alcoholism, which I'm getting a whiff of. Demon alcohol, as opposed to the kind that gladdens the heart. I've never been really down and out, though. Even during the Depression, we weren't poor, we just didn't have any money. So, I feel the psalmist beckoning me to join God and have pity on the weak and the needy and realize that their blood is just as precious as anyone's, like the psalm of the day said. Who knows where this relationship may lead me, but why worry? *Just swing one skate in front of the other and glide, as you always used to say, Charlie.*

Oh! and back to this morning—we had an unfortunate incident at the bishop's reception after the service. Madge had made her Epiphany spice cake that looks like a crown and has a foil-wrapped penny, nickel, and dime baked in it to represent gold, frankincense and myrrh. She always makes a big deal about the coins so nobody will bite into one or, God forbid, swallow one. She was in seventh heaven being totally in charge and having all attention focused on herself, especially with the bishop there! Sadly, a visitor was in the restroom during her instructions and broke a crown (dental, that is) on the dime. I actually felt a little sorry for Madge in her distress and embarrassment. I think we should pay for the man's dental repairs. Out of the evangelism budget would make sense.

This afternoon Stephen hosted a birthday party for Stephanie, "his favorite and only niece," as he loves to say. She certainly helps to fill his void of not having children. He had gone to worship this morning with his girlfriend, Alise, but then Alise had gone to a baby shower and couldn't come to the party. We haven't met her yet. Too early, Stephen says. I'm glad that he's dating again. He's grieved the loss of his marriage hard for over two years, I would say even on a theological level. "I didn't think there was anything about our marriage that God, Denise, and I couldn't handle," he said once, profoundly puzzled.

I can't believe our little Stephanie Rose is thirty-one years old! As she opened her presents, I couldn't take my eyes off her. Her face is shaped just like mine and Virginia's—square. I would describe Stephanie as wholesome, natural. She uses no make-up or hair coloring for fear that it might contain animal derivatives. She uses a rock for deodorant. (I suppose I should find the right moment to tell her it doesn't work very well.) Basically, Stephanie is medium—medium height, weight, skin tone, medium brown hair at a medium length. As I watched, I had the sensation of her little girl face morphing into her teen-age face and then into her current face. They all go together to make one of the most beautiful faces in the world, to me. When she opened her gift from her parents, a cell phone, her countenance clouded over. If Stephanie is oil, technology is water. She is surprisingly old-fashioned in this area. I think I'm less daunted by modern technology than she is!

Ethan was there. He's pleasant, if a little intense, and difficult to get to know, at least for me. He's told me ten times what his work is, but I can't really remember; something with computers. I wish he and Stephanie were at least engaged. I think they're making a big mistake living with each other; my turn to be old-fashioned. *But don't you agree with me, Charlie, that commitment needs to precede cohabitation? Besides, I think it's far more romantic not to live together before marriage. I much prefer the way we courted. Why, for pity's sake, I'm tingling all over just thinking of that day in the school auditorium when we began in earnest; it's coming back to me like it was yesterday...*

Rehearsals for Julius Caesar were going terribly. I had decided my first year of teaching—when John Fowlkes, Larry Mituski, Gordon Whatsizname, and that short kid with the deep voice were freshmen—that their senior year would be the year to do Julius Caesar, perhaps the only possible time in my entire career. When Susan Whittaker moved to town and came out for Drama Club, the die was definitely cast; she was the perfect Portia! We all seemed to sense the momentousness of the occasion. I was the happiest drama teacher around, anticipating a production that would leave the town breathless.

Then, Larry got expelled, Susan and Gordon got romantically involved, Susan and John got romantically involved, the mother in charge of costuming proved incompetent, and tornadoes came through, canceling a week of rehearsals. Now, I

29

was the most forlorn drama teacher around, anticipating either a fiasco or a cancellation.

During one of the last rehearsals, I saw the new custodian (Charlie) sitting in the back of the auditorium. He had won the entire faculty's vote for the best janitor ever after his first two days. Taking poor old Jesse Brown's place was in his favor. I figured he was on late duty and taking a break. When I saw him there the next night, I thought it rather odd.

The rehearsal was straight from you- know- where, and I had PMS even though it didn't exist then. The last thing I wanted was a janitor- spectator. I could feel him giving me the once- over, which was quite disconcerting and irritating. And when he laughed at John's blown line when nobody else thought it was funny—instead of *"Caesar should be a beast without a heart/If he should stay at home today for fear"* John came out with "Caesar should be a beast without a fart if . . . oops, sorry"—I turned and glared at Charlie and asked him to leave.

But he never did leave my life again. After everyone else was gone, and I was straightening up and having a little cry, he about startled me out of my skin.

"Miss Brinkley, this is going to be a great play," he said from the edge of the stage.

How I resented him for being there, for seeing my tears.

"I thought I asked you to leave."

"I left after Caesar's fart..." he said with that irresistible twinkle in his eye.

My heart laughed.

"but I had to stick around to lock up, and I just thought you might need an encouraging word. I've never seen a Shakespeare play, don't care much for Shakespeare, but the way you're getting those kids to say the words and move around on stage makes it all understandable. This is a great play. I love it when Brutus..."

Charlie, can you even count the Shakespearean plays you saw after that? We talked until three in the morning that night. The thrill of kisses in your supply closet and little body brushes throughout the school day when nobody knew we were in love made our courtship extra spicy. In large part thanks to you, Julius Caesar was absolutely the top production in my 45 year career!

At any rate, living together without having a permanent commitment certainly is the way of the world these days. Pr. Sauer told me recently that by far the majority of couples who come to him for marriage are cohabiting. When I pressed him on his opinion, he started giving me the party line—"certainly they should get married first." But then, he swore me to secrecy and said he really didn't care that much whether they were or were not living together. I was shocked. He said that some of the healthiest relationships he sees involve couples living together and some of the unhealthiest are between people who are not. He figured chances for successful marriages split right down the middle between co-habitors and separatists. That wasn't what I wanted to hear. That's not what statistics show either, I've read.

Since Mindy is Stephanie's generation, I wondered how Mindy might look at living together outside of marriage. I shared my concerns, explaining them quite thoroughly and quite reasonably, I thought. After listening attentively she said, "Miss Rose, you need to take a pill."

Oh, well. I still think what I think.

At her birthday party, Stephanie told us all about Colleen's wedding. Quite a spectacle, she said, and hopes they'll put as much effort into their marriage as they did into the wedding. The groom insisted on having his dog at the festivities despite Colleen's protests. At the reception, the dog went up to Colleen, raised its leg, and arched a yellow stream across her wedding gown. "Damn cur!" The groom laughed way too hard, Steph said, and Colleen tried to laugh, but it was obvious that she was totally humiliated and soon excused herself, returning red-eyed to cut the cake with grim determination and a forced smile for the cameras. Good luck, young lovers!

Oh, and the plane ride! Take-off on her return flight out of New York was delayed. They had boarded, and she was a little nervous but doing okay. After about a half-hour the last passenger, a Middle Eastern gentleman with turban and beard came down the aisle and sat in the empty seat next to her. Even though she tried to talk sense to herself, she couldn't stop her heart from pounding. The man was furious about being detained. He scowled and muttered in Arabic under his breath through the whole flight. When she was finally in her car and felt safe, she realized she was sore all over from being so tense. Such a world we live in.

Despite the agitations described, 'twas a lovely, long afternoon of family conversation and togetherness, and I thank you, Loving God. Amen.

I decided not to mention the topic of the Temples. Virginia and Stephen are very compassionate people, but they can be rather conservative when it comes to me getting involved with down-and-outers. Indeed, I hope I'm not being foolish. The thing is, Garfield and Marie are Jesus to me. I don't know how else to interpret Matthew 25:31-46. What do you think, Cute Baby? Oh, you think we should go to bed? Me too!

First Sunday after Epiphany – The Baptism of Our Lord

Isaiah 43:1-7
Psalm 29
Acts 8:14-17
Luke 3:15-17

As soon as I walked in the back door this morning, one of the Smith children told me that I needed to go the basement. Usually I avoid going down those narrow, back steps, but I sensed an urgency and carefully made my way down. Lloyd was playing the piano for the choir to practice the anthem. When he saw me he pointed his head toward the back of the room without missing a beat. There in the darkness at one of the long tables sat Garfield. In front of him was a can of pop and a paper plate with a hot dog and potato chips.

I sat down next to him. He soon told me the whole story, quietly weeping over his messed-up life. Marie is gone. He thinks she took a bus back to St. Louis. He doesn't know what's happened to Tramp, and he's been evicted from the motel. He said he feels alone in the world, and it's his own fault. He did steal the money, and it is now gone, much of it spent on cigarettes and liquor, which he didn't need to tell me because I could smell both. He's been on the street for two days. He tried going to Mindy's, but she hasn't been home. He slept for a couple hours in the laundromat earlier this morning, then came to the church asking for me. All he wants to do right now is get to St. Louis and try to patch things up with Marie. He feels she is his only connection to hope. He was a broken man, a man without bluster.

What to say? There are no words. I said something about never being truly alone, if only we can sense God's presence and feel Jesus' loving and caring. He nodded wearily and began to weep again.

I invited him to come to worship to rest and find refreshment, and then we'd see what to do next. He said he thought he would do that but wanted to go outside to take a break. I asked him if he wanted to eat something. No, he said, somebody had given him the food even though he had told them he wasn't hungry. Great. A guy walks in with a broken heart, and we throw him a couple hotdogs. Oh, well. Kind intentions.

He went outside and I threw the food away, thinking about people starving, and went upstairs to worship wondering if I would ever see him again. He edged in next to me in the middle of the opening hymn, right when we were singing, "Your Word and Spirit, flesh and blood/Refresh our souls with heav'nly food./You are our dearest treasure./Let your mercy warm and cheer us!/Oh, draw near us!/For you teach us God's own love through you has reached us." (Nicolai)

There was so much in the service for Garfield, but I don't know what he could hear. Maybe it was just more words. "You are mine," God said in Isaiah. "I will be with you; and through the rivers, they shall not drown you." Excellent news for a river-fearing non-swimmer like myself, but I don't know what it meant to Garfield. I cringed when Pr. Sauer called Jesus' baptism "the theophany of a lifetime." Why does he use those big words?! He only irritates the people who think he's a cold, distant highbrow. He went on to suggest that we begin this new year trying to discover where God is beckoning us and following those pathways even though they may be threatening and scary—and for Garfield, I thought, totally unknown, a formless void.

During the passing of the peace, a few greeted Garfield curiously. When I stood up to go forward for communion he looked up at me and whispered, "Am I allowed?"

"Are you Christian?" I asked, and when he nodded, I did too. He followed me up and partook, though he seemed ill at ease.

The Spirit of the Lord, I believe, came upon me during the last hymn and directed me to shove Garfield out the side door and get us into my car before we had to talk to anyone. As I pulled out of the parking lot, I thought, "Holy smokes, Rose! 'You have not so much brain as ear-wax,'" but I drove on home. The doorbell rang within minutes, and I was not surprised to find Madge on the front step.

"I just stopped by to make sure everything is okay, Rose," she said, trying to see around me.

"Whatever are you talking about, my dear?" I said in as patronizing a tone as I could muster, adjusting my position so she couldn't see Garfield in the living room.

"Is everything okay?"

"Why wouldn't it be, Madge?"

"Well," she said hesitantly, "I don't mean to be nosey, but . . . "

"Good. Thanks for stopping. Have a good week," I said and closed the door in her pudgy little face.

Garfield and I split my pork chop and had an enjoyable Sunday dinner. He had lots of questions about the service such as why did we use wine instead of grape juice and what does theophany mean? We looked it up in the dictionary and now, thanks to Pr. Sauer, we know that it means "a manifestation of God to man in actual appearance." Hm. I still don't know what it means.

Garfield took a shower and washed his clothes. Popcorn, oldies on the radio, and playing checkers made for a pleasant Sunday night. He seemed sad yet refreshed, maybe even peaceful. He seemed like a real person instead of an insecure braggadocio. He's sound asleep now in the guestroom.

Pr. Sauer called in the afternoon and asked me about Garfield, remembering him from Christmas Eve. He offered to help if there was a need. I thanked him and said we would probably be back in touch with him soon because Garfield did indeed have some special needs. He didn't ask if Garfield was staying overnight at my house, and I saw no reason to tell him.

Stephen called to tell me about his day with Alise. He sounds like a teen-ager. He's come a long way from wanting to go live in a cave like he did at first when he and Denise separated. For months he would slink into worship late and out early; he is definitely healing.

I called Virginia as I always do, so she wouldn't be suspicious. She and Barry went to brunch this morning with Stephanie and Ethan—a beautiful and restful day, she said. They would all be scandalized if they knew what was going on here!

Suddenly, I feel the way I felt in the parking lot. Eek. Tonight as I kneel by my bed, my prayer will be very specific and very fervent.

"God, I have given myself over to your service in providing shelter for your child, Garfield Temple. KEEP ME SAFE. In Jesus' name, Amen."

Second Sunday after Epiphany
Isaiah 62:1-5
Psalm 36:5-10
I Corinthians 12:1-11
John 2:1-11

I cannot state a single teaching from this morning's service. Was I there?! I remember the soprano section going through the stratosphere hunting for a high note in the anthem about a star. Bless their sincere hearts, they really did sound like out-of-control sirens. I remember how tired Pr. Sauer looked coming down into the congregation to administer communion to Pearl and Clyde Johnson; I was struck by his servant demeanor towards them even though Pearl doesn't miss a chance to say how much better things were when Pastor Phillips was here. Merciful heavens, I can't even remember any of the lessons—something about God working miracles, which is hardly news. I don't remember one thing about communion; now that is weird. I was out of it, perhaps because Garfield is still on my mind so much, even though he's been gone for a week.

I am very disappointed in myself because of what happened last Sunday when he stayed overnight. I was so frightened! When I went to bed, I put a chair under the doorknob and said my prayer for safety but couldn't stop thinking horrendous thoughts. The more I tried to talk myself out of being frightened, the worse it was. I replayed the nice time Garfield and I had had playing checkers and what a gentle person he seemed to be. I talked it over with Charlie. I repeated psalms and hymns and prayers. I held on to my sweet, warm little kitty, and she patted my cheek with her paw, but I could not relax.

"The children were right," I thought. "I'm an old fool for putting myself in harm's way." I considered calling Stephen and confessing. I'm sure he would have come over and stayed and only given a gentle reprimand.

Such thoughts chased each other in my brain for hours, but I didn't take any action. Stubbornness and foolish pride won out…"O weary night! O long and tedious night! Abate thy hours!" I lamented with Shakespeare's Helena. The more I tried to sleep, the faster stupid and negative thoughts raced through my mind, and I couldn't do anything about it, like when a recording on the radio gets stuck. When I heard a little noise in the wee hours I about jumped through the ceiling.

Long before dawn, I got up, dressed, made some tea, and started my morning devotions, dispensing with piano practice. I knew Garfield had been exhausted and figured he would sleep late even though he had gone to bed early. I chastised myself over and over for not trusting him—and for not trusting God. I tried to start the book Stephanie gave me for Christmas and read the first paragraph of "Female

Images of the Divine: Why They Were Expunged by the Church for Nineteen Centuries" about ten times and couldn't get a word of it to stick.

About 8:30 who should appear but Stephen! He was on his way to the airport and would be gone all week and stopped to visit before he left. Normally, I would have been delighted, but with the vagrant hidden in my guest room, Stephen's 30-minute visit seemed excruciatingly long. I was expecting Garfield to come out or make a sound that would have to be explained.

Stephen talked about Alise some more. My St. Lord, she's younger than Stephanie! We talked a little about church and how every issue seems to be a big deal lately. Finally, he left. Whew.

Around 10:30 I decided I was going to have to knock on the door and get Garfield going. Going where, I didn't know. Still feeling bad about being suspicious of him, I knocked tentatively, then louder, calling his name. There was no response whatsoever. Slowly, I opened the door just a crack, calling out again, afraid to look because he might be naked or dead. I saw the empty bed in the mirror with complete befuddlement. I searched every corner, certain that he had to be there somewhere before realizing that he simply wasn't.

When had he left?! Where had he gone?! For the rest of the day it seemed like the morning after a funeral. I bounced back and forth between feeling relieved and cheated. Finally, some of the mystery was solved when Mindy called in the evening to tell me she'd found a note from him on her door saying he was hitchhiking back to St. Louis and thanks for everything.

"So who do you think he is, Rose?" she asked.

"Who he is? What do you mean?"

"I mean as far as God's concerned?"

"Well, I think he's Jesus," I said, instantly embarrassed.

"Garfield?!" she squawked.

"I mean in the sense of 'one of the least of these.'"

"Translation, please."

"Jesus said that when people are in need it's the same as him being in need, and that when we help others, especially people who are desperately in need, it's the same as helping him."

"Oh." Pause. "Yeah." Pause. "Because Jesus loves us so much that whatever affects us affects him." Pause. "Wow." Pause. "There's the miracle—Jesus is so loving that he cares for every single one of us just like we each care for..." Pause. "our own children, our own family. That's unbelievable—it's weird that anyone could do that, could have that much love—for people he doesn't even know—for people who don't care about him—for people who are working against him." Pause. "God!"

Yes, my dear, and God cares not just for people but for the whole cosmos, for every creature, every particle. And this is heaven, this is glory, this is face-to-face with God—unbelievable and weird love without limit.

<u>Later</u>

I just read today's psalm again before turning in and jot it down here because it restates the conversation Mindy and I had the other night:

> Your steadfast love, O Lord,
> extends to the heavens,
> your faithfulness to the clouds.
> Your righteousness is like the
> mighty mountains,
> your judgments are like the
> great deep;
> you save humans and animals
> alike, O Lord.
> How precious is your steadfast
> love, O God!

Third Sunday after Epiphany

Nehemiah 8:1-3, 5-6, 8-10
Psalm 10
I Corinthians 12:12-31a
Luke 4:14-21

God's frozen people. That's what we were today with the furnace on the blink. We moved to the basement, which was filled to overflowing. Crowded, close and family-like. A good situation for hearing the "many gifts but one body" passage, although I have to admit my mind was hyperactive with pettiness while Pr. Sauer was preaching. When he talked about people in the congregation boasting of greater wisdom and knowledge, a neon sign in my brain kept blinking "MADGE-MADGE-MADGE." The thought itself was an act of arrogance, but I couldn't shake it. Communion, as usual, came just in the nick of time.

My need for divine mercy was quite intense from the moment I woke up this morning, judging myself as I frequently do, hovering around my sinfulness like a hummingbird at a blossom. "What have I done, what have I not done, how have I fallen short?" my monkey brain kept nagging.

A comical little incident before the service reinforced my mental state. As I walked by the children's choir lined up in their little robes and sashes and crosses, a plump-cheeked girl with dusty blonde braids and earnest blue eyes, apparently not feeling too well put-together, asked the child next to her, "Is there anything wrong with me?"

Her innocent question threw me right back into my childhood. Something was always wrong, and Dewayne and I didn't know what it was or when it would show itself. The modus operandi was to pretend—ignore the problem, make light of it, lie if necessary, but don't admit that anything is wrong.

So when it was time for communion, I was ready to fall on my knees and, once again, redeem my burden for peace and joy like we used to turn in our S & H Green Stamps for a new lamp. We couldn't actually kneel in the basement, however (except Madge did. I won't question her motives—I wish..."Cleanse the thoughts of my heart by the inspiration of your Holy Spirit"). Overall, the atmosphere was downright jovial, at least Florence and I thought so, with Lloyd, our organist, belting out something lively on the piano and everyone colliding and smiling and shaking their heads and excusing themselves to each other. I heard Sidney Wright and Millicent Avery grumbling about what a mess it was; if Pr. Sauer were a better administrator, this wouldn't have happened. I didn't think it was a mess at all. We were God's people, safe and forgiven and together.

And then, Stephanie came for lunch. What a treat this woman is for me! *Thank you, Creator God, for this beautiful creature who is a sister in the spirit as well as a granddaughter.*

Not that we don't argue. She turned down my vegetable soup just because it was made with beef broth. I cautioned her about being finicky and uppity; she graciously ignored me. I respect her vegetarianism, but sometimes she gets a little preachy and judgmental toward us carnivores. How I hate preachy and judgmental (especially in the mirror!).

Steph presented me with a rousing rendition of her choir's anthem, based on the Corinthians passage, singing all four parts, sort of. Her preacher had focused on Jesus proclaiming himself as the Messiah, the one spoken of by Isaiah.

"Audacious and bodacious?" Pastor Gail had asked them, then answered, "No, humbly filled with the power of the Spirit and ready to get on with his mission."

Steph told me that she and Mindy had run into each other on campus recently, and Steph found out that Mindy is in the radiology technician program. They didn't know each other well in high school. She said Mindy was a little on the wild side back then and had some really hard times though Stephanie couldn't remember details. Hearing that Stephanie teaches Women's Studies at the college, Mindy commented that she thought she needed to study men, given how much trouble she's had with them! She also said that Stephanie had a cool grandmother and asked her if I had said anything lately about Garfield.

"How involved are you with this man, Grandma?" Stephanie asked me.

I told her that I had helped him out on a couple of occasions, that he's gone back to Missouri, that he had called me a few days ago and asked me to pick up his worldly possessions at the Cloverleaf Motel—a beat-up Styrofoam cooler and a collapsing cardboard box, both tied with yellow nylon rope, and a guitar with sprung strings. I took his stuff by the church and explained the situation to Marsha in the office. She said it would be fine to store them in the area under the staircase. So now, they are safe and sound until he calls for them. I wonder if and when that will be. I wonder if Garfield and Marie are back together and if they have a chance. I wonder who else is in his life. I hope there are people he can count on who have the patience and love he needs. I hope he will let down his defenses and offenses and simply be himself.

Loving and patient God, thank you for enfolding Garfield in your merciful arms. May he be aware of your presence and strengthened by your power. As Jesus the Christ comes to him in many and various ways, may he recognize him. And a special prayer for Vickie and Jimmy Howe in their grief over their stillborn baby. Thank you for your merciful, loving presence. Amen.

Fourth Sunday after Epiphany

Jeremiah 1:4-10
Psalm 71:1-6
I Corinthians 13:1-6
Luke 4:21-30

Florence elbowed me in the middle of the sermon and nodded toward the pews ahead. Clearly, Hugh Schneider and his teen-aged daughter had a bad case of the giggles. Their shoulders and heads shook as they fought to gain control. Their behavior was highly inappropriate, of course, and when I noticed that Madge was sitting right behind them, I figured she would put a stop to it with a tap on the shoulder, but instead, her shoulders began to shake! Then, Carolyn Sauer and daughter Brittany, a couple rows ahead of us, were smitten. In an instant, Florence and I were in on it too, silently laughing until tears ran down our faces—and we didn't even know why!
Pastor Sauer and Jeremiah calmed us down.

When Pastor remarked that those in power do not appreciate loudmouth prophets, I couldn't help thinking of you at the forge back in the sixties, Charlie, right after you were made foreman. Even though you didn't work close to the furnaces anymore, you knew the danger involved and made it your personal mission to have safety standards implemented to the letter. There hadn't been a bad injury for two or three years, and we were in a recession, and the bosses were trying to cut some corners to increase profits. I remember your restless nights agonizing over the pressure you were getting from the higher-ups to lay low on safety. The Holy Spirit must have had a really good hold on you because you weren't about to lay low. Jack Simon even called me, as a coworker and as your friend, he said, to say that for your own good, you'd better give it up.

"Rosie, it would be so easy to let all this go," you told me.

But you couldn't. I honestly thought you would get fired. It's just as well you didn't want a promotion because you never got another one, but those workers got safer working conditions. You know what, Charlie, your message was prophetic in the sense that it was both judgment—"this is wrong," and salvation—"fix it and all will be better." You were/are a good man, Charlie Harris, and maybe even a prophet!

At the Rutledge Home this afternoon I learned for the umpteenth time that one little encounter with another person can change the relationship profoundly. When I first went in, I almost turned around and went right back out. The smell was horrible, which is unusual, and some unseen person was moaning and calling out for her mother. "MA-A-A-MA," like a goat, the sound reverberating up and down the hallway. I spent a few minutes in Bill's room, talking loudly to get through to him. He didn't know who I was and when I took his hand to say good-bye, he started yelling, "What are you trying to do to me?!" in a very distressed manner, so I scooted out quickly. Darn the luck, Sam wasn't around; that left Kathryn as the main one to visit. I didn't think I could endure her bitter grouchiness, but I trudged into her room reminding myself that Christ would be in our midst.

She was dozing. When I touched her shoulder, she opened her eyes and smiled at me!

"I'm so glad to see you," she cooed. Merciful heavens! Was this really Kathryn?

"I have to tell you about my mouse," she said, struggling to straighten up in her chair. "She came out about 1 o'clock, the usual time, and scampered up on the dresser and played Christopher Columbus, exploring everything. Well, she decided my peppermint sticks smelled pretty good. Can you believe that smart little mouse got one of those long sticks out of the jar and pushed it onto the floor? She scampered down and dragged it over to her hole, it took her ever so long. Now here's the funny part," Kathryn laughed. "She kept trying to push it into the hole crosswise." She stopped talking to laugh again. "That smart little thing worked so hard and finally figured out to turn it the other way and get it in that hole!"

Such sparkle in her eyes, such animation! We laughed about the feast the mouse family would have tonight and whether they might eat themselves sick. She swore me to secrecy because she doesn't want anyone catching her little gray friend. She was cheerful for the rest of the visit and even asked me about some St. Timothy people. She thanked me for coming, insisted that I take a peppermint stick, and had a smile on her face when I left. Indeed, Christ was there with us, and with that little mouse. "All creatures great and small, the good Lord made them all."

And then, when I stopped to get gas, there was Tramp! I went over and talked to him and scratched his head. As soon as I would stop scratching, he would flip my hand up, asking for more. What a sweet dog and what big, trusting, brown eyes. I told him to pray for Garfield and Marie, and I'm sure he will, in his animal way.

A word about Lydia Circle last week—"a boisterous, provocative time was had by all!" How did it start, anyway? Millicent Avery was leader; she was talking about when her baby died 50 years ago and how she beat her head against the headboard of her bed because she was in such pain. That was very moving, of course, and then she said something like, "The Lord is always our refuge, whatever happens, we can depend on him," and Carolyn said, "Or her." Millicent said, "What?" and Deedee Leppard said, "She said, 'Or her.' Inclusive God language." There was some clucking and some chuckling, and Susie Wakefield said, "Oh, for goodness sakes, girls. Nobody's saying God is male; it's just tradition, c'mon now." Well, of course, Claudia was off and running with that, informing us that the original Greek word for Holy Spirit was feminine but that, through the ages, men had changed it to the male form so that the Trinity was entirely male. When Deedee commented, "Ha! That doesn't surprise me at all," Madge attacked her with, "Deedee, you weren't even man enough to take your husband's name—you should be Deedee Brewster; that kind of thing is causing the breakdown of the American family." Well, Deedee, pregnant with their fourth child, defended herself about how she was professionally established before she got married and Chad was a secure man who wasn't threatened by departing from tradition, and merciful heavens, it was hen-squawking for awhile, with divergent opinions flying all over the place. Millicent took back control by yelling out that we would close with prayer and said a good one, straight from her heart, about "hoping and trusting in God, from birth to death, no matter what assails us, and thanks for this circle of friends where we can share different viewpoints as we study the holy Scripture and keep loving one another." Sisterhood was restored through the ritual late supper; bonding through pimento cheese, chips, grasshopper dessert, and decaf coffee.

Fifth Sunday after Epiphany

Isaiah 6:1-8 (9-13)
Psalm 138
I Corinthians 15:1-11
Luke 5:1-11

I can't believe I almost stayed home today; I would have missed Mindy! Another gray, rainy day and so cold I thought it might be a little icy—the loveliest of days to stay home. Anyway, I obviously went and was sitting there meditating and half asleep during the prelude when I felt this skinny body squeeze in, pushing me up against Florence.

I was so flabbergasted I said, "Mindy! What in the world are you doing here?"

She shrugged her shoulders and said, "I don't know. I thought I'd show up, just in case."

She told me that Garfield had called her. She tried to tell me more, talking loudly over the whole congregation singing "Brightest and Best of the Stars of the Morning," one of my favorites. Everybody around us could hear her talking, but I couldn't understand what she was saying and finally hushed her and said we'd talk after the service.

Inspired by Isaiah, Pr. Sauer told of a vision he'd had when he was in seminary. He was having difficult times with finances and family illness and was so worried that he became physically ill. He went into the bathroom in the dorm late at night and a bright cross of light was beaming through the window. The cross of light was a miracle to him, a sign from God which calmed his soul. He returned to his room and slept peacefully, waking up ready to tackle his problems. When he went back into the bathroom the next night, he was startled to see the cross there again. He then realized that it was always there, formed by the street light shining through the frosted glass. At first he was disappointed, he said, but then decided that the miracle was that he saw it when he needed it. It is a brave person who will share a vision.

Mindy didn't seem to be paying much attention as the sermon continued. She got gum out of her purse, looked around, read the bulletin. But when Pr. Sauer said that the verb "catch" used by Jesus in the gospel lesson meant "to take alive in the sense of rescuing from death," she gasped and whispered, "We have to catch Garfield, Rose."

After the service, she insisted on taking me out for lunch to celebrate acing her most recent anatomy test. The news from St. Louis is not good. Garfield is deeply depressed. Marie is living with her sister, and Garfield is not welcome there. He is staying on the street and in shelters, doing day jobs, but not steadily, because he forgets addresses or just can't make himself go. She said he talked a mile a minute, spewing that everybody is giving him the shaft but he's going to beat them at their own game and on and on. She said she had a headache when she hung up.

I think I jumped when Mindy leaned across the table and said, "What are we going to do, Rose?"

We?! Do?! We did our part when he was here; we're off the hook now, was my thinking.

"I don't know that there is much we can do from this distance," I said cautiously. "I pray for him all the time."

I sensed slight disdain as she regarded me from under her poofy mop of hair, her big hazel eyes even larger through her huge, round glasses that cover more than half of her face.

"Prayer's okay, but we need to do something," she persisted, holding my gaze. "Garfield is not a well person, and he's fighting a big uphill battle, but if that scumbag Paul could go from killing Christians to loving them, isn't there hope for anyone?"

Mindy listens more than one might suspect.

She looked at her watch and jumped up because she was late for work at the video store. She told me to keep praying and figure out what we're supposed to do for Garfield. There was a blur, and she was out the door. Without paying. Which was no problem except that I only had about six dollars and the bill was eleven. I looked around thinking surely there would be someone I knew who could loan me a few dollars. There was. Madge. Fat Madge and Robert, her fat, inactive husband. I decided I'd rather throw myself on the mercy of the restaurant then ask her for help. I sort of tottered up to the cashier to gain advantage by virtue of old age and left what money I had, and they agreed I could drive home for the rest. I went quickly to the parking lot to drive home for more. I couldn't see my car and racked my brain trying to remember where I'd parked. Oh, yes. Mindy had driven. My car was at the church.

About that time Madge came out, carrying her leftovers in refrigerator dishes from home. How easy it should have been to ask her for five dollars and a lift, but no. Oh, no. I slipped around the corner before she could see me rather than admit I was in need. What in the world is wrong with me?! I thought that by this stage in my life I would be finished with such games, such lack of confidence. My St. Lord!

I'll call Virginia on my cell phone, I thought, then realized it was in my glove compartment. I went back inside to call her but had no change for the pay phone because I'd left every penny I had as collateral. By this time, I was so mad at myself that even my low self-image didn't get in my way. I marched my six-foot frame up to the hostess, explained the situation, called Virginia on the house phone, and went back out to the vestibule to wait.

Virginia talked me into going out to her place for the afternoon and pumped me for details of my ridiculous predicament, laughing harder with each development. Barry wanted to hear my tale, too. Stephanie came by and Virginia called Stephen to come over. By that time, Barry was telling my story with far more flourish than I ever could, especially the part about hiding from Madge—"Now, picture this: Rose Harris, respected citizen, retired school teacher, our highly esteemed mother and grandmother, sneaks around the corner of a local restaurant..." I agree it's quite hilarious.

What a rich and lovely day it has been, but I am unsettled by something that occurred at worship. Despite Pastor Sauer's gifts as a biblical scholar and spiritual leader, I'm afraid he is about to crack. During the announcements, he mentioned that no one had shown up for assisting minister training last Thursday; he guessed maybe he would have to be the assisting minister—and be the altar guild—and mow the yard—and teach all the classes. Was that what the people of St. Timothy wanted, a pastor who does everything? he asked. A one-man show? Zounds, it was bad, very bizarre, very un-Pr. Sauer-like. Very un-gracious. Carolyn stared at the floor, and Brittany, being a 12-year-old, naturally looked alarmed and embarrassed.

I cornered Clarence Brown after the service—he chairs the Pastor-Parish Relations Committee—and asked him if the committee was tuned into Pastor's stress level these days. He said they were more tuned in to a bunch of people leaving the congregation, which was news to me. The Rizers have transferred to Community Fellowship on the edge of town, and the Littlejohns and a couple other families are visiting around. Disturbing information. What's going on? I inquired, and Clarence said he wasn't sure, they'd be taking it up in the committee. Since I was such a good friend of Sauer's, did I have any suggestions of how to handle this? I didn't care for his tone of voice.

"No, I don't know how to handle this situation," I responded, "except to keep in mind that the purpose of the committee is to support the pastor while being mindful of the best interests of the congregation."

Nobody ever said life would be easy, and they were right. "Your steadfast love, oh Lord, endures forever. Do not forsake the work of your hands."

Jimmy Howe told me this morning how worried they are about Vickie. They're afraid she's "gone off the deep end" because she not only talks to their stillborn child but thinks the baby is talking back. I told him I thought such conversations were amazing and sent by God. Have her write them down, I advised; see if there isn't comfort in them. The baby's name is Nathan. *Dawn on their darkness and lend them your aid, dear God.*

Now I'm going to start reading the material about icons in preparation for the retreat on Friday. *I'm not sure what I'm getting into or if God is really calling me to this, but I'll follow your advice at such times, Charlie—"Don't think about it, just do it."*

Oh, and Charlie, what do you think about this Garfield situation? I just wanted Mindy to come to church; I didn't want her to make demands on me, for heaven's sake.

Sixth Sunday after Epiphany

Jeremiah 17:5-10
Psalm 1
I Corinthians 15:12-20
Luke 6:17-26

Trust. Cursed is the one whose trust is not in the Lord but in humans, says Jeremiah. If we trust in the Lord we will flourish, like a tree planted by the water. If we don't, we will wither and die.
"I still believe in God. I just don't trust him too much anymore, since Darien died," Mindy said the other night.
Darien was her son who died seven years ago. He would be fourteen now. Goodness, strange to imagine Mindy with a teen-aged boy.
She had dropped by unannounced to discuss our plan for Garfield.
"God is calling us to this," she said, "and if we don't listen when God calls, why bother believing in him at all?"
She asked if I'd come up with anything. I asked if we even knew how to get in touch with him (Garfield, not God). Unconcerned, she said she would get a phone number the next time he called.
"I guess we could send him some money."
"No, that won't help," she said. "We're going to have to do a lot better than money. He needs somebody who cares enough about him to smack him upside the head."
"He needs that kind of support there, in St. Louis. I'm not sure there's anything we can do from here," I offered. She gave me that Mindy look of tolerant impatience and wonder that anybody would say such a thing.
We didn't make any progress with the plan, but I was glad to get better acquainted. As she left she told me to keep praying and call her if God told me the answer. I honestly couldn't tell if she was mocking or not.
She came to worship again this morning, arriving in the middle of the psalm, settling herself and her ever-present satchel, then smiling at me and leaning forward to wave at Florence. Mindy is a small commotion on the move.
When Pastor described Jesus' new kingdom of the beatitudes, he brought the Schultz family into it: Garrett, their 23-year-old, was killed in a car accident on Tuesday coming down that long hill on SR 14. Ice. All through the funeral yesterday and again this morning, I kept seeing in my mind's eye the picture in the paper of the twisted wreckage at the side of the road with the Sit 'n' Bull billboard behind it.

"Blessed are you who weep now, for you will laugh," Pastor maintained with conviction on behalf of Dolores Schultz and her family. I heard someone grumble after the service this morning that Pastor shouldn't have named names in his sermon, that he was just making things harder for Dolores. Good grief, I thought (literally!). Shall we deny death or deny Garrett, and just keep everything vague and general in regard to Jesus' startling good news?! It's for <u>now</u>, people! The good news is for <u>now</u>! The kingdom of God is <u>here</u>! Fear not!!! Weep, of course, but fear not.

Mindy stayed for the called congregational meeting after the service. Stephen had gone to early service but came back for the meeting and sat with us. We, the people of St. Timothy, were not at our best as the Body of Christ making a decision. The issue of the day was cutting down the oak tree in the parking lot. The roots are causing the asphalt to buckle, it's messy, we're losing probably a dozen parking spaces because of it, cost of maintaining it is high, and on and on, said the pros. Cons talked of children picking up acorns for generations, wedding pictures under its shade, it's sinful to destroy God's creation, it's part of our identity.

I hate to say it, but we got ugly. Michael Townshend (Claudia's husband) said families with young children wouldn't come to church here if they couldn't find a parking space. Madge stated flatly that if God wanted that tree down, he would strike it down with lightning. When Louella Rutledge was called on, she stood and recited Joyce Kilmer's entire poem, all three stanzas. Clarence Brown challenged the property committee's figures which caused Beulah Fitzenheimer, the queen of property for eons, to jump up and accuse him of calling the whole committee liars.

Poor Pr. Sauer was not cut out for such as this. ~~He sat there like a deer caught in head-lights.~~ (Censored for excessive corniness.) Florence leaned over to me at the height of the foolishness and said, "Wouldn't you just love it if Lloyd roared in playing 'Let All Mortal Flesh Keep Silence?'" I had to wonder what we would do if the double-doors suddenly opened and Jesus strolled down the middle aisle.

Stephen, always a peacemaker, helped calm things down. *You would have been proud, Charlie, and amazed too, probably. As horrible as the divorce has been for him, I see growth that I'm not sure could have happened in the marriage. He keeps maturing and he's been solidly on the wagon since he and Denise separated, not even the social drinking he used to flirt with.*

Stephen reasonably pointed out to the congregation that the tree matter is hardly an emergency situation and suggested that we table the discussion and form a task force of people with varied viewpoints to study the issue further. Everyone agreed, breathless and ashamed, I sensed.

"Wow, that was crazy," Mindy remarked afterwards, then quickly changed the subject. "The plan for Garfield is coming to me. I think I have to go to St. Louis."

"But that's 600 miles away!"

"Just a minute here, Rose! You told me you didn't exactly know why you were going to the icon retreat, you just felt you were supposed to. That's how I feel about going to St. Louis. I'm not 100% sure this is the right plan, but how will we know if we don't step out?"

Before I could reply, she squealed, "Whoa, I'm late for work," and headed for the parking lot.

"How was the icon retreat?" she yelled over her shoulder.

"Wonderful," I shouted.

"See?" she yelled, flashing a smile. "I want to hear all about it," and she jumped in her car and was gone.

I think Mindy might be a good candidate for using icons. She wouldn't be put off by their differentness. My attitude toward them began to change the minute Father Michael opened his mouth at the retreat. He explained that icons are the Word of God presented visually, just as the Bible is the written word. In fact, there is a canon of icons just like there is a canon for the scriptures. I was fascinated to learn that there is a precise process for writing an icon that includes much prayer, and every little detail portrayed, as well as the process and materials, reflects a spiritual understanding. The unrealistic/weird appearance is very intentional because they are "windows into eternity" rather than simply representations of people or events on earth. And I must tell Carolyn that Jesus' strange expression is not from indigestion, but because the two sides of his face are portrayed differently—one side is his human, earthly face and the other is his transfigured face.

Fr. Michael taught us to pray by gazing at the icon. "Look through it," he said. "Be open to its message for you."

I was especially taken with the icon of the Last Supper, which they call the Mystical Supper. Jesus and the twelve are seated around a circular table. At Fr. Michael's suggestion, I paid attention to where my focus rested; I was repeatedly drawn to one of the disciples who was turned away from Jesus and the table. I wondered if I was turning my back on Jesus with my doubts about Mindy's plan for Garfield.

God, help me understand, calm my anxieties, let me stay focused on Jesus. Amen.

Seventh Sunday after Epiphany

Genesis 45:3-11,15
Psalm 37:1-11, 39-40
I Corinthians 15:35-38, 42-50
Luke 6:27-38

I have a feeling Pastor Sauer's sermon this morning was particularly powerful, but I can't be sure because Mindy was talking through much of it. "Restoring Shalom" was his title, with God as the restorer, of course. In our first reading, he pointed out, shalom was restored when Joseph forgave his brothers. The psalm, he said, proclaimed that ultimately God/good/shalom will prevail, so we can remain faithful even when purpose fades and disorder comes. Then, Paul cites the power seen in the resurrection as the power that can overcome any evil. Finally, Jesus bids us to take control of our lives by loving and giving, even loving our enemies. Don't be a victim when others act out of fear or hatred. For the love of God, take the initiative in restoring shalom.

But right when Pastor Sauer seemed to be at the crux of the matter, Mindy started whispering in my ear. She had discovered shalom several years back, she said, when her sister Cindy stole her leather jacket and lied about it. They fought and hated each other for months. Then, about a week before Christmas Mindy was wrapping presents and cut out a picture of a leather jacket from a catalog and wrapped it in a box for Cindy with a card that said, "I'd give you this but you already have one. Merry Christmas, Thief!" But when she was doing it, she had burst into tears because she knew how horrible it was and how that was not the way it was supposed to be at Christmas. She realized how much she loved Cindy, even though she was a stealing liar.

"AND Rose, I realized I was letting Cindy call the shots," she hissed in my ear.

So, she bought the nicest sweater she could find at Goodwill, wrapped it up, and gave it to Cindy with a note that said she was tired of fighting, let's be friends, Merry Christmas. Cindy was suspicious, but Mindy was patient, and eventually they were okay again. Cindy even offered to share the jacket, and they passed it back and forth. She told me all of this in a loud whisper during the sermon! I was interested but very uncomfortable. Even Florence was giving us the eye.

I must say that Pastor's proclamation of the Word urging us towards shalom seemed to take hold at the passing of the peace. Beulah walked from the front to the back to exchange peace with Clarence after yelling at him at the congregational meeting last week. Two pews ahead, a couple I don't know were crying as they hugged, and I overheard the man say, "Let's not be enemies anymore." I quickly looked away.

On the spur of the moment, Florence and I put together a lunch party, inviting the Sauers and Mindy to go to Mom's Kitchen with us. Madge overheard, and doggone if she didn't come too. But that's okay, she got hers. In the middle of dinner, she piped up with her little pious voice and thanked Pr. Sauer for his message. She gushed on and on about how it was one of the best sermons she'd ever heard, it changed her life, etc. Well, Carolyn had played the organ out at St. John this morning and hadn't heard her husband's sermon, so she asked Madge what it was about. This funny look came over Madge as we all waited for her response. She sputtered and turned red and couldn't remember one single thing about it! Not one thing. We all laughed our heads off, especially Carolyn who whoops when she laughs. Such a thing could easily happen to me, I admit, but I enjoyed it more happening to Madge.

Pastor was the last to arrive after finishing up at the church and the first to leave to make a hospital call. He told Carolyn he would see her at home. She gave a wave, as in "Away with you!" but no eye contact. There's too much ice between those two. Something's wrong, I just know it.

Mindy and I visited outside the restaurant for a few minutes. I told her I was especially glad to see her because I thought she might not come back after that horrible meeting last Sunday.

"Shoot, Rose, I felt right at home. I know people get silly and ornery a lot, but I don't believe in people, I believe in God. It's his church. At least you church people say all the right things even if you don't always do them. At least it's sane in the church compared to out here. Church is a place where I can sit and hear myself think for a change, or if I'm really lucky, stop thinking for a few minutes."

I thought she would bring Garfield up, but she didn't. As she turned to leave, I brought him up before I could stop myself, for crying out loud! She said it looks like she's going to have to go to St. Louis. She figures I'll be the money behind it. She's just waiting for the contact from Garfield. The alarm I felt must have registered on my face because she gave me a quick squeeze before scurrying off, saying, "Remember the psalm of the day, Rose—'Trust in the Lord and do good.'"

Hm.

Yesterday, Claudia, Carolyn, Louella and I went to the annual Women's Day Away. Louella and I sat in the back seat but didn't chat much; her hearing is on its way out. Besides, I enjoyed listening to the crazies upfront. Carolyn told about Brittany stumbling during a recent ballet competition. Girls sitting behind Carolyn giggled and ridiculed. She turned around and said, "Listen here, primas, that could have happened to any one of you, and if it did, she would be sympathetic. You can do better, ladies." That incident reminded Claudia of trying out for the cheerleading squad in high school and running clear across the gym without making the required jump. Her voice was tinged with 14-year-old angst, but Carolyn's howls soon had all four of us laughing.

As for our day away—mixed reviews. I wonder if this will be the last one for me. Sometimes I feel like I've outgrown these women's days. The theme was "Going the Distance," based on Philippians, but we pretty well ran out of steam before the end. I did not connect with the speaker. I'm sorry she had a brain tumor and her husband left her and all that, but she was too absorbed in her own accomplishments and spirituality. As she was closing her final presentation, she remarked, "Okay, ladies, I've got you out of here in time to do some shopping." Into the silly, chattery response of the audience, Louella raised her finger in the air and pronounced loudly, "Remember the poor," receiving amused yet affirming applause.

The gal from the church-wide organization made everything worthwhile, though, with her sparkly accounts of a few of the peace-with-justice projects and ministries we support all over the globe—rehabilitation of women involved in prostitution, a youth garden that's a drug-free zone, homeless transition, chickens for foster families of AIDS orphans, repatriation of trafficked victims. She led us in a "devotion in motion" that fit all ages and shapes and, at the end, made a human chain throughout the banquet hall as we held hands. A spontaneous cry of delight filled the air when she proclaimed, "Now, look whose hand you are holding! Look who you're dancing with—Jesus!"

Last Sunday after Epiphany – Transfiguration

Exodus 32:29-35
Psalm 99
II Corinthians 3:12-4:2
Luke 9:28-36 (37-43)

Thank you God, for this amazing whiteness and its fresh coldness and this furry, sweet creature and this sweet, warm house and for my body which can walk in it and my mind which can wonder at it and my soul which can exult in it. Amen.

Snow. Seven inches so far. Just about everything in town is cancelled, according to the radio. Cute Baby and I took a walk in the back yard, she boxing with the big fluffy snowflakes. Now, we're cuddled by the fire, warm as toast. (Still haven't had the gas logs installed. They're just so sterile.) Florence and I had a nice chat. She's cozy, too.

Charlie, I feel so cared for. Stephen, Virginia, and two neighbors called to check on me. I hope Pastor is cozy at home with his family having a nice unexpected holiday and stress reducer.

Since I can't get to worship, I'll read over today's lessons and write down a few reflections:

Exodus 34:29-35 Moses did not know his face was radiant. That's what makes people real for me, is when they are holy without being conscious of their holiness. Some radiant faces for me are Charlie, Florence, Pr. Sauer, Stephanie, Susie and Pete Wakefield, my dear Dr. Majmundar, and, as I get to know her, Mindy, just to name a few. I think my big problem with Madge is that she always seems to be trying so hard to look radiant.

Psalm 99 God is king (Goddess is Queen, Claudia would add) over all the earth and judges with righteousness. I agree with that. However, I'm having trouble trying to get myself in a metaphorical mode and find myself asking what in the world "God enthroned on a cherubim" looks like. Since ten years old, I've been trying to shake the image of God as an old man in a robe with long white hair and beard. I have to confess that that image still creeps in sometimes, even though it seems laughable, pitiable. Michelangelo is undeniably an artistic genius, but I'm not sure he struck a good note for theology there on the ceiling of the Sistine Chapel. A man in the store the other day said he doesn't worry, he leaves everything to "the Big Guy Upstairs." I hear that sort of description all the time, and it always grates on me, no matter how faithfully said.

II Cor. 3:12 – 4:2 Paul points back to Moses in trying to make his point. And what, exactly, is that point? Something about how the covenant we have through

Christ is different than the one we had through Moses, I think. With Moses, faces are veiled. When we turn to Christ, the veil is removed and we can see God's glory. The note in my Bible re. v. 18 says, "Seeing...reflected in a mirror: combines two suggested senses of a single Greek phrase, 'beholding,' and 'reflecting.'" That makes sense to me. When we behold the Divine, truly behold it, we then reflect it. I guess that would be parallel with someone who beholds something horrible and the look of horror is reflected on the person's face.

Luke 9:28-36 The Transfiguration. How could anyone ever be the same again after witnessing such as this? Peter, James and John were transformed and transfigured, just as Jesus was, I would think. They obviously didn't understand what was happening, but at some level they were strengthened for what lay ahead. I think we were given a print of an icon of the Transfiguration at the retreat. I'll have to find that.

The St. Timothy Telegraph (a.k.a. the phone chain) just called in the person of Mercedes Scheumann to say that there will be a Transfiguration service tomorrow night to make up for missing this morning. I call Florence. She found it amusing, stating that Pr. Sauer thinks the Transfiguration didn't really occur unless he celebrates it at his church. Anyway, even though Ash Wednesday is just two days later, we will have the Transfiguration tomorrow night!

Interruption for a call from Stephanie—

Drat, if I didn't pick a fight with her! Why can't I just keep my big mouth shut?! She started it, in a way, though (says Rose, the kindergartner). We were idly talking when she said, "Ethan can be an inconsiderate slob, Grandma. When I got home from class at 10:30 the other night, he'd already gone to bed leaving pots in the sink and the stove speckled and burned with spaghetti sauce."

She should have known better than to complain to her disapproving grandmother about her live-in boyfriend.

"Well, that's what you get when you live with someone without being committed to each other," I said with a smart-alecky edge.

"At least I'm not lonely and grouchy," she retorted.

That hurt.

"I think you're being foolish, Stephanie."

"I think you're being a Neanderthal."

"I'm only concerned for your happiness," I threw in lamely.

"Nose out, Grandma!" and she hung up.

Fie, Rose! how clumsy you are with your love. "I'll not meddle in't. Let her be as she is . . ." I can't remember which of Will's plays this is from, but the line sure fits.

<u>Later</u>

I found the icon of the Transfiguration, called also the icon of the Holy Face, and stared, no, <u>gazed</u> at it for awhile. Moses and Elijah are slightly bent, their heads inclined towards Christ. The disciples are completely topsy-turvy, practically tumbling down the mountain. Christ stands erect, God-like, God. So there is my hope, my joy. While we—all of us—tumble and fumble, God is God. We are given as much glory as we can accommodate "for the living of these days."

Transfiguration (Make-up Service on a Monday Night)

Exodus 34:29-35
Psalm 99
II Corinthians 3:12—4:2
Luke 9:28-36

As I walked out to Stephen's car tonight, I looked up at the sky, and the stars were so bright I could see how the constellations were named! Even though the streets are quite passable, he didn't want me driving so he came and picked me up. Otherwise, he probably wouldn't have gone. Thank you weather! Snow and rain, worship the Lord! Stars of night, praise the Lord!

There were only nine of us—Carolyn & Pastor, Lloyd, Claudia, Susie and Pete, Madge of course, plus Stephen and me, which was fine; after all, there were only six on the mountain originally. We moved into the chapel, at which point the electricity went off. Oh, the irony! Pastor had us move the candelabra in and light up all the candles we could find. The small space took on a resplendent glow, reflected candlelight flickering wildly off a large icon of the Transfiguration positioned front and center. Christ's robe was strikingly white and the gold in the background sparkled. I had the sensation of looking into the sun and seeing a face, which made me feel close to the original event. At the same time, I knew that the light of Christ's face and robes was no light that earthlings had ever seen. And therein lies hope—we can expect more than what we can ever experience here and now. Here is good. Now is good. The Divine is present inwithunderaround. And yet, we see truth and glory only in glimpses too bright for us fully to conceive.

From our hearts we sang, "How good, Lord, to be here! Your glory fills the night; Your face and garments, like the sun, Shine with unborrowed light." (Robinson) Carolyn was the lector and her reading of the lessons from the chapel Bible, which is the King James version, was not real smooth in the dimness. She apologized, "Sorry. I haven't read-eth from this in a long time."

Jesus did not leave his burdens behind as he climbed, Pastor pointed out. He went up the mountain to pray and talk over his mission with Moses and Elijah, two others who knew about going to be with God, so his burdens were also transfigured—suffering into obedience, impending death into eternal life. His circumstance was not changed but redeemed.

This wild event, Pastor preached, was about identity. Who is this Jesus, this Son of God, Son of Man, Master, Teacher? And who were the disciples in this supernatural brightness, other than befuddled, committed followers who had cast their lot with a power and a mystery they could not comprehend? And who are we in all of this? We are those who pay attention, in astonished confusion, those who worship and adore Jesus, the Christ, attending to his words and actions, believing that Almighty God is speaking and acting through him. With him, we can rise and shine, and our burdens, too, will be transformed.

Anything seemed possible in the cold, candle-lit darkness, any burden bearable. The passing of the peace was shared by everyone with everyone, and we communed as one body, little Madge kneeling beside me. Then, back out into God's starry night. What a blessed evening.

The blessing continued when Stephen came in for his favorite, my homemade chocolate sauce over butter pecan ice cream. He let me spew about Stephanie and Ethan and yesterday's silly argument. I appreciated the opportunity and tried to express my feelings accurately while being sensitive to his situation. God knows I didn't want to stir up any feelings of guilt and sadness left over from the divorce—but, alas, I did.

I explained to Stephen that, even though I don't approve of premarital sex, that aspect of Stephanie's relationship doesn't bother me terribly as long as they're being responsible with birth control. My problem with the living together phenomenon centers on the lack of commitment. I told Stephen how shocked I was to read an article recently by a reputable spiritual thinker espousing serial monogamy, that concept of staying together "as long as we both shall love," which I find weak, cheap, and selfish. As though it's our love, completely within our pitiful power, and we are to control it. No! It is Divine Love, ultimate Love, total Love that comes not from us but through us and to us. When we depend on that Love, we have the audacity to commit ourselves, almost no matter what, to another person. "Choose thy love, love thy choice." When Stephen was still and silent, I realized I had been on a tirade and wondered if I had offended. After a minute, he told me (of course—Stephen is, by nature, an "open book," one I want to slam shut, on occasion!)

"I don't know anymore, Mom. Denise and I waited till we were married to have sex—thanks to her—and both of us were totally committed. We trusted in God for the love to carry us through, we went by the book as far as what to say and how to act, and our relationship wasn't healthy, it wasn't holy, I don't even know if it was real," and he snuffled up some tears.

Then he shrugged his shoulders, kissed me on the cheek, and left. I sat there in the discomfort of ambiguity. Fortunately, I was granted the ability on this particular night to relinquish that ambiguity to God, and granted freedom from having to figure it all out, and granted confidence to live through the tension.

Lord Jesus Christ, I entrust Stephanie into your loving care, and also my lovely Stephen, in his hurt. May I not be a nag but also may I not ignore my role as a spiritual advisor in their lives; they are certainly advisors for me, and I thank you for that. Amazing, almighty God, I simply ask that you help us all to behold your wonder in order to see beyond the darkness and confusion of this world to your brightness and truth revealed in your son, Jesus, our Christ. Amen.

Ash Wednesday

Joel 2:1-2, 12-17
Psalm 51:1-17
2 Corinthians 5:20b-6:10
Matthew 6:1-6, 16-21

Poor Claudia. She was assisting Pastor Sauer tonight, tracing crosses on our foreheads, and she dropped the container of ashes. They hit hard and flew high. What a greasy, gritty mess!

"We may be feeling pretty good about ourselves right now," Pr. Sauer began his sermon. "We've been marked with the sign of Christ on our foreheads, soon we'll drop a Lenten offering in the plate, and then receive Eucharist." Dramatic pause. "Be careful, lest we think these actions save us, lest we think we have control, lest we forget that everything we do and say here is a gift from a gracious God."

He also could have said, but graciously did not, "Claudia's little mishap here was a perfect illustration of what a mess we humans can make when we take things into our own hands."

When talking about Jesus' instructions regarding offerings and prayer, Pastor talked of hypocrites and reverse hypocrites. The reversists are those who stay away from church because there is so much hypocrisy, like Virginia and Barry. The hypocrites, for tonight's purposes, are those who broadcast their generosity and piety without truly practicing what is being preached—praying on the street corner, so to speak.

I just realized something! After the service, Madge was coming out of the broom closet when we were going out the back door. She didn't look at us, and I didn't think too much of it at the time, but now I realize that she was praying in a closet! I'll bet anything she was! Merciful heavens.

Stephanie was out this way visiting her parents and came and picked me up and went with me to the service. We patched things up after our argument the other night.

"Ethan seems to be a fine young man, Stephanie; I'm sure he is or you wouldn't have chosen him. I value your relationship highly."

"Thanks, Grandma. That means a lot to me," she said with a smile and a hug. Unspoken apologies silently accepted.

Stephanie was especially touched by the epistle lesson—Paul's testimony about beatings, imprisonment, hunger, and so forth. She was wondering if a person can be a true and strong Christian if they've known no suffering. Her grandfather's death is the only grief she has ever known and that wasn't so bad, she said, because he'd lived long and well.

"Life has pretty much been handed to me on a silver platter. I just don't know how strong I would be if tragedy struck; my belief muscles haven't been exercised much."

I reassured the dear child that her eagerness to stay strong spiritually and her commitment to Christ's Church would put her in good stead for tough times. "And, my dear Stephanie Rose," I could have added, "you will have tough times."

"Florence Lawrence wasn't there tonight. How's she doing?" Stephanie asked, and I was happy to give a fairly good report. "Sounds good. I sure do love that crazy lady," Stephanie said, and we spent some time in sweet reminiscences. Stephanie told me she had once asked Florence if she had had any second thoughts when she was deciding to marry Arnie Lawrence. "You mean because of the name? Maybe for some other reasons, but, lord, no, not because of that! I loved the name Florence Lawrence right away; just rolls off the tongue, doesn't it?!' she'd laughed."

So, here we are again—Ash Wednesday. Virginia thinks Lent is silly. "Why should I try to feel sad when I don't feel sad?" is her attitude. In the middle of a Good Friday service, when she was about six, she whispered to me, "Don't they know that Jesus rose again?"

Of course we know that Jesus rose again. That makes it even more important to remember and rehearse the incredible gift of his life—given so that we could understand, could plainly see that God's power is stronger than death—and the suffering he was willing to undergo to demonstrate that truth.

While my life has been pretty much like Stephanie's—"the boundaries for me have fallen in pleasant places"—I have experienced deep suffering twice: March 18th five years ago when Charlie died and Lent of '59 when he accidentally killed Stewart Larsen. God's grace finally broke through and made the accident bearable for Charlie, but until he grasped that grace, every time he saw Evelyn Larsen, horror would attack him from the inside out with tremors and anguish in his eyes.

Getting the call at school the day of the accident is as vivid in my mind as if it were yesterday...

I had stayed late for play practice, marking my script and eating a sandwich, when Mr. Jackson came into my room, obviously upset. Ten minutes later I was sitting beside Charlie at the police station as he recounted the accident for about the twenty- fifth time.

"I topped the hill and couldn't see a thing for the sun...I didn't see a thing...I felt a thud, a crash, a scratching on the right front," he struggled to say in a thick, incredulous voice. "I pulled over and first I saw the bike hanging on the fence. The car behind me stopped; he'd seen the boy fly over in the soybean field."

He looked at me desperately, as though maybe, just pleaseGodmaybe, it hadn't

happened.

I remember thinking, "I'll have to cancel the play," and then thinking, "What's wrong with you, Rose? So what about your play?! A child is dead!"

As we approached the funeral home the night of the visitation, one of Stewart's uncles was spouting off in a group on the porch. "The guy should be up for vehicular homicide. Couldn't see for the sun, my ass..." I know they were in pain, but what a stupid, thoughtless thing to say and how it pierced Charlie.

How many times I've thanked God for Thomas and Evelyn's graciousness. They came to our house twice: once to tell Charlie that they were going to have to file a "friendly suit" against him to be able to collect life insurance. They just hated to do it, dragging everything through the papers again, months later. And then they came to ask Charlie to be present at graduation the next year when they presented the first scholarship to honor Stewart. Charlie went to the graduation, he maintained a decent public appearance for months, went to church, took communion. Nobody had any idea how horrible our life was...

Since then, Lent has served as a comfortable shroud I can put on to protect myself from empty suffering. Lenten rites help to transform my sorrows with the certain hope that, ultimately, all will be redeemed.

Redeemer God, your joy is the only true joy. When we have sadness in this world may we always see and know the brightness of your powerful love, victorious over any calamity. In the name of the Redeemed Redeemer, Jesus Christ, your son, our Lord. Amen.

First Sunday in Lent

Deuteronomy 26:1-11
Psalm 91:1-2, 9-16
Romans 10:8b-13
Luke 4:1-13

Painfully perfunctory—silent procession and recession—dark greens instead of flowers—muted (and insipid) anthem—so horribly churchy. I thought, "What we need right now is a skinny, rambunctious redhead with magnified eyes to hustle in here, scattering propriety left and right in the name of the Father and the Son and the Holy Spirit." Mindy didn't make it this morning, though.

Jesus, Satan, and Paul all quoted the Old Testament. Every word Christ said to refute evil was from the Old Testament scriptures he knew so well. Poor Pr. Sauer went overboard trying to explain the sources and connections of the various Bible verses, who quoted which, and why. He brought in Moses, Isaiah, Joel, Jacob (the original wandering Aramean), Psalm 91, the Kings and I don't know who all else. Too many.

Right in the middle of all this seminary lecture claptrap, Julia Crawford was apparently whispering in her almost-deaf aunt's ear and the aunt said loudly to Julia, "What are you trying to say?" The question rang out across the nave, and Pr. Sauer thought he was being addressed. He instinctively turned towards auntie and stammered a paraphrase of his previous sentence. For the duration of the sermon, he paid her undue attention with earnest attempts to make his message clear. Auntie can't see much either, so here we had a preacher paying special homage to someone he thought was keenly interested in his remarks when in actuality she was totally oblivious to him. Anyway, we all sure enjoyed it, and maybe the good old Holy Spirit knew Pr. Sauer's sermon needed some comic relief!

As always, nonetheless, Pastor highlighted an important thought to carry away. "The Word is very near to you." Israel did not have to go find it. Neither do we. We do not have to go to heaven or cross the sea. The Word is in our mouth and on our hearts. And the Word for Christians is Jesus himself, always near to us through the Holy Spirit."

After Cute Baby and I had our nap earlier this afternoon, I made the rounds at Rutledge Home. Family night and pizza supper in the dining room. Bob Thurgood, St. Tim member, was there visiting his wife Mary. Bob has aged gracefully, a very attractive older man, still bright-eyed and mentally alert. He looks more like Mary's son than her husband these days. His patience and sweet touches and talk with his wife of fifty-plus years, who no longer understands who he is, were heartbreakingly beautiful. Here is an amazing story. Mary hasn't spoken a word for nearly two years, but a couple weeks ago she turned and looked Bob in the eyes and said, "Are you okay?" Shocked, he said yes, he was okay. Maintaining eye contact, she said, "I'm sorry." And that was the end of it. She went back to wherever she is and has stayed there.

"What a gift, Rose, what a miracle," he mused.

Alas, Bob has transferred to Community Fellowship. Their daughter and her family are very involved there, and he likes the upbeat worship. Oops, there goes another rubber tree plant!

Sam was enjoying the pizza, wishing for a beer. Mrs. Wheaton had obviously done her duty with the pizza; she was sound asleep but smeared with tomato sauce like a baby with its first birthday cake. Principal Hagendorf was walking around the room eating everybody's crusts. Oh, what a challenge to be in a nursing home for just a few minutes!

And another little miracle, Bill was lucid! We had a fine nostalgia session. We talked about his supervision of St. Timothy's building addition in the '70s when Pastor Phillips, fabulous pastor but inept administrator, was with us. The congregation's business affairs were in sad disarray. I'm sure Bill averted some serious difficulties by stepping in, quietly and with sensitivity, as volunteer business manager for five years until things were straightened out. I told him that I had always admired him for that. He just shrugged and said, "God. Not me." When I decided it was time for me to go, he took my hand in his and thanked me for coming, and he said—I'll never forget this—"Rose, my mind comes and goes and my body's about had it, but God stays close. Tell everyone at St. Timothy that they are in my heart, and I'll see them on the other side."

I sniffled my way home, knowing that our conversation might be the last we would ever have.

Later

I called Mindy a little while ago. She'd just gotten home from working at the video store and sounded tired. She said she'd been pretty low lately. Her classes are getting tougher and finals are coming up. Her brother is terminal with lung cancer—horrible, gruesome illness, dying much faster than Florence. Cindy of the leather jacket is trying to get the brother to accept Jesus, haranguing day and night until they have to push her out of the hospital room. The worst thing is the anniversary of Mindy's son Darien's death. He was killed in a car accident on March 18th!

"Winter should have been over on March 18," she sighed. "Now it never will be, in my heart."

I told her that Charlie had died on March 18th also.

"Wow, Rose, we're bonded. Maybe we should get together on the 18th."

"Why don't you come for dinner?" I invited, not knowing for sure if she was serious, but thinking it was a fine idea. She accepted.

She asked if I'm still praying for Garfield. I said yes and she told me that was good, keep it up. She's not too good at praying, she said.

(Hm. What is prayer anyway? "Eternal Spirit of the Living Christ/I know not how to ask or what to say/I only know my need, as deep as life/And only you can teach me how to pray. Amen." (Christierson)

Dear God, I am pondering over Garfield's situation and what, if anything, you would have Mindy and/or me do. Keep us open to the guidance of your powerful love. Strengthen us to do your will. Most of all, give us (especially her) your wisdom. Amen.

Her latest report on Garfield: He called her from St. Louis on Monday. He has been on the streets, in and out of jail, drunk and desperate, filled with despair. He talked of killing himself. He said we are the only people in the world he knows who might help him. Mindy kept telling him to give her a phone number. All she got was 378- before his time on the payphone gave out. She called information and found that prefix in the Bridgeton-Ladue (?) area. She asked if there were any Temples listed. Too many to count. No Garfield. No Marie. We couldn't think of any other names of relatives or Marie's maiden name. I said it sounded like a dead end.

"Poor choice of words, Rose, with my brother at death's door and Garfield threatening to off himself."

Oops.

Undaunted as usual, she is sure something will surface so we can connect. She is planning on going to St. Louis over her spring break in a few weeks!

"Are you crazy?!" I wanted to shout. "If you want to try and save an alcoholic street person, just go into the city, twenty minutes away, and find one. Do it in honor of Garfield if you like, but let's be reasonable." The distance, the time, the money, the dubious nature of the whole undertaking overwhelmed me. Might as well say it to a stone wall, though. She is on a mission. People on a mission are frightening.

Second Sunday in Lent

Genesis 15:1-12, 17-18
Psalm 27
Philippians 3:17-4:1
Luke 13:31-35

In the Old Testament story this morning, Abraham trusted God and followed God's instructions even though they were troubling and the outcome was unclear, and even though he followed the divine directives, Abraham asked for a sign—so I'm doing the same thing. I'm asking for a sign that Mindy and I are supposed to intervene with Garfield. I'm praying daily for a sign. Until I get one, I just don't know. Mindy trusts enough to go blindly ahead. I want more. I want to know, if at all possible, if I'm supposed to be doing this. Pr. Sauer commented in his sermon that if there were no doubt and fear in response to God's calling there would be no need for faith and courage. I've got the doubt and fear covered; now for faith and courage.

Back to scripture. Christ is marching resolutely toward Jerusalem, confident enough to get sassy with that "old fox," Herod, Pastor preached, putting words in Jesus' mouth—"Ha! It's Pilate that will have me, not you." Having made enemies in high places, our Lord seems a little heady, already triumphant over their treachery, faithful rather than fearful. Danger is subservient to the Father's will. In Christ, the Kingdom of God truly has come, not just in an afterlife but here and now, for there is no doubt in the mind of Christ that good will conquer evil, and that is the truth for us as well. Excellent sermon.

Aunt Polly (as we all call her) was a picture kneeling at the altar for communion. Ninety-four and still wearing bright lipstick, lots of it, and trying to keep her few, thin hairs blonde. Today she had on her fuchsia pants suit with matching shoes and a fuchsia, turquoise, and lime green scarf and earrings. I'll bet she's had this outfit for twenty years. The communion assistant had cut it close with the wine and had only a few drops to pour into her little glass. Aunt Polly raised it up to him with a look of pure bliss on her face and whispered a hissing, "Thanks!" and drank it through her fuchsia lips.

She was at Lydia Circle Thursday night. My St. Lord, I still break out laughing when I remember what happened. Pastor had joined us for refreshments as we were finishing our Bible study.

"Pastor," Madge piped up from the opposite end of the table, "what can we do about all these people leaving the church? It's terrible, Pastor. So far, we've lost the Littlejohns, the Rizers . . ."

And she listed several more, including Marian Cooper who was sitting right there, and who exclaimed, "I haven't left the church!"

"Oh." said Madge. "Are you Marian Cooper, then? I wondered what your name was. Anyway, Pastor, we've got to do something to stop these withdrawals, haven't we? I've been praying about this, and I have an idea," she announced, looking around proudly.

"Let's have prizes for people who don't leave."

We stared.

"I was thinking we could get some very nice religious items—Bibles, artistic crosses to hang on the wall, a personalized hymnal—special items that would be very attractive to people. Each Sunday, whoever is in attendance can put their name in a beautifully covered shoebox, and on the fourth Sunday of each month, we'll have a drawing."

We were still staring.

"Well..." Pastor said.

Carolyn snorted, trying to stifle a giggle, which caused me to explode in uncontained laughter as did everyone else at the table. Madge sat there with a confused smile. After we had howled and laughed ourselves out and were wiping away tears, she said, like a tedious fool, "No, huh?"

No, Madge. Not at St. Timothy.

"Were't not for laughing, we should pity her," shouldn't we Will?

Third Sunday in Lent

Isaiah 55:1-9
Psalm 63:1-8
1 Corinthians 10:1-13
Luke 13:1-9

Our whole family worshiped together this morning to remember and honor you, Charlie! We had dinner together afterward and then visited the cemetery. Stephen fixed a wonderful lamb roasted in a coffee marinade. Stephanie brought her fabulous whole wheat rolls. Barry made his rice and broccoli casserole. They always want me to fix your favorite dessert, Fig and Ginger Pudding, even though none of us cares that much for it. The dessert is part of a memorial ritual we've created for you over the years, and it's fun telling "Charlie Harris stories" over the pudding with rum sauce, especially since you're not there to defend yourself!

Stephanie Rose had never heard about her "Grampie" roller-skating with a broken foot after you fractured a couple bones in that accident at work. Doc Adams put a cast on it. Well, after a couple weeks, you just had to rollerskate, didn't you, you old crazy galoot?! We told Steph how you had rigged up those expandable metal skates that fit over shoes and put it on your cast. I steadfastly refused to go with you, you may recall. When Doc Adams heard about it, he blew a gasket, remember? He called you up and told you to get yourself another doctor; he wasn't about to treat any dad-blamed fool who would take that kind of risk! Well, when it was time to take that cast off, you went on into his office and talked Doc into keeping you. I can still hear you saying, "Oh, come on, Doc. I skate a lot better than I walk anyhow." Stephanie thoroughly enjoyed hearing the story and wasn't the least bit surprised at your antics.

Gathering around your grave wasn't so sad. A chilly rain was drizzling but no one seemed to care. We stood in silence for the longest time, each of us lost in our own thoughts. When a crow cawed nearby we decided it was time to go. We all know you're not there in any real sense. A cemetery is just a gathering place, a memory space.

And after everyone left, I observed my private ritual, walking in our woods. What a wise decision we made forty-some years ago to buy these two acres. How much we learned together in these woods, Charlie! How to spot spider webs and duck or go around; identify animal tracks—deer, fox, coyote, turkey, possum, raccoon, rabbit; and animal habits—remember those crazy turkeys running in circles? Remember those snakes mating in the tree? And recognize tree bark—27 different trees we identified, didn't *we? They're beginning to get fuzzy with buds. I sat on the big rock until dusk, wishing you were next to me.*

And yet, I'm not even sad tonight, though I miss you more than I can say. I am jubilant for you, for the peace and joy I am confident you now know. The richness and fullness of my life help me flow with the ever-rolling stream of time and heal the intense pain of your loss. When my time comes to be borne away, I am ready. In the meantime, what am I going to do with all this figgy pudding?!

And listen to this—tomorrow a marvelous, off-beat woman from church is coming over for dinner because her little boy died on March 18, just like you! Is it strange for me to be excited? We're not celebrating—we're commemorating. You would love Mindy a lot, I'm sure.

God, the Great Giver, you know that Charlie is the greatest gift I have had in this life, next to your grace and mercy. You know how I long for him each day. And now, I thank you again for all the comfort your blessed spirit gives—I feel his presence and I feel yours. You send him to me in dreams and memories, through objects and smells and sounds. I thank you for the goodness of his heart and the joy with which he lived—and lives—as Jesus our Christ lives. Amen.

As for worship today—Ho! I love it when Isaiah says, "Ho." Attention everyone! Here is incredibly good news for all. Free drink, free food, free grace.

When Pastor Sauer invited us once again to join Jesus the Christ on his march toward the cross, a little girl sitting upfront near the pulpit jumped up and started marching through the pews. She was a total rascal and gave her mother quite a chase right under Pastor's nose. When the spontaneous little drama subsided, Pastor smoothed it over by saying it was nice to know that someone was listening. The mother took the child out twice during the sermon. Actually, the child was taking the mother out, wasn't she? And I didn't see this, but Florence told me that at the communion rail the little girl grabbed the wafer right out of her mother's hand and popped it into her own mouth. Florence said Pastor half-smiled and half-grimaced and gave the mother another one. Children today! Of course, a communion wafer certainly isn't going to hurt her.

The sermon was bad news/good news. Bad news: there is danger. Good news: there is hope. Bad news: you're doomed if you don't repent. Good news: there is still time to embrace God's grace. I sense that time of grace keenly. Life starts anew each second.

"Repentance for what?" Pastor asked, pausing and looking into our eyes for so long I was afraid someone would stand up and start confessing something none of us wanted to hear. Finally, he continued and good news came full force—God doesn't care about our petty little mistakes and worries but only wants us to receive the treasure of unconditional love. The sin of focusing on ourselves and our problems and impurities is pervasive. Repent and know that God's love frees us from such self-centered fretfulness. That is the meaning of the crucifixion. Christ suffered as we suffer, died as we die, and overcame death by the power of God that is at work in the whole creation. Pastor practically shouted, "We, therefore, are radically free to live lives overflowing with love and joy." Amen!

March 18th - Supper with Mindy

I will never be the same. To be invited into another's grief is a treasure of immeasurable value. The evening had a rough start, however, because Mindy forgot. I couldn't believe it. My insane insecurity swooped in, and I felt like she didn't even care enough to remember. But then I remembered—this is Mindy. She's special. So I called her. Left a message on her machine. She called back about an hour later, flustered and apologetic. I told her to come on over even though I'd eaten, and the spinach soufflé was a sad sight. Silly to make soufflé for that girl. When she finally arrived around eight o'clock she ate with relish and raved about the pumpkin bread!

I had suggested she bring pictures of Darien, but she had forgotten. She painted a great mental portrait, though, with stories of a tow-headed, fun-loving, hyperactive (she refused to give him Ritalin), smart little boy. The school suspected he had a learning disability. He was being tested. In kindergarten, he had told her he thought there was something wrong with his brain. He said it just zipped past a lot of things instead of thinking about them, and when he tried to make it go back, it couldn't get there. Darien was her favorite person ever. They were so much alike that being with him was almost like being alone, she said.

She loved my favorite pictures of you, Charlie: the ten-year-old on the bike, the soldier, the roller skater, the father. She especially loved our engagement picture from my dresser—the two of us on the farm, standing side-by-side shyly smiling at each other, me in my sailor mitty, your hands in your pockets, feet crossed. She was surprised that I was a head taller than you and asked if it was ever a problem. I said no, not really, and we both laughed. But then I remembered and told her that yes, our heights had posed a problem when we argued because you intimidated me, acting like a little dog jumping up and barking in my face. I told her how we solved this problem by always sitting down to argue. And then how you took it one step farther and had us lie down on our bed for arguments. We saved ourselves a lot of arguments that way, didn't we?!

And then she told me the story of her March 18th, startling me by saying, "I feel very close to Charlie. We both killed young boys in car accidents." I'd forgotten I had told the group at Christmas dinner about your accident.

Heartbreaking, her story—it happened seven years ago today, but she told it like it was yesterday...

We were in a hurry, as usual. Darien couldn't find his book bag, as usual. He'd missed the bus, so I had to take him to school which was making me late for work. The roads were icy in spots and my tires were baldish. The seatbelt in the passenger seat was twisted, and he couldn't fasten it. I told him to climb over the

seat and sit in the floor. I was grouchy. *She began to weep.*
   I hit black ice and lost control; the car crashed two or three times, landing upside down in a field. Darien was thrown out and killed on impact, they said. Nobody saw it, but the next car stopped and called 911. People kept me away from Darien. Everything was blurry because my glasses were gone. The ambulance spun around on the same patch of ice. They took us to the hospital in two separate ambulances. I was hysterical during all of it. My mother got to the hospital and they sedated me and kept me that way for a week. I didn't even go to the funeral. I stayed on tranquilizers and anti- depressants for a long time. After a month, I went all by myself and put up a cross and flowers at the place we'd gone off the road.

   Eerie, Charlie—I realized that I've seen that cross several times and wondered what had happened and who had died.
   She said that as time went by, she tried everything to stop hurting: pills, karate, "love in all the wrong places," herbs, Amway. She got a puppy and named it Darien the Second but gave it away because she cried every time she looked at it—plus "it chewed up my whole house." She and Darien's father hadn't ever married and had broken up years before. At first, he gave her a hard time about the accident; then they had started dating again, but that had been the wrong thing. She couldn't hold a job, moved in with her mother for awhile. That was a disaster. Lived with a couple guys and then with Cindy, another disaster. Finally, she said, she was so far down she knew she was going to have to die or live, and she decided to live. She prayed for the only time in her life (so far), asking God to help her live. One day, a few weeks later, she laughed simply because the sky was so blue and the trees were so green.
   "And then I felt this voice, not human at all, speaking inside me and from way out in space at the same time, saying, 'Yes, Darien is gone from you, but I love him even more than you do, and I'm telling you, he's okay. Go ahead and laugh. He wants you to and so do I.'"
   After hearing all that, I told Mindy that your heart attack and instantaneous death, shocking as it was, seemed clean and easy; in fact, it seemed like the deepest of blessings. The only way your leaving could have been more perfect would have been if you'd been skating, huh? She was a little taken aback when I said we'd had a marvelous funeral for you. I told her how we'd given each other our planned-out funerals for our fiftieth wedding anniversary.
   "Rose, that is totally weird," she said, "but I do get it—church is your whole life so that was the perfect gift."
   We wound up at the piano, singing the hymns from your service: "A Mighty Fortress Is Our God"(Luther); "O Master, Let Me Walk with You" (Gladden/Smith); and "He Leadeth Me" (Gilmore/Bradbury). She wanted to sing my funeral songs too, but we couldn't even make it through the first

one, "Borning Cry." (Ylvisaker) She doesn't think I should use that one. "That's a terrible thing to do to your friends, and besides, nobody'll be able to sing for crying."
So now, you know Mindy, Charlie. You two are bonded indeed.

Thank you for the gift of Mindy, dear God. This precious child of yours is precious to me also. We joy in your love. In Jesus' name, Amen.

She insisted on helping me set the kitchen straight (catch the irony?), and that's when the sign came. The sign from God. She asked me when Garfield had written the note. What note? I said. There on the refrigerator on the magnetic grocery list which I never use was scrawled:

    Dear Rose You my angle form God. Went wold I do without you help. Thaks. Garfield Temple

That note must have been there ever since he snuck out in the middle of that night all those weeks ago! If that's not a sign, I don't know what is. Drat. Now what?

Mindy took it all in stride. Her only comment was, "Looks like Garfield has a learning disability, too. I'm not surprised. We have to start planning the trip, you know. Spring break is just around the corner."

We hugged good-bye and she said, "Pleasant dreams, Mrs. Angle."

Fourth Sunday in Lent

Joshua 5:9-12
Psalm 32
2 Corinthians 5:16-21
Luke 15:1-3, 11b-32

"The Joyful Father" would be a more appropriate title for today's parable than "The Prodigal Son," Pr. Sauer suggested. I agree, and I know that joy firsthand because of my own prodigal. Dear Lord, I remember it like it was yesterday...

We were having a rough summer with Stephen after his freshman year in college. Demon alcohol. Many arguments. One night he left to meet his buddies in the city. The next morning his car was not in the driveway. Before we had time to be too concerned, the phone rang. A woman asked for Stephen Michael Harris. She sounded wary, said something about not knowing whether she should have called, not wanting to get into trouble. She had found Stephen's wallet and contents strewn along the street. I sank into a chair, feeling ill. Not knowing at all who she was or if she was telling the truth, I told her that I was worried because Stephen had not come home last night.
"Oh, dear Jesus," she said.
"Maybe we should call the police," I murmured stupidly.
"Oh, yes, m'am. Yes m'am, you best do that right away. This here is a rough neighborhood. You call the po- lice right now. Bless your heart, I'm so sorry. You call them, and I wish you the best."
She gave an address where we could come to get Stephen's things.
Charlie looked ashen as I hung up the phone.
"I don't like the sounds of that," he said.
I ran into the bathroom, sick in my depths. As I closed the door, the phone rang again.
I heard Charlie say, "Stephen, where are you?"
"Thank you, oh, thank you, thank you, God," I wept.
Within a little while, one of Stephen's friends dropped him off. Charlie and I each hugged him hard, fighting back tears. He was puzzled by the enormity of our emotion and relief until we told him how events had unfolded.
He told us the missing pieces of the story. When he had gotten out of his car the night before, his billfold had apparently slipped out of his pocket. When he missed it, he went back and found the driver's window smashed and the billfold gone. The police came and wrote up a report. It was nearly 3 a.m. by then, and he'd gone home with a friend, intending to go back today and deal with the car, never dreaming anyone would call us before he did...

We have had our heartaches with Stephen over the years, and our triumphs, but no moment compares to the overwhelming joy of that early morning reconciliation. We had thought our son might be dead, but now he was alive! Lost and now found.

Reconciliation. Everybody was reconciling this morning—the Israelites, after wandering in the desert; those whose transgression is forgiven; all of us with God through Jesus Christ; the prodigal son after being lost and down and out. Jesus is our big brother who comes to our party and celebrates, not feeling cheated at all. He has lost nothing as we share in the family riches, only gained because our redemption is his purpose. Wow.

Anna Louise and Kenneth Burnside joined this morning, transferring back from Community Fellowship after several years. Got mad about something and left. Oh, well. Who cares? I don't. Reconciliation.

There seemed an unseemly amount of joy for Lent, which was just what we needed to balance out the stress and grumbling that's been going on. I remember when this Sunday was called Laetare, Latin for rejoice. We were still repentant but assured of salvation, not after we die, but here and now.

I believe this for me, I feel it for me. But what about all those who are suffering and don't know this good news? Is this redemption for them, too? Of course it is, I know the answer, but I don't know how to understand it in a meaningful way. Take Garfield. He seems to be so lost. How can/will God reclaim him, reconcile him, save him? Save him from himself? Through others, partly, maybe. Mindy and me, maybe. That's what that sweet child thinks, anyway.

She didn't make it to worship this morning, though she had thought she would when we talked on the phone last night. I had written her a note after our dinner, thanking her for a very special evening, so I thought maybe she was calling to thank me for the thank you note. She didn't mention it though, but had called to apprise me of her search for Garfield. She'd spent yesterday afternoon on the phone and the Internet with directory assistance for St. Louis. She had called 38 Temples without a nibble before giving up for the day. She sounded tired.

"Mindy," I said, trying to be gentle, "do you think maybe this is just too hard?"

"You mean not meant to be?" she said.

"Maybe."

Long silence. A sniffle.

"I don't know," she said quietly. "It won't let me go. It's not only about Garfield. It's about me—about my...my soul. It's deeper than I can handle, almost..."

Weeping.

"For God's sake, Rose," she exploded, "I killed my own child..."

I cried, too.

"...and God forgave me. God keeps telling me it's okay—Darien is okay, I'm okay. He keeps protecting me, like with David being terminal and with all my problems. Just when I think I can't go on, God sends something sweet or funny or amazing, and I get the little bit of energy I need or the answer of what to do."

The Prodigal Daughter, I thought.
"Like you."
"Huh?" I said.
"You, Rose. You are Mrs. Wisdom from heaven for me. You're so old and religious that I can lean on you and not fall over. I think God meant for us to come together—with Garfield between us, for extra fun and games, I guess.

"So, it's like I <u>have</u> to love people because my heart is bursting with all the love God puts in it, even when it's breaking. I want the whole world to know these little miracles. I want Garfield to know. I want him to wake up every morning with enough wherewithal to stay away from the bottle and be his gentle, kind self. I want him to know how much he needs God and how much Jesus knows what he's going through and how their love will give him what he needs to get well. I also want him to shut the hell up once in a while and recognize that he's not the world's foremost authority and that other people are worth listening to.

"So, I think God wants me to keep putting one foot in front of the other with this thing," she concluded with a big sigh.

"Okay," I sighed back.

Gracious, Loving and Powerful God, we give you our sighs, our doubts, our exhaustion. We fling our most grievous sins to you through our frightening darkness. You catch them and throw them over your shoulder into nothingness and your light shines through the darkness on us, your most beloved children. May our lives be our thanks. In the name of him who stands with us in the darkness, and who is the light, Jesus Christ, your son, our Lord, we pray. Amen.

Now, let's "Play ball!" Cute Baby! How much sweeter life is when baseball season opens! The Cubs already have a two-game winning streak!

Fifth Sunday in Lent

Isaiah 43:16-21
Psalm 126
Philippians 3:4b-14
John 12:1-8

The children of the church were wide-eyed and giggly when Pastor had them upfront this morning. He had started by showing several items to the youngsters:
- a family picture, noting that his dad was a pastor and his mother a teacher
- his plaque for Outstanding Civitan
- awards he'd won in his childhood for perfect Sunday School attendance and memorizing the books of the Bible
- a sheet of paper with the heading Criminal Record that was blank, indicating that he's a law-abiding citizen (speeding tickets don't count, he quipped)

After leading a little discussion about the value of these items and getting the kids thinking that, yes, these were valuable items in his life, he put them into a wastebasket. One little boy stood up, put his hands on his hips, and blurted out, "What the heck?!" Pastor then lifted up a cross with the resurrected Christ on it.

"Compared to Jesus, those parts of my life can go in the garbage. They're nice, but we don't need them to have hope. They will not give us true joy. Children, Jesus is always present with us, through the Holy Spirit, teaching about God's love. Remember that his presence gives meaning to everything else in your life."

Today's gospel lesson told about the amazing party Jesus had with his best buddies, Mary, Martha and Lazarus, right before he headed for Jerusalem for the beginning of the end. To be with friends you trust and enjoy is a precious gift, in this case, magnified by impending doom, I would imagine. I've always loved Mary's anointing, appropriately extravagant. Yes, we need to attend to the poor, but I agree with Jesus and with the note in my Bible: "Such spontaneous love will not neglect the poor."

The choir sang a dreadful, sad song (in a minor key which several of them never found) about Jesus suffering and marching towards death. They sounded like depressed clarinets, and Lloyd was playing so slowly they were having trouble keeping up (back?) with him. Florence leaned against me and whispered to me out of the side of her mouth, "Wouldn't you just like to go up there and strangle each one of them?"

She leaves tomorrow to go visit daughter Sarah until after Easter, one of their annual get-together traditions. That she feels like driving the three hours is a good sign, I guess. Sarah wanted to come and get her, but Florence thinks she'll be fine.

Thank you, God, for keeping her in your loving care.

I thought Mindy might join us in worship this morning—I'm always hoping—but when Stephen dropped in a little bit ago I found out she had been at the early service. Afterwards, she was having trouble starting her car. Stephen gave her a jump. He asked me if she was altogether okay. I said what did he mean by that? He said he thought she seemed like a "dim bulb."

"Merciful heavens, Stephen!" I said, irritated. "She most certainly is not a dim bulb; she's in a radiology technician program."

He said, "Uh-oh. Let me know which hospital hires her."

"Stephen Michael Harris! She's getting good grades," I snapped. "And by the way, she is a very dear friend of mine."

"Okay, but what about this Garfield character? How in the world do you get yourself into these situations, Mom? We worry about you."

So, I had to give Stephen a little talking-to: #1- I don't get myself into them, God does. #2 - These adventures are life abundant. #3 - Mindy Lucas is a strong and wonderful woman who does not deserve ridicule. (Being in a defensive mode, I didn't mention my first impressions of her.) #4 - Garfield Temple seems to be a good and simple person who is wounded and troubled but nonetheless God's precious child.

Stephen sat there smiling, arms folded over his chest. He said he was proud of me, actually jealous, because he didn't have the guts or the heart to get involved with the down-and-out. That's not true, of course, just his false modesty showing, all wound up with his fragile self-esteem. Why, Stephen has served lunch at the shelter every month and on Thanksgiving for years; he's very popular there, always ready to sit down at the table after the meal is served and visit with the diners over a cup of coffee, genuinely interested in their stories.

And, for heaven's sake, it took a lot of guts and heart for him and Denise to adopt Renee at age eleven; there was so much heartache when they sent her back. Stephen has said that, in retrospect, the adoption experience was the beginning of the end of their marriage, though certainly not the only reason.

I asked him about the girlfriend, Alise. He confirmed my suspicions that they had run their course. Great person, but too great an age difference, he had decided. Their last time together was a ski weekend. She had run circles around him, day and night. When she started calling him "Gramps," it was all over for him. He's taking a sabbatical from dating for awhile.

Then I surprised myself by telling him that something might be happening with Garfield. The Spirit moved me to disclose, I guess. I told him Mindy was planning to go to St. Louis next week and that I was going to finance her. Naturally, he wanted to know what the plan was. I began to feel like a dim bulb myself, since we still don't know how to get in touch with Garfield or what Mindy will do when she finds him.

The truth is, I do feel like something of a fool with this half-baked situation. And yet, I find strength in the very craziness of it. For better or worse, Mindy and I are casting our lot with Garfield, with God as our strength. I believe Stephen sensed my determination. His parting shot was, "Okay, Mom, but I expect to be informed of every development in this fiasco waiting to happen. I mean it." That was his way of offering to help.

Now I'll have to let Virginia and Barry know what's going on, I suppose. And Stephanie. And I'd better check in with Mindy. Her spring break is next week.

Later

Mindy's brother died. She sounded like an exhausted little spirit when she answered the phone. She had spent the afternoon with him at her mother's house, which was full of people. She said she was so glad that someone from hospice was there, a man named Jack. If anybody got to arguing, Jack told them gently but firmly to hush or go outside, that this was no way to let someone die. When the end came, there was quietness and relief. It had been about 24 hours since David had opened his eyes or talked to anyone. She said she couldn't believe it happened at the beginning of finals week and that she felt terrible even being concerned about finals, and yet she was. She said she guessed God would help her get through it all somehow.

"Rose, I really loved that guy," she said, in a way that made me smile. "When we were kids, he was the best one of us. He was so peace-loving but fun, too. I'm not sure what happened to David; he sort of abandoned himself. I'll miss him, but I think he's better off right smack in God's arms than he was here in this world. He just couldn't seem to stay on any horse. I can't imagine him growing old. He would have been the sorriest, little, dried-up old man. I actually feel very thankful right now to God for taking him, if that's what's happened here.

"I also feel totally out of it, and I need to go to bed," she yawned. "I just don't know how I'm going to manage all that's happening, but things usually look better after some sleep. G'night, Rose."

Postscript on Tuesday Night

I went to David's visitation last night. The parking lot was overflowing. I had to walk a block to the funeral home and as soon as I opened the door, there was that incredible, carnival-like atmosphere that always surprises me. In a way, it could be a statement of faith: laughing in the face of death, life goes on, and all that. Anyway, I hate it. *Your visitation in the church parlor with Lloyd playing triumphant hymns in the nave and people pausing to meditate was so much better for us, Charlie. I'm quite sure you were pleased, too.*

Most of the crowd was for Helen Smith who also died on Sunday. I stopped by her parlor to speak to Allen. Naturally, this crowd was well-heeled, so when a young man in blue jeans and cowboy boots loped awkwardly by the whole receiving line, the buzzing conversation died down enough that we could hear him say, after looking in the coffin, "Whoa! Wrong one." Then, he turned around and walked out with an embarrassed smile. My St. Lord.

There might have been a dozen people in David's room, at the most. They all stopped talking and looked at me. Not seeing Mindy, I approached the coffin. David was an old-looking young man with grayish-golden hair wearing a cowboy dress shirt with a string tie. A black cowboy hat lay next to him. There were three or four flower arrangements and a display of David through the ages, starting with a cracked, creased baby picture and ending with a recent one that could have been taken yesterday, except that he had a goatee and mustache in the picture.

At this point, I heard murmurings and turned around to see a woman sweep into the room like a queen. She was as tall as I am and very slim, and she was wearing a short, low-cut, black cocktail dress. A dark tan contrasted with her platinum hair, straight and smooth, which I can only describe as springing out of the top of her head like a fountain and then arching down in long bangs and to her shoulders. Her wide lips were perfectly outlined and painted with the color of faded, pink roses. Large, greenish eyes framed by thick mascara shone brightly. Looking neither left nor right, she glided straight to the coffin and placed a long-stemmed rose beside David.

The next thing I knew, a woman came up to her and said, "This is a heckuva time to stand by your man, Dolores. Where were you when he needed you, you Jezebel slut?!"

Dolores looked down at her and said, "Cindy, you're pitiful."

Then she turned and made a graceful exit while Cindy lurched along behind her yelling about her coming between David and salvation. At which point Mindy entered, intercepted Cindy, and, with the help of a man, forced Cindy to collapse into a chair, still spewing angry sobs and accusations.

Mindy came over and put her arm around my waist. I leaned my head down on hers. She turned me toward the coffin, and we stood looking at David. After a moment, she peeked at me and said, "Welcome to my family, Rose. Let's go outside and get some fresh air."

The street light accentuated her red nose and puffy eyes. Taking a deep breath, she shared her woes.

"That cheap, lousy scene you just saw with Dolores is only part of what's going on."

Then she told me that Regina (the mother) had never approved of David's beard and mustache and had told the funeral director to shave it off.

"I would have skipped my exam yesterday and gone to the funeral home with them if I'd known they were going to do that. Rose, it's like they raped him," she sniffled.

"But you know what? It's not bothering me too much. God has put this protective wall around me, as though the two of us have this secret that everything is okay; other people can play their stupid games, but I don't need to. So because of that wall, I actually think it's funny that Regina thought she was accomplishing something by shaving a dead man. I even thought about getting a phony beard and slipping it on him—not to be mean, just to be funny. But then, God seemed to say, 'No, Mindy. That wouldn't be nearly as funny as you might think.'"

The two of us had a good chuckle over it, and she hugged me and thanked me for coming. I asked her how her exams were going. She said she thought they were going pretty well, though it was hard to stay focused. I didn't bring up the St. Louis trip. Probably it won't happen now, with all that's on her.

Thank you for your protective wall around Mindy, gracious God. Good advice on the beard. Amen.

Passion Sunday/Palm Sunday

Isaiah 50:4-9a
Psalm 31:9-16
Philippians 2:5-11
Luke 22:14—23:56

Madge was lector this morning and as she was reading from Isaiah, I snuck a sideways peek at Mindy. Her face was set like flint, just like the Servant in the reading...

> The Lord God helps me; therefore I have not been disgraced;
> therefore I have set my face like flint,
> and I know that I shall not be put to shame;
> he who vindicates me is near.
> (Is. 50: 7)

I had sensed heaviness, tiredness when she sat down beside me, and I wondered if Pr. Sauer had her partly in mind as he introduced the reading of the Passion.

"Let the same mind be in you that was in Jesus Christ," he quoted from Philippians. "Jesus, our Christ, marches on, through temporary exaltation with fickle hosanna, then through humiliation and suffering, confident not in himself but in divine strength. Confident to minister to unworthy misfits, confident to offend the powers that be, confident to fail in the eyes of the world."

I couldn't help but think that we pew-sitting Christians say "Why, of course!" to the idea of having the same mind that was in Christ, and we ardently sing hymns of commitment to discipleship, "Lord, we are able; Our spirits are thine," for example, but how much harder truly to be disciples. And that is what this amazing young Mindy, hurting within her own soul, is trying to do.

And then, after the very moving reading of our Lord's passion and the sermon hymn, Pastor called Mindy forward for a commissioning ceremony! He commissioned her to go to St. Louis to try and help Garfield, "in the name of the Father and of the Son and of the Holy Spirit." That caught me, and everybody else, totally off guard.

Well. The crowd was already restless. As usual on this Sunday, attendance was high, many thinking they'd have the upbeat parade with palms this week and then come back in their new spring outfits for the grand hullabaloo next Sunday. They got more than they'd bargained for, I suspect: the entire passion story, from the Last Supper through the sealing of the tomb. So people fidgeted and whispered when Mindy was called forward.

"Is she even a member?"
"What's going on here?!"
"Garfield Temple? Where's that? Is this about Jews?"

When Pastor asked if we would support her in her mission and prompted us to reply, "Yes, with the help of God," the hesitant, lukewarm response was notable. I felt sorry for Mindy as she returned to her seat, flushed and eyes downcast, yet her face still set like flint.

What else could realistically be expected from the congregation, though? Most members don't even know what's going on in this situation—kind of like the disciples in regard to Jesus' mission. I know more about the Garfield Temple situation than anyone, and even I think the whole deal is crazy—which is why I can hardly believe that I let her take my car. She didn't even ask. I offered.

She stopped at my house after church on her way out of town. There she was in my driveway with her beat-up Escort that breaks down on her all the time. She always carries a couple bottles of oil in her trunk.

So I said, "Mindy, would like you to take my car?"

"You sure, Rose?" she said, squinting up at me in the bright sunlight.

A nod was all she needed.

"Okay," she said, and began unloading.

We switched cars around. I had her pull her car into the garage, my brain already calculating how I could manage without my car for who knows how long. Will my insurance cover this expedition? Does she have a current driver's license? All concerns floated away. We loaded her bags, notebook, maps, twelve-pack of Mountain Dew, and dog supplies into my car.

"Dog supplies?" I inquired.

"I'm taking Tramp. Did you know he still lives at the gas station? I think he might be really important in finding Garfield. Oh..." she frowned, "maybe you don't want me to take your car—with the dog and everything..."

Merciful heavens. I took in a big breath to think and burst out laughing.

"Let's get something to cover the backseat."

"You sure, Rose?"

No, I'm not sure of anything right now, I thought. We covered the seat, and I offered her some lunch before she hit the road.

"I'm too nervous to eat. What I need is more prayer," she said, oh, so seriously, and we went in the house.

Seated on my brocade and cherry wood settee, clad in snug jeans and a T-shirt that read "I've been there, but I didn't do it," she looked like a saint to me, a brave and scared and unusual saint. I suggested a few moments of silence. We sat with eyes closed, but she couldn't take that for long and began talking about a major crisis she had hit last night.

"First, I felt sick to my stomach with nerves, all knotted up. Then I started thinking about all that could go wrong and that I really don't know Garfield all that well and St. Louis is so far away and so big and how in the world will I ever find him—all those things you've been telling me. Regina and Cindy are giving me a hard time about it. They think I'm nuts. Of course, that's nothing new, but I began to doubt myself completely. I felt like a half-witted fool. Then, David came into my mind, how sad and wasted so much of his life was. And then Darien...

"I cried buckets and worked myself up into a sweat and the worst thing was, I felt like I <u>had</u> to do this, like I didn't have any choice, like I was caught in a vice. I tried to decide not to go. Screw it. Who cares? Everybody will be happy if I don't go. Garfield doesn't even know I'm coming, so I won't be letting him down. I started feeling a little relief, but then, the urge came back even stronger: Mindy, you <u>have</u> to go.

"So I started yelling at God. 'You're making me do this and you aren't even helping me! Where's some peace? Where's some strength? Where's some information about where I can even freakin' <u>find</u> Garfield?!'

"And I just curled up on the floor, Rose," she said incredulously, "and whimpered like a baby. Then, it was over. I was done and just knew that I was going to St. Louis. Case closed.

"But I was still feeling weak and mixed up, so I drove over to Pr. Sauer's house. He was at the church but Carolyn said I looked like a wreck and called him. We sat on his back porch, and I told him the whole thing about going to St. Louis. He sat there for the longest time, saying, 'Hm,' every once in a while. Then, he told me that line about being a fool for Christ. I said, yeah, that was good, but what about just being a plain fool? He said, 'Hm...well...then, it might be good for you to wait until you get more information and have more of a plan.' But I told him that I had to leave tomorrow, it's my spring break, that I've spent enough time trying to get information, that I just know Garfield needs me."

"Well then, it's time for you to settle down and trust God," he said.

"Now I said, 'Hm.'

"Trusting God sounded and felt right; what other choice was there?! So, I asked Pastor if he could dedicate me or something in church this morning, to make it more official, not just me all by myself. He went and got his little book for special occasions. Nothing quite fit. What would you call it? 'Rescue Mission' or 'Holy Pilgrimage to Try and Save a Soul?'

"Anyway, after all that, Rose, I feel like I know a little bit about how Jesus suffered in the garden. He wasn't sure of every single thing—he didn't really want to do it, but he knew he had no choice if he was going to do what God wanted him to do. So he finally gave up and trusted," she ended with a deep intake and blowout of air. She ran her fingers through her hair. She stretched her hands and feet to the extremes and then went limp and huddled on the couch. She stared at the floor for a minute and then said, "So would you please pray one last prayer for me?"

I prayed our Prayer for Vision which I have known by heart for many years:

Lord God, you have called your servants to ventures of which we cannot see the ending, by paths as yet untrodden, through perils unknown. Give us faith to go out with good courage, not knowing where we go, but only that your hand is leading us and your love supporting us; through Jesus Christ our Lord. Amen.

"That was perfect, except now you need to say one with me and Garfield personally identified, please."

So I prayed something like,

Gracious God, we pray for your beloved children, Mindy and Garfield, that they may be open to your strength and your wisdom. Lord Jesus Christ, they are sheep of your own fold, lambs of your own flock, sinners of your own redeeming. Help Mindy find Garfield so that she can reach out and share your love with him. Help him to fight against the demons. Give them their daily bread and whatever else they may need. Bring Mindy safely back to those who love her. Amen.

She hugged me and headed for the door, saying, "You forgot to tell God to not let me wreck your car, but I won't, I promise."

I told her to wait a minute and went and got the bank envelope out of my desk drawer. When I handed her some cash, she didn't even seem surprised. She stuck it in her hip pocket and said, "You're a generous and good woman, Rose. Let's just hope it's not for a lost cause."

I stepped out into the glorious sunlight of this perfect blue and green afternoon and watched her drive into the shadows of the arching trees, their branches fuzzy with bright green buds. Emily Dickinson stopped by to watch with me: "Hope is the thing with feathers that perches in the soul, and sings the tune without the words and never stops at all," she said.

Dear God, if you don't bring that girl and that car safely home, I don't know what I'll do. Please, God. Amen.

Charlie, what do you think? What are sanity and insanity in this world anyway, you know what I mean? I remember you quoting the verses about "my ways are not your ways" and "God's foolishness is wiser than our wisdom" when you set out for that roller-skating jamboree in Montreal in '52 very much in spite of my disapproval and lack of understanding. That scripture seems apt in this situation too, though I'm not sure Virginia and Stephen will settle for a Bible verse as a good reason for me to play fancy free with my car. Oh, dear.

Maundy Thursday
Exodus 12:1-4 (5-10) 11-14
Psalm 116:1-2, 12-19
1 Corinthians 11:23-26
John 13:1-17, 31b-35

What a Maundy Thursday! First thing this morning, all heck broke loose between my "raging tooth" and hot coffee, and I had to go and have that root canal I've been putting off. I got an appointment as soon as the office opened, thanks to a cancellation, and then remembered that I had no car. Mindy didn't even leave me her keys.

So I beeped Virginia. She was here within minutes and glad to take me. And then, there was a little glitch. I was brushing my teeth and she yelled, "Let's take your car Mother," and I heard her open the door to the garage.

I froze. I was still bent over the sink about to spit when her shadow covered me.

Charlie, I can't tell you how silly I felt, like a 5-year-old caught in naughtiness. The worst part was, she didn't say anything. I spit, straightened up, wiped my mouth, rolled my eyes at myself in the mirror, and turned to face her. I was "totally busted," as the young say. She didn't speak, just looked at me expectantly, like I used to do when I caught students red-handed. And then, Charlie, for a couple of nano seconds, I mentally channeled Lucy Ricardo: I thought of telling Virginia that I'm having work done on my car and that's the loaner—or say "What do you mean my car's not in the garage?! Oh no! This is awful, we've got to call the police!" But then, as you've often experienced with me, I saw the humor in the situation and I started laughing, though it came out like a cough/snort, and I said, "I guess you're wondering what's happened to my car."

She maintained eye contact with a smile hidin' behind her mouth, as Stephanie once described a young friend. So, Charlie, I came clean, like a crooked politician who decides that honesty is the best policy, once he's been caught with no place to hide. We debriefed on the way to the endodontist.

"Mother, you're 79 years old and of reasonably sound mind—I think; I'm certainly not going to tell you what to do and what not to do. But this is an incredible risk you've taken. What bothers me more than anything, Mother, is that you didn't tell me up front."

I reflected for a moment.

"I'm not so confident, Virginia," I responded, and my eyes filled with water, which was most irritating.

"Confident of what? My approval or your own actions or what?"

I reflected for another moment, distressed that tears were now leaking down my face. Mothers aren't supposed to lose composure in front of their children.

"Confident that I am an okay person, I guess," unable to fight off the urge to cry.

"Mother, what in the world?! You are one of the most confident people I know. What is this about? The Editor?"

I nodded and shrugged at the same time.

"Boy, he really did a number on you, didn't he?"

I shook my head.

"No. Yes. I don't know. I'm tired of whining about my alcoholic father. Heavens, he was dead and gone by the time I was 25, so I don't think I can blame all my personality defects on him or Mother as an enabler or what-have-you, and yet, here I am in the twilight of my life still acting and feeling like a naughty child half the time!"

I cherish the conversation that followed with Virginia's vigorous affirmation of me along with sympathy, expressed in her no nonsense manner. Like Mindy, I felt close to Jesus in my struggles and even in my little bit of physical suffering. I sensed his presence and felt loved and valued instead of naughty.

Your grace has washed over my soul like a shower, gracious Lord. Fresh and clean, I feel the sickening churnings of inadequacy quiet within me. My calm stomach and my dry eyes praise you, and from deep within, I thank your Holy Spirit for revealing the greatest reality—that I am loved. Thank you also that when I have a health problem I can have it treated and maintain a high quality of life instead of living in poor health and pain and misery and dying early. Help me to be generous to those who are not as fortunate, as I am able. I praise and thank you for your presence with everyone, through Jesus Christ, my Lord. Amen.

Amazingly, I was home by noon, as good as new, at least until the numbness wore off. Even that wasn't too bad.

I called Sarah's house to wish Florence a happy birthday. She's not feeling well, thinks she may have a respiratory infection of some kind. I hope it's that and not the cancer. She's going to tough it out until she gets back to her own doctor next week. She had another dilemma on her hands, too. Sarah has bought her a hat to wear for Easter Sunday. Sarah must have been nearby, for Florence whispered her description of the hat—a deep purple derby with feathers, suitable for a harlot flapper, she wheezed. Very un-Florence, from the description.

"There's no way I'm wearing it, Rose," she said. "Sometimes Sarah amazes me at how clueless she is. Help me figure out the way to hurt her feelings the least. I know it's a gift of love and kindness and all that. If only she weren't so ridiculously sensitive. You can tell she's Arnie's daughter on that count."

I suggested that Florence give in to whimsy, treat it like a joke and just wear it. "After all, when we are old, shan't we wear purple?" I joked.

"That would be your way, Rose, not mine," she replied, unamused.

The truth is, Florence is really enjoying wearing her own hair these days. There's not too much of it yet, but there is a chicness to its white, feathery quality. Especially compared to baldness. I'm sure she and Sarah will work it out—and I'm sure she won't wear the hat.

I called Mercedes Scheumann to beg a ride to the service tonight. I didn't feel like talking to anyone, post-root canal and chilly and tired, so it was fine with me that we arrived right as the service was beginning. I settled comfortably into the back pew with all my aches, pains and worries, very glad to be there. There wasn't a hymnal nearby, so I listened contentedly and gazed at the cross, draped in purple. Then, here comes Madge with hymnals for us. Thank you, Madge.

During the time for individual absolution, I closed my eyes to meditate as others went forward. Into the warm quietness, a major commotion broke out, caused by Rebecca, Claudia's girl, who apparently tripped on the kneeler and tipped over on her platform sandals. How sweet that a pre-teen would even be serious enough to go forward for individual absolution. I hope she wasn't too embarrassed.

Six youngsters received communion for the first time tonight, and there was foot washing, too. Pastor washed the feet of the new communicants and some of their parents. This act seemed strange and awkward. Re-enacting the last supper is okay— comfortable and proper—but merciful heavens—stinking, ugly, bare feet right upfront in the church?! I figure Jesus, knowing about Judas' plan and hearing the disciples still grousing about which of them is greatest, looked around in desperation and grabbed a towel to try one more time to get the message across. Love! Serve! Even when it's messy and uncomfortable and more intimate than you might want to be.

"In the night in which he was betrayed…" How was it for Jesus that night? He had come from God and was returning to God, yet they had never been separate. He knew Psalm 116 backward and forward and now he was living it out, lifting the cup of salvation. "Precious in the sight of the Lord is the death of his faithful ones…" How did betrayal feel? Did he feel betrayed by all the disciples because they didn't understand? Maybe I've been betrayed by Mindy! Oh, Lord, I don't even want to think that!

Zounds! I just remembered a terrible nightmare from last night; it must have come straight from Satan or maybe my toothache or maybe both. I was fixing breakfast, a very important breakfast, maybe the "last breakfast" like the last supper, but I didn't know why it was important. Then I realized it was for Mindy, before she left for St. Louis. She came into the kitchen and asked for my car keys.

I said, "Okay, but first, breakfast is ready."

"I don't want any breakfast, you silly old bat. I just want your car," she said with a pitying laugh.

Virginia and Stephen were in the dream, and they were laughing with Mindy. Then, the worst part—Stephanie Rose was there as a baby, about a year old. She was laughing at me, too, an adult laugh, a wicked, humiliating laugh. I can see her little baby face against a black background, mocking me with a knowing look in her eyes and that adult laugh. In that nightmare, my universe was destroyed. I experienced some kind of ultimate betrayal. That dream was probably in my subconscious this morning when Virginia and I were talking.

If only Mindy would call. I know this can't be a con. It just can't. It is not possible that she and Garfield are in cahoots. I feel sure I haven't misjudged her. I just wish I would hear from her. Did she get there? Has she found him?

I carried my burdens up to the communion rail and tried really hard to leave them there. At the end of the service, the barren altar and sanctuary, stripped of all paraments and objects, seemed to speak of the condition of Jesus' soul—bare yet still there, ready to be adorned in glory when the time was right. The image stayed with me as Mercedes and I snuck out while they were finishing up. Ordinary conversation with other mortals would somehow have diminished the treasures.

So, now I lay me down to sleep, dear God. I thank you for your eternal vigilance. You are watching over Garfield and Mindy. I will rest in the assurance of your gracious love and your so-called foolishness, wiser by far than my wisdom. Amen.

Good Friday (late)

Isaiah 52:13-53:12
Psalm 22
Hebrews 10:16-25
John 18:1-19:42

Isaiah says it well: "Who can believe what we have heard?" Who can believe that Good Friday is good? That all suffering can be redeemed? That Garfield can pull himself together? I find Isaiah 52-53 quite suspect. We're supposed to understand that being "despised," "rejected," "afflicted," will turn into some kind of victory?
For Jesus, yes, but for us?! Hm.
Oh, Rose, why don't you just shut up and believe it?! Stop struggling, stop thinking, stop feeling, and believe.
How I wish I could.
This suffering servant concept is decidedly unattractive. It's okay for the risen Christ. He triumphed. Ultimately, he succeeded. The Risen Christ is now socially acceptable, but not that suffering servant fellow.
I found a suffering servant on my front step when I got home tonight—Garfield. At least he was suffering; I'm not so sure about the servant part. Like the folks in Isaiah, I wanted to hide, as if he were a leper. *Held in your forgiving love, I confess it to you God, since you already know.* I felt like that worm we heard about tonight, a worm instead of a person. My heart sank to see him, instead of rejoicing. I didn't even want to touch him, the smell of nicotine and the street was so disgusting to me. He undoubtedly sensed it, and I'm afraid I reinforced his feeling of being despised and rejected.
Mindy didn't look or smell too great either. She was subdued, exhausted. Over the teapot after Garfield had gone to bed, she apologized for their appearance. She had planned for them to be all cleaned up and rested before they drove into town, but she said that St. Louis had been three tough days of making the rounds of agencies and government offices and employment places, with no good results.
"They don't like Garfield much in St. Louis, and they didn't like me much either—guilt by association, I guess. I started out trying to be polite and cheerful and 'appropriately assertive,' as Stephanie would say, but got worn down fast."
She described one closed door after another and a web of deceit and even crime that Garfield had woven for himself. Finally, bringing him back to Shippensforge was the only thing that made any sense, she had decided. They left St. Louis this morning after one last stop at a mental health center where Garfield had once received treatment. The people there told Mindy that Garfield had brought a gun to

day treatment once (a gun!) and then run away before anything could be done about it, so it would be problematic for him to go there again.

Mindy said she might not have found him if it weren't for Tramp. Monday was rainy and miserable, and she was still confused and very tired because she had arrived after midnight on Sunday and slept in the car but didn't really sleep because she was cold and uncomfortable.

"First thing Monday morning, I called his uncle, Donald S. Temple, the one Temple in the phone book who had admitted to knowing Garfield. He hung up on me, like he had the other eight times I'd called him, but his address was in the phone book, so I got directions and drove to his house. It was about 7:30 when I got there; he was just coming out to go to work. I ran up to him and poured out how I'd met Garfield and Marie on Christmas Eve. I told him about St. Timothy sanctifying me and you payrolling the trip. I could see his suspicions going down. He told me that Garfield actually was good at heart. Donald S. was the one who had taught him to play the guitar. He said that Garfield had always been a little off and then had gotten mixed up with the bottle. He hasn't seen him in over two years and neither have his children. But then he told me that Garfield had called him a while back from a Burger King and had told him that he was staying in a mission nearby.

"Donald S. left for work, and I started calling mission-type places listed in the phone book and asking if they were close to a Burger King. I got a couple possibilities. Tramp and I were trudging through one of the possible neighborhoods when he stopped and took a dump right in front of a house where a man was sitting on the porch. The next thing I knew, the man was screaming in my face, and he put me right over the edge, so I started screaming back at him and said something about Garfield Temple. Maybe I said it was Garfield's fault or his dog or something, I don't know. But this idiot stopped screaming and started yelling instead, 'I might have known this was Garfield Temple's dog! He is the poorest excuse for a man I ever…' and I was so excited and asked if he knew where I might find Garfield and he said, 'You bet I know where you can find him—right over there where he went an hour ago when I kicked his rear end out of my upstairs apartment that I'm trying to rent. Found him dead drunk in one of the back rooms. There's that worthless sumbitch right there,' he pointed.

"I looked over and there he was, passed out on a park bench. After offering to clean up the poop and being yelled away by the madman, I crossed the street and just stood there looking at the heap of humanity and I thought why in the world do I want anything to do with that worthless sumbitch? I really did think that, Rose, all the doubts piled on again, and it came to me very clearly that I could just get back in the car and leave. But after being dedicated at church and the long trip and you letting me use your car and now, the surest sign that God was in on this—I found Garfield—I knew I had to keep on. I let Tramp loose and he went right for Garfield and jumped up on him, licking his face and I thought, for God's sake, if that dog can love him, surely I can.

"Garfield was totally confused. He looked like he couldn't decide if Tramp was real or really Tramp or a dream or what. He started looking around and saw me. He didn't smile, and neither did I. He got up slowly and walked over to me and just stood looking at me. I didn't know what to say so I said, 'God sent me to save your sorry butt.' He stared at me and his eyes watered up. After that, we were partners."

She told about going with Garfield to a printing company where he had worked, to see if they might hire him back. Garfield introduced her to Alice, who hugged his neck and asked where he'd been. Mindy picked up from their conversation that Garfield had been a good worker there for a couple years. His big mouth got him in trouble once in a while, but mostly people liked him. Alice and Garfield talked about him getting shock treatments for his depression and how much that had helped him, but the insurance company or the government or somebody had stopped paying for that, so he couldn't get them anymore. His situation had deteriorated from there. Alice wished him good luck, but said she was afraid he'd used up all his chances with their company. And so the story went.

Mindy smiled, then teared up telling about delivering Tramp to Marie, who is still staying with her sister. Marie cried for joy and carried on to see him—Tramp, not Garfield. It was like seeing a mother reunited with a lost child. Then Garfield cried like a baby when Marie told Mindy that she's not mad at Garfield, she just can't handle his mental illness anymore. "I can't keep up with his downs," she said, and for her own survival, she had to get away from him. Mindy was amazed that Marie's sister and brother-in-law told Garfield they wished him the best and they cared about him, but they didn't want to see him until he had straightened himself out. They all seemed to realize that he's a diamond in the rough.

"He's a shell of a man," Mindy ended the night's report. "There's good in him, Rose, there's beauty. We can see it, but he can't."

She rubbed her eyes and said she was too tired to think. I talked her into sleeping on the couch in the family room. I think she was asleep before her head hit the pillow.

And now, in the haze of my own fatigue and perplexity, I shall gaze upon the icon of the crucifixion.

Christ is dead, it seems, his expression solemn yet somehow majestic. The sky is golden and there are angels. Yes, there is death, but more victory over death. At the foot of the cross is a black hole with a white skull—hell. Look out down there, shake and quake! God is going to beat you at your own game with this crucified guy right here. Take a deep breath, Satan, because that's what Christ is doing, and he will be descending through your shaking gates any time now.

He is well attended, a terrified John on his left, Mary on his right, gesturing toward him, seeming to say, "Behold salvation." I identify with both John and Mary. Death and sin terrify; yet I am certain—in a place beyond my ability to reason, beyond my efforts to deny—that what looks like defeat is actually victory.

And so, Mindy and I attend Garfield, knowing that Christ is in him and praying that he will be in Christ. "A broken and contrite heart you will not despise, dear God."

Merciful heavens, it's midnight! Wake up here, Cute Baby, so we can go to bed.

Oh, Lord, come to us here in this little house, to your weary, your sinful, your beaten-down. Grace us with the comfort of knowing your presence. Give us insight, give us energy, give us love for each other. Most of all, right now, give us sleep. Amen.

Easter Vigil

Selected readings from:
Genesis 1:1-2:4a
Genesis 7:1-5,11-18; 8:6-18; 9:8-13
Genesis 22:1-18
Exodus 14:10-31;15:20-21
Isaiah 55:1-11
Proverbs 8:1-8, 19, 21; 9:4b-6
Ezekiel 36:24-28
Ezekiel 37:1-14
Zephaniah 3:14-20
Jonah 1:1-2:1
Isaiah 61:1-4, 9-11
Daniel 3:1-29
Romans 6:3-11
Luke 24:1-12

"Without any doubt, the mystery of our religion is great," said Paul to Timothy. Any thinking person would agree! This is the most mysterious of nights, this re-enactment of the earliest Easter celebrations in the Church. We gather outside around a fire and then enter the dark building. When I come to this service I want us all to pretend that we are the early post-resurrection believers and hustle secretly into a dark, damp cave to worship. A candle is lit and the Word is read, starting with our ancient creation story and recounting the wild events that have shaped our faith. After each recitation, another candle is lit. Finally, we hear the simple, astonishing good news of the resurrection, Christ's and ours. New and earnest followers who have been studying the beliefs of this strange, young religion are baptized or confirmed. There is little but mystery, holy mystery that is irrationally and undeniably true.

I have loved this vigil service since Pr. Sauer introduced it the first Easter he was with St. Timothy. In the beginning, it was a midnight service. Pastor made a point of finding somebody to baptize. Several attended in those days, but the novelty wore off. After two or three years, no one was showing up except the baptism victims and their families and those who were conned into reading a lesson. Finally, Pastor agreed to change the time to 7:30 in the evening. We've gained better attendance but lost the darkness and differentness that come from worshiping in the middle of the night.

The air was cool and breezy as we gathered this evening around the fire burning in Louie Smith's outdoor grill. There were maybe 35 of us, and we were way too congenial for my mood. Way too "How-are-you?-That's-a-nice-coat.-Thanks-I-bought-it-on-sale-last-week.-I-set-out-my-onions-today-hope they don't freeze." But at least we came, the faithful few, not completely knowing why, perhaps feeling a little foolish when people drove by. Mystery isn't always exotic. Sometimes it's just plain confusing and so down-to-earth that we don't stand in awe but accept it dully, like we accept electrical surges that dim the lights.

The large Christ candle leads the way, but the breeze snuffed out the light of Christ about twenty times. Fortunately, we had a stubborn usher who kept re-lighting and re-lighting, undeterred by our awkward snickering. By some miracle the flame finally held, and we followed it through the back door. The hallway with its coat rack and bulletin boards was transformed by the silent, purposeful procession. Three times we paused and Bruce Leppard, Deedee's dad, proclaimed, "The light of Christ," in his clear, tenor voice. Each time we echoed, then moved to the next spot.

I settled in the pew next to Stephanie, cozy and content, to listen to our stories of faith, stories which we have heard over and over again. But my! Steph was feisty tonight. She elbowed me every time the word "seed" was read in the creation story. This child thinks seedless grapes are blasphemous.

"God created the miracle of plants with seeds in them! It's the divine system. Why do we think we can improve it?" I've heard her fume.

I remember her throwing a fit and refusing to eat seedless watermelon at Virginia's last summer. She loves seeds, has dozens of edible seeds in her spice cupboard. She bases her vegetarianism in Genesis 1, verse 29—"God said, 'See, I have given you every plant yielding seed that is upon the face of all the earth, and every tree with seed in its fruit; you shall have them for food.'"

Stephanie doesn't think animals should be eating one another either.

"Why, honey," I said to her during one of our discussions, "what about the food chain?"

"I don't know, Grandma, but I believe that one day the lamb and the wolf shall lie down together and the lion shall eat straw. That's how God wants it to be, but we've gotten away from the plan."

"But sweetie," I persisted, "if Uncle Stephen and everybody else stopped fishing and hunting, the world would be in a terrible mess. What about that?"

"I don't know, Grandma. Seems to me the world's in a terrible mess because hunting and fishing upset the balance. I certainly don't know how, but I believe the Almighty One would take care of the situation somehow if we tried to tip things back in order."

She once accused me of eating my cat. That is, she said what was the difference between eating a cow or chicken that someone else had killed and eating Cute Baby? They're all God's creatures, just like us.

"I would feel like a cannibal if I ate animals," she said. "That's my understanding of the Creation. Why would God create beautiful creatures with fur and spots and eyelashes for the purpose of being slaughtered?! Uh-uh."

"Jesus ate animals," I countered. "He ate lamb and fish right in the Bible."

"Yeah, well, that was Jesus' choice, I guess," she said thoughtfully. Then, "I kind of think if he came back today and saw how obsessed we are with food and how horribly we treat animals and wipe out rainforests to satisfy our insatiable appetites, he would be vegetarian. Probably even vegan."

Hm.

Apparently Pastor couldn't find anyone who needed baptizing. Instead, we all affirmed our baptism. He had a grand time, smiling broadly as he walked up and down the middle aisle flicking water from the font on us with a spritzer made of basil branches. Instinctively, most of us drew back from the flying water, though Madge leaned right into it, which was really quite sweet. I had to smile at the startled yet amused expressions of the Avery's out-of-town family guests.

Carolyn's quip as we were leaving was quite fitting. "Well, let's go home amazed," picking up on Peter's response in the gospel lesson.

Yes, home to Garfield. I called Stephen, Virginia, and Florence this morning to let them know he is back in town. Mindy called Pastor. The children insist that Garfield will stay with one of them rather than me until we can get things sorted out and help him find a place. I can't say they were enthusiastic at the idea, but I can say that they were irritated. That's okay. They don't have to do it. Mindy said I'd better take them up on it right away, before they get to know him.

I was awakened this morning by the smell of breakfast. Garfield had showered and put on my robe that was hanging in the bathroom, flowers and all. He had made coffee and was frying bacon. He grabbed me and twirled me around the kitchen for a minute, shouting, "Rose, this is the last day of the first of my life—or something like that!"

I thought, "O'boy, I'm glad you had a good night's sleep but settle down here. There's no need for such excitement just because you're fixing breakfast. You have a long way to go before it's time to celebrate."

When Mindy walked in, fresh from the 24-hour Stuff-Mart with toiletries and an outfit for him, he grabbed her and twirled her around. She looked tired and wary for a moment, but his manic optimism was infectious. She and I looked at each other and shrugged as if to say, "Hey, this is more fun than depression," and we enjoyed a raucous and delicious meal as the sun streamed into the kitchen. She gave us every detail of her 7 a.m. shopping spree—the other weirdoes there and the cashier's politically incorrect comment as she observed Mindy's purchases: "Whadja' do, honey? Pick up a bum by the side of the road?" Mindy said, "Yes, ma'm," and sailed on out to her car laughing.

In addition to the joy of food, we were privileged to watch bluebirds flying to and fro building a nest. Garfield was enrapt, as amazed and delighted as a five-year old. Tonight he's bunking at Stephen's.

So, God, we'll do what we can to help you breathe new life into the bag o'dead bones known as Garfield Temple. Guide us and guard us all. Amen.

Easter Day

Acts 10:34-43
Psalm 118:1-2,14-24
1 Corinthians 15:19-26
John 10:1-18

I didn't go to worship on Easter Sunday! In fact, it is now Tuesday. Here's what happened: Five minutes before Stephen came by to get me Sunday morning, I bent over to pick something up and my back went out. I hobbled into the bed and positioned myself carefully. When I didn't go out to the car, Stephen came in. He didn't want to leave me, but when I asked him if Garfield was with him, and he said yes, Garfield was waiting in the car, I said get me a couple painkillers and get right back out there and get that man to church! He did as he was told. The Day of the Resurrection of Our Lord was a rollercoaster from there on.

Virginia transferred dinner over here from her place. With painkillers and strategically-placed pillows, I was able to sit in the rocking chair at the table. Family plus Garfield. It would have been wonderful to have Mindy with us too, but she needed to be with her family after her brother's death and all. She said she was looking for an Easter miracle—a Lucas family get-together without an argument.

Garfield was painfully ill at ease, a little fish in a strange pond. He had a sore on his jaw and kept scratching and gouging at it. Pretty soon his napkin was spotted with blood, and Virginia slipped him another one. He was quite a different character from the guy dancing around the kitchen yesterday. Something was definitely going on with him.

He said a prayer at dinner. I'm not sure he exactly wanted to; it seemed like a strenuous effort for him. Stephanie had said an eloquent and thoughtful blessing. Then, an instant after everyone had picked up their forks and chatter was underway, Virginia heard Garfield say, very faintly, that he would like to say a prayer. She hushed everybody and segued kindly on his behalf. I shall never forget his prayer, delivered with a trembling voice:

"Dear Jesus, you had two lives and God gave nine to cats. I don't know how many I'll be allowed, but I feel like I'm starting on a new one today. Thank you for these people and please give me what it takes to straighten myself out. Amen."

He was overcome with emotion and left the room for a few minutes. I don't think I was the only one misting up, judging from the silence and averted eyes.

When I asked how the worship service was, my smart-alecky children said that, much to their surprise, Jesus Christ rose from the dead without me. Virginia said it was the usual "Alleluia this and Alleluia that," but then—now hear this!—Virginia Jean Harris McMichel said that Pastor's sermon had touched her.

Cautiously, not wanting to scare her off, I ventured a soft, "How, Virginia?"

She started with the title: "The Most Powerful Weapon for the Last Enemy, or God's Love vs. Death." Everybody said they had never seen Pastor Sauer so impassioned.

"He is definitely convinced of the truth of the Resurrection," Barry commented.

That's my pastor.

Virginia repeated his preaching refrain: "And we don't have to wait to die before we use that weapon." He emphasized that death is all around us everyday—physical death as well as the death of creativity, the death of understanding between people, the death of relationships. We can use the greatest weapon, God's love, to resurrect creativity, understanding, marriages, or whatever.

"Naturally, I thought of Eunice, Mother."

"Ah. How long has it been since you've spoken to each other?"

"Four years tomorrow. I remember that because I called her on her thirtieth birthday. I decided I wanted to apologize or whatever I needed to do to put things right after that sale she stole from me. She hung up on me that last time I called, which hurt pretty badly because I thought we were good friends; I like Eunice enormously. I felt helpless, though, and eventually accepted the death of our friendship. Pastor's sermon persuaded, or maybe reminded me, how powerful love is. So, come tomorrow, I'll try again."

My heart was warmed by this testimony, but Barry was having none of it.

"Honey, that's great. You're responding to a difficult situation in the best possible way because you are a compassionate and supremely decent person, but I'm not so sure it's God's love any more than your own decency and personal ethics that will make the difference. Frankly, I'm having a little difficulty, right here on Easter Day, with God."

He picked out a verse from Isaiah from this morning that stuck in his craw: "Those in Jerusalem will live in happiness and security."

"Yeah, right," he snorted. "Get on a bus in Jerusalem or go to the market. How secure is that? Remember that Christmas when The Church of the Nativity right there in Bethlehem itself was under siege for months, with death and destruction all around, the so-called chosen people killing each other left and right? At best, the power of God's love—or whatever you want to call it—is having a major brownout." His face was getting red and ugly.

"When you come right down to it," he was almost yelling, "it's ludicrous, the whole damn concept of enduring endless crap on the basis that sometimes it's not too bad and by and by things will be better. Thanks, but no thanks."

Uncomfortable silence.

"Sorry for the outburst. I'm not really fit for socializing today. I think I'll be better off out on the lake."

Then, Big Chief Barry-Who-Loves-to-Eat, as we fondly call him, pushed away from a plate of sumptuous honey-baked ham and candied yams and left. If I'd been quick enough to respond to his heart-felt diatribe, I would have said, "But there is new life right here at this table. Why not focus on that?"

Charlie, I also wanted to tell Barry, and all of them, about that Saturday night when you finally had your breakthrough after the accident. That was new life for you, for us. But, even though I remember it like it was yesterday, I've never been able to share that moment with anyone; it's too intimate...

Charlie was looking out the kitchen window into the woods, his hands spread palms-down on the counter. I put my hands on his shoulders, and he whirled around with a look of terror on his face.
"We have to talk," I said. "We simply cannot go on this way."
"Leave me alone," he yelled, and tried to push past me, but I blocked him. We struggled clumsily. Gasping for breath, I clung to him.
"Let me go, let me go," he panted in fury. He struck me hard on my face and then gave up. I felt him going down and went with him. He collapsed in my arms, sobbing. I held him and hugged him, kissing him all over his head and face. He cried himself out, and I stroked him. We got to our feet, clinging to each other, and walked down the hall to our bedroom.
Never was our sexual passion so desperate or so sweet. All through that night, we made up for the months of separation. With every climax, Charlie dissolved in crying, and eventually fell into a deep sleep until well into the morning, and, finally, we were a couple again...

I so wanted to share that powerful moment, the kitchen part at least, because if we don't focus on the miracles, we are, of all people, most pitiful.

When Virginia followed Barry outside, Stephen reminded us that Frank Hammond, Barry's best friend and fishing buddy since childhood, has pancreatic cancer. Six weeks ago, Frank went to the doctor with back pain, and now they're just trying to keep him comfortable until the end. So, easier to talk about what's going on in Jerusalem, maybe.

Oh, Lord God, why must you stretch our souls so? Or is it you who is stretching us? Or just random stretching? Or random sin? Or intentional sin? Help us to brave the mysterious agonies of this life in the knowledge that you are here, always, even when we are stretched to the breaking point. You were with Barry when he was out on the lake Sunday afternoon. You are with Frank and his family. You are with Garfield in his second life. May they know your presence. May Barry hear your still small voice that keeps our spirits alive and keeps us going. May all people everywhere hear you in their own ways. You raised your Son from the dead.

Your powers of redemption are stronger than any other power. Help us live the miracle. Amen.

Well, Easter dinner continued on its nose-dive. Right after Virginia came back from telling Barry good-bye, I reached for my glass and had a spasm that lasted for five minutes after they got me flat on the bed. Garfield was alarmed, but I've been through this back business enough times to know there's nothing to do but drugs and rest and give it time.

After they finished their cold dinner, Stephen and Virginia cleaned up and Garfield and Stephanie took chairs on either side of my bed to visit. Garfield said that the people at worship were very friendly. I was pleasantly relieved to hear that. (You never know.) He was surprised that they knew he was from St. Louis. I told him about Mindy's commissioning service last Sunday, shocked to think it had been only a week ago. A strange look came over his face

"Why do those people care about me? They don't even know me."

"Because of Christ, Garfield," Stephanie chimed in. "They've known his grace and love and can't help but share it. It's that simple." Steph amazes me with her open faith. She will talk faith with anybody, anytime. And I think it's kind of odd that she still uses faith words that are out-of-date, words like grace and salvation that the vast majority of her peers don't understand at all.

Garfield responded to her with a shake of his head and a smile that seemed to say, "I don't get it, but I like it."

He described a short, plump, blonde woman with Tammy Faye eyes who offered to help in any way she could. That was undoubtedly Madge, wanting to "help the underprivileged." He and Stephanie both loved the anthem the choir sang. Mindy wanted to get up and dance in the aisle, but they discouraged her. Too bad! Just as Stephanie remembered to tell me that Pastor had said he would come by in the afternoon to bring me Eucharist, as he calls communion, he rang the doorbell.

"Thanks so much for coming, Pastor, but I hate you're not with your family this afternoon," I greeted him.

"More accurately, they're not with me, Rose," he smiled. "They took off for Chicago right after the service. Brittany has a dance competition for the next three days. This week is spring break, you know. I had a cheese sandwich and a nap, and now it's a great pleasure to be here with one of my favorite sheep."

"Did you think about going along with Carolyn and Brittany?" I asked, even though it was none of my business. He could have gone to some ballgames, I thought. He's a Cubs fan like the rest of us, irrationally devoted.

He looked kind of funny. "Carolyn asked me to go along, but I had other commitments."

"I wish we'd known you were alone. We would have had you join us for dinner."

I suspect our luncheon would have been very different if he had been present, but what happened was fine, too, and real.

Pastor point-blank asked Garfield about his plans. Garfield looked at the floor with a sigh, shook his head, shrugged his shoulders, gestured palms up as he made eye contact with us.

And then, in a composed voice, he said, "Starting tomorrow morning at 6 a.m., things are going to change." His brow furrowed in thought for a moment and then he added, "I'm gonna' fight that enemy you were talking about this morning."

Pastor Sauer about fell off his chair.

"Somebody listened to my sermon!" He sounded so shocked we had to laugh.

"Garfield," he said, "there will be plenty of people to help you in that fight. In one way or another, we're all fighting the same battle."

Virginia came in to tell Pastor they had fixed him a plate to take home, and she and Stephen and Garfield left. Stephanie and I received the sacrament from Pr. Sauer. Now my Easter was complete. After he left, I slept peacefully for a couple hours, awakened by the telephone.

The ring was Florence, reporting that she will be heading home on Tuesday. I told her about my back. "Oh, yeah, hurt your back. I know you, Rose Harris; you just wanted to blow off church," she teased.

She also reported on the purple hat dilemma. Sarah had decided on her own that the hat just didn't look right on her mother and besides, Sarah had said, "Why cover up your beautiful new hair?" Grace strikes again.

Stephanie and I talked the evening away. Feminist theology, a vacation she and Ethan have planned, wonder at her mother's theological revelations and her dad's struggles.

She shared that she and Ethan had had a pretty big argument. Alas, "the course of true love never did run smooth." He had wanted her to go to Easter dinner at his folks' place. She knew it was her turn to spend a holiday with his family, but she absolutely did not want to go. It's a six-hour drive, so if they had left on Sunday, they would miss church altogether. If they had driven yesterday, they could have worshiped somewhere, but where, since Ethan and his folks have no church home?

"I'm actually rather uncomfortable in Ethan's family culture, Grandma," Stephanie confided. "They're very proper and formal, with strained smiles and arched eyebrows if anyone doesn't stay in line with his parents' expectations. Gender roles of forty years ago are strictly observed. Do you know not one person has asked me a single question about my work in the two years I've known them?! Or about anything, for that matter. I'm amazed that Ethan has come out of such a stifling upbringing so well; I love and admire him even more because of that."

She has nothing in common with his sister and can't stand to be around his twin niece and nephew, "indulged little brats who are always trying to prove how smart they are."

"I really love him, Grandma, and I want to spend the rest of my life with him but not with his family."

Uh-oh, I thought, that's not how it works, but I by-passed the opportunity to talk about the challenges of relationship, afraid that I'd wind up criticizing their living situation again. Better not to irritate my caregiver! The sweet girl stayed all night and last night too. I think I'm ready to be on my own now.

As I write, Garfield is separating my day lilies. He is doing it with great care in the mist that has been falling all morning. He's well fixed for clothing now, after Madge took him to the community closet yesterday. He calls her Midge. Ha, ha, as in midget. Rose, you are a terrible person; pull in your thorns.

Garfield's going to repair and paint my shed, and Virginia and Barry said they would hire him for a couple days of yard work. Susie Wakefield (such a saint) called me yesterday and asked if Garfield needs a job. She thinks Murray, their son who has opened his own furniture factory, might need a sander and finisher.

Stephen and I agree that the logical place for Garfield to live is Agape House, but we both have reservations because we've heard rumors that the place has a somewhat coercive religious orientation towards its residents. Also, that Brother James, the director, has had some major bookkeeping issues according to scuttlebutt and The Evening Gazette. When they drove by there yesterday and Stephen pointed the building out, Garfield asked with a worried look, "A ape House?"

The 'g' has fallen off. Definitely, a bad sign (pun intended).

Second Sunday of Easter

Acts 5:27-32
Psalm 118:14-29
Revelation 1:4-8
John 20:19-31

I just have to love Thomas the Doubter. No pious platitudes, no brown-nosing. On that last night before the crucifixion when Jesus was so earnest and eloquent and anguished and told the disciples, "And you know the way to the place where I am going," Thomas had the gumption and purity of heart to blurt, "Lord, we do not know where you are going. How can we find the way?" He didn't nod foolishly and pretend to understand, as I probably might have.

And again, Thomas plays no games with the other disciples when he misses Jesus' first appearance on that Sunday night. (Had he gone out for bread and milk or what?!) He didn't resign as a disciple, he didn't reject the others' experience, he just blundered on, insisting that he needed his own experience. After all, he hadn't seen, he hadn't been breathed on.

Some of us need to see or touch; some of us don't; the ones who don't are more blessed, I guess. There is no formula for personal faith, Pr. Sauer preached, and I thoroughly agree with him. To think that the gift of faith must come to us in a certain way or at a specific time is balderdash.

I peeked at Garfield during the service and wondered about his life of faith and what goes through his mind during worship. How much of the goings-on can he comprehend since it's all so new and different for him? This morning he seemed troubled and distracted. He didn't even smile when I pointed out the bulletin blooper: "Thine Is the Gory." Maybe he didn't get it.

And he showed little response when two infants were baptized. My heart hurt for both of them. Clarice Renee is the daughter of Derrick Evans, Mary Jane and Jerry's son. Clarice Renee's mother, who is not and apparently will never be Derrick's wife, was not present. She is moving to California with the child, according to Mary Jane.

The other babe was William Jayce, Chad and Deedee's newest, born on Wednesday! Heavens, it seems like about ten years ago when Chad and Deedee were baptized! What a behavior problem Chad was when I taught his third grade Sunday School class—so curious, so smart, so smart-alecky. Years later, he wrote me a note of apology for his third grade behavior. We all enjoyed his and Deedee's courtship, both of them St. Timothy kids, and their sweet, simple wedding and the chatter over Deedee not changing her name, and the baptisms of their other three children. Chad leaves for Iraq Wednesday. He was given just enough time off to attend the service. In his desert camouflage fatigues, surrounded by both sets of grandparents and Deedee and the three older children, he wept and most of us did too. After the service, Danny ran up and hugged him hard and said, "D-d-d-on't go, Chad. You m-m-ight get killed."

May Chad be saved from his enemies and all who hate us, please God.

Back to Garfield. Despite outward showings, I have no doubt that his faith is genuine. I felt love in his gentleness when he helped me get in Stephen's car this morning, taking every precaution to ease me in with my sore back. I saw love in his cheerful kindness when he and Stephen came home with me and took over my kitchen. Working with what food I had on hand, they fixed a strange but tasty Sunday dinner of smoked sausage, cranberry sauce, corn, and hashed brown potatoes. Garfield makes a mean hashed brown. We sat at the kitchen window and chatted for a long and pleasant time after the meal. I got out the binoculars and bird book, and he was excited like a little boy when we identified some of our winged friends. He went out to check on the bluebirds. Stephen went to the grocery to restock my pantry while Garfield cleaned up the kitchen, whistling as he worked. By the time they left, they had done up all my laundry, vacuumed, and filled the birdbath and feeders. They were a great odd couple to keep me on the road to recovery.

So, I wonder what faith means to Garfield. I can't help but contrast myself and other religious people who try so hard to be faithful and good. He considers himself to be such a low-down sinner that "what's the use?" And then, out of nowhere, yet naturally, love and gentleness float out of him, praising Almighty God, and he doesn't have a clue. He doesn't know his face is shining.

He told us that he had thought about calling Marie last night to tell her about his new life and see how Tramp is doing, but he didn't because he was afraid he would only cry. He intends to call her tonight, their first contact since he left St. Louis.

Mindy got him in to see her psychiatrist last week who prescribed an antidepressant.

"Man, I hate taking this stuff! It flat-lines me into a zombie, but I know what happens when I slack off. I feel like hell with it and go to hell without it."

Tomorrow he starts half-days in Murray Wakefield's cabinet shop and, for better or worse, he'll soon be moving into "a ape house." Meanwhile, he and Stephen are like a couple of old bachelors, taking turns fixing supper and watching TV in the evenings with popcorn and apple juice. He's gone to AA with Stephen the last couple weeks.

"He really is a good guy," Stephen said the other day. "I don't think he's messing with us; he knows he's fighting for his life."

Mindy keeps Garfield in cigarettes, a strange graciousness. "Here, friend. I'll pay for your lung cancer until you get back on your feet and can pay for it yourself." And he's asthmatic! Mindy can't stand smoke and has never smoked herself. Nonetheless, she thinks smoking is a crucial safety valve for him.

"I doubt Garfield will live to a ripe old age, Rose," she said the other day. "He might as well have the smoking pleasure if it steadies him a little. Besides, my grandma died of lung cancer, just like David, but she never smoked a cigarette in her life. She said she almost wished she had smoked since she had to go through all that suffering anyway." I have a very hard time watching anyone I care about smoking, in light of Florence's excruciating illness and approaching death.

Thank you, gracious God, for simple blessings—birds in my backyard, pills and pillows, friends and family, gently falling rain, happy memories of a good marriage, a quiet afternoon to rest, being able to gather in Christ's body and worship you. Amen.

Third Sunday of Easter

Acts 9:1-6
Psalm 30
Revelation 5:11-14
John 21:1-19

The gospel lesson this morning was the disciples' strange little fish breakfast on the shore with the risen Christ. Imagine how Peter must have felt to be able to reconcile with Christ after that horrible night in the courtyard! On this early morning, the Risen Christ presided over a three-question liturgy for Peter, as Pastor described it—Do you love me? Do you love me? Do you love me?—gracing Peter with the opportunity to declare his love three times and wipe out his three denials.

After a short period of estrangement from Garfield, I, too, felt the warm glow of reconciliation when he looked straight in my eyes and said, "Peace, Rose," during the passing of the peace.

Our difficulty had started on Tuesday afternoon when he called me from the church office. He had gone there to reclaim his belongings, and nobody knew where they were. I drove right over, my first time to drive since my back went out, and went straight to the closet under the stairway on the north end of the building where I had put his ice chest and guitar. Gone! There was very little in that space at all.

As we climbed the stairs to the office he said, "I sure hope it's not lost. Every song I ever wrote is in there." Oh, dear.

I called Sidney Wright, Property Chairman. Gruffly, as usual, Sidney said they had thrown the stuff out at a workday in March. Nobody knew what it was, it just looked like junk, he said. He thought maybe somebody had taken the guitar home, but he couldn't remember who. Fie!

I stood with my back to Garfield and the receiver on my ear after Sidney hung up, but I finally had to turn around.

"I'm so sorry…" I started out, but the look of betrayal in Garfield's angry eyes stopped me. He turned and walked out. I didn't go after him because I didn't know what to say. Never has the phrase "one person's treasure is another's trash" been so painfully true. Oh, dear God, I wish I'd labeled it; I should have put my name on it. And I confess that I thought of his belongings as junk, too. What's the big deal in losing a broken down Styrofoam ice chest and an old guitar? That was before I knew all the songs he had ever written were in there.

I called him later at Stephen's.

"That was a big part of my life, Rose. It's like I don't matter, just throw me away."

"No one feels that way about you, Garfield," I said, then remembered some not so nice remarks about him at circle meeting the other night.

Millicent Avery said that I wasn't very discriminating when it came to people. I thanked her for the compliment, but we were on different wavelengths. In her smoother-than-smooth way, Millicent continued—

"We mustn't look down on the unfortunate, but it's hard to hold out much hope after the lives of deprivation they've led. And I really do think the poor fellow would be more comfortable with his own kind of people. He's more Church of Christ-y, don't you think?"

<u>Who</u> would be more comfortable, Millicent?

Anyway, I kept apologizing to Garfield over the phone until I realized that the more sympathy I gave him, the more he wallowed in it.

When he whined dramatically for the fourth or fifth time, "Maybe it didn't look like much to somebody else, but that was my life," something in me snapped.

"That was not your life, Garfield! Your life is in your and God's hands. If you're going to make it, you're going to have to stop feeling sorry for yourself. You're going to have to write new songs. Move ahead, let the past be the past."

"I thought you were my friend," he muttered bitterly.

"I think I am. Friends can say what they think to each other."

"Thanks a lot," he said and hung up on me.

So this morning was especially sweet. After the service, he invited Florence and me to come over and see his new place. He moved into Agape House yesterday.

"Ladies, come into my little corner of the world," the playful Garfield said as he opened the door to his room and made a sweeping gesture with his arm.

My eyes immediately rested upon a guitar, his guitar, I thought, looking at him in surprise.

"Yes, it's my good old gee-tar," he said with a big smile. "Sid had it re-strung for me."

Sid?! Sidney Wright, of all people, tracked down Garfield's guitar and had it re-strung. The same Sidney Wright who grouches about every little disorder at the church, Sidney Wright, who thinks people on welfare should be shot at dawn, Sidney Wright, who lets everybody know his offerings go solely to the building fund because he doesn't want his money to go to the undeserving. Sidney is also a guitar player, which I never knew. Sid. What next?!

The folks at the house invited us to stay for dinner, becoming quite insistent when we were concerned about imposing on them. Garfield seemed to want us to stay too, so we did.

In the table blessing, Brother James said something about God having a-hold of Garfield since Wednesday night and God won't ever let go because Garfield has made his decision, has accepted Jesus for his very own, his personal savior. The path behind was crooked and dark, Br. James preached more than prayed, but the path ahead is straight and bathed in the sunshine of Jesus' love. Florence and I exchanged a little rolling of the eyes. I wanted to point out that God has always had a-hold of Garfield, even before we knew him, even before he moved in here. It's not us, Brother James. It's God.

But I behaved myself (at that moment) and proceeded to enjoy the crustiest, most delicious fried chicken I've ever tasted along with creamy mashed potatoes, sweet and buttery corn and homemade German chocolate cake. Hospitality par excellence. There are many advantages to Garfield being here: good food, walking distance to the cabinet shop and St Timothy, supervision.

Florence and I sat on the screen porch with him after dinner and visited for awhile. Garfield had been in touch with Marie.

"She doesn't hate me, I know that. I'm not sure if she loves me anymore, but she wants me to get well. She doesn't hate me," he said again, looking at the floor and pondering. "I hope and pray we can be us again."

"And how is she?" I asked.

He smiled. "She's beautiful, she's kind, she's a good mother for Tramp. She's working graveyard with a construction crew, making good money. She said she was glad I called."

He seemed peaceful as we said good-bye.

On our way out, we found Br. James changing the billboard sign, and I simply could not resist engaging theologically. He was putting up the motto, "Life is a test. God is the teacher. Are you passing or failing?"

The dialogue that ensued surprised me, and I will try to recapture its essence here:

"Brother James, thank you for the excellent hospitality, but I'm afraid I must take issue with the thought there on your marquee."

"Huh?"

"If God graded us, none of us would pass, I daresay, but we have a gracious God, slow to anger and abounding in steadfast love. I wonder how the harshness of your message might affect Garfield and others who are already feeling like failures. It seems to me that they are more in need of hearing grace than judgment."

"Ah, but God will repay them for their iniquity and wipe them out for their wickedness, Sister Rose. The Lord our God will wipe them out!"

"But all have sinned and fall short of the glory of God…"

"Do you deny that we are what he has made us, created in Christ Jesus for good works…?"

"No, but we have been saved by grace through faith, which is a gift from God, through the resurrection and redemption of our Lord Jesus Christ," I tried to quote, adding pointedly, "Saved not by the results of our own works, so no one may boast."

"'Oh, but who can endure the day of his coming, and who can stand when he appears? For he is like a refiner's fire and like fuller's soap...O Lord, how long shall the wicked exult?!"

"You're trying to scare people into salvation! There is no fear in love, but perfect love casteth out fear, and God is perfect love."

"Yes, but He will redeem us with an outstretched arm and with mighty acts of judgment. Judgment, Sister Rose! We all stand before the judgment seat of God. Each of us will be accountable. The Holy Bible tells us in black, white, and red that even by our words we will be justified and by our words we will be condemned. How can I neglect the Holy Scriptures and turn my back on the souls who come to me in this place as though I don't care whether they prosper in righteousness or suffer eternal damnation?!"

"If God is for us, who is against us, Brother James? It is God who justifies. Who is to condemn? Surely not you or me!"

We had been yelling and, at this point, the steam began to go out of us.

"The wicked will not stand in the judgment, nor sinners in the congregation of the righteous; for the Lord watches over the way of the righteous, but the way of the wicked will perish," he offered earnestly.

"Garfield is not wicked," I protested.

"His ways are wicked, his deeds are wicked. The wicked are those who do not choose God's way. Watch out for the deceitfulness of sin, Sister Rose."

"Misguided, not wicked."

"Wicked in the eyes of God. Garfield must fear God and keep his commandments."

"As must we all, as we are able, but the Father sent the Son into the world not to condemn but to save."

"Those who believe in him are not condemned; but those who do not believe are condemned already."

"We have seen his glory, the glory as of a father's only son, full of grace and truth. That truth will set Garfield free, not our efforts."

"That's right," Brother James said abruptly, returning to his task.

Florence and I looked at each other for a moment and started walking to the car.

"Wow," she said. "Who won?"

Good question. God, I hope.

Dear Lord, may Agape House be the right place for Garfield right now. Amen.

Fourth Sunday of Easter

Acts 9:36-43
Psalm 23
Revelation 7:9-17
John 10:22-30

"Alleluia...Christ is risen," Pr. Sauer mentioned more than proclaimed, as though caught off guard, at the opening of the service this morning.
We responded in kind with an anemic, "Christ is risen indeed. Alleluia..."
If the words hadn't been printed in the bulletin, I doubt if pastor or congregation would have thought to say them. Exclamation points seemed to be replaced by question marks, the miracle and wonder that echoed in the rafters three weeks ago reduced to "alleluia this and alleluia that." What a challenge to keep the resurrection front and center in our lives!
We're back to the usual crowd. I didn't detect a single person who might have been left over from the mob on Easter Sunday or any visitors. Unless you count Garfield. He almost seems like one of the old gang already. I thought maybe he would start attending Sunday worship at the house since he goes to their week-night services. They're more informal there and perhaps at an intellectual level that he's more used to. Oh dear, I sound like Millicent! I just thought our liturgy and ritual might be difficult, but he said he likes the service, that it seems holy and that it's more about God and less about people.
The most compelling part of the sermon for me was a true story. Starting with the story of Paul raising Dorcas from the dead, Pastor pointed out how distressed her community was by the passing of a person who did so many good works. We, too, might be concerned in a similar situation, asking, "Are _we_ supposed to fill that void?!" Pastor answered that question with a story he had read in the newspaper. A week ago in a rural community, a man was on his way home after an evening of working at his church. He stopped and picked up two kids, one of whom he had mentored through a church program. The boys stabbed him to death, dumped his body, and stole his car. Immediately, there was a huge void where that man had lived. The day after his funeral, his wife said that her husband had shown her how to cope with his death, how to heal the wound. He had shown her by the way he lived, she said. She plans to get involved with troubled young people like the ones who killed her husband. The resurrected Christ, Pastor concluded, calls us to step into voids and serve others and help heal our broken world. I marvel at the faith of that husband and wife and the power of the resurrection in their lives.
The appointed psalm was the 23rd. Through the years, I remember being bored by it, like a pretty hymn that is sung about 50 times too many. Sometimes, I think

we could just announce "23rd Psalm" and move on. The older I get, however, and the closer I move towards that "valley of the shadow of death" the more I love that psalm. I wonder how many times I've said it so far in my life. Probably 25 times on Tuesday alone, come to think of it.

How many exactly, Charlie, did you count? You were with me. I feel that you're always with me, you know. I feel like you see and hear everything I do and know every word I write in this journal. We certainly had some long conversations Tuesday afternoon, even if I did have to make up your part. I always wanted to do that anyway, ha!

I still can't believe it happened, and I still defend my right to walk in the woods, *but I guess I'll never go there alone again, Charlie—another last time.* I hate to admit that I'm getting unsteady on my feet; I'm so unreasonably healthy for my age that I feel like I shouldn't have to limit myself in anyway. But, okay, okay—it's just not worth risking another fall.

What happened: When I carried the garbage out after breakfast Tuesday morning, blue skies and a warm breeze beckoned me to meditation on the big rock. I was on my way back to the house, must have been about 9:30, when I stepped in a hole and pain seared through my left ankle. I was too far from the house for anyone to hear my calls. I tried to crawl when I couldn't walk, but the back pain was too much.

So I lay there for a long time, finding pictures in the branches and the clouds and tried to stay calm. Every once in a while I would yell as loudly as I could, but my voice isn't what it used to be. I had plenty of time to repeat the 23rd Psalm and every other scripture and song and poem I know by heart over and over, including some soliloquies, mainly, "All the world's a stage...," my all time favorite from <u>As You Like It</u>, but not helpful this time because the "last scene of all…mere oblivion, sans teeth, sans eyes, sans taste, sans everything," seemed far too apt. I felt that I could die there. Aching and cotton-mouthed, I wondered how long it would be before anyone even missed me. I thought of Muriel Jones—four days! I desperately tried crawling again, but my back said NO!

As evening shadows began to cover me, I started thinking how alone I am, not really a part of anyone else's daily life. My people all love me, but they would not necessarily miss me after six or eight or ten hours. I envisioned Cute Baby as a little Lassie, but she was in the house, probably wondering where I was.

It was a long time for an old lady, Charlie, and I felt so very, very old. Foolish. Helpless. Useless. Worthless. Disconnected. Despised. Don't even try to talk me out of thinking that old people are despised when their bodies and minds fail, Charlie. I know better. I'm still pretty able, physically and mentally, so I'm not despised yet. Just disregarded. I can see it in people's eyes when I'm out in public. They don't look at me, especially younger people. A quick glance, "Oh, she's old," and that's the end. But I know what I may well face in a few years because I myself have despised those who are in the process of losing their faculties.

There. I said it. I don't want to have such feelings, I don't mean to, but it happens. I love and care about aged people, but the ugly truth is that I find their declining conditions irritating, inconvenient, unpleasant. Especially at Rutledge Home. Flakey skin, dubious odor, boney. Despicable. Untouchable. Nobody wants to kiss a hollow cheek with skin flaking off. I wanted to die when I was lying there. You heard me, Charlie. In the chilly darkness, when my bladder gave way and my bowels burned, I prayed and wept, "Just take me, God."

But then I heard Virginia yelling and knew I was saved, and tears turned to joy.

Merciful heavens, I've had a good life, constantly surprised by big and little moments of grace, like the outpouring of love and attention from the children and Stephanie since I fell. How loved I felt when Barry and Virginia left at midnight after helping me get a warm shower, cooking me a meal, and tucking me into a soft, luxuriously comfortable bed.

I had adamantly refused to go to the emergency room, so they took me to see Dr. Majmundar on Wednesday morning. The ankle was sprained but everything else was fine, albeit sore and swollen. "Mrs. Rose, you are most solid for an ancient one," Dr. Majmundar commented. I felt admired, a nice contrast to how I felt in the woods.

Mindy brought pizza dripping with grease one night (miraculously, it didn't bother my stomach) and pumped me for details of my disastrous day. She cheered me up with her bad day at the beauty parlor—pinkish hair. Regina thinks she should sue, but she thinks it's hilarious. Garfield brought flowers. Pastor visited. We talked a lot about Florence. He says she has been very straightforward with him about getting ready to die; in fact, they have planned her funeral. Stephanie called; she wanted to come out but was sick at her stomach three nights running. Lydia Circle brought food and cleaned my house on Saturday.

Gracious God, okay. I will go on living. In the dark woods, you were there. You are my shepherd; I shall not be in want. Amen.

Fifth Sunday of Easter

Acts 11:1-18
Psalm 148
Revelation 21:1-6
John 13:31-35

Who are we to stand in God's way? That's what Peter the Rock asked himself in this morning's lesson. Is that not always a pertinent question for us as the Church? The obvious problem to me, though, is what, exactly, is God's way? How do we know for sure? What if I think God's way is to go right and Madge, or whomever, thinks God wants us to hang a left?

On sexual orientation, for example. Pr. Sauer had to go and bring that up again. I don't know how the Church is going to get out of this issue alive. So many strong feelings, based in experience, based in Scripture, based in love of God and wanting to be faithful. Pastor keeps urging us to participate in the study about sexuality sent from headquarters, but that isn't happening at St. Timothy yet. The study is supposed to be about human sexuality, in general, but it's the gay and lesbian issue that dominates. If we ever do have the study, I don't think I'll participate. I certainly have thoughts and opinions, but I've logged so many hours in Sunday School and discussion groups, much of it dry and worthless, that I can't stand the thought of attending again. On the other hand, I think that old people like me should be represented. "Here I am, Lord—send somebody else," as the saying goes.

Anyway, Pastor talked about how Gentiles were excluded from the Church at first. Baptizing the Gentiles, when it finally happened, was painfully controversial. For some sincere believers, baptizing Gentiles went against Scripture and teachings. The same thing happened when the Church finally went on record against slavery. We find unthinkable that abolishing slavery could ever have been debated, and yet arguments and emotions were just as real and as strong on that issue as they are regarding sexual orientation today. Only a few years ago, it seems, we were struggling and arguing over ordaining women. I remember that unbelievable story of a person in opposition to that change kneeling for communion and digging her (?) fingernails—to the point of drawing blood—into the hand of an ordained woman who was serving her Christ's body. Female clergy still have an uphill battle sometimes, I'm afraid, but I think most of us accept pastors on their individual merits, regardless of gender. At least, it's been a good while since I've heard anyone argue that God Almighty is against ordaining women.

So, with each new controversy, we pray, we listen, we decide together, and we move ahead the best we can, trusting that, whether we've erred or done the right thing, God is with us, blessing and/or redeeming our efforts.

What conversational adventures we had hashing all this over at dinner—Mother's Day and my birthday rolled into one. I hobbled into Virginia's house on my crutches and the day was perfect! Virginia had expanded our family to include Florence, Mindy, and Garfield, and the whole crowd had surprised me by showing up and surrounding me at worship. There could be no more special gift for a church lady like me!

All showed up except Barry, that is. Frank Hammond died last week. As soon as I arrived, he made a point of telling me that he stayed home and cooked this morning "rather than endure the intellectual insult of God." I'd not heard Barry at that extreme before. He must really be hurting. What to do, what to say? *God, be with him and grant him peace.*

A flock of opinions and insights fluttered congenially around Virginia's dining room table. Stephen and Stephanie Rose got into a tussle because he playfully challenged her biblical foundations for vegetarianism, citing Peter's vision with the message to eat any of the animals, none are unclean.

"So?" Stephanie responded. "That attitude toward animals 2000 years ago was just as misguided as attitudes today. Besides, the real point was accepting Gentiles into the Church; you know that, Uncle Stephen!"

Mindy told us about a dream she once had which she interpreted as a divine revelation. The revelation was that homosexuality doesn't matter. She could remember no content of the dream (just as well, perhaps), only waking up with the clear understanding, "completely from outside of myself because I never could decide what to think," that our sexual orientation makes absolutely no difference to God.

"So I don't have to worry about that one," she concluded.

"O'boy, I can't go along with that," Garfield shook his head. "Homosexuality is sick."

As he started on one of his know-it-all tirades, we all appreciated Florence cutting him off with, "Mr. Temple, won't you fill your mouth with another serving of this scrumptious corn pudding?"

Virginia spared us her little speech about how the male and female bodies fit together perfectly which is what makes her wonder if homosexuality could possibly be natural. Stephanie spared us her little speech about how we all have characteristics of both genders in our nature and the biggest homophobes are those who will not accept the cross-gender parts of themselves.

What about same sex marriages, what about gays adopting children, what about ordaining gay people, we chirped at Mindy, as though she now had expert credentials.

"Don't know, don't care," she responded serenely.

"What about promiscuity among gays?"

"Promiscuity's always wrong," she replied. "Now let me eat," as she shut down that topic for the day, shoveling a mound of Stephanie's quinoa-apricot salad into her mouth and making a funny face.

"Why did Jesus say that love was a <u>new</u> commandment?" Garfield asked. "Wasn't loving one another part of the Old Testament?"

Hm. Virginia got the Bible and verified what we were thinking—love is not mentioned in the Ten Commandments. I would say, nonetheless, that loving one another is the foundation of divine laws. And love is woven through the Old Testament, including love of neighbor. Maybe the newness was that it was given by Christ, the long-awaited messiah. Also, embodied by him. In leaving the disciples to go to his death, the commandment to love one another was a parting shot, his greatest legacy; his followers would love each other as much as he loved—enough to give their own lives.

Everybody loved the verse from Revelation where God will wipe away all tears.

"And until then, we just have to keep passing the tissue back and forth," Mindy commented.

Barry presented his famous raspberry torte, my absolute favorite, an 80 candle perched on top. Garfield pulled an envelope out of his pocket and handed it to me with a "Happy Birthday, birthday girl!" I couldn't speak for a moment when I realized what it was—a new song, written just for me. "I Believe in Angles." This was a good-natured response to Mindy teasing him about his misspelling of angel (prompting him to enroll in a GED program).

He serenaded me with the simple minor melody, which lilted into major for the refrain:

> I was sinking low, in so many jams.
> Didn't know where to turn, hardly gave a damn.
> Because of my mistakes, my life was in a tangle.
> Right about that time, God sent me an angle.
>
> Refrain: Thank you God for all your goodness,
> For helping to relieve our stress.
> For angles full of your great love,
> For peace and guidance from above.
>
> When God's angles speak, life is not so bleak.
> My strength builds right up, I am not so weak.
> Angles can be young, and angles can be old,
> Redheads or grayheads, just so they are bold.

Chances are, it won't make the hit parade, but it's precious to me.

Having Florence there was precious, too. She is getting worse, I'm sure. Her color's bad and so is her cough. She winces a lot, just barely, but I see it, so there must be pain. Fie! We tried to have a conversation as we drove home from the party but finally gave up because of her coughing. She's private and she's stubborn and she hates to admit that she's not doing well, but when she got out of the car, she pointed to me, touched her folded hands to her bowed head, and pointed to herself. A little pray-for-me charade. Then, she went hacking and wracking her frame up the sidewalk and into her house. I sat there bawling, envisioning her hugging her mint green toilet bowl trying to heave something up once and for all, trying to find the strength to get up and collapse onto her bed and lay there moaning, like I've seen her do before.

What do I pray? "Ask for anything and it will be given." Okay.

God, please heal Florence. Take the cancer away. Let her live longer and die peacefully. Amen.

There. I said it, God. Now what happens? Why would you heal Florence when you didn't heal Frank Hammond?

She's too old, God! Can't you see she's too old for this?!

Yes, she smoked all those years, but we didn't know how deadly it was. Eventually she quit. She was determined and never looked back, just rearranged her priorities and did what needed to be done. Doesn't that count for something?!

Show your mercy, damn it! If ever anyone needed mercy, Florence needs it now. She has loved you and served you faithfully. Spare her this suffering!

Take me instead. You know I wouldn't care if I dropped dead tomorrow if you would just take this suffering from her.

Stop teasing her, God, do you hear me?! Just take her. Why the back and forth, the hospital, the treatments, the misery? Just take her!

"Why, O God, do you take so long to tear my heart to pieces?"

You make me so angry I don't know what to do.

If this is how you treat your friends...

I guess I should humbly bow and pray, "If it be your will..." but I don't feel like doing that, God! What is your will? What exactly is the divine will regarding suffering? What is the divine purpose of a splendid person like Florence, or anyone else, suffering like this?

I've had it up to here. If you don't do something for Florence, I'll go over with Barry. I'll sneer at you and jeer at you and steer clear of you.

What's the difference?! Who cares? What good does it do to believe in you if you won't stop the suffering?

Sixth Sunday of Easter

Acts 16:9-15
Psalm 67
Revelation 21:10, 22-22.5
John 14:23-29

"Pastor Sauer, what in the 'H' is a paraclete?" Mindy giggled as we greeted him after the service. Bless his heart, he deserved to be put on the spot.

Apparently getting caught up in his own earnestness and wandering from his prepared sermon, he had slipped into academic lingo and said something like, "The coming of the Paraclete laid the foundation for Jesus' words and actions to serve as the kerygma of the Christian community, then, now, and always."

What kind of way is that for a preacher to talk?! Dear Sir, we are neither seminarians nor studied theologians. Why, Jesus himself wouldn't use such language! I've been to more seminars and lectures than the average person in the pew, and I was puzzled enough by that statement that I missed whatever he said next.

I do realize that, like Jesus was doing with his disciples, Pastor is trying to get us ready for the Ascension. Our dear spiritual leader is trying to alert us to the ways that Christ remains with us even though he is gone. Enter the Paraclete, "a Comforter, an Advocate," as he explained to Mindy.

"Cool," she responded.

Oh, well. I forgive Pastor for his high falutin' language. Perhaps everyone did, after the conclusion to his sermon. An experience is worth a hundred thousand words.

"Before departing this world, our Lord gave us the great gift of peace," he stated, coming down into the congregation, "and the promise of his continued presence through the Holy Spirit. I invite us to use an ancient greeting to experience these gifts."

And he had us get up out of our seats (!) and form a circle all the way around the pews (!) and exchange the peace of Christ (!). Pastor demonstrated first with the person next to him, who happened to be Jack Brewster, Chad's father. Pastor placed Jack's hands on his shoulders and his hands on Jack's shoulders. Then he said to him, "Christ is in our midst," and prompted Jack to reply, "He is and always will be." I could see in Jack's eyes how much this meant to him, Chad being in Iraq and all that goes with that. Then, Pastor and Jack showed us how to kiss each other (!) on opposite shoulders, simultaneously, in a bobbing motion. Pastor then moved to the person on the other side of Jack and exchanged the peace in the same way. Jack fell in behind him and so on, the circle turning on itself until each of us had exchanged this intimate, spiritual peace with every other person present.

For the first few exchanges, most of us were silently waiting, listening and watching Pastor and whoever was opposite him, out of our comfortable pews, way out of our comfort zones. There wasn't very good space to maneuver (especially with my crutches). We didn't even know some of the people we were kissing. The Paraclete was there, however, and as more of us were exchanging, the volume and motion increased, and I sensed people relaxing. Christ, indeed, was in our midst and that peace that we simply cannot understand prevailed.

When Florence and I were partners, we mouthed the words like silent meows, too overcome with happiness and sadness to make a sound. My outrage over her suffering began to fall away at this undeniable presence of Love, of Christ. The outrageous, unreasonable truth entered: our sufferings are not as they appear—the crucifixion was not as it appeared—God is God, is Good, is Love and made Christ victorious over death—that is true for us as well. That's what passed between Florence and me.

The insult and the scandal of "where-are-you-when-we-are-suffering-God?!" finally loosened its grip; the monstrous mystery lay down and slept. I breathed deeply for the first time since I prayed that prayer last week. (I can hardly read the prayer because the ink is blotched and smeared from my tears. I didn't even realize I was crying when I wrote it, that's how angry I was.) Florence is healed. She may not be cured, but she is healed because she is whole spiritually, despite the ravaged state of her body. She can say to the cancer, "I do not fear you, for you can kill my body but you cannot kill my soul." Her courage and honesty through each day, each crisis, including her gallows humor, are stronger than the evil forces of the cancer. The love she has lived is truer and stronger than death. "Many waters cannot quench love."

When I said "Christ is in our midst" to Danny, he responded, "Yeah-yeah, Rose," in his simple, staccato way. He may know this peace better than most of us because he doesn't have the intellectual capacity to puzzle over it.

Garfield cried and Mindy laughed. Sidney grimly said his part and moved on, muttering under his breath, "This is taking too long." Time had been suspended for me until he said that. Poor Sidney was stretched. Oh, well. He obviously understands something about the presence of Christ because he did get Garfield's guitar fixed and buddies around with him, a true miracle of love.

Pr. Sauer made visible how he loves each one of his sheep in the St. Timothy fold, regardless of how lovable we may or may not be at any given moment and regardless of how a given sheep may feel about him. Pastor is Christ-like, in that regard. Even though he and I have an especially close relationship and much in common spiritually, he cares about each person as much as he cares about me, which gives me great joy—paracletes and kerygma notwithstanding!

The powerful peace of that strange circle of ordinary people kissing each other was a beautiful gift of love. I must admit, too, that my reaction to this experience may not be typical. There were undoubtedly some who experienced it very differently, took offense, felt uncomfortable. The way things have been going, someone might even transfer out over it. And I will say to them, "Go in peace, serve the Lord, somewhere else."

Sidney was right that it took a long time. It was one o'clock when I got home. After lunch and a nap on the deck in the warm, sunny breeze, my aches from all that standing and bending over to kiss shoulders are just about gone.

I can't remember the last time I've been to Rutledge Home due to my various feeble conditions. I really feel like going. Who might be willing to drive me out there? Mindy?

Later

Merciful heavens, that was more than I'd bargained for! When I asked Mindy, she said, "Sure," but then, "Well, now, wait. Let me think about this for a minute. Do I really need to be going into a smelly institutional residence with a bunch of senile droolers?" Pause. "Okay, I'll take my chances."

She cheerfully picked some of my gorgeous lilacs so we could leave bouquets. We went to see Sam first, and he and Mindy hit it off. He was looking good, sitting in a chair, his colorful African hat perched on his white hair above his thick-lensed horn rims, as usual. A few dozen birthday cards for his 98th were standing on his windowsill. In his rich, gravelly voice, he recited his poem for Mindy about his and Irene's first meeting:

That Wonderful Cloudy Day

It was cloudy and gray on that wonderful day
And I didn't expect a surprise.
But God sent a surprise in that fathomless way
When you looked into my young eyes.

My heart was yours and light broke through
Those gray and cloudy skies.
The world seemed new and inside I knew
That you would be my prize.

A deep, strong love and many lives
Began 'neath those cloudy skies.
In sixty years as we take and give
Love's grown because God is wise.

Clouds may come and clouds may go
But the light of our love need not vie
With any power on earth below
For e'en death, God's love will defy.

Mindy went right over and hugged him. He told her all about Irene, how they were blessed to have each other for 73 years, how she went home to be with Jesus on August 28 almost 3 years ago. Mindy and Sam made a date for another poetry recital, and she happily agreed to read to him. Sam's always looking for readers.

I automatically headed for Bill's wing, forgetting that he died last month. I found his graveside service very sad, despite Pr. Sauer's best effort to create an atmosphere of victory. Heavens, if Bill had died twenty years ago, the nave would have been packed. He'd outlived almost everyone who knew him. His only child is in the advanced stages of Alzheimer's. A nephew who lives nearby was the only family member at the service. Florence and I and four or five others made up the rest of the congregation. A long life well-lived deserves more honor.

Mrs. Wheaton thought Mindy was someone named Scarlett. She clutched her hand crying, "Scarlett, Scarlett, I knew you would come." Mindy played along, fending off questions with nonspecific answers, but Mrs. Wheaton got really mad when she asked how Ralph was doing and Mindy said he was doing just fine. The ancient woman's eyes narrowed and she said, "Aha! You're not Scarlett. Get out of here, you imposter! You want my money, like the rest of them. Just get out! I'll call the police..." and on and on as we made our exit, laughing our way to Kathryn's hallway.

We could hear Kathryn groaning with her arthritis as we neared her room. Her hands and feet looked more kinked than usual. I asked about her mouse friend, thinking it would be fun for Mindy to hear about that, but Kathryn said she hadn't seen it lately. And then, without warning, she started into a story about herself, about a kind of pain that made the arthritis seem like nothing in comparison. She's been crippled and in pain for fifty years, God's punishment for her sins, she said.

"I should have known. In a way, I did know. That's why God can't forgive me. I knew it was wrong—but I didn't know it was Satan. Oh, how clever Satan is!"

Mindy looked at me as if to say, "Whoa. What are we getting into?" and we sank down into chairs.

As she wove her tale, Kathryn seemed less and less aware of us, gazing and talking into a space long ago and far away. She told the story as though it happened yesterday and yet as though she had told it a hundred times before...

If only it had been raining, I don't think it would have happened. My heart had been in a swoon all morning because of the perfection of that spring day, the kind of air filling your lungs that makes you want to love the whole world. If only Mother and Father had waited to go to town until Linda and Tommy got home from school. I should never have been left alone. I wasn't strong enough. I thought I was strong. Mother and Father had warned me about eternal damnation since I was a little girl. I knew what the stakes were. I knew about God's anger. I went to church every week, I prayed every night and read my Bible every day. I thought I was strong...

Her eyes scrunched in anguish for a moment, but then she continued.

Ours was the first motel in the area and the cleanest. Mother and Father kept everything absolutely spotless. They couldn't stand anything out of place or dirty even for a moment. I felt protected by that cleanness and order. I thought I was clean, but I was filthy inside. The Prince of Darkness knew. He waited for the right moment, the moment when I would feel so sure of myself that I didn't think I could do anything wrong, and then he deceived me.

I should have known Mr. Lewis was an instrument of the devil. I remember when I registered him. I was surprised that he was a salesman because he was so polite and kind compared to most. He looked right into my eyes when he talked, and he was always smiling. He charmed Mother and Father and Linda and Tommy too. He seemed so honorable, so good. How could I have known?

He had played cards with us the night before. He had asked Mother and Father endless questions about the old country. After Mother and Father went to bed, I—heaven help me—I read him the last letter Chester had sent me from Korea. He acted like a big brother, so kind and sympathetic. It was all in Satan's plan.

Kathryn scowled and Mindy and I raised our eyebrows at each other, frozen in our chairs to hear what was coming next.

Mr. Lewis came to the front desk at exactly 12:45 that day, after Mother and Father had left for town. I caught my breath at his handsomeness and excitement rippled through me. I should have known evil was moving in. We talked and laughed. He asked for an extra towel. As he took it from me, he held his hand over mine. He leaned across the counter...

Why?! Why did I do it? He made it all seem so right, he made it seem good, like this was what God wanted. I was cruelly deceived.

She dropped her head into her knotted hands.

Father wrote Chester immediately. He divorced me as soon as he got back. I was now considered to be a mother in name only. For all practical purposes, Mother raised my children. The arthritis began that fall. Satan has had his way with my life. He has ruled...

Kathryn stopped talking and looked at us in the dim light, surprised to see us.

"You need to go now," she said.

She pushed the button to recline her chair and closed her eyes. We walked into the hallway squinting, the sweet smell of lilacs trailing behind us, and out to the car in silence.

"Rose, didn't you want to do something for her? Kiss her or say a prayer or tell her she has it all wrong about God? I wanted to do something, but it didn't seem like it would really matter now. I mean, after all these years, it seems hopeless."

"Yes," I answered, thinking that it's no wonder Kathryn is bitter. The ecstasy and the agony. I never had known much about her family. She and her parents moved to town and joined St. Timothy twenty or twenty-five years ago but never got involved. I remember those three sitting together in worship, rigid, unsmiling, leaving by the side door. Linda and Tommy, she said. I had always assumed that she had never married or had children. Merciful heavens, to think of Kathryn carrying that twisted burden all these years!

Dear Jesus, the ruler of this world had no power over you, you stated so simply. That devil ruler has controlled poor Kathryn's life, her parents' too. I pray that she may somehow know your peace, that you will send the Comforter to her right away, that somehow her strife may be ended in this world, even before "your divine light eclipses night forever." Make me an instrument of your peace. Good night, Christ Jesus.

Ascension Day Service (Evening)

Acts 11:1-11
Psalm 47
Ephesians 1:15-23
Luke 24:44-53

"I ain't never been in there," a voice said from the shadows as I started up the front steps of the church tonight. "I live right across the street, and I ain't never been in there. What is it, a church?"

He was drunk.

"Would you like to come in?" I invited like a good Christian, hoping, like a bad Christian, that he would say no and go away.

"What does it look like in there?" he asked dully, gazing through bloodshot eyes and breathing heavy, alcoholic breath at me.

"I'm Rose Harris," I said, and extended my hand. "You're welcome to come in."

His hand was rough and heavy. "I'm..." he thought for a moment. "Arfur." I didn't know if he meant Arthur or what.

He shuffled in behind me and there were Pastor Sauer and Madge, the assisting minister, and Paul Wakefield who was carrying the processional cross, robed and about to start down the aisle, the cross lifted high. A thin chorus of "Alleluia! Sing to Jesus" had begun.

Pastor looked at me questioningly and said, "Good evening" to the fellow.

"This is Arfur," I said. "He wanted to see the church."

"I ain't never been in here," Arfur said. "What is it?"

"This is St. Timothy," Pastor said, extending his hand. "How do you do. I'm Marcus Sauer, the pastor here."

"I'm John," Arfur said, shaking Pastor's hand and moving toward the doors to look into the nave. He looked up into the vaulted arches and all around as we watched.

"Is this a church?" he asked, looking at Paul.

Paul nodded. The congregation sang, "Alleluia! Here the sinful flee to you..."

Arfur John looked around some more, holding us hostage with his drunken, unexpected appearance as we tried to be compassionate, welcoming church people. Pastor and his crew should have been down front in their places by now.

"We're preparing to worship. You're welcome to join us," Pastor Sauer said.

Arfur John looked at him blankly. "I ain't never been in here before. This the first time I ever been in here."

I could see people in the pews turning around, wondering what was going on. Lloyd was playing very slowly which didn't help the already anemic singing.

"Please join us," Pastor invited one last time and then quickly mobilized the troops and started down the aisle.

"My St. Lord, now what do I do?" I was thinking, when Arfur John turned, staggered to the door, and left. I went and took my place.

There were only about 20 of us in that cavernous church nave and despite Pastor Sauer's best effort to prepare us for the Ascension, I suddenly felt as disoriented as Arfur. But it was my heart, not my head, that brought me to this place. I needed to be there, with those few others, and gained far more from this strange, little gathering than from being at home watching TV or doing laundry or even writing or reading.

We had come, as always, looking for glory, trying to hold on to Easter, longing for "meaningful answers to life's persistent questions," as Garrison Keillor's private eye puts it. Longing to breathe deeply without having to remind ourselves to do so. As the service went on, I felt less like a loser and a fool and more like a person of faith, a witness to God's power. The language, the music, the humility and earnestness of those gathered, the bread and wine, all conspired to inspire me. Being there had to do with Florence being back in the hospital and with poor Kathryn caught in her own personal hell. Being in this place had to do with medical missionaries in Yemen being shot to death by an Islamic extremist who covered a machine gun with a blanket and carried it into the hospital like a baby. The reason for being there stretched back over time, softening the hard, heavy times with Mother and the Editor and helping me see them for the loving parents they tried to be, indeed were.

At one point in the service, sirens drowned out our singing and blue lights flashed across the stained glass windows. We were gathered in the name of the Triune God on behalf of whomever was on the receiving end of that emergency. And on behalf of Garfield more than ever. Brother James dragged him out of the Sit 'n' Bull late one night last week, Garfield's second tumble off the wagon since he moved into Agape.

Pastor made a statement that seemed presumptuous at first, then supernatural, then almost natural: "We can ascend with Christ and sit with him and see the universe from his perspective." Hm. Wow.

"Furthermore," he continued, "Christ is here with us, he is and always will be, through the power of the Spirit. We can, therefore, relate to the universe—and its sirens and flashing lights—with a power fueled by an informed hope."

So, it was my sacred privilege to be there, to join with the Venerable Bede singing "A Hymn of Glory," a hymn he wrote fourteen centuries ago, and to tip the vessel of wine to my lips, side by side with others equally unable to explain why they were there. The eyes of my heart were enlightened.

The paragraph printed in the bulletin—absurd, I should think, to anyone not at the edge of the chasm one has to leap to find faith—struck a chord in my soul: "The risen Lord enters the invisible presence of God in order to be present in all times and in all places to the Church and to the world. Where shall we find the risen and ascended Lord today? In his word and his bread, in his people and his washing with water and the spirit, and in all who cry out for mercy."

So many cry out for mercy and yet they "ain't never been in this place," they "ain't never even seen it." So it is the job of the 20 of us, and the others who didn't happen to be present tonight, and the others around the globe and throughout history, to see and find the risen and ascended Christ in those who cry out for mercy, including ourselves.

Seventh Sunday of Easter

Acts 16:16-34
Psalm 97
Revelation 22:12-14, 16-17, 20-21
John 17:20-26

"It's us! People of St. Timothy, do you realize it is us Jesus is praying for in John 17, verse 20?! You—and me," Pastor Sauer earnestly implored this morning, and then turned abruptly out of the pulpit and came down into the center aisle. "Over 2000 years ago in some crowded little room in somebody's normal little house, the Son of God was getting ready to know what glory truly is and he looked at Peter and James and John and the rest of his earthly helpers and he looked at God and he prayed for us! For all who will ever hunger and thirst for righteousness and long to be at one with God and with each other."

Pastor had a desperate almost wild look in his eyes. He became as still as the eye of the hurricane and then suddenly chopped the air with his hands, imploring, "Listen! Listen! Listen! Listen!listen!listen!listen!" Then his shoulders slumped and he went and sat down.

Yikes. We were most uncomfortable, I have to say. Riveted but uncomfortable. I doubt if those visitors I saw a few pews ahead will come back. I couldn't help but wonder when Pastor's next sabbatical is coming up.

Garfield leaned over to me and said, "We were all listening. Why didn't he say something?"

"I think he'd already said what he wanted us to hear," I whispered back. He thought a minute and nodded.

Garfield has become like a sponge, soaking up whatever spiritual thoughts and experiences he can, and then, of course, wanting to rant and rave about everything he's come to believe. His belief system seems a strange mixture, at this point, of Brother James' works righteousness, St. Timothy's emphasis on grace, bumper stickers, and country gospel music. "There's no such thing as the next best thing to Jee-zuss..." "Jesus is tougher than nails..."

Garfield honored me with a glimpse into his life of faith the other day. I was in the basement of Your Hardware Store, with its hundred-year-old bins of nails and screws and its smells of oil and coal and its obsolete pipes and wires. I had gone down with Bob to get a certain piece of white plastic tube connection I needed for Stephen to fix the drip under my sink. If I'd known the feet coming down the stair steps were Garfield's, I would probably have ducked into one of the aisles. I was not in the mood for him. But he turned the corner at the bottom landing and appeared right in front of me. He was picking up some supplies for the woodshop.

Bob got us both set with what we needed and went back upstairs. I think the dim light and the subterranean setting encouraged Garfield to be his vulnerable self. He let out a cry for mercy that I'm sure was sent by God as well as directed to God.

"Rose, why do I still have doubts about God? Everything is going great for me right now, better than I can ever remember."

He hesitated, looking up at the rough beam a foot over our heads as though something was written on it.

"But it's the weirdest thing, Rose. Every morning when I wake up..."

He stopped and looked at the beam again, struggling, his eyes filling up.

"...every morning when I wake up—I wish I wouldn't."

He put his hand over his eyes for a minute.

"I like all the ideas I hear at church. I want to believe that Jesus is always with us, shining like a light in the darkness and some day there will be only light, no more night. I really want to believe that the Spirit gives us hope and strength to get through all of our trials. In broad daylight on Sunday morning it makes sense, but it seems like when the sun goes down, so does my faith."

Bowing his head, he confessed, "That's why I went drinking last week. I get so scared. I feel like such a loser. I hardly have the guts to force myself out of bed in the morning," he choked out.

"I know," I thought. "You feel like a monster is chasing you and the alcohol numbs the terror for awhile, just like for Dad and for Stephen."

The opposite of you, Charlie. Except for the horrible spell after the accident, you would practically jump out of bed at 5 a.m., ready and rearing to go. I would hear that chuckle of yours, for no apparent reason. What a gift, your zest for life!

I was not given that gift. I can understand Garfield's feelings. I didn't point out to him that part of his gloom was the human condition, and part perhaps his upbringing, and part undeniably his mental illness and addiction problems. He wasn't asking for explanations. He wasn't really asking for anything. The only appropriate response seemed to be to acknowledge his plight, to stand there with him for a few minutes.

"I know," I said, and put my arm around his shoulders, and gave him a little squeeze.

"I need to cut things down to size," he continued. "Stephen's always telling me not to worry about anything except dead ahead. That helps. Like right now. I'm standing here safe and sound and sober with a good friend who cares about me enough to give me a hug. That's enough for right now."

We climbed back up together and before I knew it, he was embroiled in a heated debate with Bob over which kind of something-or-other was the best, and he knew because "...I built this skyscraper in St. Louie once and..."

Charlie, too bad you're not around to inspire Garfield; I think you two would like each other. He's a character, yes? I know you could help him carpe diem. Actually, I think he's doing awfully well, given his load to bear.

Okay, back to the service this morning. The main theme of Jesus' prayer was unity, Pastor emphasized, stressing diversity in unity. We don't have much diversity, I thought at first, only the Duys, resettled so long ago from Vietnam, and Anna Kim, adopted from Korea, and the Crawford's little mixed race grandchild. As Pastor talked, though, I looked around and realized that diversity reigns:

- Madge with her well-meaning but tiresome piousness;
- Louella, peculiar as a snowflake in Miami;
- Claudia with her extreme and profound feminism;
- Mindy with her fresh, down-to-earth faith;
- Lloyd, our very talented organist, who everyone knows is gay;
- Danny, lacking in intellect but a genius in human relationships;
- Thomas Tyndall, just the opposite of Danny;
- Genevieve Lachman in her gorgeous new home;
- Louie and Rita Smith waiting for their Habitat house.

Thinking of variety, I see Mother's flower garden along the fence, with all hues of creeping phlox to six-foot tall sunflowers, violets, lily of the valley, tulips, iris, hydrangea, day lilies, morning glories, hollyhocks, each at a different point of blossoming and withering. I can see Mother on her knees—in a dress, hair slightly lavender—lost in pleasure, lovingly clipping and pulling and separating, so that all could flourish and not encroach on each other. She nurtured that garden into a glorious unity as the Holy Spirit does with us when we <u>want</u> unity, when we allow the Spirit to do its work.

Pastor talked about diverse opinions, admitting that he was generally uneasy with disagreement but that false harmony is not unity. Jesus' prayer for us is not to be unified in opinion or lifestyle or politics but unified by a love that trusts and transcends our diversity. I caught a glimpse of such love when Rachael and Rebecca (Claudia's girls), one the crucifer and the other the acolyte, hesitantly exchanged the peace of the Lord and a giggle after first rolling their eyes upward at the very idea of being peaceful with each other.

So, Holy Spirit, at our congregational meeting coming up about whether or not to cut down the tree, let us argue, if necessary, but let us love one another in the midst and in the aftermath of that argument. Amen.

The prayer list is getting so long again you wouldn't think there'd be enough of us walking around to hold services! We prayed for some child's friend who has a stomach virus which hardly seems necessary, but I'm sure the child asked for the name to be on the list, and what's a pastor to do? Tell the child his friend is not important enough or that God doesn't care about stomach viruses? I'll just do like Susie Wakefield suggests—say "Amen" after each one and think about the person. The whole list probably doesn't take sixty seconds, but I've heard folks actually get upset about how long it takes. Merciful heavens.

I lingered after the service, visiting with this one and that, in hopes of having a word with Pastor Sauer about his "condition." Debonair, dignified George Hapless gave me a laugh. We were chatting when his grandson came up to him and said he had made five A's on his report card. The proud grandpa clapped him on the back, shook his hand, and rewarded him with a ten dollar bill. The boy's face lit up with excitement; he grabbed the money and ran off, exclaiming, "Oh, goody! Now I can get my ear pierced." I wish I'd had a camera to catch the look on George's face! I talked with two people about their foot surgeries, Claudia about her impending "D-n-C" ("dustin' and a-cleanin'"), Louella about the march she's organizing for better recycling services, and Sidney about the tree controversy. He's of the "If God wants it down, he'll take it down" persuasion. Finally, I did get my moment with Pastor.

"Pastor, I'm concerned about you," I blundered in. "You seemed almost distraught at the end of the sermon when you were urging us to listen."

He squinted at me in concentration. "What did I do?"

"Well, you chopped the air with your hands and repeatedly told us to 'Listen!' You came down from the pulpit, remember? And then, after urging us to listen, you stopped abruptly and went and sat down," I told him as I searched his face.

"I did? That sounds bizarre," he said in genuine surprise. "Well, Rose, I can only answer your straightforward concern with a straightforward response: # 1, that apparently was not me talking because I have no recollection of it whatsoever. It must have been—let's hope it was—the Holy Spirit. # 2, I am having difficulties, Rose, and I ask your prayers," and we held each other's eyes.

"Of course."

"Thank you," he said and turned and walked away.

Whatever Pastor's difficulties may be, Gracious God, I ask your blessings upon his struggles, and upon Carolyn too, that they may come closer to you and more fully understand the richness and the goodness of your ways. With confidence that you are present and that you are powerful, I pray in the name of the one who so gloriously embodied your power, Jesus Christ. Amen.

I'm going to send Pastor a card with that August Wilson quotation: "Your willingness to wrestle with your demons will cause your angels to sing." I'll send one to Garfield too.

I'd better wrap this up and turn on the TV for the ballgame. Also, Stephanie called and is coming for a visit. What a perfectly lovely way to spend Sunday evening. No doldrums tonight.

Later

Oh, my dear Stephanie. I would gladly have suffered an evening of doldrums in exchange for her not having to bear a new burden. I knew she had something of great magnitude to say when she wanted to go for a walk in the woods, which I was ready to do, happily leaning on her shoulder. She settled on the big rock and told me. My sweet child, my own heart, is pregnant.

I understand quite well that being pregnant and unmarried does not carry the onus it once did. I don't have serious concerns when I stop to think about the situation, but neither do I have good feelings about this for Stephanie. She smiled a big smile when she told me and tried to make her eyes sparkle. Of course, I wasn't shocked—I know she and Ethan have been sexually active, and contraceptive methods are not 100% effective.

I certainly couldn't express dismay, though, after her pre-announcement instructions: "Please tell teachy-preachy Grandma to go back to the house because I have something really important to tell you and I need your love and support."

When she said, "Ethan and I are going to have a baby in December," I instinctively felt humiliation, as in "bringing shame upon the family name," which really shows my age. That is only one sentiment of many, though. *Indeed, I'm not particularly unhappy about the pregnancy, are you, Charlie? Probably not.* They're old enough and mature enough to be fine parents, and the prospect of me getting to see, hold, know Stephanie's child brings me great joy. Mother and grandmother have been my favorite roles in life, with teacher right behind; I'm sure great-grandmother will be marvelous, too. Most certainly, there are far worse situations than this. We parted with a hug, but "she is much out of quiet," methinks.

Giver of Life, may the love, peace, and joy that is You be present with Stephanie and Ethan as the baby grows. May their love grow along with the child. Amen.

Pentecost

Acts 2:1-21
Psalm 104:24-34, 35b
Romans 8:14-17
John 14:8-17

White hot. Touched and consumed by the Spirit, lighting whatever is nearby and into the "dark and furthest corners" of the world. That's the image Pastor Sauer—and hymns and scripture—set for us this morning.
White hot with the Spirit. The opposite of Bryan Bowman. Bryan is Randy's boy. Randy still lives on the farm. Marilyn, Randy's wife, has been intermittent in church attendance ever since the marriage, even though Randy never comes. On my way into the building, I happened by their car at the wrong moment and heard the mother rage quietly at the child who was staring sullenly ahead with jaw set, "You get in there and get yourself confirmed or you're grounded for the entire summer!" He about threw the car door off its hinges and slammed it shut, then stalked into the church, his mother running to catch up with him.
So I wondered what Bryan would say when it was his turn to make public profession of his faith, to promise to continue in the covenant, live with us, hear God's Word, proclaim the good news, serve people, strive for peace with justice.
I was hoping he would yell out whatever was in his heart: "No! I don't promise anything! I'm only here because my mother threatened to ground me!" It would have been fine with me if he'd said, "I don't believe all this stuff. I'm never setting foot in this place again, just like my dad. This doesn't work for me. I don't know what in the heck you're even talking about." But that's asking a bit much of a fourteen-year-old. Bryan mumbled the promise and, like the rest, asked God to help and guide him. Can the Holy Spirit kindle such wet wood as this for the Church? Maybe, in time, after the boy's been weathered and dried out some by living.
I think back to Virginia's confirmation. She was about that age. We didn't force her. She just did it, along with her friends and peers, along with 4-H and menstruation and passing to the next grade. And apparently, it didn't take with her either.
How strange are the workings of the Spirit. We can guide and goad, nurture and encourage, but we certainly can't control the Holy Spirit or the human spirit. Who knows, though? Maybe Bryan will someday remember that his mother cared enough about him and about the Body of Christ to bully him into attending to his spiritual life. Maybe at just the right moment, the memory of his petulant promise will come drifting back to him and mean something. That is the undying prayer of

we who are ceaselessly drawn to the Church. Virginia is the main object of my prayer, of course.

And mercy, I'm not saying that people who don't go to church are not spiritual. What foolish thinking that is. Virginia is spiritual. Maybe Bryan Bowman is too. Being touched by the Spirit of God happens anywhere, anytime, not only in worship, not necessarily in worship. In fact, we can hide from God real good sitting right there in the pew, and we can obscure God for each other even as we engage in ministry. Like last week when Claudia unplugged the noisy ice maker during our Bible study and forgot to plug it back in, and the kitchen flooded during the night. Sidney called her up the next day and reamed her out over the phone. She apologized, but he just kept ranting until she said, "Sidney, what about forgiveness?!" He yelled, "Confound it, this is not about forgiveness! This is about ruining the kitchen floor!" Sigh. Still, I don't know how I would get by without this place and these people. I doubt that I would maintain much of a prayer life or worship or meditate if I tried to live a spiritual life separate from a community.

Take this week, for example. Please. How do you spell nincompoop? I feel like everything I've touched has turned to dust which I wanted to blow away immediately. The silliness started on Tuesday when I joined the $67.50 club because I confused the speedometer and tachometer on Stephen's classic Corvette. He'd asked me to walk over to Clyde's garage and drive the car out to him. I was kind of surprised to see the needle at only 25 when I was whizzing down Washington St. through the heart of town. "Wow, so this is what it feels like to drive a sports car," I thought. "My Baby Does the Hanky-Panky" was blaring, and I couldn't distinguish the radio from the heater knobs without taking my eyes off the road, so I just let it blare.

I don't know how long the swirling blue light had been following me when I heard the siren blast. Officer Jason Blume said he clocked me at 61. I can't believe that child gave me a ticket. Why, I taught his mother and his grandfather! I don't think either one of them would approve. Stephen paid for it, appropriately, but I'm plenty tired of all the jibing I've had to endure since it came out in the Police Blotter in the paper. Stephen definitely needs to quit calling me Flash.

I almost fell into a bout of agoraphobia after that. I grabbed my daily devotional the next morning, hoping for inspiration to combat the weak-kneed feeling I was having just thinking about going grocery shopping. The Bible verse was, "Beware for the devil is prowling around like a lion, looking for someone to eat." That made me laugh which gave me enough energy to get in the car and go, but I was in sad shape. I was afraid I might reverse green lights and red lights or trip and fall on my tender ankle—or who-knows-what!

In the store, I kept ducking in and out of aisles whenever I saw anyone I knew. Standing in a stupor in front of the orange juice, unable to make a decision between extra pulp, old fashioned, traditional, low pulp, no pulp, calcium added, etc., I heard Claudia call my name. We had a conversation and I think she told me something significant, but as soon as she went on her way, I had no idea what she had said, and I was a jumble of nerves again. When I wrote my check I was amazed that my handwriting was steady and legible.

What in the world?! An eighty-year-old woman who has raised a fine family, had a respectable career, and served her community and church well, continues to have crises of confidence—absurd! The truth is, nobody knows how weak I am. People think I'm strong and faithful and kind and cheerful. They have no idea the self-doubt and self-absorption that plague me. They don't know of my confusion and lack of discipline. They don't know how often selfish and ugly thoughts fly into my head even as I kneel to receive communion. They don't know who I really am.

When will I ever be free of this sense of inadequacy?! Florence says when it comes to guilt trips, I always have my bags packed. When will they ever be unpacked?! If I believe anything about God, if I understand anything Christ taught, it is the message of grace! And yet if believing is feeling, God help my unbelief.

I can't help but think about Dad and his demons. He told me once, in a rare moment of honesty and intimacy, that he had always felt like a monster was chasing him and would one day catch him. While it saddened me to think of this kind, talented, hardworking man living with that monster, it explained his behavior, too—the drinking, the irrational anger, the long periods of sleep and withdrawal. So maybe my demons have come to me by way of genes and environment, but then I have to ask, can't God overcome genetics? Oh! enough of this! I'm reminding myself of a bestseller I saw in the bookstore the other day— Women Who Think Too Much and the Brains That Devour Them.

God, you are gracious. You know me and you love me. Please keep coming to me with this truth. Set my heart on fire with your amazing grace, that it may burn away every doubt, humiliation, and mistake. Keep me safe in the Body of Christ. Amen.

Garfield will be with us only two more Sundays. A week from Friday he'll be getting his GED. With that goal achieved, it's time, as he said, "to take a deep breath and jump back into real life." Back to St. Louis.

"I'm scared," he told us over dinner today. On the spur of the moment, I had called him and Mindy last night and invited them over for pot roast after worship in an effort to force myself out of my little dance with dysfunction. (It's working!) Pastor came too. I heard him say after services that Carolyn and Brittany were out of town for ballet again, so I invited him to join us. He made a couple drop-ins at confirmation celebrations, arriving after we had all finished eating, but we had saved dinner for him.

Everyone raved about the food. The carrots and potatoes were perfectly browned along with the roast, it's true. The yeast rolls succeeded, and Mindy threatened to lick her salad bowl for my homemade poppy seed dressing. All I served for dessert were huge strawberries with powdered sugar which were as scrumptious as they looked. My special guests' pleasure made going to the store last night and getting up at 5 this morning completely worthwhile.

Anyway, Garfield told us he was scared, but that was nothing new, and he figured there would never be a better time to go home.

"I've got some money, some clothes, some education, some work experience, some self-confidence, some real friends and, best of all," he said to Pastor Sauer, "I've let the Holy Spirit into my heart. I'm not even white hot let alone red, but there's a spark that will keep burning, God-willing."

Mindy and I looked at each other with raised eyebrows and hopeful smiles; he was acting unusually down-to-earth. He spoke calmly, without twitching or trembling or swaggering, apparently relaxed, leaning forward slightly with arms crossed on the table. He wasn't like Philip in the gospel lesson this morning— "Lord, show us the Father, and we will be satisfied"—asking for a personal, dramatic experience or appearance of God (a theophany, perhaps). In his sermon, Pastor had interpreted Jesus' response to Philip as, "Keep your eyes on me." Watch the everyday actions, listen to the everyday words. Then you will know God. Garfield is showing signs that finding God in the everyday is going to be a better weapon against his demons than miraculous revelations or dramatic experiences based only in emotion. "I ask no dream, no prophet ecstasies, No sudden rending of the veil of clay, No angel visitant, no op'ning skies; but take the dimness of my soul away." (Croly)

"Here's my plan," this confident Garfield said over dessert. "Tonight I call Marie and let her know what's going on. Tomorrow I call the downtown St. Louie Y and see about staying there for awhile. I work at Manpower until I can find a job working with wood, like what I'm doing. I love it, I'm good at it, and as long as I mask and take my meds, I can keep my emphysema under control.

"Pastor, I want you to help me find a church back home; maybe you could even call a pastor and tell them I'm coming. Mindy, I need you to help me pack; I'm no good at that. Rose, you could fix me a lunch for the bus ride—and everybody keep those prayers coming!"

He ended with, "I know you all get really sick of me sometimes; who wouldn't? But I hope you know how much I appreciate you." Well put, dear friend, and we hope you know how much we love you.

Well, Charlie, I'm going to settle into a pleasant, summer evening now, probably sit on the deck amidst the vibrant greens of flora and fauna and birdsongs and frog croaks, reading and thinking of the nice dinner and dozing and praying for Bryan Bowman and Garfield Temple and whoever else appears in my consciousness, or unconsciousness, for that matter.

Florence, of course. She's with Sarah, hacking her insides out, perpetually exhausted, resigned to whatever happens, with her usual crusty faith. She told me she went with granddaughter Angelica to a heavy metal concert!

And Stephanie. I tried to call her a bit ago but no answer. She's nauseated every day around suppertime and extremely fatigued. Worst of all, she sounds so sad to me.

And I'll fantasize about the Cubs winning the pennant. They're in first place in their division. I know it's early, but this could be their year, Charlie, as we've said since we were kids. I won't thank God for their excellent success; if I did, I would have to conclude that God is a Yankees fan, which is unacceptable.

Trinity Sunday (First Sunday after Pentecost)

Proverbs 8:1-4, 22-31
Psalm 8
Romans 5:1-5
John 16:12-15

"Those who have done good will enter eternal life, those who have done evil will enter eternal fire. This is the catholic faith. One cannot be saved without believing this firmly and faithfully."

So concludes the Athanasian Creed which we professed today to emphasize the meaning of the Trinity, and those last three sentences bothered me greatly. The rest of this crazy creed is perfectly okay by me—a poetic way to fathom the unfathomable a bit. Not made for the literal minds of the present age, however, and the congregation seemed challenged by both the length and the language. "What in the hell was that?!" I heard Sidney say. I was, however, disturbed by that ending, and couldn't wait to get to Pastor Sauer after the service.

"Pastor, what about that closing statement of the Athanasian Creed?! Isn't it contrary to our understanding of ourselves as both saint and sinner? We're not dependent on our good works for salvation, only God's grace!" I was so agitated and confrontational he might have thought I was blaming him!

"Ah, Rose, that statement would indeed be bothersome if we look at it that way," he started, obviously delighted to engage. "We need to go back to the 4th century and understand that the writers of that statement defined evil or bad people as those who obstinately disregarded belief in God and had no inclination to live in a godly manner. They weren't talking about people of faith who, despite our best efforts, do that which we ought not and don't do that which we ought, regularly asking God's forgiveness."

That helped—not that I have any desire or need whatsoever to have an opinion on who is assigned to eternal fire.

The Trinity is a fine way for me to understand the ultimate power behind the universe and how that beneficent power is present in our world and in our souls. I believe the creeds to be true <u>for the Church</u> and <u>for me</u>. I accept the creeds and live by them. I do sometimes wonder, however, if the Trinity is supposed to be ultimate truth for everyone.

How would I have fared as a person of faith in the days when professing what you believed could be a matter of life or death? In light of modern thought and contemporary ecclesiastical/religious culture, the Trinity hardly seems worth dying over. So, if a stern, squinty-eyed inquisitor had asked me, "Do you believe in the

Holy Trinity as ultimate Truth?" I would have looked him straight in the eye and said, "Youbetcha." I can see the headline: "Hypocrite Heretic Not Burned at Stake."

Why three persons? Why not four—or seven? Why not thirty-two? Surely Almighty God has that many "faces." How about a quartet instead of a trinity? Let's add Lady Wisdom! Seriously, I know the Three are from the Bible, from the witness of Christ and the witness of faith. Again I say, the Three-in-One work perfectly in their majesty and mystery for me.

The Trinity concept didn't seem to cause Mindy undue concern. She leaned over Garfield at the end of the sermon and joked to us, "Huh? I thought the 'Father, Son and Holy Ghost took the last train for the coast.'" But she did compliment Pastor on his sermon and proudly shared her image that the Trinity is like lemonade—"Just try and separate the lemon juice, water and sugar! Can't do it—and it quenches our thirst!"

She stopped by on her way home from work a little while ago, catching Cute Baby and me napping during game two of a doubleheader. We ate some melon and left-over macaroni and cheese for a little Sunday night supper.

"What in the world is this, Rose? Who are these three women?" she asked, leaning forward to look at the icon of the Trinity I had propped up on the kitchen table.

"They're not women, they're male angels. They represent the Trinity."

She stared for the longest time, then said, "I don't get it. What's it mean? I thought the Trinity was God the Father, God the Son, and God the Holy Spirit, not three men angels who look like women with big hair."

"If you really want to know, I'll try to tell you, but it's all rather involved."

She cocked her head and widened her eyes, silently indicating, "I wouldn't have asked if I didn't want to know." Forsooth, the question was bigger than I wanted to answer, but I breathed deeply and began. The scene is actually based on Genesis 18 when the Lord visits Abraham and Sarah in the form of these three angels, I explained.

"You mean, God turned into a man? or three men? or three angels? I don't know if I like that. God should be God, and God is not like humans at all."

I tried to explain that we don't understand the Scripture as literal, physical, scientific accounts but rather as faith stories that witness to ultimate truth. I passed on the definition of myth that I once heard from a thoughtful child: "A myth is a story that's true on the inside but not on the outside." We interpret the Bible with a respect for its mystery and complexity, I told her. Images like those in icons are created to help us in our understanding of God's Word. When she nodded, I continued with what I could remember of Father Michael's comments about the icon of the Holy Trinity.

"The one on the left is the Father who is motioning toward the Son. The Son and the Spirit are both oriented toward the Father, from whence they came. The three form a circle, and, if you use your imagination, they also form a chalice."

"So this one's the Paraclete?" she asked, pointing to the figure on the right.

"A representation of the Paraclete, yes."

She nodded.

"Imagine yourself within this holy circle in the presence of God, the mystery," I invited her, just like Father Michael had invited us at the icon retreat. "Let your mind descend into your heart. Listen and hear the divine heart speaking to yours. Bring your joy and sorrow into this place."

She gazed...and gazed. I tiptoed into the living room, sank down into the rocker, and contemplated the intriguing connection Father Michael made between the Genesis 18 story and Christ, a "prefiguration," he called Gen. 18. The Old Testament story points to God the Creator sending the Redeemer son who gives us new life through the Spirit. The tree of life is in the background. Abraham and Sarah's house symbolizes the dwelling place of the Divine. The mountain symbolizes the spiritual heights where we pray and meditate. The choice meat in the chalice that was served to the guests becomes the Lamb of God chosen before the creation to take away the sins of the world. This understanding totally transforms otherwise weird stories from another era and culture into the inspired Word of God!

Through my musings I heard Mindy softly humming, talking, weeping. "Weep your tears into the channel, till the lowest streams do kiss the most exalted shores of all," little one. Darkness was upon us when she came in, handed me the postcard-sized print of the icon, knelt down, and put her head in my lap. I rubbed her back and remembered the incredible sweetness of rocking my sleepy babies. After a bit, she raised up and asked, "Can you get me one of those icons of the Trinity?"

I insisted she take the print, of course. I'll get another from Pr. Sauer.

And so, faith is a gift that comes to us, not an achievement or a product of personal piety, nor can we lay faith on someone else. Now, listen to what you're saying here, Rose, and be as certain as you can that you're not viewing other people as somehow inferior because they haven't yet received the gift of faith. What an unkind attitude that is!

And here's another sadness surrounding the brokenness at church: the memory of what Claudia had told me in the grocery store last week popped into my poor old brain the other day—they're leaving St. Timothy. Damn! As soon as I remembered the news, I picked up the phone and called her.

"Why?!" I demanded in my sorrow.

"Lots is going on with us, and we don't need more conflict in our lives, especially not at the place we go for relief and strength." She hesitated. "Rose, Michael and I are struggling with our marriage."

"Oh, no, not another one," I thought.

"I think we're going to be okay, but we are involved in major work, and we've got to have a healthy, peaceful community of faith. Plus, you know how the masculine understanding of God crushes my spirit. And we've also lost patience—Michael and I agree on this—on the Church's stance on homosexuality. We don't want to be part of a denomination that makes judgments about people based solely on sexual orientation. We've been visiting the United Church of Christ in the city; it's not perfect, of course, but I think it's the place for us right now."

When she said she would miss me, I started crying from sadness and sheer frustration, and I had trouble stopping.

Oh, God, this brokenness in our Body of Christ is so hard. Please do something to save us from ourselves. Amen.

Second Sunday after Pentecost

2 Samuel 11:26-12:10, 13-15
Psalm 32
Galatians 2:15-21
Luke 7:36-8:3

Out of her depths she cried, the woman in Luke 7. Imagine going into a household where you're not wanted or respected and totally losing control of your emotions, crying, probably sobbing and shaking, mucous all over the place. Your tears fall on the guest of honor's feet and then you cry more and then wipe your tears off his feet with your hair.

Granted, there were different customs then. Jesus was reclined at the table, stretched out with his feet behind him and the practice of people following religious personalities around was apparently tolerated, even as they intruded into private homes. Nonetheless, this woman must have been experiencing spiritual agony and ecstasy to do what she did. Garfield did a similar thing in worship this morning.

We had a Service of Farewell and Godspeed for him, ending with the words "...as Garfield has been a blessing to us, so now we send him forth to be a blessing to others; through Jesus Christ our Lord." We added our Amen! and Pastor started to pass the peace, which would have made a really nice little package. Instead, Garfield abruptly dropped to his knees, hanging on to the communion railing for dear life, and crying in great heaves. Few of us could understand the depth at which he was operating, not having experienced the depth of separation from God that he has known. I suppose we don't know the full force of forgiveness either. Like the woman crying on Jesus' feet. After a moment, Pastor Sauer placed his hands on Garfield's head and said, "Garfield, your sins are forgiven. Faith has saved you from despair. Go in peace." Tears fell, and Garfield was well-hugged when we passed the peace.

The hymn that followed, "God! When Human Bonds Are Broken," (Kean) was exquisitely applicable to Garfield at this time of re-entering his natural habitat and, once again, starting over:

> God! When human bonds are broken and we lack the love or skill
> to restore the hope of healing, give us grace and make us still.
> Through that stillness, with your Spirit come into our world of stress,
> for the sake of Christ forgiving all the failures we confess.

You in us are bruised and broken;
hear us as we seek release from the pain of earlier living;
set us free and grant us peace.
Send us, God of new beginnings, humbly hopeful into life.

Use us as a means of blessing;
make us stronger, give us faith
to be more faithful, give us hope to be more true,
give us love to go on learning: God! Encourage and renew!

Pastor's sermon hinged on one word. Of. Instead of in. Imagine that. An important matter of faith hinging on of instead of in! How boring that sounds, and how could it possibly matter that much? Well, here was the gist of it: Galatians 2:16 was the phrase in question, "...we know that a person is justified not by the works of the law but through the faith of Jesus Christ." Traditionally, the preposition has been translated as in—"faith in Jesus Christ." Modern scholarship is now suggesting of instead. Pastor explained that rather than justification depending on our faith or belief (in), we are justified because of Christ's faithfulness (of), which is our model and gift. A big difference. Yes, the crux of the matter, actually. We can't do faith, only receive it. Then, overwhelmed by divine love and mercy, respond. Like the woman.

"Her sins, which were many, have been forgiven; hence," Jesus says, "she has shown great love." Like Garfield.

We had a great going away party for him last night. Guests included his boss, Murray Wakefield, Sidney, Madge, Pr. Sauer and Carolyn, Mindy, Stephen, Stephanie Rose, GED teacher Eleanor, and Brother James—his team. Florence would have come if she'd been up to it.

He enjoyed himself and seemed genuinely overwhelmed at the gifts. Pastor gave him the "Icon of the Empty Cup," especially for alcoholics. Mindy, Stephanie and I went in together and presented him with a nice notebook, including composition paper. Stephen gave him a fancy duffel bag and Brother James a book, The Joy of Righteousness. Murray had cut out wooden shapes of Agape House and St. Timothy's building and his wife had meticulously painted them. Very special. Garfield ate three pieces of Madge's carrot cake and raved about it so much that she wrapped up more for him to take on the bus trip. But he was too emotional even to talk when Sidney gave him a brand new guitar. My St. Lord, what an extravagant gift!

After the others left, Stephanie, Mindy, Garfield and I sat out on the deck late into the night with the frogs and cicada thundering musically and all the lights off. The sky was alive with stars and stardust. Stephanie had been subdued all evening and into our contemplative silence came her quiet sniffling and weeping—out of the depths.

"Stephanie, what's wrong?" Mindy inquired immediately.

After a brief hesitation, she told us that Ethan has been gone for a couple weeks. She told him to leave when he suggested one time too many that she have an abortion. My poor baby. I'm not surprised about Ethan, but will never say so (unless she asks).

"It's meant to be," she sighed, describing their relationship as perpetual tug-of-war. The final disagreement—over having the baby or not—was one in which she could not even engage, she said.

The evening might have concluded with a pity party for her if Garfield hadn't seen a falling star and reacted with, "Don't worry, Stephanie. Our lives are just like that star streaking across the sky and then going out. Nothing is that big of a deal."

"Way to be sensitive, Gar," Mindy chided him, and we chuckled.

Still gazing into the heavens, he apologized, then continued. "I don't mean we're not important, but we're so tiny and temporary. In the whole universe, Earth is like an anthill. When disaster hits, we run around like ants do if you dig your toe into their hill, with carcasses all over the place, hardly knowing what hit them."

"You're doing a fine job of cheering everybody up, Garfield. Just keep going," Mindy teased.

He didn't need any encouragement. Sitting on the edge of his chair, he pointed upward and said, "Look at that bright light right there. It could be a UFO flying through space on a vacation cruise and right as they get over us in about a hundred thousand years, they could empty their toilet not even knowing we're here, and, poof! that's the end of civilization, just like that. The Taj Mahal, the Grand Ole Opry, everything gone."

We howled and groaned.

"I heard we all have stardust in us," he went on with his head still tilted back. "Wow! How can anybody look at the night sky and not believe in God?!"

"Because they think it's pure science and physics and random big booms and black holes without anybody in charge," Mindy promptly replied to his rhetorical question.

Garfield: Well, they're ignorant.

Mindy: Not necessarily.

G: What?! You're sure about God, aren't you?

M: Not always. I can't shrink God into a small enough, tight enough package to be sure all the time. I don't have any trouble believing that God is the God of science—of evolution or the big bang or whatever. But, holy smokes, our galaxy is huge and there are millions more of them out there. The hugeness and the mystery

is too much for my little pea-brain; sometimes I wonder if the big boss of it all even knows who I, Mindy Lucas, am...
Silent gazing
M: ...but God, the loving Creator who knows what color my hair is on any given day is the way I want it to be, so I choose a loving God over nothing.
Silence
G: You can't choose God. God chooses you.
M: Okay.
Silence
G: You know, some of those stars we're looking at are dead. They burned out a long time ago, maybe millions of years ago. We're looking at their light which has taken all this time to reach us, but they're dead, they're done.
Silence
M: I heard on the radio that the sun is going to burn out in seven billion years.
G: (Alarmed) Did you say million or billion?!
M: <u>B</u>illion, as in <u>b</u>urn out.
G: Oh, thank God. I thought you said million.
M: What difference does that make, silly?
G: You're silly. Billion is a lot longer than million. It means we have more time.
M: Who's <u>we</u> and more time to do <u>what</u>?
G: People. More time to plan our escape to another planet.
Silence
M: Rose, what's that line? "God made us just below the angels" or something like that. Look at those stars! and there are universes we can't even see! It gives me the willies. God is over it all and creates it all, more than we could ever even imagine, and more or less gives us this little earth and everything on it to enjoy and take care of.
G: Your point is?
Silence
M: God is great and God is good.
G: Let us thank him for the stars.

Amen! I say to these backyard gazers.

Third Sunday after Pentecost

Isaiah 65:1-9
Psalm 22:19-28
Galatians 3:23-29
Luke 8:26-39

Pastor was standing tall in the pulpit preparing to preach and giving us that intense look that seems to say, "Okay, everybody focus. These are the words of eternal life and, even though I'm not positive what it all means, I am going to do my best, informed by the Holy Spirit, to interpret them to you," when a bat came swooping in, kamikaze style, like it was the superhero and Pastor was the villain. Pastor ducked and we hardly had time to react before the bat circled around and headed straight for us, like the veritable bat out of Hades. We undulated like the ocean, ducking, straightening up, ducking again with stifled screams and gasps as the little creature circled and soared.

Sidney was happy as could be; I think he'd been waiting for this moment. Almost immediately, I saw him stretched precariously over the balcony railing trying to nab the bat with a swimming pool net on a long pole. That was folly, of course. I was waiting for the pole, or maybe Sidney himself, to land on somebody's head. Pastor Sauer commanded in a voice stricken hoarse by terror, "Let us reassemble in the lower level of the church," and bolted for the sacristy. At Lydia Circle once, Carolyn had told us of his bat phobia, hilariously imitating him pulling the sheet up tight over his head when there was a bat in their house.

As we surged through the double doors, a child whimpered, "No, Mommy! There's mouses in the basement."

"Well, at least they don't have wings," comforted big sister.

Pastor had the ushers go back upstairs to get the bread and wine and his sermon notes. A table was pulled front and center and altar guild personnel hastily set things up in their dedicated, loving way. We sat down at chairs and tables in the linear dinner formation. I wound up next to Madge who shared that the bat had been asleep on one of the speaker boxes all through Sheila Smith's wedding yesterday. And then we were reassembled and Pastor, looking as though he had been swooped at and missed, gave us that concentrated stare again and plunged in.

"When is help not help?" he asked. When it's not wanted, was the answer. Here's this poor, pitiful fellow out of Luke 8, wandering around naked in cemeteries, restrained for his own good, breaking loose and running wild, knowing only the agony of mental illness. Jesus cures him, transforms him into a sane, calm person who can think and enjoy life. And what thanks does Jesus get from the man's family and neighbors? You would think they'd fall at his feet in awe and gratitude that the man is now well, that they don't have to take turns guarding him anymore. But no—

"Go away, please." they tell Jesus. "We were doing fine without you. We had learned how to handle this situation; we had accommodated this poor chap. Yes, you've healed him and made him truly alive, but we don't understand how this has happened, we weren't in control, this is mysterious and frightening, we were far more comfortable dealing with his illness then with this change. Besides, you drove our hogs over the cliff, you ruined our livelihood!"

Pastor Sauer gave several contemporary examples of that same human response to divine power, that unwillingness to relinquish control and surrender our lives to divine guidance: abusing our bodies with food and other addictions, staying in a job that's not good for us, not getting help when there is an abusive relationship. If he'd used a situation to describe my lack of trust it would have been comparing myself to others for validation rather than resting in God's affirming love. Imagine if we could only trust God for strength and insight instead of holding fort within ourselves against the Holy Spirit!

And then, of course, Pastor had to go and apply the message directly to St. Timothy. That's when people started bristling. He challenged us again to participate in the sexuality study from church headquarters, charging that we were more comfortable ignoring this issue and didn't want to risk the discomfort and change brought on by wrestling with a difficult topic. I understand Mary Jane Evans, as Christian Ed. chair, has been somewhat obstructionist; in fact, the other day in the hallway I overheard her say, "Studying sex is not <u>Christian</u> education!" Pastor said God is offering important gifts through the sexuality study, and we could trust God and each other to proceed with it.

He further challenged us to get involved with prisoners and persons with mental illness rather than maintaining the status quo by simply sending socks and underwear to the institutions at Christmastime. Great, I thought. Now those poor souls won't even get new socks and underwear. He practically double-dared us to misbehave at the upcoming congregational meeting to decide about the tree.

And he exulted. "Good news, people of St. Timothy! God has given what is needed in all these situations; accept the gifts!" Good sermon, Pastor.

I thought of Garfield as our demoniac and that Jesus had driven his demons out. He looked so neat and rested and normal when he got on the bus last Monday morning with his new guitar and duffel bag. Pastor Sauer drove him into the city to the bus terminal, and I went along. The bus left at 7:00, so we rode in together in the fresh, cool dawn. There wasn't much to be said after all the festivities of the week-end. The three of us were quite tired of saying good-bye, hugging, passing the peace, saying thank you and good luck. So we talked mostly about the Cardinals and the Cubs. I'd packed Garfield a lunch to go with Madge's carrot cake. In his last glance and wave as he mounted the steps in brilliant sunshine, he reminded me of Stephanie boarding the bus on her first day of school. She looked back at Barry with an excited little smile and said, "I'll be darned if I'm not scared half-to-death!" And then she was gone. Barry still gets choked up telling that story.

And now Garfield is gone, and my eyes mist and my heart has a strange little ache when I contemplate him trying to make it in St. Louis, even as I think of all the headaches, literal and figurative, that we will be spared by his departure. I think many of us feel like he's been our child, under our care and teaching and nurture. Now, it's up to him. We can only watch from a distance.

I know Mindy feels that way. She called one night last week and confessed that she'd looked forward to him leaving and how much it would simplify her life, but now that he's gone, she misses him and worries about him.

"We did our best, Rose. Now it's up to him."

No. We're wrong. Now it's up to God. It's always up to God. Not us. Not Garfield. God.

Dear Saving God, save Garfield from the clutches of sin. Help him not to separate himself from you. Help him rather to feel your love and presence each morning when he wakes up weak and frightened and half-sick, feeling like an alien forever wandering in a strange and foreign land. Help him to remember your promises, to take courage no matter how demonic the demons, and to trust in your saving power, fully manifested in your son, our Lord, Jesus, the Christ. Florence too. Amen.

I went over to do her laundry the other day and to frame a family picture taken when Sarah was about ten which she wanted on her nightstand. Out falls her hair again. She was feeling relatively fabulous, though, finally free of nausea after several days but too weak to do anything but lie in bed. She ate up every detail of news about Garfield, Stephanie, and our beloved, off-balance pastor. Each conversation we have is more precious than the last.

"I finally have you right where I want you, Rose—waiting on me hand and foot," she joked when I helped her sip some water.

Our eyes locked, and I couldn't think of anything clever or lighthearted to say. Intending to smile, I was suddenly crying instead. I sat down on the edge of the bed and we hugged and wept on each other's shoulders. I thought of a long-ago hug when our friendship was young, and she had miserably confided to me that she was being unfaithful to Arnie. We were sitting next to each other on her porch swing, and I felt awkward but put my arm around her, and she laid her head on my shoulder and cried. How many hugs, laughs, tears, arguments, and just plain fun we've had since then! *I can never thank you enough, dear God, for this precious friend.*

"I wish there was something I could do for you, something that would make a difference," I said as we tried to stop crying.

"There is," she said. "Fugue 1, C Major."

I went to the piano. Bach's gentle but lively exercise weaned us from our grief, momentarily. Thanks to J. S. and God for this wonderful music that speaks to the human soul.

When I walked back into the bedroom, she said, "Thank you. Go home now, Rosie. You have filled me with deep pleasure and peace, and I think I can rest."

"May the Lord watch between thee and me, while we are absent, one from the other," I said, taking her hand.

"Get out of here, Rose, before you ruin this lovely moment with all your damned holiness," she smiled, which kept a smile on my face all the way home.

Well, for better or worse I'm going down to visit cousin Josephine. It's been four years. She doesn't pressure me, but she's so alone that I feel obligated. I'm the only cousin who ever visits anymore. Being there is not awful. I love her big old house, and I enjoy being in the South. It's quiet, and who cares that much about food anyway? We don't starve. Her incessant talking is a little wearing at times—breathy, thick slurriness from medication, no eye contact, almost as though she's talking to herself. No emotion except a little excitement closer to hysteria once in a while when she starts spinning her fantasies and that high-pitched tee-hee-hee of hers kicks in. I hope she's gotten over the delusion that the principal of the high school is infatuated with her. I don't guess she could ever damage his reputation because the very idea is too absurd.

I'd prefer taking the bus down like I used to, but it's just too hard on my old bones. I'd better finish packing right now. Stephen will be here bright and early to get me to the airport.

Fourth Sunday after Pentecost

I Kings 19:15-16, 19-21
Psalm 16
Galatians 5:1, 13-25
Luke 9:51-62

Worshiping at Josephine's little country church is not easy for me. For one thing, the garish painting of Jesus praying in Gethsemane which is positioned behind the altar puts me off. I had a chance to examine it closely this morning, suspecting that it might be a paint-by-number, and saw a long black hair painted into it. The cousin of one of the wealthier members painted it and, once ensconced, politics has taken precedence over piety.

Physical interpretations of Jesus, especially behind the altar, often disturb me. I doubt that Jesus himself would like them. If he wandered in and saw one, he'd probably say, "Who is that supposed to be?" I find it presumptuous to impose one individual's mental image of Jesus the Christ on the whole worshiping community, but these artistic renditions are usually there to stay unless there's a fire or a building project and the artwork in question can be shifted to a chapel or mysteriously disappear during the chaotic period. Maybe my developing attraction to icons is because the iconographer intentionally creates an other worldly representation of holy scenes and people which are not made in our image, are not of this world.

Josephine's Preacher Duncan was blunt this morning about whether or not to participate in the community Fourth of July God and Country service coming up. Josephine had warned me that he was dead set against mixing church and country and that the congregation was splitting right down the middle over it.

"The hand of the Lord is upon me!" he bellowed. "His Word is in my mouth! He has come to me and told me to deliver the Word unto you. The Word of the Lord is at hand, the Word of the Lord lives among us! God's Word is that God and nation cannot be uttered in the same breath! Our God is the God of the cosmos, not only of one nation! Our God is the God of eternity, not just of selected historical moments!"

The people in front of us got up and left, and I heard rustling behind us, too.

"God chose the children of Abraham to spread the Word of salvation far and wide, to all people! Christ hung and died on the tree for all people! It is the devil's work to invoke the blessing of almighty God on one nation! Almighty God blesses as he sees fit. It is not our role to interpret that we are more blessed! Almighty God blesses justice and peace! It is our duty only to do justice, love kindness, and walk humbly with our God, not to puff ourselves up with arrogance and pride and military power!"

More people left.

"The wages of sin is death!" he fumed, except he said, "The wages of si-yun is deh-yuth!" which sounded far less threatening.

Whew. Exhausting. I prefer our conflicts to theirs.

They reckon a lot down here and declare (de-clah-yah) too, as in, "Well, Ah declah-yah, Josephine, it's been a long kinda' tahm since cousin Rose has blessed us with a visit. Ah reckon it's been three or four years, hadnit, Miz Rose?"

The seven-member choir did their level best. Sincerity is beyond question, as with the average choir. A peroxided blonde, who probably took the average age of the choir from seventy-something to sixty-something, personified this devotion. Head held high, nostrils flared, beatific expression, head moving in rhythm. "Leaning on the everlasting arms."

So, that was Sunday morning worship. Now, here I sit with Josephine sweltering, I say sweltering, in the shade of her lush Bougainville vine. No baseball all week because she doesn't have cable, but at least sitting on the porch breaks the monotony of sitting in the house for hours with little to do or say. Our stomachs are comfortably filled with macaroni and cheese out of a box, and I find it hard to believe I head home tomorrow. As I write, Josephine is in her customary position on the porch swing, chattering about nothing and staring intently into the street as though some special friend will drive by any minute and need a wave.

Josephine is definitely unique. Okay—odd. The children used to call her "Cousin Weirdifine." How to describe her—child-like? naïve? stupid? And yet, I am always surprised to sense a certain invisible substance. I learned more about her in five minutes in the grocery store parking lot yesterday than I've learned in 75 years. We were walking back to her car when we heard a woman yelling.

"What the hell are you thinking, you fool?! What the hell are you even thinking?! Goddamn it to hell, you look at me when I'm talking to you, young man! And don't you so much as think about saying one word back to me, not one fucking word, do you hear me? I can still beat your sorry ass if I have to. I am your mother and you will respect me, goddamn it!"

She was an obese woman, mobile in a wheelchair, positioned to get in the driver's seat of her specially-equipped van. The son was a lanky 14- or 15-year old with acne. He was wearing sneakers, a T-shirt, and short jeans that he'd probably grown out of since last week. He was standing at the end of the van, his forehead pressed against it in agonizing humiliation. Passersby took furtive looks; those of us farther away stared.

The miserable fat lady railed on, and I was so engrossed that when a short, square woman in a white dress with big red polka dots entered the scene, it took me a moment to realize that it was Josephine. She spoke to the woman who told her to mind her own business, but Josephine kept talking. The woman continued yelling, the boy continued dying a thousand deaths, and Josephine continued talking quietly. The woman let out a sound of despair and covered her face with her hands. Josephine talked for another moment, then returned and we climbed in her car. The woman still had her face covered and the boy still had his forehead against the van when we pulled out of the parking lot.

"What did you say to her, Josephine?"

"I told her that God gives children to be loved and that it's wrong to yell at them and wrong to be cruel. I told her that my father used to yell at me a lot, the way she yelled at her son, and that sometimes I thought maybe I would kill myself. 'Do you want your son to kill himself?' I asked her. I told her to get a-hold of herself, that she's the mother and that those bad words are like little knives cutting into her son. I told her that if she would just be nice to her son he would love her again and everything would get better and she wouldn't be so sad," she said in her sing-songy way.

What if those words are life-changing for that mother and son?! What agony that woman has obviously suffered, what bondage to sin that such violence could spew from her mouth and allow her body to balloon to that deadly size. She cannot free herself, but maybe, just maybe those words of judgment, forgiveness and hope spoken through the little Christ of weird Josephine will encourage her to set out on a new path. Maybe not, but I admire Josephine for doing what she did.

Later, on the plane

I'm glad to be heading back to my own routines and at the same time I'm savoring the unusual and rich experience of cousin Josephine.

"Poor Garfield," she said, as I hugged her good-bye a little while ago. "I hope he and Marie can get back together and be happy. Tell Stephanie that I love her and her baby. Maybe Virginia will get back to church, but it really doesn't matter, Rose, really. Better for Barry to stay away right now. I believe Stephen will find the right wife, and Denise will find the right husband. Florence will be with you even when she dies pretty soon. I wish I could meet Mindy. Thank you for coming," and she sort of hugged me back.

A grandfather and child I observed while we were waiting to board are sitting behind me. The girl's head is a little large for her body and misshapen, and her face is flat with a broad, flat nose. She has no eyes, only sockets, and she talks non-stop in the fashion of a bright and curious seven- or eight-year-old. Grandpa has patiently conversed and answered questions, but in the midst of her ceaseless chatter, I just heard him say, "Now listen, darlin', we don't have to talk all the way to Atlanta. Once we take off, we can stop talkin' for awhile."

With that sweet image, a pleasant warmth of contentment is settling over me. Thinking of all the love in my life and all the joy that my people and circumstances have brought, I say with the psalmist, "The boundaries for me have fallen in pleasant places."

Thank you, indeed, good and gracious God, for blessings upon blessings. Thank you for Josephine, an injured yet brave and loving person, a gift for me and for the world. Thank you for helping me to see you in her and to understand how precious she is. Through Jesus, my Lord, Amen.

Fifth Sunday after Pentecost

Isaiah 66:10-14
Psalm 66:1-9
Galatians 6:1-16
Luke 10:1-11, 16-20

There was quite a baptism this morning. Nobody knew who they were—an overweight, disheveled young woman with a black child. When they started up to the front, I heard Madge whisper, "Who are these people?" I wanted to turn around and say, "Oh, shut up Madge. God knows who they are!" even though I was thinking the same thing. After the service I heard Pastor tell someone that the woman has just moved to town. She is the sister of a man who used to go to our former pastor's present church. Hm, it doesn't take much to get baptized these days, does it?

Well, oops, Rose, that's the point—God bestows this gift on helpless infants. There is not a single thing a baby can or must do to receive divine grace. It doesn't matter who your daddy is or your mother. In baptism, we are simply recognizing how God is, the way the universe is set up. We are loved, we are precious, we are liberated from sin and death. I always chuckle to myself when the congregation welcomes the new baby as "a fellow worker in the kingdom of God." Shall we put the baby on the Stewardship or the Church Property Committee? The Nursery Committee, I suppose!

And as for the acceptability of these particular persons—the main point of today's gospel is that ALL are invited. How unfaithful of us not to rejoice when "they" show up, "they" being anyone. Anyone who comes in the door. Did Jesus ever wrinkle his nose, even internally for an instant, because he didn't personally know people who responded to his invitation or because they were unsightly or smelly or socially awkward or sick or poor? Quite the contrary, I think. He was not surprised when they came; he expected them. He welcomed all with love and mercy. We, in contrast, often try to possess our congregations and control, consciously and subconsciously, who comes.

I hate like anything to admit it, but it's a shock to the system when somebody like Garfield or the young mother of this morning walks in. I think that sometimes we are too tired to welcome strangers, what with everything else that's going on. By the time we tend to this member's divorce and that one's stroke and that other member's fire, etc. etc. etc., people who are not in our inner circle can seem like a burden. If we could only have the mind and strength of Christ, we would expect these people and rejoice when they appear rather than feeling uncomfortable or taxed, for heaven's sake. I certainly miss the unusual Mr. Garfield Temple and

Mindy too, who hasn't been around much lately. I especially miss them now that Florence is able to come to worship only sporadically.

Pastor was stepping into the pulpit when I came in. I had trouble pulling myself away from Vanessa and Serena Williams' Wimbledon match. Oh! those gorgeous, strong bodies. Such grace and strength. Strangely, the tennis match provided a segue into what Pr. Sauer was saying about Isaiah 66 with its strong female images portraying Zion, and then God, as both mother and warrior. Claudia nodded her head emphatically when Pr. Sauer preached that God is not exclusively male, that the human image of God was, from the beginning, created male and female. She probably felt like standing up and cheering. I think her family turned up because of today's congregational meeting about the tree—Michael is the unofficial leader of the cut-it-down contingent. Maybe they won't leave after all. Please, Claudia, be patient with us!

Sidney's response to the female image of God was predictably different. He came up to Mercedes and me after the service and said angrily, "Ladies, you are not now and never will be God," and turned on his heel. We burst out laughing without saying a word. Was Sidney thinking *he* was God? or might be someday?! Merciful heavens, if he would spend ten minutes talking to Stephanie and/or Claudia about their concerns and opinions regarding feminism, he would find female images of the Divine pretty tame.

We gathered in the basement after worship to eat a light lunch and then tackle the tree dilemma. We seemed ridiculously cheerful and polite, given the underlying tension, as we served ourselves dainty chicken salad and pimento cheese sandwiches and weak lemonade. Both sides had enlisted members who rarely attend worship to be present for the big vote. Stephen presented the Task Force report which included financial and arbor science information as well as comments, concerns, and questions from the focus groups. Their recommendation was to let the tree stand. A quiet gasp from the cut-it-down/change/progressive group hung in the air.

I was proud, grateful, and relieved with the discussion that followed. No grandstanding, no false piety attempting to sway emotions, no excessive celebration. Rather, reasonable discussion with individuals speaking to both sides of the issue, some choking up as they expressed deeply-felt opinions. God's will and the workings of the Spirit were invoked genuinely and appropriately.

"I like the tree. It's G-g-g-od's tree," Danny stuttered with his lips against the microphone, his words reverberating loudly.

"I like the tree too, Danny," Susie Wakefield gently responded when it was her turn, "but it's very old and it's damaging our property and it might be making people stay away from our church because they can't find a place to park. God wants us to welcome people to our church."

The vote was 69 in favor of the recommendation and 66 against. The tree will stand. I sensed a miraculous peace, however, in the midst of this profound division. Michael Townshend expressed the mood well.

"I think we have succeeded today, because in our disagreement, we have been honest with each other, we have listened to each other, we have respected each other. Now, the decision is made, and we are called to continue our mission not as winners or losers but as God's children."

Amen, brother! This morning's meeting was the Church at its best. I called Florence with a full report, and she was proud of us too. She started another round of chemotherapy two weeks ago with strong, experimental chemicals which are liable to be very rough on her. "Florence, what's the point?" was on my lips when she snapped, "Don't ask me what the point is, Rose. I've made the decision." Okay, friend. I'll be by your side every step of the way.

As regards the Church and its crazy goings-on, Stephanie and Mindy and I had a little conversation about it yesterday afternoon, arriving at that topic by a circuitous route. Poor Stephanie had hit rock bottom with a crash, actually a series of crashes, and stopped by for some "Grandma time," as she puts it. Being pregnant and alone would be more than enough for anyone to handle, and her pregnancy is not being an easy one—sickness, fatigue, swelling. I'm sorry for her problems, and yet I have an emotional distance, knowing that she will be fine in the long run, indeed will benefit from the difficulties. I'll help her and lend support in whatever way seems right; being a good listener may be the most important help. *As you know, God, I don't always succeed at that.* For example, perhaps I was too harsh when I refused to discuss the topic of female scents with her yesterday afternoon. She was telling me that she's feeling very pressured by a deadline for an article she's having published.

"I just don't know if I can do it, Grandma; every time I sit down I'm in an agony of not being able to write. I think, who cares anyway? It's not like the world is sitting out there waiting for this article," she rambled. "I feel inadequate to the extent that I'm so wrapped up in my own limitations that insecurity is really ego, you know? I freeze up when I think of how people might disagree with what I write…"

"What's the article about?"

"The female bouquet."

"Wedding bouquets?" I asked in puzzlement, knowing full well that she wouldn't be writing about wedding bouquets.

"No, of course not," she snorted. "Vaginal scents. In our culture, women are negative about their natural fragrances and use douches and…"

"OK, that's enough."

"But Grandma," she persisted, "we try to deodorize away our God-given being. There are women who scrub themselves raw trying to..."

"Stephanie Rose, that is enough!" I shut her down.

Her expression was that of a beautiful doe looking into the face of the hunter who had just shot her. Her eyes filled up and in a moment she was sobbing. I was sorry, but honestly, I'm an old lady and do not desire to contemplate the political significance of the odor of our private parts and how we deal with it. And I think it should be my privilege not to discuss that particular topic—even if my granddaughter is, apparently, an expert.

Anyway, here was my precious grandchild, crying her heart out with all the anger and sadness about Ethan and fears of what lay ahead as a single mother. And there was more.

She has somehow deleted all her students' grades, right at the end of the first summer term when it's time to average them up. They're due Tuesday. She had a faint thought that Ethan might have broken into her apartment and tampered with her computer for spite. I hardly think so. She probably forgot what she named the file, though she bit my head off when I suggested that. Ethan's not the type for such dirty tricks, in my estimation, but her suspicions seem to confirm the rightness of their not marrying. So, she has spent countless hours attempting to reconstruct enough from memory to assign and submit grades and is now living in mortal fear that some students from this peculiarly cantankerous class will contest their grades and she won't have documentation and…yakkity-yak. Why didn't she just give them all As and Bs, I thought, and forget it. But that's not how Stephanie works.

And there was MORE. Between sobs, she started telling this barely coherent story about a mistake that has been made with her phone bill that she's been trying to correct for six months—endless phone calls, getting names of those she's spoken with, threatening on both sides, yakkity-yakkity-yak!! I didn't fully understand some aspects of the situation and every time I asked a little question, she acted like we were in a courtroom and I was the prosecuting attorney and had just broken her emotionally. Mercy, child, you're drowning in self-pity, I thought, and felt like quoting from Richard III—"I'll join with black despair against my soul, And to myself become an enemy." Obviously, this billing problem was not for me to help solve, or perhaps even know about. I was feeling quite paralyzed when the doorbell rang, the door opened, and we heard a cheery yoo-hoo.

"We're in the den, Mindy," I yelled, like a person in a sinking life raft calling to the captain of the ocean liner.

"Steph, what's wrong, baby?" Mindy said, rushing over and sinking down on the sofa next to her.

Whew.

I went outside to weed flowerbeds, leaving the gals to talk without reserve about feminine issues and pregnancy and the horrors of this technological era. As I weeded, I said a prayer of thanksgiving to Jesus Christ and the Holy Spirit of God Almighty for sending Mindy and for my sweet Cute Baby kitty cat who was affectionately rubbing against me, not saying a word, only purring. I'll never quite understand how people get along without pets.

The girls were chattering merrily and fixing some supper when I came in the back door, barely able to straighten up and hoping against hope that I hadn't overtaxed my back.

"Guess what, Rose!" Mindy greeted me. "I'm going to be Stephanie's birth coach," and they smiled at each other like husband and wife. *Thank you again, God, for Mindy.*

"And guess what else! Marie and Garfield are dating! Candlelit dinner in an Italian restaurant last night, then a walk in the park with Tramp."

"Who called you?" I asked.

"They both did, actually, about 1 a.m. our time, but I wasn't in bed. I hadn't left work until midnight and Shaquan, my co-worker, had talked me into taking home this crazy movie about Jesus—but he was named Bryan—by Python somebody, have you ever seen it? Python is sick. So it was okay with me when the phone rang with good news, which we don't usually expect in the middle of the night, do we? Garfield's working day jobs with Manpower and also doing some janitorial work at that church Pastor Sauer called for him, living at the Y still, has opened a bank account, thank you, and his next official act, according to Marie—who said it more like it was her idea than his so I don't know about this one—is to start going to AA meetings. I'm so happy I think I'll go and worship tomorrow to give God the glory."

"That would be great," I said, adding, "Why have you stayed away for the last six weeks?"

"How do you know I wasn't there last week when you were at your cousin's?"

"Were you?"

"No."

"Is something wrong or did something happen that makes you not want to come?"

"No. I just don't always get that much out of church. I'm glad it's there for me when I'm ready to go, but sometimes it seems more trouble than it's worth. I'd rather sleep in and then paint my toenails or clean or something and watch junk on TV instead."

"You're not like Grandma and me, Mindy. We can't live without the Church," Stephanie offered pensively. "Having a place to praise God, wrestle with God, wonder about God is crucial for me. I hate to think about a Sunday morning without the poetry and music and scripture and bread and wine that float around, feeding my body, mind and soul, not to mention the people.

"I want you to meet Gail, my pastor. I don't know what I would do without her and all my other church peeps since I got pregnant and Ethan and I split (pause for choking up). Alice calls a couple times a week to check on me. Jason and I get together for lunch every month, primarily to laugh. Harriet—she's ninety-two—came over the other day with bubble bath, carrot sticks and chocolate chip cookies and stayed to chat about pregnancy. They are the Church!"

Mindy smiled, nodded, and asked, "Can I still be your birth coach, even if I don't go to church every Sunday?"

"Like, uh, yeah," Steph said in her valley girl voice.

Come to think of it, Mindy didn't make it to worship this morning either. Oh, well.

Sixth Sunday after Pentecost

Deuteronomy 30:9-14
Psalm 25:1-10
Colossians 1:1-14
Luke 10:25-37

"Faith is not rocket science, friends," our guest preacher began the sermon this morning. I winced. My composition students knew better than to use clichés; I took off five points for each one unless they could justify usage on grounds of artistry or irony. However, I quickly forgave the preacher's literary transgression because of the very powerful message that followed.

"Moses was telling the people of faith who were floundering and failing in a foreign land to take heart because they know what they believe; they say it all the time, it is the Torah, the teachings, learned as children. God's law is part of their very being, written in their hearts, revealing what is true and right, what brings life and not death."

She gave us a little seminary lesson (but didn't get carried away!). The lessons for today are action-packed: the Deuteronomy passage ends with the Hebrew word for "do" while the Greek word for "do" is present at the beginning, middle and ending of the parable of the Good Samaritan in Luke. Do it! Get busy!

I thought of mission statements and why I hate them. We already know what our mission is. God has put it on our lips and in our hearts. We need to do it. Like the lawyer questioning Jesus, we don't need more information; we need to act on what we already know. I remember spending an entire Saturday at the church writing a mission statement. At the end of it, I thought, "Merciful heavens, we could have sheet-rocked a Habitat house in that time." Now that would have been a mission statement!

The preacher dovetailed the text nicely with my favorite lines from the confession: "Forgive us, renew us, and lead us, so that we may delight in your will and walk in your ways..." In other words, she observed, abundant living and true joy is what God promises; when we are truly alive, we take delight in what God wants and what God is, and we give and do as naturally as the myrtle breathes its sweet fragrance into the air, to use Kahil Gibran's image. No sacrifice. We give and do because we are loved, not so that we will be loved. We have faint glimpses, quick sensations of such a life, like the congregational meeting last week. Someday, we will know fully. Now, in this present reality, we seldom give and love unconsciously.

She was right about that! This present reality is often typified by the called circle meeting we had after worship to plan lunch for the Habitat crew next

Saturday. It was the Sloppy Joes vs. the Tuna Fishes. What a brouhaha! We settled on pizza, and I couldn't help but think of the days when people didn't think so much about what they would eat but simply ate what they had, gratefully.

Speaking of brouhaha, Pr. Sauer called around 8 o'clock last Tuesday morning and asked if I could go with him to Rutledge Home to help with Kathryn. He said she had staged a naked sit-in at the nurses' station. What??!! Kathryn?!

We were greeted by Pam Turner, my former student, St. Tim member, fine person and well-trained nurse. She briefed Pr. Sauer and me about Kathryn's behavior, which she described as atypical, oppositional, socially inappropriate, indifferent to consequences. When they had gotten her back to her room, she had put up such a resistance they couldn't dress her. Kathryn?! Pastor and I were speechless as we walked down the hallway to her room.

She was in her bed, trembling with rage.

"They----ig----nored----us," Kathryn glared, fierce and frail.

The rest of the story: This making of a radical started a few weeks earlier with her toenails. The ask-and-wait routine was not getting them trimmed, so one day she rolled herself down to the nurses' station and parked her wheelchair in front of the doorway—not an easy task with her arthritis—and declared that she was not moving until trimmed. It worked. Those on duty apologized, laughed a little, and did the job.

Then, one morning around 5:30 she heard Mitch in the next room begging to sleep later. "Sorry. We have to have you ready for breakfast before shift change," said the nursing attendant. Later, Kathryn and Mitch and a few others requested a meeting with the administrator who told them a later wake-up was impossible, for several reasonable reasons. So, fueled by her success with the toenail incident, she organized a protest. Yesterday six or seven residents walked and rolled around the nurses' station chanting, "Sleep later!"

"At first, they smiled at us condescendingly, like we were cute little children," Kathryn recounted. "Then, they decided to ignore us. They went about their business like we weren't even there and let us go round and round until we were exhausted, which didn't take long.

"I hardly slept at all last night, just lay in bed feeling foolish and powerless, asking myself what I could possibly do, handicapped by my old, crippled body. I thought of how I had once defiled my body, gone against God's laws. And then, right before dawn—I was dozing, I think—the idea came to me: 'I'll use my body for God's purpose, to relieve suffering.' I got out of my gown and into my chair [that must have taken an hour!] and put a blanket over myself and had Mitch push me down to the TV lounge. He didn't even know what I was going to do. I pulled the blanket off and had that sign in my lap," and she motioned to a piece of paper on the windowsill which said LATER SLEEPING HOURS!

"The staff was busy getting people up. As residents came to the lounge, they gathered around, and I explained the situation. When one of the staff finally saw me, pandemonium broke out. They were hollering and tripping over themselves to get me out of there, as though I were hideous—and dangerous!" and Kathryn smiled a little smile.

Pastor and I stared at each other in wonderment. I suggested Kathryn let me help her get dressed, so Pastor left the room.

"Let justice roll down like wheelchairs," I quipped, as we got her dressed, washed her face, and combed her hair.

"And righteousness like an ever-flowing dream," Kathryn quipped back.

Pastor came back in and the three of us chatted briefly, discussing possible solutions to the wake-up policy, including an offer from Pastor Sauer to mediate another meeting. When Kathryn seemed serene, we got ready to leave, and he playfully but seriously asked her if she would behave herself now.

"I'm making no promises," she replied, with a sly and determined expression.

As we departed, Pastor and I agreed that this aged activist is far more interesting than the embittered old sourpuss we've known for twenty years. But what next?!

Seventh Sunday after Pentecost

Genesis 18:1-10a
Psalm 15
Colossians 1:15-28
Luke 10:38-42

When the phone rang right as I was leaving this morning, I knew it was Virginia begging off. We had made plans last night to meet for worship.
"Sorry, Mother. This day has gotten too hectic. I've wound up with three showings!"
On the Sabbath, Charlie! Where did we go wrong!?
I'm hardly disappointed anymore. Virginia's spiritual life is on God's timeline, not mine. As it turned out, I was relieved she didn't come.
The summer choir was a disgrace to music itself, bless their hearts. Hugh Schneider read the scripture lessons. Why do they let Hugh read?! He can't read. He droned on through the amazing story of the three visitors to Abraham and Sarah and the majestic hymn to Christ in Colossians like a first grader doggedly reading through unfamiliar words. During the sermon, the acolytes slept and Lloyd worked crossword puzzles. Not exactly a picture of vitality, and Virginia needs vitality.
Also, Pastor's sermon was rather in-house, so Virginia probably would not have appreciated it. He implored us, as pastors always do, to be like Mary rather than Martha and choose the "better part."
"People of St. Timothy, if you would choose the better part, I would not be standing before you frustrated and confused as the spiritual leader of this congregation."
Oh, dear. More frustration.
"At monthly meetings, the council devotes two minutes to spiritual reflection and then three hours to repetitious discussions about housekeeping matters, very little of which are directly connected to our purpose as the Body of Christ. St. Paul urges us to embody the hope of glory, to share the nature and purpose of our God with the whole hurting, groaning creation, to interpret the mystery of Christ's presence and love to those who know nothing about it.
"Let me be clear—the work of hospitality is vital. I love our dinners as much as anyone," he said, patting his middle-aged paunch, "and I appreciate how well our building is maintained. But let us not attend to these tasks with more vim and vigor than we put forth in worship, in studying the Scripture, and in meaningful wrestling to connect our faith to everyday, everywhere, everything, everyone."
So here we are on a tightrope between last week's directive to DO—a la Martha—and this week's directive to be still, listen, learn, like Mary. I must say,

though, balancing acts in the life of faith make sense to me. "Lord, Speak to Us, that We May Speak."

As for the frustration and confusion of our spiritual leader, we'll keep those prayers coming. I hope the Sauer's two-week vacation coming up will be restful and help him shake this sense of desperation he seems to be feeling. Granted, I would probably feel desperate too, if I were in his collar. Four more families have left St. Timothy.

Madge stopped me after the service to ask about Garfield. I told her what little I had heard over the last month or so: the beginnings of a reconciliation with Marie, steady work, a bank account, involvement at the church.

"Sounds like we've saved him, Rose!" she bubbled, then added piously, "By the power of the Holy Spirit." My St. Lord, Madge.

Last night I fixed sirloin tips with green pepper and onion over rice, Florence's favorite, and popped in with it after worship today. She ate a little, to please me, but didn't want much because of the horrible metallic taste in her mouth from the chemotherapy. She has had a pretty good week, and while I was there, Sarah and her daughter, Angelica, arrived. They will help a lot, and Florence is always glad to see them come—and leave. Continuous argumentative banter is their m.o., she says. Angelica presents as a pierced, tattooed, fluorescent blue-haired, unhappy teen-ager.

"I don't care about any of that," Florence says. "I just wish we could carry on an intelligent conversation, but she's too sullen and angry. She is so different from the two older ones, and who knows why? Angel, as they call her—I've always thought that was part of the problem right there—took her parents' divorce much harder than Clay and Allison. She was at a more tender age. Sarah spoiled her horribly, and Bill was usually away. Right from the beginning, Angelica was a demanding little girl no one enjoyed too much."

I hope they manage to have a good week. Cute Baby and I will mosey through the Sunday paper now, and, with any luck, "sleep, perchance to dream." I've been staying up too late—the Cubs are in California. I'll probably head back to the church later for the ice cream social.

Later

Wow. I don't know about dreaming, but I surely did sleep! The next thing I knew, Stephen was shaking my shoulder and talking about ice cream which seemed completely ludicrous because I had been in such a deep slumber that I didn't know where I was or what day or time it was. I stared dumbly at him laughing at me before I could figure things out.

At the social, he and I sat at a table with Aunt Polly and Danny and the Sauers. The social doubled as Aunt Polly's 90th birthday party, and we had brought money gifts in denominations of 9 (instructed through the St. Timothy Telegraph) to give in her honor to her favorite cause, the Church's fund for world hunger. $1,134.18! She looked beautiful in an orange pants suit and coordinated lipstick but was suffering with a nasty summer cold.

Carolyn seemed to be feeling her last name (Sauer). I asked where they were going on their vacation, and some truth came out, with a bite.

"Well," she said sharply, "Marcus has decided that a meeting scheduled at the last minute is more important than the vacation we've had scheduled for six months, so he'll be joining us for whatever time is left. First things first, you know."

"C-C-Carolyn, don't you love P-P-Pastor anymore?" Danny blurted.

Brittany said crossly, "Danny, you talk too much."

Pastor stared into his ice cream.

Okay, that's it, I decided right then and there. I'm calling Pastor tonight.

Stephen and I talked about Pastor on the way home; he's concerned too, naturally, but what to do? Plus, Stephen has bigger matters on his mind—he is moving to Chicago! He has no choice if he wants to stay with his company. Plus, he admits he is attracted to making a fresh start.

Fie! I understand that a fresh start can be wonderful, and I would never say a word to make Stephen have a second thought about moving, if that's what he really wants. I'm excited for him. But drat, I will miss him.

Later

I called Pastor and he's coming over Tuesday afternoon. *Gosh, I wish you could be here, Charlie. You gave Pastor wise counsel on several occasions. I don't know what I'm getting into. Come to think of it, I don't even know what to say to him.*

"You seem a little whacked-out these days. Something wrong?"

Or maybe, "You need to pull yourself together. Can I help?"

Maybe let him direct the conversation. "Pastor, how do you feel things are going at St. Timothy?" But whatever is going on with him is about more than congregational matters, I suspect.

Maybe just, "How's everything going, Pastor?" Non-judgmental, open-ended.

You had a way of accepting Marcus Sauer as he is, Charlie, and valuing his gifts while recognizing his shortcomings. You could be both frank and kind. Like when he wanted to have the Easter Sunrise service in the graveyard at 5:24 a.m., technical, scientific sunrise.

"Pastor, that's a fine idea you have," you told him. "God surely appreciates it. But Pastor, the people won't appreciate it. Now, God knows you love him because God knows your heart; you don't have to prove your

devotion to God. But the people, Pastor, are yours to love, too. They don't know your heart, they don't have that power; you have to demonstrate your love in your actions. Asking them to get up at 4 o'clock in the morning and go into a dark, wet, cold graveyard does not come across as loving and caring."

Oh, my wise little Charlie, a man of few words, but when you spoke, people listened and thought. How I miss you, especially at times like these. I will rely on the presence of your sweet spirit Tuesday afternoon.

Eighth Sunday after Pentecost

Genesis 18:20-32
Psalm 138
Colossians 2:6-15
Luke 11:1-13

This morning's preacher ignored the lectionary altogether and told a rambling story about what God had called him to do over the years, and then sat down at the piano and played and sang a religious song you'd hear on an elevator. Nothing he had to say grasped me nor was I able to grasp on to anything. I noticed Mercedes nodding in agreement at everything he said and finally realized that she's developing some palsy-type activity.

And alas, Garfield's fallen off the wagon in St. Louis.

The only meaningful part of the service for me was the bread and the wine, and that was enough. As I knelt to receive, gratitude for Tuesday afternoon with Pastor flooded through me.

I had started out, "Well, how are things going, Pastor?"

He bowed his head and closed his eyes, his normally square shoulders hunched. He began mumbling, and I leaned across the kitchen table trying to catch his words.

"Major conflicts...congregation...people leaving...marriage...shambles...don't know if...not the real problem... the real problem is...is..." His chest began heaving and his face twisted.

"Rose," he gasped, "I think I'm losing my faith."

"Get out of here, you bum!" I wanted to say.

I wouldn't have minded a little enigmatic smile with a soft-spoken, 'I have my doubts, even if I am ordained.' That would just validate his humanness; I could relate to that, easily accept that. But don't come at me with tears and agonized, breathless silence. For God's sake, you're my spiritual leader, my pastor! I'm the one who needs comfort and reassurance from you! Part of me sat across the table from him in love and silence, and another part of me ran out the back door.

More mumbles.

"...no good to anyone...totally inadequate...a pitiful example of humanity...

"Who am I to suggest to anyone how to live or what to do or what God is like— I don't know what God is like!" he yelled, angrily throwing his hands in the air.

"My ego is a jumble of pulses in my brain that will not stop, will not stop, constantly taunting me with guilt, shaming me with accusations of phoniness and hypocrisy. I measure my every step, each thought, each action, and pass judgment

—was it appropriate, proper, genuine, acceptable? Could I have done better? Should I have said that? Should I not have said that?! I am in hell."

I waited, feeling strangely distant from his agony, acutely aware that Christ was in our midst, that the Holy Spirit was very present with peace and insight. These painful, uncomfortable moments were holy.

"I am viewed as inadequate by members of the church," he went on, "because I can't cover all the bases; I miss a meeting, I don't return a phone call, I didn't know someone was in the hospital. Any and all of these transgressions may well result in someone leaving the congregation. My wife finds me inadequate because I'm at the church too much and neglect my family. Everybody's right! I can't do it all!"

He buried his head in his arms on the table. Cute Baby hurried across the room and jumped into his lap. He shot up, his arms forming a circle around his head. She marched up his chest and patted his cheek with her paw, looking earnestly into his face. He pushed her off onto the floor. She padded back towards the den, turning and giving him one last, concerned look as she exited. He sat with his elbows on the table and his face in his hands for a few quiet moments, then heaved a sigh that seemed deep enough to turn him inside out and wiped his face with a napkin.

"Pastor, drink," I said, pouring tea and offering cucumber sandwiches. Silent together in our thoughts, we drank and nibbled.

"Sometimes I think my beliefs are based primarily in a refusal to accept that there is no God. Is my belief that Jesus Christ fully reveals and expresses the reality of God grounded in my very being or am I grasping and clinging to that belief because the alternative is unacceptable?"

"Grasping and clinging is how human beings get through life, each of us deciding what we want to grasp and cling to."

"I'm hanging by a thread, Rose."

"A holy thread, Pastor, a strong thread provided by the Holy Spirit," I said, remembering several occasions when the roles had been reversed and Pastor had said something similar to me in the midst of one of my attacks of doubt.

We relaxed into conversation about our feelings of inadequacy, times of closeness to God, times of distance. Our minds sparked off each other's thoughts, quoting poetry, remembering tidbits we'd heard on the radio or read, describing movies and plays that had stuck with us. When we'd finished off the pot of tea and devoured the food, we took a bathroom break.

After a minute of arguing with myself about whether or not to, I opened a bottle of wine to mark the uniqueness of the occasion and offered my oatmeal-raisin-pecan cookies, the best ever, in my humble opinion. We talked on and on, about—icons, Shakespeare, country music ("Seems like I can't talk to God without yelling anymore..."), Charlie, Carolyn, Garfield (needs to get to AA, needs to write songs), Madge (love but don't like), homosexuality, heterosexuality—with much laughter, and a few tears.

When is the last time I laughed that much? With Charlie gone and Florence out of commission and Stephen preoccupied with moving and Stephanie preoccupied with pregnancy, I hadn't realized how laughing has dwindled in my life lately.

"Well, Rose, what shall I do?" Pastor interjected abruptly. "Share your vast treasure store of wisdom."

I was actually feeling a little wise.

"Start with your family," was my advice.

"Verite in vino" gave way to disclosures back and forth about the challenges of marriage and intimacy.

We were astounded when the clock struck five. A funny look crossed his face.

"Oh, wow—I was supposed to lead a Bible study for Dorcas Circle at 3 o'clock. Now I guess two or three of them will transfer to Community Fellowship. Oh, well, I'll just tell them I was boozing it up with Rose Harris and time got away from me."

Ha!

And then, "Rose, would you pray for me?"

The part of me who had run out the back door thought, "I can't do this," but the other part of me got up, walked around the table, put my hands on his shoulders and tried to pray a bold prayer for mercy.

Good and gracious God, we know your love and trust your mercy and yet we forget and feel alone and overwhelmed. Look upon your servant, Marcus, in his doubt, in his worry, and help him to be aware in each aspect of his life, of your presence and power. Help him to see your divine nature at work in the details of his circumstances as well as throughout the cosmos. Renew his spirit so that he might run and not be weary, walk and not faint. In the name of Jesus Christ, your child, our Redeemer. Amen.

Now, they're on vacation.

Please, God, may they sense your presence and guidance each moment, to get them through these troubled times. Help them play. Amen.

Ninth Sunday after Pentecost

Ecclesiastes 1:2, 12-14; 2:18-23
Psalm 49:1-12
Colossians 3:1-11
Luke 12:13-21

Vanity of vanities, indeed. Should we ever delude ourselves into thinking that our efforts will save the world, we can look back to this sabbath day to know the folly of such a thought. Rarely does a series of crazy bloopers like this morning's occur in one simple worship service.

The guest preacher made an announcement before the service that we could not understand at all, but we figured out from her gestures and the intermittent croaking noise she was making that she had unexpectedly lost her voice. As she walked back down the aisle to assemble for the procession, the small summer crowd sat there with blank looks of expectation (if that's possible).

The processional hymn—"The God of Abram Praise," verses 1, 5, 6, 8, and 11—was understandably a fiasco. Even Lloyd got lost and came in with a thundering chord to start the last verse after we had already sung it.

Louie Smith was assisting minister for only the second or third time and was so nervous his hymnal was shaking. He got mixed up and prayed the offertory prayer instead of the prayer of the day, which would not have been a big deal except that after he sat down he came back front and center and said, "I have to apologize. I think I said the wrong prayer just now. Here's the right one," and then prayed the offertory prayer a second time, bowed to the people instead of the altar, and sat down again, red-faced.

The first line of the sermon was, "After we have rendered unto God what is God's and loved our neighbors as ourselves, we are to eat and to drink and to be merry." From there on, it was a hoarse and raspy message with frequent pauses for water. Idolatry was mentioned a few times and bigger barns were compared to 3-, 4-, and 5-car garages. We all heard the word "balance" clearly, because as the preacher was emphasizing with her hands that following God's will provides balance in our lives, she nearly stepped off the back of the pulpit platform, teetering for a moment. As soon as she smiled, pent-up tension billowed out in laughter.

A little boy whom I don't know played a 2-line piano beginner's arrangement called "Bells Are Ringing" from Beethoven's 9th during the offertory and had three false starts before finishing. Precious! We wanted to clap but naturally restrained ourselves, smiling broadly and whispering our delight instead.

Then, as Louie came forward to receive the offering, his cincture/belt came loose and trailed like a snake behind him until someone in the choir reached out and grabbed it as he went by. We joined him in the offertory prayer, the words quite familiar by now.

Communion was lovely, our guest officiant whisper/croaking, "Brother/Sister, the Body of Christ, given for you," and Louie nervously pouring the Blood of Christ into our tiny glasses, careful not to spill a drop. And then, the craziest blooper of all. As the pastor was wiping out the sterling silver chalice after communion, it fell apart! The stem and pedestal are apparently connected to the bowl with a rod and a bolt. The bolt had worked loose and parts fell onto the floor with a clink-clank-clunk as she stood looking at the bowl in her hand and then down at the jumble on the floor. We shared an oh-brother-what-next? chuckle, and she and Louie picked up the pieces and covered them with altar linen.

In the midst of all this, it seemed fitting for Louella to choose this day to protest the coolness of the air conditioning by sitting up front wrapped in a blanket. Fine, but why her old Navajo picnic blanket out of the trunk of her car with leaves and debris clinging to it? Couldn't she at least have worn a new quilt from the quilting circle?!

So, nine weeks after celebrating the coming of the Holy Spirit in wind and flame to inspire us and assure us of salvation, we seem to be off balance again. We are keenly aware of and embarrassed by our liturgical efforts which mirror our efforts in the world— but we survived. God's name was glorified, Body and Blood did their work, and we went in peace to love and serve the Lord. Thanks be to God!

And Mindy decided to show up, which is always a deep blessing for me. She thoroughly enjoyed the proceedings, unlike Madge who was clucking around about what a shame it all was and she wished she'd been assisting minister. Vanity of vanities...

"Goof-ups are the rule for me, not the exception," Mindy observed after the service. "You know I come from royalty, as far as dysfunction goes. I'm only a princess though, not a queen. That would be Regina, with Cindy next in line to the throne," she chattered under the oak tree where we were visiting comfortably, despite harsh sun and high temperatures.

"By the way, I went to see Kathryn the other day. I can't believe her! 'God is my guide,' she kept saying when I was asking her about her protests and all. 'God is my guide,' she'd say with a little smile. And did you hear that they're going to get to sleep later?"

Yes, I had heard. The Holy Spirit apparently moved the hearts of the powerful—after three more ancients threatened to stage naked sit-ins, one of whom has a great-nephew who is a reporter for The Evening Gazette.

"How's Stephanie?" I asked, knowing Mindy had seen her since I had.

"She's very sad, Rose. I don't know if you realize how much she loves Ethan."

I was startled. I've been thinking "good riddance" in regard to Ethan. Rose! how can you be so dense, insensitive, short-sighted?! Did you think your smart, healthy, independent granddaughter would welcome a man into the most intimate parts of her life without loving him passionately? You've been treating their relationship as though it were a high school romance. Wake up and get beyond your narrow viewpoint!

Next, Mindy informed me, "Garfield called again. He wants me to come and get him, Rose. He says he can't make it."

I remember staring into heat shimmers and having nothing to say.

"I told him no," she continued. "He cried over the phone. Said he can't stand himself, that 'if being a fool were cool, he'd be the hippest guy in town' and kept putting himself down. I'm pretty sure he's not taking his meds. He got in a fight and got kicked out of the Y."

"What about Marie?" I asked.

"She told him she'd meet him at AA anytime he wanted her to, but that's all she could promise. So I said to him, 'OK, fool, then what's the problem? Go. Meet her at AA. That's easy.' 'Nothing is easy for me,' he shot back and said I didn't understand his life at all."

She sighed, and we headed for our cars, and when we got there, we hugged hard and long and went our separate ways.

God of power and might, of love and wisdom, shine your face upon Garfield Temple like a searchlight on high beam. Force him to know that he is safe, that Christ gave up his life so that he, Garfield, can truly live. Make him believe in his heart that if he will just keep on through the foggy misery of his mornings, the fog will lift, his heart will lighten, he will be able to persevere. Help him recognize the love that so many have for him and help him to be strengthened by it. Guide those of us who care about him to do what we can, by your grace and for your purpose. Amen.

Florence is feeling so much better after being off the chemo that she almost came to worship this morning! I'd seen her perking up all week, which perks me up. Virginia and I spent a couple hours with her this afternoon. We made peach milkshakes and sat on her back porch after a thunderstorm had cooled the air. Virginia and I told her about Aunt Polly's glorious funeral yesterday. As the saying goes, she preached her own funeral sermon by the way she lived. Pastor Koch, on duty for us while Pr. Sauer is gone, had called me and a few others to get some personal stories about Aunt Polly. The human linchpin of the sermon was her relationship with Gary, and merciful heavens, Gary was there, crying his eyes out and wiping his nose, attendants on either side of him. Here's the five-year-old news clip I saved:

Local Woman Beaten

Mrs. Pauline Woknovich, 337 N. Cypress, was found unconscious in her home this morning with injuries consistent with having been beaten. She was admitted to Baker Memorial Hospital where she remains listed in stable but serious condition.

Police investigators report no evidence of forced entry and suspect the assailant was an acquaintance. There is evidence of theft. Anyone who has any information that may be helpful to this investigation, please call 437-9340.

Everybody knew Gary had done it. What a sad turn of events in their remarkable story of friendship. Aunt Polly seemed to tame the wildness of Gary's inner turmoil. His dual diagnosis for developmental delay and mental illness have kept him in and out of institutions since his teen years. People were amazed how he settled down when he started working for Aunt Polly. His ability to do odd jobs and his helpful spirit were just exactly what she needed, but everything fell apart that hot autumn day. Aunt Polly said he'd been raking leaves.

I remember they caught him pretty quickly, hiding in his dad's garage. Aunt Polly ordered that he be brought to her hospital room. "He needs to see what he's done," she said. Gary was sincerely and grievously sorry for his offenses. Aunt Polly didn't press charges. A month later he beat her up again and was unpredictably violent thereafter, landing in the high security section of the state mental health center. He and his dad still went to Aunt Polly's for Thanksgiving every year, joining in with her family. She visited him once a week, up until taking pneumonia recently.

Aunt Polly had no fear of death. More than once I've heard her say that she had died and was raised in Christ at her baptism. For her, eternal life was in full swing right here and now. What amazing transcendence for a woman who I doubt ever traveled out of the state. Reminds me of Julius Caesar: "It seems most strange that men should fear, seeing that death, a necessary end, will come when it will come." Add faith to that philosophical resignation and fear makes a hasty exit.

Lydia Circle served the funeral meal. We went all out, making our very best recipes; after all, it was Aunt Polly. I made my extra rich pineapple upside-down cake with real whipped cream. Carolyn brewed fresh mint iced tea. I think everybody drank at least three glasses of it. And, indeed, it was a fine celebration of a life well-lived, a pleasurable party which affirmed life itself. To God be the glory.

Tenth Sunday after Pentecost

Genesis 15:1-6
Psalm 33:12-22
Hebrews 11:1-3, 8-16
Luke 12:32-40

When I was a child I would sometimes feel an overwhelming desire to go home even though I was at home. I would be looking in the mirror brushing my hair or lying in bed waking up or curled in the big chair in the music room reading when an eerie, melancholic longing to go home would come over me like a cloud covering the sun. Without a moment's notice, I longed with a physical yearning that sometimes made me cry for a home that was not to be found in this world, and yet part of that very longing included the fantastic knowledge that someday I would find such a home. Then, the cloud would pass over and the sun would shine normally again. I don't think I've ever told anyone about these episodes, but Pastor's sermon this morning made me feel once again that he and I are soul mates.

"Have you ever had a longing to be at home even when you were at home?" he asked. "Or have you ever felt at home when you were far removed from your house?"

Abraham and Sarah, he pointed out, abandoned any traditional notion of home. Time and again, they moved on to parts unknown with no clear destination in mind. Home moves into the heart at such times, Pastor suggested. To be at home in the Lord is to feel some measure of contentment and peace even when we can't sleep in our own bed. To feel at home in the Lord places life on a new level.

Sometimes it's hard to feel "at home" even in worship. We were passing the peace this morning and everything was moving along just fine, when suddenly, there were three false starts right in a row, hands sticking out in midair. We all froze for a second and then sat down and looked straight ahead without saying a word. We just gave up! Merciful heavens, it was hilarious, even though no one laughed. The mess-up didn't do much good for the cause of passing the peace, I guess. Some still don't like the peace much, but we're good sports, and we keep trying. Pastor Sauer has grounded the experience in the ancient tradition of making peace with each other before going to the altar for communion, a time of *shalom*—the abiding peace that only God can give. It's not just chat time—"Hi, how are you? Is your cold better?" or "Let's go out to eat Thursday." No. "May the peace of the Lord be with you" means, "Susie and Pete, I wish for you the comfort of God's peace even though your son was killed last year, and you can hardly get out of bed some mornings because the pain is so intense." Passing the peace is about being at home with each other and with God.

Another silly incident—Mary Johnson's shoes made me think of Mr. Ivensen trying to police the acolytes into wearing black oxfords years ago. He took his job as acolyte coordinator very seriously and served for many years with an attitude of great reverence. I didn't like the children's sneakers and sandals sticking out under their gowns too much myself, but I didn't think it was that important. But Mr. Ivensen did, and persisted until black oxfords were required, and then we had a terrible time getting acolytes. He did it himself, half the time. Anyway, there I was, kneeling at the altar with my head bowed, trying to think holy thoughts, and here comes Mary Johnson picking up the communion glasses wearing patent leather shoes that look like a piano keyboard. I couldn't help smiling at her. She smiled back, but I don't think she knew I was laughing at her shoes.

I'm glad to have Pastor and Carolyn back from vacation. She and Deedee were talking and I came up behind them and put my arms around their shoulders and quickly asked, "Good vacation?" She nodded and smiled, but I saw mixed reviews in her expression.

Well—the phone just rang and it was Garfield. A surprise. He was upbeat but I fear he protesteth too much. The conversation went something like this:

G: Hello, Rose. Is that you?
R: Yes, Garfield. I understand you're having some tough times.
G: For a while there I was. I even called Mindy and asked her to come and get me; I was feeling a little homesick for Shippensforge, I guess. That's pretty desperate, isn't it? Ha ha! But I'm A-OK, now, I'm on the up side of down. Tell everybody not to worry about me. I swear I'm going to fly right through this storm with You-Know-Who as my co-pilot. Wait a minute, I'm the co-pilot, he's the pilot, let's get that straight. Yeah, Rose, I was back drinking and things were going downhill fast. But, you know, "the drinking bones connected to the lonely bone," and I don't want lonely, I want Marie, so I've pulled myself together, with God's help. And God works through AA, I'm here to tell you that. Tell Stephen I'm in AA. He'll be glad. Marie's standing by her man. I'm going to be alright, okay? Tell everyone I'm going to be A-OK. I'm going to AA every night, that's what you have to do sometimes, and I'll be going every night until I'm out of the danger zone. You still there?
R: Yes, I'm here. I'm happy you're in AA. Going every night sounds like an excellent idea. And, yes, those people are from God. My father joined in the '30s when AA was brand new. They'll help you hold steady until you really are steady. And remember, bad days are usually followed by good days; believe me, I know. Don't give up, Garfield!
G: No. Never. I'm good, I'm A-OK.

Another pleasantry or two and we hung up. I kept thinking about Garfield and people like him. In his soft and tender voice, our Lord, Jesus the Christ, calls us to come home, to be at home in the miraculous love of God. Oh, wanderers! Wanderers of the world, who don't know where you're going or why, turn toward this voice that calls out to you, follow its bidding and find peace, find joy, find hope for each tomorrow. *Thank you, God, for the life-saving, life-giving people of Alcoholics Anonymous. Amen.*

People like Stan Wampler and his wife, June. What good people they were. Who were Dad's other AA buddies? It's hard to remember; they were not around often—usually just during crises—strange, off balance times. Merciful heavens, I remember the morning after the fire like it was yesterday...

"Well, kids, your illustrious father burned down his newspaper office last night," Dad announced to Dwayne and me as we were eating breakfast. "That's the kind of father you have, a no-brained fool who doesn't have enough sense to..."

"Clarence," Mother said, "don't..."

"Don't what, Helen?! I've already done it, I've done it now," and I think he was crying, and she gently guided him out of the kitchen and up the stairs and my stomach did confused somersaults.

When she came back down, she explained that Dad had been working late at the office and had fallen asleep at his desk and his cigarette had started a fire.

"Don't talk about it, children," I remember her saying. "You'll only make him feel worse."

A while later, I was sitting in the big chair on the front porch when Stan and June came. I quickly pulled my thumb out of my mouth, wiping it on my shorts, and sat up straight. I watched as they walked up the little hill and the front step, Stan balding and wiry, and June, hefty, huffing and puffing behind him. He rapped on the front door and walked in calling, "Anybody home?" June knelt down and pulled me to her ample bosom.

"How are you doing, little Rose?"

I was uncomfortable because I hardly knew her, but also comforted, and I squeaked out, "Okay."

"Your father is a good man," she said looking me in the eyes. I nodded. She hugged me again and went in. I walked around the yard for awhile and then edged in the back door into the kitchen, Dwayne behind me. The four of them were sitting around the kitchen table, the Editor holding his head in his hands. Stan reached over and put his hand on Dad's shoulder, but before I could catch any of their murmurings, Mother told us to go outside...

Those childhood memories are edged with wonder—at their love, I now realize, and how they came around at the worst, stinking times, frail, wounded people banding together to support each other in their frailty and woundedness, "Little Christs," all of them, whether they knew it or not. "What wondrous love is this, O my soul!"

I'm feeling pretty low tonight, worried about Garfield, afraid I'll have a third almost sleepless night; seems like a glass of wine might help, but how can I, after just thinking about how alcohol ruins so many lives. The thing is, when I drink a little alcohol, my mind is opened, on fire in the most fabulous way, and I am unafraid. So, yes, I will have a pleasant glass of wine to take the edge off my stress, and thank God for it.

In regard to Garfield, and everything else, I shall close this day of sabbath rest with Reinhold Niebuhr's serenity prayer:

God, give us grace to accept with serenity the things that cannot be changed, courage to change the things which should be changed, and the wisdom to distinguish the one from the other. Amen.

Eleventh Sunday after Pentecost

Jeremiah 23:23-29
Psalm 82
Hebrews 11: 29-12:2
Luke 12:49-56

"Rose!" Danny yelled at me from across the parking lot as I got out of my car this morning. "C-c-ome and look at the t-t-tree. It's not there!"

He raced over and pulled me by my arm to the center of the lot where the oak had stood until a thunderbolt unbelievably sheared its trunk of a foot-wide strip of bark from top to bottom in the early hours of Tuesday morning. The whole town was awakened by the storm; "All the foundations of the earth were shaken," it seemed. After seeing the damage, even those who wanted to preserve the tree at any cost knew there was no hope.

I joined the spectator crowd with my lawn chair for a few hours on Thursday to witness the amazing spectacle of the death of so great a life. The arbor specialists started at the top in their cherry picker and worked their way down, sectioning off the leafy branches one by one, and then cutting down the huge trunk in chunks.

Late Saturday afternoon when the job was almost finished, Pastor held a little service. The workers stood aside, hats in hand, while we counted the rings (107), read Psalm 96, reflected together about trees—the tree of life, Christ was lifted up on a tree, and so forth. Louella recited Joyce Kilmer beautifully as dusk crept across us—all in the name of the Father, the Son, and the Holy Spirit. Then, the workers ground the stump until, at dark, its dust mixed with the good earth. By next Sunday we will have glistening black macadam with white parking lines, and newcomers will have no personal knowledge of our tree.

Praise to the Lord, the Almighty, that the great oak controversy in the congregation was over and reconciliation prevailed before this cataclysmic event occurred. To everyone's credit, no one claimed the lightning strike as an act of God except the insurance company.

I think if the tree's spirit could talk, it would say to us, "Perhaps you will think of me occasionally and of our sharing of life and death. Perhaps I might inspire you with the thoughts that greatness comes from that which is small and ordinary, like an acorn, that change is inevitable, that adversity is part of existence, and that the best we can do is stand tall and share our beauty with the world. And if you look at the space which once was mine and think of me, perhaps you will give profound thanks for God's creation, which it has been our delight to share." Farewell, old friend.

The opening words of Pastor's sermon this morning were, "Jesus' incarnate presence is no picnic." He doesn't have to tell me. I understand "mother against her daughter and daughter against her mother." Yesterday Barry answered when I called Virginia to see if she wanted to come to the tree ceremony.

"I don't believe you people! A funeral for a tree! Rose, I love you like a mother, but you are downright unbalanced when it comes to church. You get involved with all these misfits, you give away your money when you might need it in your last days. How many times were you at the church last week?"

"Five," I responded weakly after a quick mental tally.

"The week before?" he demanded.

"That's enough, Barry. Where I spend my time and money and with whom I choose to associate is my business."

"If I have to shell out to keep you in a nursing home, it will unfortunately become my business."

Ye gods.

"I apologize, Rose," he quickly went on. "I didn't mean that the way it sounded. It's just that you church people are crazy. You live a life of delusion that messes up other lives. I honestly think the world would be better off if organized religion disappeared tomorrow, along with all of its corruption, greed, and hypocrisy."

"Barry, all that I do and give and think is not for an institution, it's for God," I said, knowing that he couldn't/wouldn't even begin to understand what I was saying.

"Whatever. I'll give Gin the message, but I'm sure she won't want any part of it."

He then asked how I was doing, and we had a few minutes of pleasant conversation. Pleasant, but not so very meaningful, diminished by my acute sense of the gulf that exists between Virginia/Barry and me. Virginia once said to me point blank that she has always resented my allegiance to the Church. I tried to convey to her on that occasion that my allegiance is to God—the Creator, the Christ, the Spirit. To me, the Church is the Father's vehicle, the Son's body, the Holy Spirit's ballroom, not an end in itself.

"Okay, then, I'm jealous of Jesus. It's all the same to me," she sassed.

The burden to bear for modern people of faith in our culture, I think, is not discrimination or persecution but rather the indifference of those around us to the Body of Christ. "Spirituality is wise but religion is stupid" seems to be a popular contemporary attitude.

This morning, Pastor preached that we will inevitably know alienation from others as people of God, both within and outside of the corpus Christi. In response, there is nothing that a Christian should want more than shalom, the peace of God among and for all.

"Pursue peace with everyone. Standing as we do in a great cloud of witnesses [including people who have been sawn in half, for Christ's sake!], don't drop out, cop out, burn out, or lay out, but rather, let us 'lift our drooping hands and strengthen our weak knees' to persevere as God's people."

Pastor reminded us that as a community and as individuals we are called to make sure that "no one fails to obtain the grace of God," that "no root of bitterness" poisons the community, and that no one gives up faith and becomes "an immoral and godless person."

Easier said than done, I say to Pr. Sauer and to the author of Hebrews. Ha! As if they don't know that!

I'll bet I wasn't the only one who thought of Franklin and Janet Lawson when Pastor talked of people giving up the faith. We were delighted when they joined St. Timothy because we finally had black members; most of us yearn with a deep longing for diversity. They were the only African Americans in town except for that lovely white-haired man who was produce manager at the grocery store. Franklin had a great spirit, and Janet's cheerfulness, sharpness, and hard work transformed our kids' programs. She was fabulous with children, very creative. Then, she got caught up in the re-location controversy and ran for parish council on a platform of re-locating out on the by-pass. When she was narrowly defeated, she and Franklin stayed involved for a while, but gradually withdrew. Everybody was heartsick when they stopped coming. How many of us went to them, time after time, when they left St. Timothy? I think Claudia still keeps in touch with Janet.

We called on them when they went inactive, remember Charlie? Remember how we struggled to get our courage up even to do it? Who were we to be butting into someone's private life?! But who are any of us in the Body of Christ if we don't care enough to risk offending people in the name of love?

We had tried to schedule a visit, but when they kept putting us off, we decided to drop in unannounced. I remember climbing the steps of the old Victorian house they'd restored. The steps were gray with yellow, burgundy, and lilac accents. Merciful heavens, I remember it like it was yesterday...

Charlie and I looked at each other apprehensively. He took a quick breath and punched the doorbell which chimed coldly. Franklin answered the door.
"Why Rose and Charlie, what a surprise."
Awkward moment.
"May we come in, Franklin?" I said.
He looked me in the eye, hesitated, smiled. "Certainly," and he stepped back and opened the door.
"Janet's not home," he explained as we walked into the sitting room. "She's working late."

Never one to beat around the bush, Charlie said, "We miss you at St Timothy's. What's wrong?"

Franklin tried to make light of the situation. "The truth probably is we got overly involved too fast," he commented with a strained chuckle. "Then, there's the sleeping- in thing on Sunday, our only chance. By ten o'clock, we're both in our offices. Since Janet took the assistant superintendent position, she just can't dance fast enough, you know? I'm trying to make a go of my own law practice. It's all just a matter of shifting priorities. Nothing's wrong."

We knew better than that. Janet had gotten involved with that circuit court judge, Heineman; the affair was no secret.

"Franklin, we've heard you and Janet may be having some problems, and we want you both to know how much we love you. We want to help if there is anything we can do," I said.

"You need to be in church, Franklin," Charlie said.

Franklin's expression was hard to read, a mixture of emotions. He slid forward on the edge of the sofa, rested his arms on his thighs, clasped his hands together, and looked down. Before he could reply, a door in the back of the house opened and closed. Janet's heels clicked across the wood floor and she entered the room behind us, facing Franklin, who kept his head down.

"Why it's Rose and Charlie," she said after a brief pause and came around the sofa to grasp our hands. "How are you both? It's wonderful to see you. What brings you by?"

"Because we miss you so much at church, Janet. We all do. We want to be sure you know that."

"I appreciate everyone's kindness, I really do," she began as she sank into a chair, kicked her pumps off, and launched into her story of having invested so much of herself in the congregation and then feeling rejected when she wasn't elected. She had thought of herself as a dove of peace, she said, and got shot down.

"My sense is that St, Timothy, by and large, just doesn't want to grow. They're content to sit there downtown, landlocked and static. That doesn't work for me. I am a growing, living organism; if I'm not growing, I'm dying! I've got to experience life to the fullest, every minute of it. I've got to pack it full and reach out and constantly discover new people and new ideas and new places. Status quo stifles me, I find routines deadly, there's a huge world out there waiting..."

Franklin rose and excused himself and trudged quietly up the stairs. Janet bowed her head for a moment, then looked up at us.

"Franklin and I are going through a difficult time; we've grown apart; he doesn't understand me..."

"He's a good man," Charlie said quietly, "and you've made a vow to be faithful."

"It's time for you to go," Janet said, standing up.

"Janet, find a church, even if it's not St. Timothy," I pleaded. "You need a place where your spirit can grow along with the rest of you."

She had opened the front door. We went out without another word, and the door swiftly closed. Charlie squeezed my arm as he opened the car door for me...

Franklin and Janet moved back into the city shortly thereafter. Franklin's law practice is apparently doing well; I read about him in the paper occasionally. Janet is assistant superintendent of a school district west of here. She's married twice since her and Franklin's divorce ten years ago. I still miss them, two beautiful people whose lives are in God's gracious hands but lost to the community of believers, I fear, at least for the moment.

Okay, time to wrap this up—after the service, Mindy and I compared notes on Garfield, agreeing that he sounded too good to be true. At least his news is good rather than bad. She had talked with Marie, who is hopeful but cautious. Madge was assisting minister this morning and prayed: "Oh Father God, make us your instruments to show mercy to all your wandering and wayward children with mixed-up hearts and minds, that they may find their way back to you, especially Garfield Temple."

Yes, dear God. Please. Amen.

The Day of Garfield's Death (entered Sat. August 24)

I was getting ready to go work at the food pantry. I had practiced at piano, eaten toast and tea, weeded for a few minutes in the cool dew when the dirt gives way so easily to the tug on the roots. I had just gotten out of the shower when the phone rang.

"Hello," I said, not expecting anything untoward.

"Rose, he did it," Mindy said.

My mind screeched to a halt. I took in a slow breath through my nose, my eyes fixed on a hummingbird on the deck.

"Garfield?"

"Yes."

Silence. What to say? It was over. Garfield was over.

"I told him to, Rose."

"Told him to what?"

"Told him to kill himself."

"What do you mean?! Why?! Mindy, make some sense!"

"Rose, can you come over? My car won't start," she said shakily.

I called the church to leave word for Pr. Sauer, dressed, jumped in my car and—I am not kidding—the "William Tell Overture" blared out from the radio the instant I turned the ignition key; I jabbed the off button. In five minutes, Pastor and I were sitting in Mindy's living room.

"He called around 6:30 this morning, totally whacked out, drunk out of his mind, strung out too maybe," she began. "He rambled on that it was no use, he couldn't take it anymore, he should never have been born—his tired old song and dance. He had the gun, he had the bullets. Then, he hung up. I was going to call Marie, but before I could find her number, he called back.

"This time he kept saying good-bye and thank you. He told me to tell people good-bye and thank them and named about a dozen names—you two, Sid, Stephen. 'Tell everybody good-bye and thank you,' he said. I told him I was going to call Marie and there would be help on the way. He hung up again.

"I quick called Marie, and she said she would call the police and try to get to him. A minute later Garfield called again, all agitated and completely irrational. He said he was going to take Marie and Tramp with him. He started crying," and now Mindy was crying, "He said he couldn't stand to be separated from them, the only ones who had ever really loved him.

"I tore into him." She closed her eyes, her face twisted. "'Don't you dare kill anyone else, Garfield!' I said. If you have to do yourself in, okay, but don't you dare kill anyone else!' After a minute, he said, 'You're right, Mindy. I'll only kill myself,' and hung up.

Right after that," she sobbed, "he must have pulled the trigger."
Pastor and I sat stunned, listening to her weep.
"Where was he?"
"In the church. In their big room where they have dinners where there's a phone on the wall. That's what Marie said. She called the pastor and went with the police to the church, and they found him lying on the floor next to the phone on the wall. It was seven o'clock when they found him."

The three of us sat in silence for a few minutes. The clock ticked and a couple of pesky flies buzzed around. I closed my eyes feeling very old and very tired and pictured Garfield lying in that fellowship hall in the faint light and quietness of early morning and thought, *Dear God, let him be at peace.* We held hands, and Pr. Sauer said a beautiful prayer of which I can't remember a word.

Pastor excused himself to return to his vigil at the hospital where Marsha, church secretary, is having a mastectomy. I dropped Mindy at the day care center and went on to the food pantry. Garfield was everywhere. I saw him in the faces of people coming in for food assistance. He was the dead squirrel in the street as I drove home. The blood of the chicken I was thawing for supper was his.

I went and sat on the edge of the bed in the guest room looking out on the backyard that he loved so much, and the dam of emotions broke with a flood. It was Tuesday morning when he did it.

Twelfth Sunday after Pentecost

Jeremiah 1:4-10
Psalm 71:1-6
Hebrews 12:18-29
Luke 13:10-17

Pastor Sauer once told me that whenever he stepped into the pulpit, he felt unworthy and inadequate.

"Oh, dear," I responded, thinking that would be pretty uncomfortable.

"Oh, it's quite alright; it goes with the territory. There's not space for the Holy Spirit to enter if one is filled with confidence."

Pastor's brave and faithful sermons mean even more to me now, since I have been privileged to enter his spiritual struggles. This morning he stood in the pulpit seeming to listen intently to something within the silence, and we began to wonder if he would ever speak. Then, God touched his mouth.

"Like the bent-over woman in the scripture came, we too have come to worship, figuratively bent over by life's burdens. We have come to stand in the presence of the holy, and we too, unexpecting like the woman perhaps, will be exposed to the gracious and healing power of Christ."

Virginia reached over and took my hand when he talked about Garfield. God was Garfield's midwife, listener, rock, Pastor said, drawing upon Psalm 71. And now in death, God is no less present with him, releasing him from the power of sin and death, the power of the devil. Garfield is healed and peaceful and standing tall, no longer bent over with the burdens and diseases of this world. We, too, are liberated to stand tall, to participate in a modern day sabbath miracle, a miracle we experience each time we eat the bread and drink the wine of God's mystery.

Mindy was nodding her head as tears streamed down her face, and I had the urge to lean forward just a bit and cast a sideways glance past her to see how Garfield was reacting, the same kind of urge that makes me flip the light switch five or six times before I actually assimilate the reality that the electricity is off. Garfield is dead. "Look at Garfield. He's not there." We will never hear his bluster or see his soft-heartedness or smell his nicotine or feel the rough scratch of his stubble again, except in the memories that will keep him near us.

Virginia astounded me when she rang the bell and walked in the house this morning about 10 o'clock. I hadn't even dressed and had a little thought lurking on the edges of my mind that maybe I was too sad and weak to worship today, simultaneously acknowledging the serious absurdity of such a thought.

"Mother! Why aren't you dressed? You can't stay home. You have to go to church!" she shrieked.

"What in the world are you doing here?" was my response.

"I came to take you to church because of Garfield. I thought you would want to have family with you."

In the name of all the gods, what next?! It was nice having her along. I guess. How very odd that I long deep within my soul and pray for her to sit beside me in worship, and then this morning, I had this strange feeling, almost as though she was an unwelcome intruder, a non-member who was there for the wrong reasons and didn't know the proper protocol. Why wasn't my heart filled with gratitude and joy at her presence? Merciful heavens! Was it because I wasn't in control, because she came on her own rather than in response to my urging? I certainly hope not! Maybe my feelings were partly because she wasn't that fond of Garfield.

Be that as it may (or may not), worship was sharp and filled with meaning and beauty. I did a double take at the brightness of the orange day lilies and the perfection of the white calla lilies amongst the glistening greenery left over from a wedding yesterday. Even though the choir consisted of only three sopranos (including a ten-year-old), one alto, and two men, their voices were unusually attuned, and I could understand every word—"The Lord Is Ever Watchful." The artistry of the green and gold paraments on the pulpit and lectern with their silken embroidery of the lamb on one and the wheat and grapes on the other seemed more brilliant today than they have the other eleven Sundays they have been hanging there. The eternal flame, which I often don't even notice, glinted off the gold altar cross.

"You have filled all creation with light and life..." Pastor proclaimed in the Eucharistic prayer. My grieving heart leapt in affirmation! I was determined through my tears to believe these words, and yet determination had nothing to do with the conviction that rose from the depth of a reality beyond the one I normally know.

The greatest reality is that Christ has died, Christ is risen, Christ will come again! And because of this, I know that Garfield has died and somehow risen, and some-mystically-how, is not a failure but a redeemed child of God, loved beyond human imagination.

Which didn't stop us from having a weeping circle after the service. Sidney was especially distraught. He and Garfield had enjoyed a good guitar relationship, but his grief was over more than losing the friendship.

"He can't be saved," he finally choked out. "Suicide victims can't go to heaven."

"Where you gettin' that, Sidney?" Mindy squinted through her red eyes.

"It's in the Bible," he moaned.

She looked at me, and I shrugged, unable to call up relevant passages.

Madge sniffled, "Yes, I think it is. I'm worried about that too, Sidney."

"G-G-Garfield's in heaven with Ch-Charlie," Danny declared, hugging me around the waist.

Mindy said, "Well, I don't believe for one minute that God gives up on people who are in so much pain and anguish that they can't go on living. I just don't believe that. You're selling God short, Sidney, and not being a great friend of Garfield's either, to think of him as so worthless or weak that even God Almighty would abandon him. I'd just wipe that idea off your brain, if I were you."

I thought of Cassius' words—"life, being weary of those worldly bars, never lacks the power to dismiss itself..."

At that point, Pr. Sauer joined us, and we immediately asked about suicide in the Scripture. Quite predictably, our question was more than answered. Saul, Abimelech, King Zimri and others were mentioned. Some people interpret "Thou shalt not kill" to include suicide, he told us. The inspired authors who reported on situations relating to this matter, however, made no moral judgment nor did they provide direct instruction concerning suicide, according to Pastor. He quoted I Corinthians 3:17, a verse commonly used to cast judgment on persons who take their own lives: "If anyone defiles the temple of God, God will destroy him. For the temple of God is holy, which temple you are."

"That verse, however, is clearly referring to the temple as the community, not as individuals," Pastor said, closing the discussion with, "The common saying about suicide is that it is a permanent solution to a temporary problem; I think this could most definitely be applied to Garfield and many others with mental illness. Our friend struggled hard; inspired by the Holy Spirit, we helped him in that struggle. To our eyes and hearts, the struggle is lost, but we know that the wisdom of this world is foolishness to God, and we can rest assured that Garfield is not outside God's circle of mercy."

Sidney looked confused (the coincidence of the name Temple vis á vis the I Corinthians passage probably didn't help any) but comforted.

"Pastor S-S-Sauer, when are we going to b-bury him in the ground? When is his f-f-funeral?" Danny stuttered.

And so, we began to plan a memorial service.

And the service won't be just for Garfield. Mindy had a sudden thought and asked in a funny little voice if the memorial service could be for Darien as well.

"I didn't go to his funeral," she whispered.

Of course it could be for Darien too, Pastor Sauer quickly assured her.

Now, we have something to look forward to, something beyond the present sadness and confusion. In moments like this, I understand Father Matthew Fox's (or is he still a Father? I think he was excommunicated) words which I wrote in my journal years ago: "The mystic teaches us to trust all bottoming out, all emptying, all nothingness experiences as the matrix of new birth."

And so, I thank you God, even for this bottoming out, even for this ache in my heart, for now I know for certain that we grieve because we know only part of reality. I trust your love and mercy to help me discover the greater truths which Jesus, the Christ, embodied and shared. Amen.

Thirteenth Sunday after Pentecost

Jeremiah 2:4-13
Psalm 112
Hebrews 13:1-8, 15-16
Luke 14:1, 7-14

"To God be the glory, great things have been done!" Pastor Sauer began the sermon at the memorial service this afternoon.
"What great things?!" he continued. "The contrary might seem to be the case. Garfield Temple and Darien Brown are tragically dead; they have each had their moment and they are gone and we are left to mourn them and miss them. We are up against hard realities. What is the meaning of their brief lives? What is the meaning of our prayers and hopes for them? What do we now believe about God and resurrection, and how do we express those beliefs?
"We believe that Garfield and Darien are alive and well, that they have been resurrected, and that they are in the presence of the Most High, the Source of all life, in a way that we cannot yet know but for which we hope. We testify to that belief by saying it. Say it, people of God! Christ lives and we too shall live! Say it to yourselves, say it to each other, say it to those who are cynical and despairing. And we testify to that belief by living it. Live with joy, live with hope, live with grace toward all people."
We had planned to hold the service in the chapel, but so many came that we had to move to the nave. Madge and I wound up receiving people as they poured in the front door.
I was glad to see Brother James—honestly, I was; I insist I was glad to see him—and surprised by his entourage: three characters who, I learned, had become acquainted with Garfield and Marie during their layover in the city before coming to town last December:

- Mary – Skeleton-thin. A scabby area of dry scalp showing through her stringy, gray hair. Huge, unseeing eyes with hauntingly blue, quivering irises. Wearing a granny dress stylish in the 60s. She looked so familiar, and I just now remember that I've often seen her on the corner of Broad St. and 3rd Ave. singing and shaking a tambourine with another tambourine turned over to hold donations.

- Hank – Mobile in a beat-up wheelchair. He "left his legs in Vietnam" I heard him explain. Overweight. Droopy mustache, shaggy beard.

- Iam! (that's how she signed the guest register) – Tall, muscular black woman with yellow eye whites wearing ragged camouflage and a beret. Identified herself as a "reclamation specialist"—she makes her living picking up bottles and aluminum cans for recycling

Scores of Mindy's family were there. She was flabbergasted time and again as another relative arrived and absolutely dumbfounded when Darien's father, Larry, walked in.

"When I called him about the service," she had told me earlier in the week, "he said, 'A little late don't you think? What's it matter now anyway? The kid's dead.' Of course that was a huge hurt, but I still felt really bad for Larry. I said, 'It's okay, Larry. I'm not trying to pressure you to come. The point for me, however, is gathering together before God with people who know what they believe and let their belief and their love rub off on me. It's just too hard to try and make it on my own. And I want you to know that you are more than welcome to join us.'"

We told Pastor to invite everyone for the dinner afterwards, to "let mutual love continue." We had not prepared nearly enough food, though, so Sidney and Stephen went out and bought some buckets of fried chicken and trimmings. Merry chatter, along with tearful memories, filled the basement as we broke bread together.

I met Larry's Uncle Marvin, a very distinguished old gent who elegantly kissed my hand upon introduction! He reminded me of some character actor whose name I can't recall—tall, groomed mustache and bushy eyebrows over playful eyes. Uncle Marvin and I had a conversation about what a unique and fabulous person Mindy is. Melinda, he calls her.

Mary, the blind person, liked the last hymn, dubbing it the "Hello—Good-bye Hymn":

> Peace within the Church still dwells
> In her welcomes and farewells;
> And through God's baptismal pow'r
> Peace surrounds our dying hour.
> Peace be with you, full and free,
> Now and through eternity.
> --Nikolai F. S. Grundtvig in the 1700s

Madge had baked her carrot cake in loving memory of Garfield.

"Garfield loved my carrot cake," she said sadly at dessert time.

I was sitting across the table—she took her first bite—a look of confusion and distress—her mouth fell open, full of half-chewed cake—tears filled her eyes.

"Oh, Rose! I left out the carrots!" she said quietly. "Oh, no," she moaned, putting her fork down and holding her head with both hands. "The bowl of grated carrots is sitting in the refrigerator, I can see it. I never put them in. How could I have done that?!"

She covered her face with her hands and wept. "Oh, Garfield, I'm sorry, I'm so sorry."

Danny was sitting next to her watching her as though she were crazy.

"Whatsamatter, M-M-Madge? Garfield doesn't c-care, he's dead."

Madge cried harder.

"Garfield's probably laughin' because he thinks it's funny, he's probably laughin' with Jesus in heaven," Danny comforted, stretching his short arm across half of her back and patting her.

A gentle chuckle started as people up and down the table asked their neighbor what Danny had said. Even Madge had to join in the laughter before it was over.

Cindy, Mindy's sister, had put together a picture board of Darien's short life. Seven Halloween costumes, seven visits to Santa, seven to the Easter Bunny, quite a few shots with Aunt Cindy. The family gathered around it, quietly reminiscing.

So, Charlie, are you looking down, husband of mine? Are you getting acquainted with Garfield and Darien? Perhaps. I find comfort in thinking that you might be, but I don't really think you are. You're changed, like the seed changes into wheat, you're still you but resurrected in a different form now. And you know what? Even if you're not the same and even if we won't be re-united as good old Rose and Charlie, I don't care. I'm just sure, along with Margaret Mead's Madam Chang, that life is never lost. And the spirit of who you were while you were here is still so very present with me.

Come to think of it, Charlie, your spirit fits right in with that crowd of misfit, loser nerds from the fringes of society who were at the table today. I can imagine all of you at the roller rink—Br. James pushing Hank in his wheelchair, blind Mary confidently gliding along with you holding her hands, Iam! flying low and hanging on to her beret. Here comes Garfield, showing off, falling down, getting back up, with Marie gracefully moving along at her own steady rhythm next to him. And there are Mindy and Larry with Darien in between, and everybody's laughing to beat the band. Jesus is playing the organ.

Fourteenth Sunday after Pentecost

Jeremiah 18:1-11
Psalm 1
Philemon 1-21
Luke 14:25-53

I missed worship at St. Timothy because I went with Sarah Floyd, friend and former colleague, to her church in the city. They had a ceremony called "The Mingling of the Waters," an annual event on the first Sunday after Labor Day. People brought samples of water from places they had been over the summer. They told the source or meaning of their water. For example, one woman's water was from the pond in her backyard and symbolized the peacefulness of that place as she recovered from a kidney transplant. Two men brought water back from a gay and lesbian convention. Sarah brought water from the Jordan River, from her Holy Land trip last spring. They all poured their water into a lovely, hand-thrown pottery bowl. Then, the minister gave a brief meditation about the waters being mingled and the whole creation coming together.

The only lesson read, from The New York Times (!), posited that Deuteronomy, strictly interpreted, would result in the execution of most of us. We sang some nice, very poetic songs, which struck me as being rather people-centered, as was the one prayer. The folks were warm and friendly, and the service was meaningful in some ways, but I missed God and Jesus and the Holy Spirit. Not that they were absent, of course. For me, they were in, under, and around everything that happened, even if not formally invited or acknowledged. Afterwards, Sarah and I ate a pleasant lunch at her favorite place in the city, The Lion and Lamb Restaurant and Cultural Center. All vegetarian, quite delicious and we could watch people doing Tai Chi while we ate in the lovely, quiet garden.

When I got home I was eager to see the Cubs extend their winning streak, but there was a phone message from Florence telling me to come right over. She greeted me at the door with the news that her brother, John, had called and would be arriving shortly. I searched my mind—sister Jean, brothers Frank and Elliot, but John? I couldn't place him.

"I had forgotten about him, Rose," she told me on the way into her living room. "How in the hell do you forget you had a brother?!" She stared at me incredulously and sank into a chair.

"He was the oldest, and I was the baby. He left when I was five, he told me on the phone. We weren't a close family, as you know, about as connected emotionally as strangers in an elevator. Thinking back, I vaguely recall there was some kind of trouble and John left, but nobody ever explained anything.

"Wait a minute," she said, sitting forward in her chair. "I remember one time asking Jean where he was. We were on the back porch. I could smell burning leaves. I said, Where's John?" Jean said, 'Gone.' That was it. Over the years, he was never there, never mentioned...I forgot he had ever existed."

The doorbell rang, and I froze on the couch. After a few moments of murmuring in the hallway, they came into the room, and she introduced me to John, a slight, eighty-something man with a shock of beautiful white hair like hers.

"Rose has been my best friend for over fifty years, John, and I asked her to be here. I'll just tell you straight out, this is a terrible shock."

"Is it?" he asked with interest. "You honestly didn't know where I was or anything about me?"

"John, I hate to say it, but I forgot about you totally. I never even thought to ask about you. I was so little when you left. I never saw a picture of you, your name was never mentioned."

He nodded solemnly and began his story.

"I was banished from the family because I wouldn't fight in World War II. I was a conscientious objector. Do you remember the CPS, Civilian Public Service? Most of the workers were pre-theology students. Mennonites, Quakers, and Brethren financed the program. I was assigned to a camp outside of a little town in Montana. Forest management. Tough work, that's how I lost this," he said, holding up his left arm with a gray glove on an apparently false hand.

"When we went into town, the storekeepers refused to sell to us, restaurants had signs saying 'No skunks allowed.' After the war, doors were slammed in my face left and right as far as employment. It wasn't easy living with the scorn of my country—but all of that was a cake walk in comparison to losing my family," he said, his voice breaking.

"I didn't sleep at all the night before I left, February 1, 1942. Dad had told me that if I didn't join up, I was to leave and never come back. I prayed and cried after you had all gone to bed. 'Thou shalt not kill,' kept ringing in my ears. I asked Jesus, 'But what about Hitler? He's killing!' and the answer was, '<u>Thou</u> shalt not kill.' And I knew I couldn't do it, under any circumstances. I felt cowardly and weak and undutiful. The worst part, though, was knowing the shame that I would cause my family."

He told us about his life working with the Mennonite Church. He has served in twenty-some mission locations, spent a year in a Salvadoran jail in the '70s, contracted malaria in West Africa. He's never married and lives in a small apartment in a Mennonite retirement village in California. Words from "Cymbeline" came to me: "Thou mayest be valiant in a better cause; But now [then] thou seems't a coward."

We sat in silence, bathed in autumn sunlight.

"I came back for Frank's funeral in '45," he said, startling Florence.

Frank fell in New Zealand just a few months before the end of the war, I remember her telling me.

"I didn't have the courage to talk to anyone. That was the last time I saw any of you. I've stayed in touch with our cousin, Elizabeth; remember her?"

Florence nodded her head.

"I'm not far from her in California. She is a very, very fine person. She told me about your cancer, Florence. Coming here seemed like the right thing to do."

"And you're my brother," Florence responded, shaking her head in wonder.

Fifteenth Sunday after Pentecost

Exodus 32:7-14
Psalm 51:1-10
1 Timothy 1:12-17
Luke 15:1-10

Think of yourself as both the sheep and the shepherd; think of yourself as the coin and the woman, Pr. Sauer advised, as he helped us through the scripture lessons this morning. First and foremost, we are lost and can trust that God is always on the search for us. Starting with Adam and Eve and throughout the biblical witness, God searches for us whenever we go astray. And to be sought and found by a loving God Shepherd, the lamb did not have to pray or plead or bleat out a signal or promise to be a good lamb if rescued. All the little wooly thing had to do was get lost. Enter God, and the story of salvation begins anew.

Second message: We are God's agents, like the woman with the coin, called to seek out the lost and rejoice when they are found. Go all out in your efforts, Christ tells us through these parables. Every soul is beloved and deserving. Pastor pointed out that Jesus is addressing grumblers, the poor old scribes and Pharisees, whose legalistic and traditional ecclesiastical community is being disrupted by Jesus' indiscriminant love. Their social and religious boundaries are being blatantly disregarded by our Lord at every turn.

Shame on those uptight, merciless scribes and Pharisees, I thought for an instant, but then, my experience with Louise Felder thirty-five years ago popped into my brain, and smugness vanished. No one was surprised when Louise got fired from the school district; her performance had been at half-mast for some time. Stories of her unabashed favoritism toward certain students and rumors of serious parental complaints had been circulating. Finally, she failed one too many students who had clearly passed and was fired in disgrace. Something was obviously very wrong in Louise's life, and I felt called to be a friend, to offer support and be a point of God's grace for her. As the scandal thickened, though, I kept backing away. One late afternoon, she returned to school to pack up her room. I started to go next door to give her a hug or whatever—decided to call instead—decided to send a note instead—did nothing—she moved away—I have no idea where she went or what became of her.

My drawing away seemed so reasonable at the time, so very acceptable. But perhaps I had a Pharisaical and scribal attitude, thinking that forgiving would have been condoning, that I would have been contaminated by befriending her, that sinners forfeit their social standings and the "righteous" are justified in shunning them. In light of my sinfulness—and Louise's and everyone's—God's "grace overflowing" is amazing, especially when described by Paul, reformed murderer. And the earnest, panicky pleading of that fool, conniver, adulterer <u>and</u> murderer David in Psalm 51 confirms my faith in a God who never deserts us, whose Holy Spirit is always, always present and full of mercy to answer our pleas.

Interpretation of the scriptures continued into Sunday afternoon at Rutledge Home. I love it when that happens! At the end of the reading of the Old Testament lesson this morning, Mindy, who I had thought was possibly sleeping, jerked to attention and looked at me, truly confused, maybe even alarmed, and asked in her outside voice, "God changed his mind?!!!" And she would not let it go. This afternoon we were visiting Kathryn, and Mindy thought of that statement again.

"How can God change his mind?!" she erupted. "God is God! How does God even have a mind, he created minds! I don't think God thinks. People think. Animals think a little bit. God's above all that. God doesn't need to think, he just <u>is</u>. He is the beginning and the ending, which there isn't one, but it's all God. And if he does have a mind, how could he ever change it? God is <u>God</u>! If God changes his mind, how can we ever count on him? How do we know he might not change his little old mind?! And who's going to make him change it? Is he going to go Democrat or Republican according to who prays the most or begs the most or something? Does God…"

"Mindy, stop!" Kathryn yelled.

We took a little breath and sat there blinking and thinking for a minute.

"I just don't believe God changes his mind," Mindy said petulantly. "Do you all?"

I said, "Hm." Profound as usual.

"Well, what was God changing his mind about?" Kathryn asked.

"Oh, yeah, that brings up another little problem," Mindy said. "God was going to wipe out the Israelites for making this calf out of their earrings and Moses begged him not to be so hard on them, so God says, 'Okay, Moses, maybe you're right, maybe I was a tad harsh. Okay, have it your way. I won't wipe them out.' Oh! I can't stand it!"

"So you wanted God to wipe them out?" Kathryn asked.

"No! I don't like that part either. Sometimes I just want to throw out the Old Testament where God smites and fights and floods and all that mean stuff. Rose, you're a smart Bible girl, help us out here."

"Well, first of all," I waded in, "if you want to throw out the Old Testament, you're a Marcionite."

Her eyes narrowed. "Wha'd you call me?"

"Those are people led by a theologian named Marcion in the 1st century who rejected the Old Testament, feeling that it contradicted the gospel message of Jesus."

"Yeah, I think I might be one of those."

"Well, now, just a minute," I said. "Think about this possibility…"

And I offered my personal hermeneutic (not exclusively personal, I trust, grounded as it is in many years of listening, exploring, reflecting, and living, all within the community of faith, guided by the Holy Spirit) which I state in a formal way here, for self-clarification, as much as anything:

> The Scripture, old and new, is the inspired Word of God, a gift to the people of God, to understand the nature of God, and to live according to that divine nature. The Scriptures were recorded by people of faith traveling through time and space, interpreting the divine will and divine action in their own lives as revealed to them. Human, fallible, limited in their powers of interpretation and subject to their culture and history, these people faithfully did their best to express the truth about God. Because Christ is both human and divine, his actions and words most fully reveal the divine nature, so we look at all the Scripture through the eyes of Christ.

"Are you trying to say that some parts of the Bible are truer than others?" Kathryn challenged.

"More true, more important, more fully revealing of the true nature of the Divine. The test is to analyze through the teachings of Christ. If something contradicts what Christ said, we go with Christ. Like 'an eye for an eye and a tooth for a tooth.' The Old Testament people considered that divine truth. Many hundreds of years later, Christ said, 'I show you another way. Love your neighbor as yourself. Love your enemy.' We go with Christ."

Kathryn responded firmly, "No. It's all got to be either true or not true."

Mindy chirped back in. "You mean maybe God <u>didn't</u> change his mind? Maybe Moses just <u>said</u> that God changed his mind because Moses wanted to get a certain message across to the people because they were going back to idols or something? Or maybe Moses just <u>thought</u> that God had changed his mind so he wrote that down?"

"Maybe," I said, refraining from pointing out that Moses didn't write down anything. "The Bible is shrouded in mystery. That's why we need the Holy Spirit."

"It's a crazy book, alright," Mindy mused. "Kathryn, let's color your hair."

"I'm going to try something that combines red and gray," Kathryn told me, as Mindy started getting supplies out of her satchel.

"Whose idea was this?" I asked, surprised.

"Mindy's," Kathryn answered with a big smile.

"Did you get permission?"

"Permission from who, Rose? It's Kathryn's hair," Mindy said.

They looked at each other, and their laughter shot up like a geyser and splashed off the ceiling.

"How are they going to color her hair when she can hardly stand up?" I thought. Amused and happy not to be involved, I excused myself to go visit the others.

I picked up a poem from Sam that the Stewardship Committee had commissioned him to write.

Stewardship
by Sam Benshaw

Planting flowers, saying a prayer;
fixing the furnace, showing that we care;
Preparing Christ's body and blood, preaching the Word;
reading the Greatest Story ever heard;

Giving our money, giving our time;
raising our voices in music sublime;
Grateful hearts give back the blessing,
Father, Son and Spirit confessing.

Excellent.

I made the rest of my rounds, and when I got back Mindy was blow-drying Kathryn's hair. Her smile and her hair were glowing when we took leave.

"Have you heard from Stephanie lately?" I asked Mindy on the way home.

"Actually, we had lunch on campus the other day. She's eating like a horse, two horses, I guess; okay, a horse and a colt. She looks fabulous. Oh, and Ethan's been calling her."

"Is that a good thing?"

"She was a little upset at first, but she's getting used to it. He wants to be a dad, and that makes her happy."

Okay. Here's hoping this is a good thing. *Guide them, loving Father-Mother God.*

Egad! I just remembered one more item to report and then to bed with me.

I can live the rest of my life more peacefully now. I no longer have to live in dread of my cell phone going off during worship. I was so hoping to go home to my God without this happening. I have lived in fear of this moment; I have tried to be vigilant and manage my communication system so this wouldn't happen. I have—*as you well know God*—been disdainful and self-righteous towards others whose phones have rung at inappropriate times (Pharisaical again!). Well, my dreadful anticipation of being the transgressor is over. The ultimate humiliation has come to me, and if the darn little phone were to ring during worship again, it will never be as bad as this time. I have fallen.

Thank you, Lord, for this humbling experience. Thanks a lot.

Charlie, I sense your loving smirk. By the way, it was a wrong number!

Sixteenth Sunday after Pentecost

Amos 8:4-7
Psalm 113
1 Timothy 2:1-7
Luke 16:1-13

Today was Youth Sunday. Drums. Saxophone. Piano. Guitar. I sure do love the children, wouldn't miss their Sunday for anything, but—give me that old time liturgy! Nevertheless, contemporary hymns I'd not heard before expressed our faith beautifully, although they were played so fast I couldn't even begin to sing. I was surprised at Mindy's reaction to the service, which expressed my sentiments as well: "That was nice, but it's kind of thin and watery compared to the usual."

The kids presented the gospel lesson as a skit, seriously under-rehearsed. Ad lib seemed to dominate.

"Nice bling-bling," said the boy playing the dishonest manager to the boy playing the rich master, upon which the two of them had an attack of giggles as we sat clueless staring at them and trying to laugh a little so they wouldn't be embarrassed. The manager in the skit overacted, approaching one teen-aged family and then another with a villain persona, manipulating them into altering legal documents and returning the papers to the boss. The boss adolescent had no idea what to make of it. He accused the manager of cheating and the manager replied, "But I did it for you. They're gonna' kiss up to you now, just watch." After an awkward silence, the boss boy said desperately, "Watch what?" and they stood there giggling and red-faced until a pretty blonde child with her navel exposed walked in front of them holding up a poster board which said, "YOU CANNOT SERVE GOD AND WEALTH." My St. Lord.

Brittany Sauer evened things out with the most beautiful liturgical dance I have ever seen. Wearing a pink leotard with a loose white garment over it, she stretched and whirled in praise to a lovely contemporary tune and for a moment I forgot troubles and woes.

Several of the teen-agers had written petitions for the Prayer of the Church. One young woman picked up on the epistle lesson, praying with teen-aged fervor that our president would "change our national priorities so that we, and all the people of the world, especially the Iraqis, 'may lead a quiet and peaceable life in all godliness and dignity.' Help us to love members of Al-Qaida and terrorists everywhere; we pray for their souls." The response, "Hear our prayer," was noticeably weak, which is what often happens when Matthew 5:44 is lived out in the here and now. Of course, we all had Chad on our minds. Deedee is very vocal about her feelings; I heard her talking to some people after worship, tension evident in her gestures and voice.

"This is ludicrous. He enlisted to build, not destroy. He's not a security expert; he should be in New Orleans, building bridges after Katrina, not plunked down in a war zone with only three weeks of training." Chad is included in the prayers every week, of course.

Florence and John were there this morning. He has moved in with her and all indications so far are that the arrangement is supremely serendipitous. Florence looked pretty good but just couldn't seem to get comfortable in the pew. Sarah and Angelica were there too. We waited together in the narthex while Florence received hugs and inquiries from people, and I overheard Angelica snap at her mother, "So what if she's old?! Life is still life and pain is still pain!"

Sarah looked like she'd been slapped and she turned and headed for the bathroom, leaving Angelica with a confused scowl on her face. I wonder what Sarah had said. That it would be better if Florence would die or something like that, I suppose. John caught my eye, and I could tell he'd witnessed the interchange, too. We smiled sad smiles and shook our heads. Oh, dear God, death is so hard. Charlie. Darien. Garfield. Florence on her way.

Pastor Sauer was with Florence yesterday. "She is a woman at peace," he told me. "We planned her funeral. As you can well imagine, Rose, she said the most important thing is that the funeral be more about Christ than about her."

I nodded my head and smiled through my tears.

Oh, Lord of life and death, keep us safe and strong as we struggle with the ultimate mysteries. Help us to cherish your wonderful gift of earthly life even though it doesn't last as long and isn't as easy as we might wish. Let your love flow through us to each other as we struggle against the dying of the light, in the certain knowledge that another light shines far brighter and can never be extinguished. In the name of Jesus Christ, our Lord, whose brightness fills the cosmos, we pray. Amen.

Seventeenth Sunday after Pentecost

Amos 6:1a, 4-7
Psalm 146
1 Timothy 6:6-19
Luke 16:19-31

Pastor talked this morning about the ongoing debate between Jesus and some of the Pharisees about what God says concerning the rich and the poor. In the course of these discussions, "the Pharisees, who were lovers of money, heard all this [Jesus' teachings on money], and they ridiculed him." Jesus responds, "You are those who justify yourselves in the sight of others; but God knows your hearts; for what is prized by human beings is an abomination in the sight of God."

If I'd been there, I'm afraid I would have said, "Oh, Master! such incendiary language! Don't you know they're out to get you?! Did you have to say abomination? Couldn't you have just said, is distasteful in the sight of God? You're talking as though you are one with God! What are you trying to do, get yourself killed?!"

Yes, I think I might have been quite the chicken-hearted disciple/advisor. Sometimes I think I am a chicken-hearted disciple, avoiding conflict, choosing conciliation when confrontation might be the faithful action. I know one thing, I'm no Louella Rutledge.

Louella, our holy eccentric, is one of the wealthiest people I've ever known. For one thing, she has six homes—her large family home here in town and then two houses in Mexico, one in Honduras, one in Turkey, and one in Russia, homes which she has financed for families in need. I guess you could say she owns Rutledge Home, too, since the family trust keeps it going. In many ways, Louella exemplifies the contentment Pr. Sauer, grounded in Timothy, described this morning: enjoying sharing as much as we enjoy having. She has "taken hold of the life that truly is life."

Admirable, and yet Louella is something of an extremist and can be irritating with her constant challenge for the rest of us to follow her lead. She was extreme with the chocolate chip boycott in the 70s and 80s. I remember how our women's circles were outraged when we found out that companies were giving mothers in Africa powdered formula knowing full well that they had no source of clean water in their villages. Church women all over the country mobilized when the companies refused to change their practices even when more and more babies were dying. Despite my righteous anger, though, I was embarrassed one Saturday when I stood with Louella outside the grocery store handing out printed information, and she pulled out a little hibachi and started a fire to burn coupons. Chicken-hearted disciple, that's me.

Pastor took us deeper than the issue of wealth and poverty to the underlying teaching of Christ in today's gospel: the interpretation and honoring of the Scripture. Bring an open heart and mind to the reading of the Bible, earnestly seek divine truth, Pastor urged. Don't fall into the trap of appropriating certain aspects of the Law to justify our preferred way of life and disregarding other aspects.

You have fallen deeply into that trap, Jesus seems to be saying to the Pharisees (and to us?), creating a great chasm between yourselves and the Divine. Because of your love of wealth, you hold in primary importance the words in the Torah about the righteous prospering and ignore laws requiring mercy and sharing of wealth with the poor. Being a rich person in the global scheme, I wonder if I'm trapped. Certainly doesn't hurt to be vigilant about traps that detour us from the divine plan.

Pastor Sauer had quite a day. He had to chase down a five-year-old who wasn't keen on getting baptized. The little girl is the stepchild of Ruby Goodson's granddaughter. Ruby is a former student of mine. How can this be?! My former student's great-grandchild is running around, and I'm watching her! Anyway, the child's infant brother was baptized, too, and was preciously calm, but the little girl fussed at everything. When she saw Pastor coming at her again to make the sign of the cross on her forehead, she took off and hid behind Ruby. Did Pastor Sauer give up and let her be baptized without marking her with the cross of Christ forever? Oh no. He came straight on with his sweet oil and a kind smile and sealed the deal on the twisting, shrieking little child of God!

Okay, Cute Baby, time for a nap before Stephen calls. A postcard from him arrived Friday: "Mom! Big, happy news. Let's have a phone date at 5:30 Sunday. Stay well. God bless. Stephen." I think we better rest up for this one, little bitty kitty.

Later

Stephen's in love with his pastor!

Pastor Penelope Schultz. Merciful heavens, I've always categorized Penelope with Kalamazoo—crazy but actual names. Pastor Penelope. Pastor Penny. Oh, dear, I hope she goes by Pastor Schultz.

"She's quite a woman, Mom!" and Stephen began to catalogue her virtues until I zoned out, fatigued by his unbridled enthusiasm, frankly. "Lovers and madmen have such seething brains!"

But let me see, how did he describe her?

- the most relaxed person he's ever met

- the most compassionate person he's ever met—evidenced by her father with dementia living with her and a troubled, teen-aged niece coming to live with her next week (Yikes!)
- everybody at the church is crazy about her (hm—that seems unlikely)
- musical—sings in an early music ensemble
- she's published a book but she is totally down-to-earth
- her potato soup and cheese blintzes are out of this world
- her sermons are captivating

And on and on. Wow. Penelope Schultz has obviously captured his heart for the moment, and it sounds mutual. They've had several dates including a picnic and symphony in Millennium Park. Stephen went to one of her concerts, and she went to his Rotary function. Apparently, they are established in the congregation as a couple. Wow.
I hardly know what to think, Charlie.
I'm going to call Stephanie.

A few minutes later
Stephanie's known for weeks. Humph, he tells his niece before he tells his mother?! Oh, well. I'm glad they're close.
Stephanie's high-strung emotions continue. We didn't talk about Stephen and Penelope much; I could tell she was upset.
"Grandma," she wept in a quivering voice, "my supper is ruined. I spent at least twenty minutes fixing myself this fabulous sandwich. I had julienned red and green pepper, celery, broccoli, sweet onion, and two kinds of olives—with the julienne knife from the set that Ethan gave me for Christmas." Her voice faltered for a moment. "I put the veggies on thick whole wheat bread toasted to perfection, Grandma, and melted soy cheese on them. I sprinkled sunflower kernels and spread nayonnaise and some herbal balsamic dressing on the bread. I cut it in half and took one bite of it—I always have to do that immediately; it was so good—and then I put it on the patio and came back inside to get a drink and then decided I had to go to the bathroom—I always have to go to the bathroom these days. When I went back out, a raccoon was eating it! A raccoon! It had eaten almost every bit of it except for a few pieces of things strewn about. Oh, Grandma," she groaned, as if to die.
I thought of her love for animals and almost said, "Well, Stephanie, think how much the raccoon enjoyed it!" but thought better of it when I realized that that's exactly what Mother would have said.

"I do not choose an urban lifestyle to have raccoons eating my dinner," she lamented.

"Well, sweetheart, do you still have all the ingredients so you can make yourself another sandwich?"

Click. She hung up on my rationality. I was still sitting by the phone thinking about calling her tomorrow when she called back.

"Sorry, Grandma. I'm ready to tell you what's really wrong," she said, taking a deep breath followed by silence. "I <u>think</u> I'm ready..." Breathing, silence. "Okay, I'm ready," and she read me a note she had received from Ethan's family. Essentially, it said,

Dear Stephanie,

We felt compelled to be in contact with you because of our deep love and concern for Ethan. We cannot condone what has happened, and while we understand that Ethan bears some responsibility for this unfortunate pregnancy, we feel that the woman should have exercised greater control. Ethan is emotionally unstable at this point and is not able to make sound judgments. If you care for him at all, please sever the relationship so that you can both move on with your lives. We wish you no additional problems.

Sincerely,
Randolph and Linda Franklin and
Kirsten (sister) and Husband Whomever

No wonder the raccoon got her goat! She spewed anger in between sad, confused weeping. I offered sympathy and told her the wild story of Kathryn's parents interfering in her marriage—it seemed to fit—and then Steph started talking about watching "Adam's Rib," the old Hepburn-Tracy comedy. We ended up laughing. By the time we said good-bye, she was ready to make herself another sandwich.

Thank you, Holy Spirit, for strength and comfort and nourishment through the tough and tender times of life and for Stephanie's healthy pregnancy. Help her to be aware of your peaceful presence. Thank you also, God, for amazing blessings for Florence. She's not getting better, we know that, but for her strength and clarity of mind and endurance through pain, I praise your name, knowing that you are the source of it all. Especially for brother John and his tender, loving care, a thousand thanks, dearest God. Amen.

Eighteenth Sunday after Pentecost

Lamentations 1:1-6; 3:19-26
Psalm 37:1-9
2 Timothy 1:1-14
Luke 17:5-10

How anguished we are, how speechless. How like a village of zombies the church seemed this morning. Chad Brewster has fallen. We just found out. The family called Pastor early this morning.

We dispensed with the hymns and the anthem. Pastor let the reading from Lamentations suffice as the Word:

> The steadfast love of the Lord never ceases,
>   his mercies never come to an end;
>   they are new every morning;
>   great is your faithfulness.
> "The Lord is my portion," says my soul,
>   "therefore I will hope in him."
> The Lord is good to those who wait for him,
>   to the soul that seeks him.
> It is good that one should wait quietly
>   for the salvation of the Lord.

Then, the body and blood, given for us. As I knelt, I thought of Chad's body and blood.

Evening

After trying unsuccessfully to nap, I put on "Adagio for Strings" and gazed upon the icon of the crucifixion to wait quietly for the salvation of the Lord with Cute Baby curled in my lap.

How I wish you were here, Charlie. We would hold hands and cry together and probably fall into bed to hold and comfort each other. Are you greeting Chad, can you sense his closer presence? Perhaps...

Nineteenth Sunday after Pentecost

2 Kings 5:1-3, 7-15
Psalm 111
2 Timothy 2:8-15
Luke 17:11-19

"If the fear of the Lord is the beginning of wisdom," Pastor began the sermon, "I am about to morph into Einstein. For I am afraid of the Lord, people of St. Timothy, but I am more afraid of myself. And I am afraid for you and for what you are allowing to happen to this congregation."

Mindy leaned against me and said, "Uh-oh. He's off."

"Our lessons focus on gratitude. Only one out of ten people whom Jesus had healed turned back to give thanks. Are we any better? The best way to show gratitude is to worship the Lord, our God. Worship is a treasure, developed and handed down from one generation to another over thousands of years, and yet when the Sabbath comes, how many of us stay at home?"

"None of us!" Danny yelled. "We're all right here, P-P-Pastor Sauer," he stuttered in unarguable logic.

As we chuckled, Pastor's face sobered. "You're right, Danny. You have caught me preaching to the choir."

"P-P-Preach to all of us, Pastor Sauer, because I-I-I can't s-s-ing," Danny spoke out, playing to the crowd for another laugh, which he got.

Pastor came down into the center aisle, leaving his notes behind. He apologized for a negative beginning of the morning message, saying that he was going to address his remarks to the faithful few—there were maybe 100 of us—in gratitude that we had chosen the better thing. Then, he rambled on about the importance of storytelling and how the story of Naaman had been known to Jesus from his earliest days, and something about the gospel lesson being two stories put together, the first about gratitude and the second about the Church in that day being blind to truth, and that Jesus Christ is the ultimate earthly manifestation of God. Points but no power.

Pastor was indeed off, just plain off. In the midst of our puzzling congregational conflict, we are all off. The devil confounds.

Our grief over Chad has brought some unity as we mourn together and pitch in to cook, clean, help with children and logistics, and whatever the family will let us do. During a 48-hour prayer vigil, someone was in the chapel around the clock praying for the family, offering thanks to God for Chad's brave, abbreviated life. The funeral has been set for Saturday. The Brewster and the Leppard families, led by Deedee, are inspirational towers of strength.

But the crazy conflict in the congregation persists, exemplified all too well by a piano and organ duet arrangement of "Fairest Lord Jesus." Janice Smith (openly anti-Sauer) was speeding at the piano and Lloyd (pro-Sauer) was at the organ trying to slow her down, glaring at her and nodding his chin stiffly a tempo. She doggedly ignored him and sailed along a beat or two ahead. Sad and silly imagery for the state of the congregation. I truly do not understand what is going on.

Millicent Avery called last week to invite me to a meeting she and some others were hosting to talk about the "current unpleasantness."

"Does Pastor Sauer know about this meeting?" I asked.

"No. We don't think he needs to be involved. We love St. Timothy and can't stand to see it going downhill. The church is more than its pastor, you know, Rose. We were here before he came, and we'll be here when he leaves. We just want to talk and see what we can come up with to stop the flood of people leaving."

I declined the invitation. Nothing about their plan sounded healthy or kind.

And now, it's time to drive back to the church. Gr-r-r-r. I can't believe that I have waited my whole life to see the Cubs in the playoffs, and now I have to go to the church and talk about sex! I don't *have* to go, of course, but Pr. Sauer conned me into it. This afternoon, we begin our discussions of human sexuality.

"We really need your mature wisdom and experience, Rose, and your open-mindedness," he cajoled as we spoke after the service this morning. So, here I go…

Later

The Cubs managed to win without me, so I can watch tomorrow. As usual, I'm glad I pushed myself and went to the discussion group, which was facilitated by a well-prepared Pam Turner—nurse, teacher, woman of faith, and very sharp person.

An amazing dialogue ensued between Lois Rizenhouer and Brett Babcock. Brett said he was saving himself for his future, as-of-yet unknown, wife. Lois, who is enjoying that mouthy independence of octogenarians, challenged him.

"For crying out loud, Brett, you're thirty-five years old. I can't imagine a God who would create the fabulous gift of sex and then not want you to enjoy it. Waddayah doin', son, hanging on by your toenails?! What if you never get married?"

"Mrs. Rizenhouer!" he responded, shocked. "You were my Sunday School teacher when I was little, one of the best I ever had. I can't believe you think that!"

"Well, I do. I never taught you that physical love between a man and a woman was wrong, excluding adultery. I'm not suggesting one-night stands or shacking up. In fact, I'm not suggesting anything, just thinking that perhaps you are needlessly missing one of the greatest pleasures God has given us because of puritanical ethics which have wreaked havoc with the divine order, as far as I'm concerned."

Several came to Brett's defense, of course, strongly affirming his virginity, but I sensed from the look on his face that he was intrigued by Lois's viewpoint.

Lloyd spoke about everyone needing love and affection. Susie told the story (that most of us have heard or told about someone) of her niece who is lesbian and tried ever so hard throughout her growing up years to be heterosexual and couldn't do it and was miserable and psychologically fragile and since coming out of the closet is obviously happier and well-adjusted and one of the finest people you'd ever want to know. Hugh Schneider said everybody might as well calm down and get ready for whether or not to ordain androids. Somebody asked what Jesus said about homosexuality. Nothing. Edwin Smith asked what about Genesis 19, Joshua 19, Leviticus 18 and 20, Romans 1, 1 Corinthians 6, and 1 Timothy 1? Which is, indeed, a perfectly legitimate and very important question. After all, we are people of the Book.

Pam offered principles for interpreting Scripture which fit perfectly with my personal hermeneutic. I find them extremely helpful:

- observe "peaks and valleys"—some parts of the Bible are more important than others
- honor tradition—the interpretations and teachings of the Holy Catholic and Apostolic Church should guide us and not be changed lightly
- bring experience to bear on how we understand the Scripture—trust the Holy Spirit to allow experiences to move our hearts
- use our God-given brains—ask what makes sense, both in the original and modern contexts.
- look at everything through the lens of Jesus Christ's teachings

I can't imagine that we of such diverse experiences and opinions will reach a consensus on sexual matters and faith, but what a gift to be able to disagree in an atmosphere of love and mutual acceptance. Ah! the Church.

One more item before I have my Sunday night calls with the children. Philipp Nicolai, whose touching hymn we sang a few weeks ago, was featured in the bulletin in "Church Commemorations" this morning. Nicolai was a pastor in Germany in the 1500-1600s. Thirteen hundred of his parishioners died in the plague, 170 in one week. Yes, I guess he knew about sadness. Actually, that is beyond sadness into cataclysm, chaos, hell, I should think, and yet, his faith, the same faith that we profess each Sunday, was unshaken. He wrote hymns to comfort his congregation during those times. Imagine, in the face of such suffering to sing out:

> What joy to know, when life is past,
> The Lord we love is first and last,
> The end and the beginning!
> He will one day, oh, glorious grace,
> Transport us to that happy place
> Beyond all tears and sinning!
> Amen! Amen!
> Come, Lord Jesus!
> Crown of gladness!
> We are yearning
> For the day of your returning.

If Phillip Nikolai could keep the faith under those conditions, surely we can keep it in our world and in our little group called St. Timothy, and be bold enough to proclaim that amazing message, like he did, even as we mourn.

Oh, God, shower your healing blessings upon us, especially on Deedee and the children and Jack and Helen Brewster and Faye and Bruce Leppard. And on the warring nations. Amen.

Chad's Funeral

2 Samuel 1:19-27
Psalm 37:1-9
Romans 8:18-39

What a difficult funeral to preach, but Pastor ably proclaimed the faith. He likened our grief to King David's after Saul and Jonathan fell in battle. We too feel defeated. Chad, our "beloved and lovely," was not saved from death. Our earnest prayers on his behalf seem to have come to nothing. After David's heartfelt lament over his loss, he asked the Lord God what to do. Even in his sorrow, David remained faithful to the God of Israel. We, too, can appropriately ask what God would have us do now. What are people of faith to do when it seems that evil has the last word? How are we to live in a world where death claims so many innocents, now one of our own, magnifying the sadness we experience everyday when we hear the death count?

Then, he began to preach about "who are the evil ones?"

His question made me wonder if he had heard what I heard at the funeral home last night. The whole town was there and the crowd so packed I don't know if Pastor was nearby. I was behind George Hapless, who had a disturbing exchange with Deedee right by Chad's coffin.

George began the way we all do—"I'm so sorry. I don't know what to say." Then, "Always remember, my dear child, that Chad's life was not wasted. We will win this war because of sacrifices like his."

Red-eyed and exhausted, Deedee looked him in the eye and said, slowly and deliberately, "His life was wasted."

"Deedee, no! Chad is a hero! He's made the ultimate sacrifice!"

"Yes, he's a hero, the bravest man I ever hope to know, and he was proud, Mr. Hapless, proud to be an American soldier, until we lied our way into this war. His life was wasted along with thousands of others."

"No," George pleaded. "It's about freedom and justice. We're fighting the terrorists, the evil ones…"

"Our country is evil too, as far as I'm concerned. And Chad joined the National Guard to build bridges, not to fight. I wish he'd never…"

Her father stepped in and led her away, saying, "C'mon, honey. You need a break."

Oh, it was a rough moment. Poor George left in an aura of distress. The rest of us stood soberly in line, talking about supporting our troops but not discussing or debating the war itself.

So, I wondered if Pastor had heard that exchange when he continued the sermon with, "Deep within our souls we are outraged and grievously agitated at evildoers who deal in death and destruction. And who are the evildoers? Are they the people who killed Chad? Saddam and Bin Laden? Our own leaders? The psalmist was addressing people who had the same internal churnings. Turn your anger over to Yahweh, for the Almighty One laughs at the wicked and holds your hands, rescues you from the wicked, provides refuge in time of trouble."

I'm sure I wasn't the only one thinking, "Wait a minute—Chad wasn't rescued from the wicked." Pastor responded.

"Yes, Chad perished physically, but ultimately, our God has rescued him. I cannot convince you, brothers and sisters, I cannot prove this. The choice is for each of us to make. Either we embrace faith when it comes to us and trust in the Lord, or we do not."

I was consoled in a very powerful way. Phenomenal power had also issued forth when Deedee rose at verse 38 as Pastor was reading the passage from Romans 8. The family stood too, some with quizzical looks, and then the rest of us, and when she began repeating, "Neither death nor life..." with Pastor, so did the congregation.

As we slowly left the church behind the flag-draped casket, I heard a thirty-something man ask the woman he was with, "What did you think of all that?"

"I thought it was a crock."

God of Power and Might, I thank you for your presence with that woman who thinks faith is a crock. Through this hard and wonderful life, I praise your name for the times of joy you will bring to her, and moments of peace. How I wish she could know Christ. Amen.

Twentieth Sunday after Pentecost

Genesis 32:22-31
Psalm 121
2 Timothy 3:14-4:5
Luke 18:1-8

"Is anyone besides me sick and tired of focusing on St. Timothy's troubles?" Pastor began his sermon.

Those of us settling in the pew to read the bulletin announcements or rest our eyes snapped to attention.

"As your spiritual leader, I can give you no better instruction during these trying times than that given in our epistle lesson: 'In the presence of God and of Christ Jesus, who is to judge the living and the dead, and in view of his appearing and his kingdom, I solemnly urge you: proclaim the message; be persistent whether the time is favorable or unfavorable...carry out your ministry fully.'

"Besides struggling with conflict and division in the congregation, we are deeply grieved over the loss of Chad. We each face individual problems as well. Some of you may be wrestling with depression or obesity or cancer or other illness. Others may be caught in difficult relationships you don't know how to handle or tied up in knots because of financial concerns.

"And, again, I say to you: PROCLAIM THE MESSAGE...CARRY OUT THE MINISTRY FULLY.

"Even in the midst of great difficulty and anxiety, we are called to persevere in prayer and hope, living into uncertainty as disciples. The gospel word for us this day is that God the Creator will breathe life and strength into our congregation and into each of us, the same breath and life breathed into Adam and Eve.

"Hang on, people of St. Timothy! Do not refuse the struggle! The fight against misunderstanding, against injustice, against confusion, is a worthwhile fight, and God is always on the side of those who are willing to fight. God neither sleeps nor slumbers. Through Christ, with Christ, in Christ, by the power of the Holy Spirit, our Creator will ever bless us and redeem us."

Carolyn cried, Mindy cried, Susie and Pete cried, the Brewsters and Leppards cried, of course. I cried too, hope and strength in liquid form. Tears came to my eyes again when the Evans sisters sang Florence's favorite, "Lift Thine Eyes," in pure, sweet harmony. She wasn't up to coming this morning, but I saw John leaving the early service.

I was not at all prepared for the passion and confidence of Pastor's sermon after the phone message he left me last night: "Rose, twelve hours from now I am supposed to proclaim the Word of God to people searching for truth and meaning, and I have nothing to say. Call if you get home before 10."

I didn't get home until 11, after going to dinner and a movie with Mindy and Stephanie (now I remember why I rarely go to movies anymore—even the best are "Hollywood" as opposed to real life, and I simply am not into Hollywood), so I went to the church early this morning to check on Pastor.

Madge had him cornered, shrieking about what to do to confirmation students who don't attend worship. (Valid concern, horrible approach.) Pastor was poorly shaven and bleary-eyed. When he saw me, he patted Madge on the shoulder and we walked down the hallway—he was limping, I noticed—into his office.

"You look awful, Pastor," I greeted him.

"Thanks," he smiled. "I am scarred and I am weak, Rose, but I am at a new place this morning.

"Last night after Carolyn and Brittany were settled, I went out on the porch and sat in the darkness. Powers both demonic and divine, it seemed, attacked me full-force. There was terror in the air. Feeling like I was doomed if I sat still, I walked all over Shippensforge, wrestling with unbelief as though it were a physical enemy.

"I tripped and crashed down on cement. My knee hurt like hell, but I kept walking. I didn't know what else to do. Next, I was sitting on a bench by the fountain at the library. I decided to leave the ministry; I felt relief but no peace, so the struggle continued. 'I don't know who I am, and I don't know who you are!' I shouted into the sky.

"And then—in a minute or an hour, I don't know which—peace came over me in the most unremarkable, gentle way, and, Rose," he said looking at me as though I had just entered the room, "I knew who I was. I am a pastor. I am a husband. I am a father. And I can't explain it really, but I also knew that if I had discovered that I wasn't a pastor or husband or father, God would have been just as present and just as gracious."

"I limped home as the first rays of sunlight grew strong and—and—here I am. I still don't have any idea what to preach, but God will provide."

Forty minutes later, he was standing in the pulpit, and God did, indeed, provide. What a man, this pastor of ours, and what a God! After that powerful proclamation—the body and blood!

"Lamb of God, you take away the sin of the world." I love singing this each Sunday as we head up for Eucharist. I believe it with all my heart. And, I wonder what on earth it means. What does it mean for the man who was next to me in line at the grocery store the other day? He was on crutches and made some comment about how hard it was to get around. I asked him how he had injured his foot. His reply: cancer—surgery—another deeper, higher surgery—experimental therapy that didn't seem to be working—then "me and my wife started having problems"—split up—lost job—lost insurance—can't get insurance because he has cancer. Our Lord Jesus Christ gave up his life so that this man could live fully with hope and peace and love. Lamb of God, you do take away the sin of the world, but sometimes I would like to know exactly how? I believe, Lord, help my unbelief.

And now to Rutledge Home with me. George Rizenhour moved in last week, and I can't wait to see Kathryn. Wow, I never would have imagined six months ago that I would count her as a friend and look forward to seeing her! Mindy and I think there is a romance blossoming between her and Mitch, her neighbor in the next room, although she blushingly denies "any such thing." The place is rapidly changing since the two of them started chairing the RCC, as she says, making it sound like a subcommittee of the UN. Residents' Concerns Committee. Children from a day care center are coming to visit, there are fewer rules and more parties. Go, Kathryn! What's more, going there will provide a lovely diversion to the ennui eating at my edges since the Cubs didn't make it to the World Series.

Thank you, Almighty One, for your son, our Lord, always present with us through the power of the Holy Spirit and for the constant redemption we enjoy through his resurrection. We long daily and urgently for suffering to cease and for questions to be answered, and we know in the depth of our hearts that you hear us. As your servant, Marcus, persists in his struggle, help the people of St. Timothy to persist through these difficult times, fixed on your unchanging, unending grace. Amen.

Twenty-first Sunday after Pentecost

Jeremiah 14:7-10, 19-22
Psalm 84: 1-7
2 Timothy 4:6-8
Luke 8:9-14

I have done it now. Fie! how I wish I could take my words back. I feel like—no—I am the biggest phony in the world. Hypocrite. Self-congratulator. Self-aggrandizer. Arrogant fool. Oh, fie! and again fie! Would that I could cut my tongue out. Well, I guess I could, and I'm not going to, but I sure do feel horrible.

What was I thinking?! I am not really prone to put others down or to be negative, especially in public. Maybe if I record this distressing incident here, word for word, I can begin to purge myself of the profound regret that is overtaking me. I'm almost too upset and ashamed to confess, even in the privacy of this journal…

Here's what happened: We had a reception after worship this morning to honor all those involved in worship ministry—the altar guild, choir, ushers, acolytes. Things were winding down, most everyone was gone. Mercedes, Susie, and I were chatting outside the kitchen, ready to clean up. The pass-through window right behind me was open.

"Well, let's get to it ladies, so we can go home," Mercedes said. "I thought Madge was on the clean-up crew; is she still here?"

"Oh, Lord, let's hope not," I said (taking the Lord's name in vain). "If Madge helps, we won't be home till suppertime. She'll have to have every teaspoon in its place and every crumb wiped away. I have never seen such ridiculous attention to details that don't matter. I feel for her poor family."

"She's unique, alright," Mercedes put in.

"That's for sure. Madge Humphrey personifies works righteousness," I rattled on. "Always thinking she's better than the rest and trying to be holier. The arrogant Pharisee we heard about this morning comes to mind…"

Susie lifted her finger quickly to her lips with a warning look just as Madge walked through the door from the kitchen, her face very red, looking as though she was fighting back tears. She made a beeline for the door without speaking to us.

My heart sank and is yet sunken. Fie! Madge is not my favorite person, but I certainly did not intend to insult her right to her face. And now, alas, I remember Pastor Sauer saying in his sermon that we have missed the point of Christ's story if we think we measure up better than the Pharisee. Rose, you old fool! The truth in that parable is about God's grace, not our goodness or lack thereof. Not about your merit or Madge's or anyone else's. The story is about how God sees us, not about how we see ourselves!

I've learned about divine grace the hard way this time. Now, what to do? Maybe I'll share my dilemma with Pastor and Susie and Pete this afternoon when we travel to Rossville for the The Tree of Life's organizational service.

Florence and John were at worship. She didn't stand up at all; for the first time, Pastor took communion to her in the pew, and she and John left after that. Ah, so she dies.

The Organizational Service of The Tree

Great service, most uplifting (except for a bad choral rendition of "God's Green Tree"—terrible theology, terrible poetry, terrible music, terrible singing). The congregation is formed of a motley crew of 58 people including but not limited to a young man with several prominent piercings and big, big hair who read the lessons; Mist-Over-the-Water, of the Wawasee tribe; a couple from Finland who had found The Tree on the Internet before moving to the area; two families of migrant workers from Mexico; a retired pastor and her husband; and the mission congregation's pastor and his family of four children, three from different countries. Today's Church.

Fittingly, the new congregation planted a tree—a vibrant oak sapling—but they put it right in the middle of the parking lot! The Wakefields and Pastor and I smiled together at our private irony. My heart hurt a little like it might for blissful newlyweds, and I thought, "Beloved brothers and sisters, you don't know what you're getting into. Praise the Lord, say your prayers, rejoice, and be ready for some heartache."

In the car on the way home, I shared my faux pas concerning Madge. Pastor and Pete said forget it. Susie agreed with me that I need to get face-to-face with Madge and apologize. Oh! how awful.

Wednesday

I went over to Madge's to set things right. My attitude was more of wounded pride and false humility than the true humility and remorse I had hoped to feel. Her house didn't help any—plastic pumpkins and ghosts outside; lamination everywhere inside—vinyl runners on the carpet and vinyl furniture coverings, cellophane on the lampshades, glass tops on all tables, nothing out of place, and enough frou-frou, including her yippy miniature poodle, Pet, for the whole town.

She seemed very happy to see me, and I translated that to mean that she was savoring each moment of seeing me humble myself. We sat down at her kitchen table, and she chattered incessantly about the several kinds of window treatments she had tried to screen the sun from the kitchen table (in vain), what she was fixing for supper, how Wednesdays were crowded for her because Thursday was recycling day, which grocery stores had the best price on which items, how much time she had spent preparing for next week's Bible study, and so on, until I had to interrupt abruptly because she was only taking breaths in the middle of words.

"Madge, I need to clear up things about what happened at church Sunday."

She squinted.

"I feel awful about what I said when we were getting ready to clean up after the reception."

"What you said about what? I had to rush home because Paul called and said Pet had gotten out."

We looked intently into each others' eyes, both of us processing, and she beat me to the punch. A look of recognition, and then alarm, and then hurt.

"You were talking about me, weren't you? When you said acting holier—you called me a Pharisee, didn't you? I never dreamed you were talking about me, but now I see that you were."

"Please forgive me, Madge. I am a sinful person and, even though I know better, my mouth sometimes spits out thoughts before my brain engages. You are a fine and important member of St. Timothy, and I had no intention of hurting you," I said, delivering my rehearsed speech.

She looked forlorn for a moment, and I expected full-blown drama. Instead, she said, "I know I'm that way," and heaved a sigh.

"Do you want a cup of tea with a shot of peppermint Schnapps?" she offered, getting up to fix it, and then asked me if anyone was having a shower for Stephanie.

"Just because she's pregnant out of wedlock is no reason not to have a shower. Every expectant mother needs a baby shower with games, gifts, and refreshments. If nobody else is doing one, I'll do it."

My head spinning a little, I looked and listened while she planned the who, what, when, where, why, and how of the shower and handily prepared the tea. We each drank two cups, the perfect amount for a lovely buzz.

I heard you Charlie, saying shame on me for enjoying a buzz, do I want to be like my father? and so forth. Not to worry, I assure you. Getting off the hook with Madge and knowing her in a different way was a moment of grace that called for celebration. Funny, I felt the Editor's presence; he was enjoying our loose-tongued conversation about his great granddaughter's shower for her illegitimate child and how Madge was sorry to end our conversation, but she had to get going because her library books were due. The Editor got a kick out of that.

The Twenty-second Sunday after Pentecost

Isaiah 1:10-18
Psalm 32:1-7
2 Thessalonians 1:1-4, 11-12
Luke 19:1-10

So much for Good News this morning—Pastor preached a powerful sermon about God seeking and saving us in the midst of the crazy mess we've made of the Creation and, often, of our own lives, just like Jesus sought and saved Zacchaeus and blessed his home with salvation. And then Pastor Sauer did an about-face and refused to commune Genevieve Lachman!!!! Oh! my heart is still faint thinking of him skipping over her, the Executive Director of United Way, chair of the Social Concerns Committee, a moving and shaking pillar of society on behalf of those in need, so devoted to her career of service that she made a conscious choice not to marry, she told us at circle meeting once. When Pastor ignored her at the altar, I didn't trust what I had seen and brushed off the incident with just a passing moment of curiosity but then found out that he had withheld the sacrament intentionally.

I was the last person in line to greet him after the service, behind Pearl and Clyde Johnson. Clyde was hanging over his walker and arched his neck to look up at Pastor and ask, "Did you know you skipped over Genevieve Lachman with the communion?"

"Yes, Clyde, I did, and how are you folks this morning?" he answered.

"Not so well, with that kind of thing happening," Pearl said under her breath, and they moved on, shaking their heads.

"I was exercising my duty as a called and ordained minister of the Church of Christ, Rose," he explained before I even asked. "Genevieve is living in severe contradiction of the very meaning of the sacrament. As her pastor, I have invited her to confess and repent; she has refused. I cannot, in good conscience, continue to serve her. You are my confidante, Rose. I am indulging this information only to you and two others in the congregation," Pastor said, moving me into the nave and closing the double doors.

"Genevieve is embezzling United Way monies."

I was too shocked to speak.

"Someone came to me with the charges; I have done my homework and found the charges to be true. After deep and difficult prayer, two lay leaders and I confronted her; she is caught in the clutches of angry denial. My sense is that she will, in time confess and repent; for one thing, the story will be in the open soon."

He paused and looked at the altar.

"When I came to her with the sacrament, I thought, 'No. Your worship is an abomination to me and, I believe, to God. The taking of Christ's body and blood is pointless under these circumstances.'"

"Have you ever denied anyone before?" I wondered out loud.

He shook his head.

"You did what you had to do then."

"Thank you, Rose," and he opened the door and walked out.

I made my way slowly to the front and sank down at the railing, praying for us all.

Later

I had thought I was finished writing for today, but then the doorbell rang. There on the front step was Carolyn Sauer.

"Rose, I'm going nuts. I've got to talk to someone, and you're her, honey!"

She talked as she walked in, her shiny brown hair swinging, and marched in circles through the living room-dining room-hallway-kitchen, her clogs shuffling on the floor every step of the way, and verbally careened from one tirade to another against her husband's inattentiveness to his family and the craziness in the congregation. There was no point trying to follow her around, so I settled at the kitchen table with Cute Baby. We could hear every word

"And I don't know if you noticed this morning, but he refused the sacrament to Genevieve Lachman! Refused the sacrament! What the hell?! I didn't know he could refuse the sacrament to someone! Any fool would know what something like that will do to the congregation. I'm so frustrated with Marcus I could just twist his balls off."

"Watch your language, Carolyn," I yelled, even though I knew exactly how she felt. But I figured if I was going to be her confidante as well as Pastor's, I had better set some standards as to how she would talk about him, one of my favorite people. If she heard me, she didn't let on.

"It's as though he's stuck his head up his butt, lost all concept of cause and effect. And does he even think about what all this is doing to Brittany and me?! I'm sure he is acting on principle; he is extremely principled, and I admire him for that. But what about the principle of loving and protecting your family? Isn't that in the Judaeo-Christian tradition somewhere, for Christ's sake?!"

"You're right, he was acting on principle," I yelled out in reassurance.

Silence.

She moved slowly into the kitchen, her mouth open, her eyes wary, and sank down on the other chair.

"You know why he did it, don't you?"

I nodded despite the fury I saw in her eyes.

"He won't tell me. 'This is of the highest confidence,' he says to me. To <u>me</u>, Rose! To his partner of the heart," and she gasped for air. "As though I'm interested in tawdry gossip, as though I don't have any right to know what's tearing our church apart, as though," she sobbed, "as though I can't be of any help to him."

She wept herself down, and then looked at me and asked, "What am I supposed to do? I don't know what to do. He is shutting me out in so many ways. Did you know the Townshends have left?" and she teared up again. "Claudia didn't even tell me. Neither did Marcus. What am I in all of this, chopped liver? Could I borrow your cat?" and I walked over and put Cute Baby in her lap. The one petted and hugged and the other purred and cuddled.

She pulled a piece of paper out of her pocket and tossed it across the table to me.

"I wrote this. I want you to read it," she said as I unfolded it.

Psalm to Jesus

Hear me, Jesus; feel how I hurt.
Sleep will not come and emptiness hurts in the pit of my stomach.
I have prayed, I have sung silent hymns and cried quiet tears.
There seems to be no end to my anguish.

I have searched the darkness for answers and found none.
Conversations play over and over in my mind, but provide no comfort.
I am derided and deserted by friends and enemies alike.
Reality has lost its meaning in the midst of confusion and falsehood.

All is twisted and confused; clarity is out of my reach.
My head aches with confusion; doubt attacks, I cannot duck it.
My weakness disgusts me and becomes another enemy.
My own weakness mocks me.

Oh, come to me, Jesus; calm me quickly.
Fill my emptiness with the bread of life; fill me and do not abandon me to myself.
Take me beyond this time and space; show me your glory so that I will know my smallness and relinquish it to your care.

May my mind be filled with the strength of all that is good; for surely there are few as blessed as I.
Family and friends, health and life's necessities, satisfying work and stimulating

activities are mine and they are sufficient.
Comfort me with the knowledge of God's unending goodness.
Sustain me through this night and bring me to the morning refreshed, miraculously refreshed to be your sister, to walk in your way.

I was overwhelmed; I hadn't realized how deeply affected she was.

"Will you talk to him, Rose? Will you tell him what's happening to me? He can't hear me. Please talk to him."

"Carolyn, I would hardly know what to say. Maybe you need to..."

"We've been in counseling. Things were better for a while, but now we're stuck in the same old ruts again."

She paused and the look in her eyes underscored her next words. "I'm really scared—please, Rose."

I started to protest again, but she quickly cut me off.

"Marcus respects you and he trusts you. I think he would take you seriously."

I felt like I have to try, Charlie.

Oh, great. Now I'm advice to the lovelorn and personal counselor for the Sauers.

Help me, Jesus, to be your sister, to walk in your way, to share your love, to know and teach your wisdom. Thank you for bringing people into my life and providing me with the great gift of friendship. Help me be equal to the tasks presented to me. Amen.

All Saints Day

Daniel 7:1-3, 15-18
Psalm 149
Ephesians 1:11-23
Luke 6:20-31

Tonight I helped serve the annual dinner before the All Saints service to families who have lost loved ones in the last year. Carolyn was helping, too, attractive in her wholesome slimness in a black jumper and ivory blouse. I found the right moment to tell her I haven't forgotten about talking with Pastor.
"Don't take too long, Rose. We're going down," and she turned abruptly and headed for the ladies' room.
So, once dinner was ready and we were waiting for people to arrive, I hurried up to Pastor's office. His desk light shone brightly in the otherwise dark room. Not knowing how to begin, I just stood there.
"Yes, Rose?"
"I'm feeling quite awkward," I started, hoping for an invitation to proceed, which did not come.
Fumbling for words, "Carolyn asked me to talk with you."
No response.
"She's concerned, as you know, about your marriage."
The Great Stone Face
Helplessly, "How are you feeling about your marriage these days, Pastor?" wincing inwardly as I spoke, feeling like I was drowning in a mud puddle.
"I don't mean to meddle, but Carolyn wants to be your partner of the heart and she feels like she is being shut out, especially by your schedule, and…"
Oh, I was so miserable. How did I ever get into this mess?! I thought.
I sat down in the chair facing him.
"She's hurting badly because of the conflict in the congregation. And, you know, things could be worse, Pastor. Carolyn wants more of you, she loves you and wants the relationship to grow. It's not like she wants to leave you."
He looked out the door.
"Would you please say something?" I pleaded after a moment.
"I can't seem to do anything right with Carolyn. She wants more time together, but …"
"The relationship <u>needs</u> more time," I cut him off, wary of his defensiveness. "I'm sure you've heard or thought of the idea of the three persons of marriage: the husband, the wife, and the relationship. Think of the relationship as a growing, living organism which needs attention, time, tenderness." I felt like saying

"lunkhead!" at the end of my little speech but refrained. We heard footsteps and Mercedes peeked in to beckon us to dinner.

"Carolyn and I are very different, Rose," he said as he stood up

"I should hope so. Celebrate that differentness, Pastor, revel in it! But remember, celebrations and revels take time."

"The "t" word, huh?" he said with a tired smile. I nodded.

Please God, help these two lovely children along.

Thinking that Virginia might want to come to the service to honor Aunt Polly, who she especially loved, I impulsively phoned her from the kitchen. But she couldn't come because she had to watch "American Idol." I guess we all choose our heroes—and sheroes, as Stephanie says.

Clyde Johnson died Monday, and the situation became quite difficult. Pearl was sore at Pastor for not communing Genevieve, and she did the unthinkable: when Clyde passed on, she called Pastor Phillips instead of Pastor Sauer! Pastor P. wound up calling Pastor S. and they did the funeral together this afternoon. Heavens, Pastor S. was upset! I certainly understand what a grave insult Pearl visited upon him, but she was in grief and also she and Clyde were particularly close to the Phillips, who were here for over twenty years. Pastor is exhibiting some siege mentality, methinks.

During the service we read the names of those in our congregation who had died over the past year, nine of them, eleven if you count Garfield and Darien, which we did. A chime was struck after each person's name, leaving a sweet, somber sound in the air for a moment of reflection. We called them saints. Saints! It hit me right between the eyes that they are saints, not because they are good, but because they are God's. When we sang, "We feebly struggle, they in glory shine," I had to smile thinking of how *you are the lucky one, Charlie. I love this world and this good, old life of mine, but "feebly struggle" often describes life perfectly Even when we are personally having a good day, we only have to listen to the hourly news report to know that we as a planet are feebly struggling.*

Pastor preached, "In the Church of Christ and in accordance with the divine and eternal purpose, we believers live united with God through Christ and the Holy Spirit. Together, we in the Church anticipate the complete unity we will know in the heavenly life, the unity now known by the brothers and sisters we here remember." Pastor ended with Paul's powerful and poetic prayer from Ephesians: "I pray that the God of our Lord Jesus Christ, the Father of glory, may give you a spirit of wisdom and revelation as you come to know him, so that, with the eyes of your heart enlightened, you may know what is the hope to which he has called you, what are the riches of his glorious inheritance among the saints, and what is the immeasurable greatness of his power for us who believe, according to the working of his great power."

Florence is so close to this wisdom and revelation and enlightenment, these riches and the knowledge of immeasurable, divine greatness. For the first time, I feel some joy about her passing on. "Come, death, and welcome!"

Samantha Jackson was communion assistant. I found myself thinking some more about sainthood and about the idea that the truth and miracle of communion do not depend upon who administers it. I suspect some people may find it difficult to receive the holy sacrament from Samantha. We all had a hard time when she left Al and went on that wild binge. Al's forgiveness and acceptance are amazing; more than once, I've heard people say he's a fool for taking her back. How many times do we have to hear the story of the prodigal before we realize that Jesus really expects us to reflect God's awesome grace?

Charlie, I wonder if you know which of our number entered the Church Triumphant this year. And if you do know, I'd like to know exactly how you know! Just in case you don't.

> *Evelyn Blake*
> *Garrett Schultz*
> *William "Bill" Jackson*
> *Lucille Jenkins*
> *Lloyd Jenkins (the next week)*
> *Nathan Howe, infant*
> *Pauline "Aunt Polly" Woknovich*
> *Harry Smith*
> *Garfield Temple*
> *Darien Brown (7 years ago)*
> *Chad Brewster*
> *Clyde Johnson*

And now I lay me down to sleep with "heaven dreams" swirling in my brain, visions and hopes about what comes next, swimming in a sea of maybes, for we will not know until we know fully.

Mysterious Most High, I thank you for mystery. For its wonder, its excitement, its promise. As we contemplate death—others' and ours, tragic and unremarkable—help us hear your Word, deep within us, that all is well. Still our thrashings. Enlighten the eyes of our hearts. Through death's conqueror, Jesus Christ our Lord, Amen.

Twenty-third Sunday after Pentecost

Job 19:23-27a
Psalm 17:1-9
2 Thessalonians 2:1-5, 13-17
Luke 20:27-38

Genevieve wasn't in her usual place this morning; the story of the embezzlement was on the front page Thursday. $323,000 over ten years. I thought of her during the singing of the psalm, how that her foot had slipped, but that she is still the apple of our gracious God's eye, the object of divine yearning for her repentance. And then, there she was at the communion rail, right across from me! I was between Stephen (home for Thanksgiving dinner) and Mindy.

I know everyone was wondering what Pastor would do.

He seemed about to bypass her again, but, with head bowed, she stretched forward and stopped Pastor with her arm like at a railroad crossing, her palm open and trembling. He looked at her bowed head and closed his eyes. Then—the Body of Christ, given for Genevieve. Given for a thief whose bowed head was her confession, whose shame kept her eyes downcast. As she drew the bread toward her mouth, Pastor's robe brushed her hand while he was moving to the next person, and her bread fell on the floor! Mindy gasped and Genevieve's head and several others including mine turned, and we stared at the morsel on the red carpet. Pastor stared too, for a moment, and then calmly pressed another piece into her hand. When Stephen and I were getting in the car to head out to Virginia's, I saw Pastor throw the fallen piece out in the grass for the birds to eat.

Gracious God, thank you for your mercy of Christ's body and blood for Genevieve and for all of us. Thank you that your Holy Spirit prompted her to fall on her knees next to us at your altar. May she be aware of your presence and grace through this long ordeal of hearing, trial, probably prison. May we attend to her in your name. Amen.

So, Thanksgiving dinner, yes, early, to accommodate Stephen. He and Penelope are making a trip to her hometown of St. Paul for Thanksgiving so he can meet her family and friends. I thought having him home would be more fun than it has turned out to be—still a pleasure, for goodness sake—he's my child and hasn't been home since Gar's and Dar's memorial service, over two months ago, though that seems impossible. It's just that he can't keep his mind on anything but Pastor Penelope Schultz. Starting Friday night when he and I sat down to a cozy supper of chicken and dumplings, she has been the topic of his conversation. I tried to go into some depth about what's happening in my life—Shippensforge news, Pastor and St. Timothy, Florence's condition—but he was a horrible listener and the next thing I knew, we were back on his romance every time.

He is gravely worried because in the past few weeks, Penelope has been reminding him of Denise. Her habits, her expressions, even her physical appearance.

"Why didn't I see it from the beginning, Mom?" he lamented. "I'm so confused now I don't know what to do. I think we're good together, but when I saw a list of the lists she needed to make on her kitchen counter the other day, I broke out in a cold sweat. That is so Denise-ish!

"Our sex life is fabulous," he said and I cringed, "but so was mine and Denise's at first. And I sure don't know about being a clergy spouse. She's got me involved in things that I don't really want to do, but she doesn't take no for an answer very readily. On the other hand,…" Yakkity-yakkity-yakkity-yak! Same chorus, next verse until midnight Friday and over breakfast Saturday, so preoccupied and agitated that he seemed to hear none of my reflections or questions. I got some relief when he spent most of Saturday with Stephanie. She whispered to me when we went into Virginia's for dinner this afternoon, "Grandma, he's driving me crazy talking about Penelope!"

Stephanie is radiant and huge with child, Mack, to be precise. She and Ethan both like the name. Mack?! "Hey, Mack, whaddya' think you're doing?!" "Hey, Mack, you can't park there!" Okay, so Mack it is. Our precious little Mack. Ethan painted Stephanie's guestroom for the nursery, including a mural of animals which reminds me of Eichenberg's peaceable kingdom, and also paid for all the baby furniture, so there is a sweet nursery ready for my great-grandson. (Hey, Mack, how do ya' like your room?!) And a mommy and a daddy ready for him, too, I guess. Here he comes, ready or not!

Thank you, God, and guide them.

Turkey and trimmings by Virginia and Barry were absolutely scrumptious from the artichoke crostini and white wine punch to the pecan pumpkin cheese cake. Everyone behaved nicely, except for you-know-who's incessant references to you-know-whom. I would look at Stephen and think, "I wonder that you still be talking: nobody marks you." Barry was hilarious at one point, saying, "Steverino, what's Penelope think about the Bears' chances for the Super Bowl this year?"

"She doesn't like football," Stephen said flatly, taking no notice of our snickers.

As much as I love my family, the get-together seemed labor-intensive. Furtively, I looked around at each of them and suddenly felt fractured with great distances between us. So much of relationship, I thought, is spent hanging in there until things get better.

Think of our long years together, Charlie. Don't you agree that so much of our relationship was merely existing together with no expectations, maintaining a certain vigilance, waiting for the moments of closeness, of hilarity, of passion?

At any rate, I'd had enough of everybody by 4 o'clock and wanted to get home in time for a program on NPR—"What Makes Mozart Tick?"—somebody thinks he might have had Tourette's, of all things—so I was happy when Steven dropped me off and headed back to Chicago.

I also wanted to call Florence. John answered the phone and said she was sleeping, somewhat peacefully. I haven't seen her since Thursday when I stopped by with flowers and some apple cider fresh from the orchard that I thought might go down easy. She laid stock still with her eyes closed and didn't talk much but wanted every detail about Genevieve. I read her the newspaper account and told her what I'd heard. She knew about Pastor Sauer not communing G. and also about Pearl Johnson not calling him when Clyde died.

"Rose, St. Timothy is a mess. I think you ought to hightail it out to Community Fellowship..." She opened one eye just long enough to see the look on my face and smiled her sassy smile.

Oh, God, how I will miss this woman! Help me, God, I cry unto you. Help me.

I told John to tell her about Genevieve taking communion this morning. I also asked him how he was doing.

"Bittersweet, with an emphasis on the sweet. We've had these months to know each other, find peace with each other. Now that she can't talk much, we don't need words. Being together feels so right, so guided, so blessed."

Thank you, Mother-Father God.

Oh! I said it again. Father-Mother God. Claudia's influence.

And now, let's hear about what makes Mozart tick, Cute Baby. Wouldn't you just like to know?

Twenty-fourth Sunday after Pentecost

Isaiah 65:17-25
Psalm 98
2 Thessalonians 3:6-13
Luke 21:5-19

"Third Isaiah offers a vision of peace, harmony, and well-being to a people recently out of exile who are enduring difficult struggles with conflict, dissension, and insecurity," Pastor began the morning's message.

Madge flipped back and forth in her Bible, trying to find 3 Isaiah. I assume third Isaiah is a term well-known to biblical scholars based on identifying sections of the book according to style, time of writing, etc., but not identified in our common Bibles as such. Pastor, Pastor, you're too academic for us! He probably didn't even know he said "third Isaiah."

"The prophet delivers this Word from God to enliven hope in the hearts of those suffering grief because their young and old are dying too soon and because they have been forced out of homes they built with their own hands and prevented from harvesting the food they labored to plant.

"We, the Church, are called to keep alive the great prophet's vision of peace, people of St. Timothy, not only in regard to the new heaven and earth described in the lesson, but in our very own troubled world. When our finest, like Chad Brewster, and thousands of innocents are dying in Iraq, we must not lose heart but press on with determination, staying true to our faith in divine goodness and greatness. We are called to expect divine action that will bring about peace with justice and to give witness to that action with sacrifices of time and money and lives, perhaps even opposing princedoms and principalities in the name of Almighty God."

After the service, Susie was mad because she thought Pastor was supporting the war, and Sidney was mad because he thought he wasn't. Being angry at the pastor seems to be the main activity at St. Timothy these days.

I stayed after worship for a covered dish dinner and session for making advent wreaths. Mindy and Madge and I were in line together and when we neared the food table, Madge cried, "Oh no! I didn't know this was covered dish; I thought it was catered; I can't stay!" and started to leave.

"Why not?" Mindy questioned, grabbing her arm and turning her around.

"Because I didn't bring anything."

"So? I didn't either; it doesn't matter."

"Oh, but it does," Madge insisted. "Some people worked yesterday, some got up early this morning to fix their food; fried chicken and chocolate pound cake don't just fall out of thin air. I wouldn't feel right eating when I didn't bring anything."

"Get over it, Madge. There's plenty. Bring double next time, and don't deprive of us your fabulous company," Mindy sweet-talked her, pulling her back into line.

Madge smiled and stayed, and she actually was fun, though she seemed worried that covered dish security might come by at any moment and ask her what she had brought.

I overheard a conversation between Pastor and Millicent Avery that I liked. Millicent wanted pastor to be at the altar guild Christmas party on a certain night, and he said he was sorry, but he had other plans. So she said that they could change the date to suit his schedule, and he said, "Please don't change your plans. I won't be able to come at all, Millicent. I simply have to let some activities go. You'll have a fine party without me, I'm sure." Yea, Pastor!

Mindy and Cindy stopped by about 6:30 tonight, perfectly timed to keep me from sinking into any blues. They needed help changing the phone number on 500 lavender flyers introducing "Nails and Skin Care by Cynthia." As we worked at the dining room table, they continued an obviously on-going argument, Mindy saying how tacky the flyer looked with one phone number crossed out and another written in and how that would not inspire confidence in Cindy as a professional, and Cindy insisting that she wasn't going to buy another ream of paper and she probably wouldn't want customers who were so hoity-toity that a little correction would bother them anyway.

"Besides," Cindy said crossly, "I didn't know a month ago when I made these up that I was going to have a kitchen fire and car trouble in the same week and have to move and spend money on the car. I've pretty much had it with God, to tell you the truth."

"Whoa, so are you done at Gateway Chapel?" Mindy asked, surprised.

"Yeah, since the preacher started going out with the secretary. As a three-time divorcee, I need a little better spiritual example than that, and David dying and Dolores getting his entire estate, even if it was only $87, and those two big planes crashing yesterday, I'll bet it was terrorists. I've had it. Just forget it all. If God lets all this happen, I don't want any part of him."

"Oh, that's real smart, Cindy. Life is hard and filled with tough stuff, so you decide to have nothing to depend on, nothing to cling to. Very intelligent. Be sure to stay away from church too, from people who just might help you save your life."

Cindy took a breath to retaliate, but instead wadded up a flyer and threw it dejectedly across the room. Then another, then another, Cute Baby leaping in the air trying to catch them, until Mindy grabbed the pile, telling Cindy to wad up the ones that weren't yet corrected, not the good ones!

"You know what, Miss Know-It-All-About-Religion?" Cindy said after launching a half-dozen more missiles for my ecstatic little kitty. "I poured my heart and soul into Gateway Chapel for almost a year and what good did it do me? I can't see that life is any better."

"You just don't get it, Cin. Sure, life is full of bummers, but # 1, most of them are definitely not God's doing. Is Darien's death God's fault when I was driving too fast and Darien didn't have his seatbelt on? Is terrorism or your pastor fooling around God's fault? and # 2, all of this shit—excuse me, Rose—that we have to wade through is more or less unreal compared to heaven or whatever you want to call it. You know what? We won't even remember all this heartache after all is said and done."

What was that look on Cindy's face? Amusement? Skepticism? Grudging agreement?

"What a deal we have!" Mindy mused. "God had every right to be angry at me when I kept messing up, but kept comforting me instead. When I thought I'd never have hope or peace or happiness again, he kept giving it."

She paused for a moment, and then said, "Cindy, look at me," and Cindy did.

"I wish I could say something that would soften your hurting little heart; I wish there were some way you could let go of your petty angers and doubts and fears and free fall into grace. I am as surprised by joy as I can be; God has taken the terror out of my life and replaced it with a true joy that doesn't disappear because of what happens."

Cindy covered a fake yawn, and I noticed what a mess her nails were.

"Good for you, sister. I hope he does it for me sometime."

And they went out into the darkness together to stuff lavender flyers into mailboxes and paper tubes.

Thank you, wondrous Spirit, for giving Mindy words and a wisdom to speak truth and salvation to her loved one. Amen.

After <u>Masterpiece Theater</u>—I am a sucker for Henry VIII's tragic and despicable story, even as a repeat—I'll try to get a good night's sleep. Tomorrow Virginia is taking me shopping for a winter coat (it seems like I just bought my green one a couple years ago, but she swears it's been 14), and then we're going to shop for Stephanie's shower and probably have lunch out. In the evening, I'll sit with Florence.

I stayed two hours with her this afternoon, and she slept fairly peacefully the whole time. When John came back, we sat by her bed and visited. That man did a stint with Mother Theresa! He didn't think he could stand being around people who were dying, washing their filth off, treating their open sores.

"But God surprised me, as usual. Washing people and sitting with them into death became the most privileged work I could ever hope to do," he said, not taking his eyes off Florence's face. Through these humble acts, I thought, John is prepared for this moment, for any moment. Like Mindy, he will trust and not be afraid. With joy they draw water from the wells of salvation.

On second thought, I think I've probably had enough of Henry VIII. I believe I will gaze on the Theotokos (Mother of God) for a bit instead, and try to soak up some of that mystical peace she and the child present—and then,

"Lord of all gentleness, Lord of all calm, Whose voice is contentment, Whose presence is balm; be there at our sleeping and give us, we pray, your peace in our hearts, Lord, at the close of the day." Amen. (Struther)

Christ the King Sunday

Jeremiah 23:1-6
Psalm 46
Colossians 1:11-20
Luke 23:33-43

Rational discourse about deep mysteries and the cosmic truth of Christ are sorely inadequate—and so we sing. The music throughout this morning's worship touched me profoundly.

Our brothers in Christ, Matthew Bridges and Godfrey Thring, did a wonderful work when they wrote "Crown Him with Many Crowns" a hundred fifty years ago. Mindy really liked that hymn. She was writing during the offering (while the choir sang "Who Is This Glorious King?" Answer sung boldly by Bruce, the bass section: "The Mighty, Holy One") and here is what she was writing:

Different things Jesus is called in the hymn Crown Him with Many Crowns
- king
- lamb
- virgin's son
- God incarnate
- fruit of the mystic rose
- stem "   "   "   "
- root "   "   "   "
- babe of Bethlehem
- Lord of love
- mysteries
- Lord of life
- Lord of peace
- Lord of years
- potentate of time
- Creator
- Redeemer

"That is a bunch of crowns! My favorite is 'potentate of time,'" she said, showing me the list. "Potentate means top banana, right?"

My favorite part is an image of people so "absorbed in prayer and praise" that wars cease. If only we would all crown Christ as the Lord of peace and allow his power to "sway his scepter from pole to pole!" If only.

We sang "A Mighty Fortress," the appointed psalm being #46, and I thought about Carolyn's comment at circle regarding this great hymn of our heritage.

"I guess I believe that last verse—that God's Word will win the day—but when the organ roars and everyone belts out at the top of their lungs about losing their child or spouse, I can only whisper sing."

During communion we sang the simple Taize tune, "Jesus, remember me, when you come into your kingdom," over and over, till we were about hypnotized with it.

The last hymn was that contemporary tune that marches up and down the scale, "Thine the Amen, Thine the Praise." My! that melody and poetry transport me to a safe and exciting place. What a team, Herbert Brokering and Carl Schalk! Artist saints.

> Thine the truly thine the yes
> thine the table we the guest
> thine the mercy all from thee
> thine the glory yet to be
> then the ringing and the singing
> then the end of all the war
> thine the living thine the loving
> evermore evermore

Pastor preached, "The second thief knew a king when he saw one, unlike the Roman soldiers who mocked and derided our Christ with titles of power and esteem because they had no sense of his godliness. Jesus could have saved himself, physically, but then we would all be lost, for the ultimate power of the Divine would not have been manifested. What would have been gained by Jesus avoiding the cross and then dying when he was old? No! It had to happen the way it did. An easy out for him would not have vanquished death and given us hope for eternity. 'He died, eternal life to bring, and lives that death may die.'" Well-spoken, Pastor.

Indeed, Christ is more than we can ever imagine, and I strongly sensed his eternal spirit at Stephanie's shower yesterday. Seriously, the spirit of Christ manifested in the midst of a ladies' baby shower for an unwed mother in a church basement. As people began to arrive, everything felt sad and difficult—Marge way too controlling, Stephanie not feeling well and not wanting to be there, Mindy coming off a bad argument with her boyfriend (whom we didn't even know she had). Carolyn seemed in the same mood as Mindy. Steph's friend Alice had baked a cake shaped like a baby buggy—goodness! who even remembers baby buggies—which had fallen off her backseat on the drive out and looked more like a stroller.

We stuffed balloons under our shirts and played charades with things you do to a baby. And then, the inevitable, tasteless renditions of childbirth experiences, one after the other. Water breaking and so many centimeters dilated; My St. Lord, save us. I want to say, "My dear, that is your own private water; there is no need for everyone else to hear about it."

And then, the most amazing grace started creeping in as we were tearing off strips of toilet paper and estimating how many panels would reach around Stephanie and Mack. Two women came in carrying a large gift that looked very much like the travel system Virginia and I had gotten Stephanie. I asked Mindy if she knew who they were, thinking they might be from the college.

"Holy smokes! I think it's Ethan's mother and sister! Steph didn't want to invite them but Madge insisted. No one dreamed they would come from so far away."

Madge hurried over to them. Stephanie stiffened and looked at her mother with wide-eyed alarm.

"Everyone! Yoo hoo, everyone!" Madge yelled. "This is Mack's other grandmother, Linda Franklin, and his Aunt Kirsten." Linda, a tall, square-shouldered woman with perfectly coiffed salt and pepper hair and just the right pantsuit for the occasion, smiled socially and nodded. Kirsten, a younger version of the mom, very sorority-looking, flashed a smile too, and waved.

Virginia went over to meet them, and I followed along. Stephanie approached, trailing toilet paper, and didn't appear to have any interest in social protocol—I know her look of deep indignation that precedes excoriation. Before she could get going, Ethan's mother spoke, in a private voice.

"Stephanie, I apologize for that letter we sent. You are the mother of Ethan's child. Please accept my apology and allow us to be part of our grandchild's life."

Stephanie swallowed hard and shook Linda's outstretched hand.

Madge clapped her pudgy paws and did a little dance or something (did she actually jump up and down?!) and called out, "Fantastic! Okay, everyone; it's time to open presents!"

Virginia said to me afterwards, "Mother, I could have killed Madge for a minute, but then a voice said to me, 'For what? Has any harm been done?'"

Opening presents was rich and joyful. The grandmas outdid each other in offering to exchange their respective travel systems for whatever Stephanie needed. *Florence's gift was the red wooden truck you made for Sarah, Charlie, hanging a U-turn to come back to your great-grandchild after the Lawrence children and grandchildren have played with it—and Florence about ready to leave us; it's all just about too much sometimes.*

The whole affair was beyond my wildest imaginings—which is exactly how the spirit of Christ works. This morning during worship, I looked around and saw the Brewsters in their pain and the Sauers in their ministry and struggles and Mindy with her offbeat, joyful faith. I thought of the conflicts in the congregation along with the ministries that bring new life to so many people. I thought of Florence, almost dead, and Mack, almost born, and how we are privileged to come together, Sunday by Sunday, loving one another and forgiving one another when our love falters, listening to ancient voices and voices of today speak truth, finding moments of peace and sanity in a noisy, crazy world.

You have rescued us from the power of darkness, gracious God, and transferred us into the kingdom of your beloved son, in whom we have redemption, the forgiveness of sins. Therefore we will not fear, though the earth should change, though the mountains shake in the heart of the sea; though its waters roar and foam, though the mountains tremble with its tumult.

Amen

Amen

Amen